Praise for Jaye Carroll's If the Shoe Fits

"What really makes it stand out is the consistent humour with which the author imbues [the] characters . . . An interesting and entertaining first novel"

Irish Immigrant Newsletter

"A charming and infectious novel"

Irish News

"Slick, entertaining and insightful writing"

Mayo News

"An impressive debut"

Woman's Way

"Fun and frothy"

Evening Herald

"Carroll's writing never falters"

Ireland on Sunday

"Very much in the Poolbeg style, successfully twisting romantic fiction . . . A fascinating and largely successful experiment."

Belfast News

GW00362346

Praise for Jaye Carroll's If the Shoe Fits

"A definite talent for the witty one-liners"
"A tight little story that will keep you reading all night.
A real page-turner."

Irish Farmers Monthly

"fun and very readable"
"perfect holiday escapism reading."

Irish Independent

Loving
the Stars

Also by Jaye Carroll

If The Shoe Fits
The Sweetest Feeling

Loving the Stars

JAYE CARROLL

POOLBEG

Published 2002
Poolbeg Press Ltd.
123 Grange Hill, Baldoyle,
Dublin 13, Ireland
Email: poolbeg@poolbeg.com

1 3 5 7 9 10 8 6 4 2

A catalogue record for this book is available from the British Library.

ISBN 1 84223 069 7

Cover designed by DW Design
Typeset by Patricia Hope in Palatino 10/14
Printed by
Cox & Wyman

www.poolbeg.com

About the Author

Originally from Canada, Jaye Carroll now lives in Dublin, Ireland, with her four children. She is the author of the best-selling novels *If the Shoe Fits* and The *Sweetest Feeling*.

She now writes full-time, but in the past she's worked as a waitress, receptionist, dietician, and cereal packet designer.

In her spare time, she feels guilty about not working.

Jaye Carroll is currently working on her fourth novel, as well as a lengthy dissertation on why Irish road signs show distances in kilometres and speeds in miles per hour.

Acknowledgements

They say it's hard work being an author, and, well, at times it is. But I suspect that it's a lot harder to be friends with an author. Imagine having to put up with sudden, mysterious disappearances, unreturned phone calls, missed social engagements, all because the author in question is working like mad to become as famous as Madonna (and is sadly still only at pre-Madonna status).

So, for not killing me or, worse, shunning me, thanks to . . .

Alix, Amanda, Anita, Anna, Aveen, Brona, Crystal, Denise, Gabi, Gaye, Helen, Jack, Janet, Jo, Kawen, Kerrie, Martina, Mary, Mary Jo, Morgan, Olivia, Paula, Rachel, Rhona, Sheelagh, Tanya, Theresa and Tríona.

Not to mention the Y-chromosome brigade . . .

Chris, Damian, Eoin, Frank, Frank, Gary, Harry, James, James, James, Jim, John, Justin, Liam, Martin, Mike, Mike, Mike, Owen, Paddy, Padraig, Pádràïg, Paul, Robert, Robert, Shane, Tim, Todd and Willy.

And of course all the people I've forgotten. Sorry about that. I guess I shouldn't always leave this bit to the last minute.

Everlasting gratitude to Lee, who understands me better than I understand myself, and puts up with a lot more than anyone will ever know.

Jaye Carroll,
Dublin, December 2001

For Doreen, Pat, and Joan

Chapter One

I was woken by the door crashing open and a hideous creature roaring at me. It seemed to be speaking some kind of language, but the words made no sense.

The creature had pale skin, sunken eyes, hair all over the place, and fluffy slippers.

Gradually I came fully awake.

My mother was standing in the doorway, glaring at me. "I *said*, Ellen's on the phone."

"What time is it?" I mumbled.

"Just gone seven. In the *morning*."

I considered saying, "Tell her I'll phone her back," but thought the better of it.

I'd arrived home about four hours earlier. Ellen and Robbie had dropped me off. And now here was Ellen phoning me at this ungodly hour. My hungover, exhausted brain told me that something must be wrong.

I made a feeble attempt to put on my dressing-gown and crawled downstairs. "El? What's the matter?"

1

The only reply was a muffled sob.

I sobered up rather quickly. "What happened?"

"We broke up," Ellen said.

"Oh shit. Why?"

She paused, then said, "He was going on about needing some time apart and spending more time with his friends. All that sort of thing. So I said that if he wasn't happy, he could sod off and have all the time he wanted with his friends."

"I see."

"And then he said that if I was going to be like that, there wasn't any point in us going on. So I said that was what I meant, and he said he knew that. And that anyway, there was someone else."

"Bastard! Who is she?"

Ellen sniffed. "I don't know. He says that nothing's happened yet."

"Which means that something probably *did* happen," I said, then regretted saying it.

I wasn't sure why Ellen was so upset. She'd mentioned a few times that she wasn't really happy with Robbie. He seemed to treat her as a sort of trophy girlfriend. They were forever going to parties and things just so that his mates could see him snogging a beautiful girl.

But to tell the truth, she treated him more or less the same. Still, that wasn't something I was going to mention.

"Look," I said, "I'll come over if you want." Since I could barely stand up, I prayed that she'd say no.

2

"No, it's okay. I'll come over to your place later. Sorry for ringing so early."

"Don't worry about that. Get some sleep and I'll talk to you later."

We said our goodbyes and I hung up. I was making my way back up the stairs when my Dad's voice called out. "Andi?"

"Yeah?"

"While you're down there, put the kettle on."

"Dad! It's seven o'clock in the *morning*!"

A pause while he considered this.

"And some toast, pet."

* * *

It was a rare Saturday, both Ellen and I having the day off together; we worked in a pound shop right in the heart of Dublin. Not the best job in the world, but we had a laugh most of the time.

Ellen called over to the house at about two in the afternoon, when I was just about thinking of getting up.

She came up to my bedroom and sat on Eimear's bed while I got dressed.

"So tell me the whole story," I said.

It turned out that there wasn't that much to tell. Ellen and Robbie had been going out for the best part of a year, and now it was over.

What really bothered her about the break-up was summed up in one sentence: "If he only wanted me

around to show off to his friends, then what does that
mean when he dumps me?"

There was no easy answer to that one. "I don't
know . . . It means that he's a prick. I mean, why were
you going out with him?"

She shrugged. "Because he was nice."

"Not any more," I said.

"Dean was furious," Ellen said, giving me *that* look
again.

Dean was Ellen's twin brother, and he and I had
gone out for a few months a year and a half earlier.
When we broke up, I told Dean that I wasn't in the
mood for going out with anyone, and I'd rather that we
were just friends, for the moment.

Normal people should be able to get the hint – but
not Dean. He'd been waiting patiently for me to get
back with him. And so was Ellen.

Ellen and Dean were very close, so I couldn't just tell
Dean to get lost. Ellen would have taken it as badly as
her brother.

So because of that, I'd only had a couple of dates in
the previous eighteen months, and I wasn't able to tell
Ellen about them.

And lately, Dean's patience had been showing signs
of wearing thin.

* * *

We decided to go to the local pub that afternoon. My
Dad and his mates were lined up at the bar as usual,

and there were people sitting in what Ellen and I thought of as "our corner", so we had to sit in the posh part.

The drinks were barely on the table before Ellen started up about Robbie, while I was managing the difficult task of nursing a drink and a hangover and trying to be sympathetic at the same time.

"What should I do? Should I call him? Maybe we were just getting all worked up over nothing . . . But *he* started it. And he barely said a word all last night, remember?"

I didn't remember that, but I said I did.

"So he was probably just too scared to break it off and so he started the fight. And last weekend he was all silent and moody and he wouldn't say what was bothering him. That's supposed to be one of the signs."

There was more like this . . . I felt sorry for Ellen, but not *that* sorry. I'd never really taken to Robbie, and I'd always got the feeling that they weren't really going out with each other. They'd just been passing the time together.

Ellen spent about an hour going over past events and reinterpreting them in light of the break-up. It was all, "Now I know why he looked at me funny like that that time. Remember? And I *said* that was strange. And I asked him but he said there wasn't anything wrong or anything. If I'd known then . . ."

Me, I just sat there and listened, throwing in the occasional "Bastard!" to show that I was still on her side.

"And remember last year at the festival in Kilkenny? And I saw him staring at that bitch? The one with the knock-off Jimmy Choo shoes? And he said that she just reminded him of someone he went to school with? I should have known. Even then he was probably thinking of breaking up."

"I doubt that, El. It was the day *after* that when you started going out with him, remember?"

She paused. "Oh yeah. But even so."

Shortly after that – just when it seemed to me that Ellen was on the verge of changing over from being hurt to being "kind of relieved, actually, in a way" – Dean and his silent friend Joe arrived.

Dean raged for a few minutes about the damage that he was going to do to Robbie next time he saw him.

"You know what we should do?" Dean asked Joe. "We should put sugar in his petrol tank, that's what!"

Joe said nothing, which for him was par for the course.

"And we could superglue his wipers to the windscreen!" Dean suggested.

"Just forget it," Ellen said. "It's over now. And I'm glad. He was a wanker."

"I always hated him," Dean said.

"You did *not*," Ellen said. "You were always asking me to bring him along on Thursdays."

"That was just because I thought *you* liked him."

There was a lot more like this. I glanced at Joe and he smiled back. I got the impression that he'd spent the morning listening to Dean rampaging on about what a bastard Robbie was.

Joe was the quietest of our little quartet: I'd known him for years, but we'd never really been friends. Joe was my age – twenty – tall and thin, with uninteresting straight brown hair and average brown eyes. Not particularly good-looking – at least, not in the traditional sense – but certainly not ugly.

A lot of people who met Joe mistook his quietness for stupidity. They assumed that because he never said anything he didn't have anything important to say. I believed that, Ellen believed it, and Dean – Joe's only friend as far as we knew – believed it too.

Whenever we went out, Joe would sit with the rest of us, barely speaking, almost never contributing to the conversation. He didn't smoke, hardly touched a drink, and seemed content enough to be an observer.

Once, I'd asked Ellen what she thought of him.

She shrugged. "He's all right."

"No, I mean, would you go out with him?"

She gave me a puzzled look. "Go *out* with him?"

Clearly, she'd never looked at him that way either.

Joe's role in life seemed to be the straight man for Dean's slagging. Looking back now, I can see that Joe's lack of reaction wasn't because he didn't understand – as Dean believed – but because he didn't care. You could say what you liked about him, and he still remained placid.

If he'd looked a bit more vacant, we might have

7

imagined that Joe spent most of his time daydreaming, but Joe never looked vacant – he was always aware of what was going on and what was being said.

And as we finally discovered, he was aware of a lot more than that . . .

Chapter Two

The shop where Ellen and I worked was called "Sound as a Pound" and did a modest amount of business. We were paid a pittance, but we didn't care – I was still living at home and Ellen had absolutely no financial worries: her parents were rich.

Pound shops are great . . . Almost everything in the shop costs a pound. There's none of that "and ninety-nine pence" crap that you get in every other shop. I mean, it's not like anyone was ever fooled into thinking that £5.99 was substantially less than £6.00.

In the pound shop, we didn't have to always make sure we had a stack of pennies in the till. And writing the prices on the cards was a lot simpler. Plus, when a customer came to the till with a full basket, all you had to do was count the items and add "pounds, please". The customers liked that – it made everything so simple.

Okay, so there were a *few* things that were three for

a pound, and one or two things cost two pounds, but that still didn't make for any taxing arithmetic.

The only downside were the customers. They complained about *everything*. The prices were too high. They couldn't find something that they were looking for. The shop was too hot, or too cold, or too crowded – once, an old woman informed me that if the shop was less crowded we'd attract more customers.

There was always someone getting offended by something or other: when we put up the Christmas or Hallowe'en decorations, we had people complaining that it was too early.

Once a guy who worked in an office across the street complained to our boss that we were putting shiny things in the window display: at certain times of the day, when it was sunny, the sunlight was reflecting up through his office window and getting in his eyes.

But for the most part we got along reasonably well with the customers and had a relatively easy life.

But nothing lasts forever.

* * *

It was the Thursday after Ellen's break-up with Robbie. She now claimed to be completely over him, and spent most of the day telling me that she'd barely even thought about him all day.

It was late in the evening, and we were dealing with the after-work crowd. Mostly they were casual customers who wandered in for a browse, got fed up with having to squeeze past the slow-moving customers who couldn't decide which bottle of ultra-cheap washing-up liquid to buy, and wandered back out.

But there were enough paying customers to keep both of the tills in operation. I wasn't paying much attention to anything until I encountered the old man. He seemed to believe that he was living in the middle ages and the marked prices were merely a starting point.

He dumped a stack of stuff on the counter: two blank video cassettes, a horror novel, a large roll of Sellotape and a packet of fifty Rawlplugs.

"Five pounds, please," I said.

He looked at me over the top of his glasses. "I'll give you three."

I exchanged a glance with Ellen, who was in the middle of a transaction with another customer. Ellen just grinned and turned away. "Sorry," I said to the old man. "I'm only allowed to sell them at the marked price."

He thoughtfully scratched the white stubble on his chin, and rose to the challenge. "All right, then. Four pounds. That's all I have on me."

"Then you'll have to put something back," I said.

He took in a sharp breath and made a disgusting clicky, slurpy sound with his false teeth. "I need all of them. Look, these videos are a *pound each*." The way he said it, you'd think that every other shop on the planet sold video cassettes in packs of ten for fivepence.

11

"Sorry, I'm not allowed to negotiate."

The old man gestured behind him, towards a bunch of ultra-cheap and remarkably shite children's videos. "How come *those* videos cost the same, but they have stuff on them?"

It was always difficult to argue with someone like him. It was pretty clear that he was lonely, and just wanted to chat with someone. I'd no problem with that, and there had been times in the shop when I would have loved someone to talk to, but not when we were busy.

Behind him, the line was beginning to build. Irate customers bobbed up and down, trying to peer past the people in front of them to see what was going on. A few of them abdicated to Ellen's queue, which was moving a lot faster.

Eventually – just as I was about to call Dave the sullen security guard over – the old man decided that he didn't want to buy anything after all. He abandoned his items on the counter and ambled away.

The next person in the queue was Sharon, a friend of my mother's. She handed over three badly-painted ornamental cats (three for two pounds), a bright blue toilet brush, and two bags of fizzy cola bottles (two for a pound).

"How's it going, Andi? How's your Mam? I haven't seen her in ages. Tell her I'll drop over during the week. And how's your Dad? How's retirement suiting him? I know I wouldn't mind giving it a go myself!" Sharon was like that – well able to carry on an entire conversation without giving the other person a chance to get a word in edgeways. She gestured in the direction the old man had gone. "Some people! You must be sick to *death* of customers like that," she said to me with a knowing grin.

"Oh, I don't mind," I said, taking her money and stuffing her purchases into a plastic bag. "He probably just wants someone to talk to. It only bothers me when they hold up the queue." I handed her the bag.

"I know what you mean," she said, not taking the hint. "I used to work in a butcher's, Did I ever tell you that? God, it must be twenty years ago now. Maybe more. And there was always someone coming in and asking for a particular cut and it had to be exactly a certain weight and wrapped in a certain way. And then like as not they'd just change their minds and leave or ask for something else instead."

Behind her, the rest of the queue were getting even more annoyed. "Uh, yeah," I said. "Thanks."

"And there were always young lads coming in and asking for ninety-five pence worth of mince for their mothers. And we'd say, 'Don't you mean a pound's worth?' because we knew that they were going to spend the other five pence on sweets."

I decided on a tactic Ellen had shown me: I cheerfully pretended to be interested, and then asked Sharon to step aside while I served the customer behind her. She finally got the hint and left, but not without reminding me to tell my mother she said hello, asking me about my sister's forthcoming wedding, and enquiring after my oldest brother.

That day I sold about eighteen packets of clothes pegs, fourteen novels, over a dozen pretend cacti, a whole boxful of lucky bags, enough sweets to keep a dentist in business for years, enough make-up to paint the Sistine Chapel, and hundreds of "knick-knacks" (plaster cats, dogs and ducks, candlesticks, flowerpots, tennis balls, packets of ten greetings cards showing unattractive watercolours . . .).

* * *

Being Thursday, the shop officially closed at nine. Ellen and I started wrapping up at about half past eight. The boss usually came in just after closing to collect the money, and we'd learned that it helped if he came in and found that the place wasn't a complete mess. We'd also learned to rearrange the shelves a little so that he could see some gaps where the sold stuff had been.

Not that Gerry was the sort of boss who would care too much about that sort of thing. He was the most easy-going person I'd ever met.

At nine exactly, Dave the sullen security guard muttered "Seeyiz" and went home. Ellen locked the door and stood by it while I rushed the last few customers through the till. As always, there was someone who didn't seem to understand that the red-on-white "Closed" sign, the shutters pulled halfway down, and the locked door meant that we weren't open. "But I only want a tea towel!" she said, in that cheerful trying-to-engage-our-enthusiasm way.

I could see Ellen debating whether to tell the customer to sod off or let her in. In the end, Ellen relented and the woman dashed around, reappearing at the counter a minute later.

"Sorry about that, pet," she said to me. "I don't want to hold you up."

"It's all right," I said. "We have to wait for the boss anyway."

"But sure, it's always the way, though, isn't it?"

"Sorry?"

She waved the tea towel. "I've been meanin' to pick one up for ages, and sure every time I get home don't I remember that I forgot? I was only sayin' this morning that I better not forget today, and there I was halfway home and I remembered that I *did* forget. I would've got one ages ago only you know how it is – we were doin' up the kitchen and I got the young lad to do the paintin'. You know, the cupboard doors. We had the paint and grain stuff – have you tried it? It's brilliant! And he ended up cleanin' the brushes on my good tea towels. Jaysus, I'm tellin' you, I could have feckin' *murdered* him!"

I had the sudden fear that this woman was going to engage me in conversation for the rest of my life, and then Gerry arrived to collect the day's earnings.

* * *

15

Ellen and I were out of the shop and in the pub by half past nine. It was my turn to get the drinks in, and when I got back to our table Dean and Joe had arrived.

Dean smiled and nodded at me as I sat down. Joe just looked placid as usual.

"How's it going, Joe?" I said.

He shrugged. "Fine. Yourself?"

Before I could answer, Dean asked me the same question. "How are you? Anything new?"

"Not really . . ."

Ellen elbowed me. "Shut up. It's starting."

We looked towards the little stage that had been set up at one end of the pub. One of the barmen was fiddling around with a microphone. He tapped it a couple of times, the words "Is it on?" boomed out and scared the bejesus out of everyone, and then he said, "Ladies and gentlemen, put your hands together for Ireland's newest stand-up comedian, making his debut performance tonight. Please welcome Tony O'Hehir!"

At our table, we applauded and cheered as loud as we could. We'd been regulars at "stand-up night" for a long time, and we'd seen more than a few comedians die on stage even before they'd opened their mouths.

Tony O'Hehir looked about thirty, very tall, good-looking though a bit on the skinny side. He had kind of spiky hair like Freddie Prinze Jr., though his angular face was more like Seth Green's. He wore thick-framed glasses that didn't suit him at all. I wondered if they were part of his on-stage costume – it certainly didn't look as though anyone in his right mind would actually *buy* glasses like that. Except Elvis Costello.

He stepped up to the mike and paused for a second, looking around. The pause stretched out.

"Shit," Ellen muttered. "He's going to be torn apart."

The assembled pub-goers and hardened joke-hearers stared at him. He stared back.

Someone shouted out, "Get on with it!" and everyone laughed.

There was another pause while the laughter died down, and then Tony started speaking rapidly, barely stopping to take a breath: "So I went to the cinema the other day. I don't know what the film was like because I fell asleep and on the way out there was this lad with a clipboard and he was asking everyone what they thought of the movie and he stopped me and said, 'Can I ask you about the movie? What did you think of it?' 'It was shite,' I said to him. 'It was way too loud and it kept waking me up.' So he said, 'What, you fell asleep?' And I said, 'Yeah, but it's okay because I didn't want to see it anyway.' So he said, 'Then why did you bother coming?' And I said, 'Well, the seats are a lot more comfortable than they are in the park.'"

There was a smattering of undeserved polite laughter, and Tony continued.

"Did you ever get that thing when you're carrying a load of plastic bags down to the bin and just as you're putting them in, one of the bags falls and splits open and the head rolls out? And it's rolling down the street and everyone is stopping and staring at it? And you're there with the rest of the plastic bags thinking, 'Shite! Now everyone will know!' And they call the police and you're there going, 'No, those body parts were in the bags when I got them.' And the cops are taking you away and you accidentally say, 'I wouldn't bother checking under the floorboards in the flat because there aren't any other bodies in there.'"

This one got a better response. Ellen nudged me. "What do you think?"

"I think he's trying to be Eddie Izzard and Steven Wright at the same time," I said. "He's okay."

Dean nodded knowingly, even though he didn't know. "The material is a bit weak, but his delivery is good."

"Right," contributed Joe.

At the microphone, Tony was talking about dogs. "I hate them little dogs that think they can just rape your leg and get away with it. This happened to me. I was out walking my mate's dog and it started humping my leg. So the next day I reported it to the police. Next thing you know the dog's solicitor is talking to me and my solicitor in his office, and he's going, 'My client says that you didn't refuse,' and the dog's just sitting there beside him with this smug look on his face. And then next thing you know the dog's sold his story to the papers, 'He said he'd take me for a walk, but I knew what he really wanted,' and, 'If he didn't want sex, he wouldn't have dressed like that, wearing those new jeans and just asking for it.' And then all of a sudden they're interviewing the dog on the television – they had him in a darkened room with the light coming from behind, and they had an actor dog doing the voice – and the interviewer's going 'Now, people always think that the dog's the one to blame, without ever looking at his side of the story. What do you say to that?' And the dog thinks about this for a few seconds, and says, 'Woof!'"

Tony paused for the laughter to fade. "I heard that the dog was looking for a ghost writer to tell his story, so I decided to go for it – I needed the money. And now the book's just come out and I've got to sue myself for slander. I had to give myself a court summons, but I wasn't in, so I just hung around until I came back, and then I jumped out at myself and handed me the summons." He paused again. "And I said, 'What's this?' 'It's a summons.' 'What's that mean?' 'It means summons in trouble.'"

Tony O'Hehir finished his set after about ten minutes. On the whole, he wasn't bad – not brilliant, but we'd seen a lot worse. He received a good round of applause, thanked everyone and left the pub. As he passed by our table, Dean said, "Well done. That was great!"

Tony looked a little embarrassed. "Thanks," he said.

Once he was gone, Dean said, "He was all right. Better than most first-timers."

"True," agreed Joe.

19

"He wasn't bad," Ellen said. She turned to me. "What do you think?"

I shrugged. "That stuff about suing himself . . . That's really old. It's the sort of thing Woody Allen used to do. The rest of it was okay, though."

"I didn't know that Woody did stand-up," Dean said. That annoyed me, because I knew that Dean *did* know about that. He was trying way too hard to be friends.

Maybe, I said to myself, this is a good sign. If he's trying to get things moving again, relationship-wise, then maybe he's giving it one final go before he gives up entirely.

On the other hand, I added silently, Dean hasn't been clever enough to take the hint before now, so why should this time make any difference?

I toyed with the idea of telling Joe to tell Dean that I wasn't interested, but that wasn't as easy as it sounds. Joe seemed to be permanently in Dean's shadow, and it wasn't fair to put him in that sort of position. Besides, it would be strange: in all the years I'd known him I'd never spoken to him without Dean around.

So it seemed that for now I'd just have to continue with the standard battle plan: ignore Dean and hope he took the hint.

Chapter Three

Ever since we were kids, Ellen and I had been best friends. She lived across the road, and we went to school together and played with each other every day. That was until we were about eleven, when her family moved to Kilkenny.

Ellen and I stayed in touch, writing to each other about once a week on Pierrot notepaper and being careful to sign our names across the seal of the envelope just in case anyone in the post office was tempted to open our letters.

Dean and Ellen weren't identical twins, but there was still a very strong resemblance. They both had mad black curly hair when they were kids, and fairly pale skin. By their late teens, Ellen had let her hair grow out, and now it was less curly and more Catherine Zeta-Jonesey. By contrast, Dean kept his hair very short, in the style of his hero Adam Sandler.

They were close as kids – Ellen always said that

Dean was her best friend apart from me – and they played together a lot, though this didn't get Dean beaten up because every boy in the area was in love with Ellen. Besides, Dean had always been big for his age. When Ellen and Dean reached their teenage years, they did the usual "teenage rebellion" thing and insisted to their parents that dressing them alike wasn't cute any more – it was scary.

The summer after I finished up in secondary school, I spent six weeks staying with Ellen's family. I was eighteen, and it was my way of getting away from my own family and avoiding the "why don't you get a job?" discussion.

It was the first time I'd really travelled anywhere on my own. The previous times I'd stayed with Ellen's family, I'd been driven there by my parents – a long, horrible journey filled with "and don't do this, and don't do that, and I've told Ellen's mother to phone me *immediately* if she smells smoke or drink off you".

This time, I went by train – my parents had sold the car a few months earlier anyway. I think my folks were glad to get rid of me: Roddy was married and lived in Cork, Ciarán had gone off backpacking around Europe again, John was living with a married woman in Rialto, and Eimear had just moved into a flat. It was the first time in about thirty-five years that my parents would have the house to themselves.

I hauled my bags off the train and stood looking around while the crowds milled around me. After five minutes, I was pretty much the only one left on the platform.

An old woman sidled past. "Are you all right, dear?"

"Yeah, I'm fine," I lied. "I'm just waiting for someone."

She told me about the hedgehog in her garden, informed me that it was a hot day, then wandered off again.

I put my rucksack over my shoulder, picked up two of my bags and pushed the other one along with my foot, meandering awkwardly towards the public phones. Once I found a phone that wasn't vandalised and would accept coins, I put down my bags and spent a good few minutes going through them to find my purse.

This done, I phoned Ellen on her mobile. There was no answer, so I let it ring, and gradually I became aware of a mobile phone ringing somewhere behind me. And then I heard laughter.

I turned around to see Ellen and Dean about ten metres away, laughing their heads off.

* * *

The first couple of weeks were great. Ellen's house was *huge*. There were five bedrooms – three with en suite bathrooms, a great kitchen filled with every electronic convenience you could imagine, separate dining-room that they actually used, a sitting-room *and* a recreational room.

It was about four times the size of my house, which was a two-bedroomed mid-terrace with no front garden and a door that opened right out onto the street. Worse, at one stage there were seven of us at home – the sitting-room had been converted into a bedroom for the lads.

There was no doubt that Ellen's parents were very well off: years before, her father had inherited an old house on the North Circular Road. At the time, he could have sold it and made a lot of money, but he was wise and instead divided the house up into flats and rented them out. It wasn't long before he'd bought another old place, then another . . . By the time of that visit, Ellen's parents owned over twenty houses scattered around Dublin. It was almost a full-time job just going around and collecting the rent.

* * *

That summer, Ellen and I hung around with her ex-schoolfriends and went for long walks when there was nothing else to do – which I suppose was most afternoons. In the evenings, we watched videos or went to the pub.

And Dean was with us pretty much the whole time, tagged as always by the human shadow called Joe.

To me, Joe seemed to be completely devoid of any personality of his own. Sometimes a whole evening went by without any of us even talking to him. On the other hand, you could spend the whole night slagging him – and we often did – and he just grinned and said as little as possible.

24

Dean was the opposite: you would have had to kill him to shut him up. He was like Ellen in that respect: the two of them talked incessantly. Once or twice they finished each other's sentences, and everyone would pounce on it and go, "Wow! It's like you've got one mind in two bodies!" and things like that. Funny how no one ever noticed when they *didn't* finish each other's sentences. No one ever said, "Wow, it's like you're two individual people!"

On the third week, Friday night, Ellen went out on a date with some guy we'd met in the pub a few nights before. Naturally, this was accompanied by much slagging from me and Dean.

"Don't mind us," Dean said to her. "The rest of us will be fine without you."

"Unless you think that we should all chaperone you?" I suggested.

"Not in a million years," Ellen said. "The lot of you can fuck off and do whatever you like."

So Dean, Joe and I went down to the pub as usual. None of their other friends were around, so the three of us sat together and chatted for an hour or so, and then I went up to the bar to get the drinks in. As I was trying to catch the barman's attention, I glanced back and saw Dean and Joe involved in a conspiratorial conversation.

About ten minutes later, Joe finished his drink and declared that he was expected elsewhere for a prior engagement and that he would have to depart. Actually, he said, "I'm goin' home. Seeya."

That left me and Dean . . . I'd known him as long as I'd known Ellen, but this was the first time since we'd reached adulthood that we were alone together.

Dean was a nice guy, most of the time. He was fun, fairly good-looking, and, well, available. One thing led to another and it wasn't long before Dean and I were an item. The only reservation I'd had was that Ellen might not be happy about it, but she was fine, and later she told me that Dean had been interested in me for ages.

Going out with your best friend's brother can be awkward, especially when you can remember rescuing him from a bully at the age of six. And when you can remember how he used to chase you around the street with a watering can, or when *he* can remember how you bawled your eyes out when you were nine and discovered the truth behind the Santa Claus conspiracy.

Dean and I remained a couple for about five months. The reason I broke up with him was simple: he was beginning to bore the hell out of me. Plus, his feelings were inclining towards the physical, and there was no way I could see myself having sex with him.

He was still living in Kilkenny, so I would go down to stay with them for the weekend, or he – and sometimes Ellen – would come up to Dublin to stay with us. Dean would stay downstairs in the boys' room, and Ellen – if she came – would stay in my room. After the third time Dean came on his own, my mother figured out that we weren't simply friends any more, and so she and Dad took to staying home whenever Dean was there, just in case.

Dean would arrive fairly late on Friday night, so we'd stay in and watch telly. On Saturday morning we'd usually go into town, stay there for the day, and end up in a pub somewhere. We'd get home fairly late, and he'd be quite amorous. Luckily for me, at least one of my parents always stayed up until we'd gone to bed.

One night, my Dad caught Dean trying to sneak upstairs into my room, and had a blazing row with him on the landing. I hadn't even known what Dean was up to: I'd been fast asleep and woke up to the sound of my Dad shouting his head off. Next thing we knew, Dean was banned from the house unless Ellen was present.

Pre-marital sex was not something my parents approved of. I was eighteen or so, but they still thought of me as their little girl. My mother routinely had nightmares that I'd end up pregnant, an unmarried mother, doused in sin and eternally refused entry into the Kingdom of Heaven. Even worse, the neighbours would gossip about it.

At that time, Dean was working in a factory in Kilkenny, packing computer bits into boxes. I was unemployed, actively avoiding work and pretending to my parents that I was thinking about going to college – they didn't push too hard because they couldn't really afford to support a college-going daughter.

A date with Dean tended to go something like this:

I'd meet him at his friend's flat, and we'd head off to the local pub.

"So, how was your week?" he'd ask.

"Fine. Yours?"

"Busy. Remember I was telling you about Doyler and how he was holding everyone back?"

"Yes," I'd lie – I couldn't remember from week to week who Dean's co-workers were.

"Well, Neil gave him an absolute bollocking on Wednesday! Took him aside and said that he wasn't pulling his weight and that we were all carrying him."

"Wow. What happened then?"

"Then Neil said that Doyler didn't know one end of a CPU from the other and that he was the most computer-illiterate person he'd ever met. Which reminds me, we're going to be getting the new Pentiums soon. Probably on Monday. Actually, it probably won't be Monday, because we've got nowhere to put them at the moment. Did I tell you that they're thinking of converting the storeroom into another assembly area?"

"No," I'd say. "Which one?"

"The small one," Dean would reply, looking at me as though I was mad: why on Earth would they want to convert the *large* storeroom? "Anyway, it better not be Monday because you know what it's like on Mondays trying to get something done when everyone is hungover. So anyway, Doyler told me later that he was thinking of leaving."

"Where's he going to go?"

Dean would shrug. "Don't know." He'd sip his pint, sit back and look around to see who could see him sitting with his girlfriend. "Neil said that Doyler told him that Nicky said that he was a complete fucker and then he turned around and he was standing right behind him!"

"Wait, who was standing behind who?"

Another "isn't it obvious?" look from Dean. "Doyler was standing behind Neil when he told me."

I couldn't see what the big deal was. "So?"

"Well, you had to be there. You should have seen his face, though."

I didn't have the energy to ask *whose* face I should have seen.

On the way home, Dean would half-drunkenly try and kiss me, and if I was half-drunk, I'd usually let him.

That was how it was for about five months, the last four of which I spent wondering how I was going to break up with him.

* * *

We were in the pub, as usual . . .

"Look, Dean, there's something we have to talk about," I said.

Dean wasn't paying attention – he'd been flicking through a computer magazine and was drooling over a particularly exciting keyboard or something.

I nudged him. "Dean."

"Huh? What?"

"Look, we've been friends for what, more than ten years now, right?"

He nodded.

"And you and Ellen are my closest friends."

"True. That's why you and me get on so well together."

I sighed. This wasn't going to be easy. "Okay, right . . . I think we should break up."

From the look on his face, you'd think I'd just turned off his computer when he was only three dead bad guys away from a high score. "What? Why?"

"Because . . ." I'd had four months to think about it, and still couldn't come up with a good reason that didn't break his heart. "Because sooner or later, you're going to meet someone else and break up with me and I don't want to ruin our friendship."

"No I won't. I don't want anyone else."

"And what if *I* meet someone else?" I asked. "That sort of thing could happen."

"Listen, Andi, if you've already met someone, just tell me."

"There's no one else," I said. "But, well, the truth is I just don't want to be going out with *anyone* right now."

Dean let out a long, deep breath. "Okay . . ." He was silent for a few moments, then said, "Christ, I don't know what to think. I thought you loved me."

"I never said I loved you." Seeing the look on his face, I quickly added, "I mean, I do love you as a friend, but I don't know if it's the kind of love that could grow into something else."

Dean said, "Well, *I* love *you*. There, I've said it. Is that what you wanted to hear?"

Get the fucking hint, I mentally told him. "No. It's not. Look, Dean, you've never gone out with anyone else, have you?"

He looked around in a mild state of panic in case anyone else in the pub had heard me – which showed me that he couldn't have been *that* heartbroken. "Not really."

"Well, I have, and the longer it goes on, the harder it is when you do break up. So I think that we should just break up now and be done with it."

"Yes, but *why* do we have to break up? There's nothing that says we can't stay together forever."

"Jesus, this isn't a fucking debate," I almost shouted. "Look, you're one of my closest friends and I don't want that to change." In truth, of course, I just didn't want to lose Ellen's friendship. "I don't know how I'm going to feel in the future, but for now I don't want to go out with you. Besides, I think we're both too young to be making lifetime commitments."

Finally, the message seemed to be sinking in. "Okay . . . Maybe you're right." He finished his pint and sat back. "Friends, then?"

I nodded. "Friends."

"Okay."

Chapter Four

After Tony O'Hehir's set, the next comedian was someone we hated – he was of the Bernard Manning school of comedy, though without Mr Manning's charm and sophistication. Still, a lot of the other regulars loved him. His name was Bosco Byrne, overweight, middle-aged, red of face, unbuttoned of shirt, missing of hair and floppy of jowl.

Bosco opened his set with the sort of joke that was standard for him: "The wife sez to me, she sez, 'Bosco, are yeh ever goin' ta get a fuckin' proper job?' So I sez to her, I sez, 'listen you, if I go an' get a proper job yiz'll only spend all me fuckin' money.'"

We waited for the punchline, but apparently that was it. Bosco's fans laughed and cheered and shouted, "Fuckin' right! Ha ha ha ha!"

"Jesus, I hate this guy," Dean muttered.

"The young fella comes up to me," Bosco continued, "an' sez, 'Da, can I have an encyclopaedia?' So I sez to him, 'No yeh fuckin' can't, son. Yeh can walk to school like I did.'"

"That joke's older than he is!" Ellen said. "He's only one step away from mother-in-law jokes."

A few minutes later, Bosco proved her wrong: he was *no* steps away from mother-in-law jokes: "The wife's mother came to stay, an' she's always on at me. 'Bosco, look at the fuckin' state of yeh. Yeh're fuckin' drunk again.' And I says to her, 'I might be drunk, but you're ugly –'"

Ellen glanced at me. "The Winston Churchill joke?"

I nodded. "If I hear that one more time . . ."

Bosco leaned on the microphone stand. "Me mate Mick, now, can't hold his drink. It was his birthday, an' we took him out for a few jars. Well, he wanted to keep up with the rest of us, so he had eighteen pints and ten bags of peanuts. Sick? Don't fuckin' *talk* to me about sick! On the way home he pebbledashed three houses!"

* * *

After Bosco there was an intermission, during which everyone piled up to the bar. Dean and Joe joined the throng, and Ellen turned to me.

"I think that Robbie phoned the flat yesterday."

"You *think*? How do you mean?"

She toyed with her almost-empty glass. "Well, there was a message on the machine but whoever it was just hung up."

"But sure that could have been anyone."

"I know. But I have a feeling that it was Robbie and he wants to get back with me."

I stared at her. "You're not thinking about it, are you? I mean, after he just dumped you like that, you'd be mad to go back with him. I mean it. You're much better off without him."

"So what's happening with you and Dean?" she asked, clearly not in the mood to hear me say negative things about her ex.

"Nothing," I said. "Why? Has he said anything?"

"No, I was just wondering. Mam said that he's been moping around the house the past couple of months. She said if he gets any worse she's going to throw him out so that she doesn't have to look at him any more."

"I suppose he's staying with you tonight?" I asked, even though I knew the answer. Ellen had moved back to Dublin a few months earlier. Having wealthy parents seemed like a good deal: Ellen had a great flat and didn't have to pay any rent. On the downside, Dean always stayed in her place at the weekends.

Since he'd left the factory – or, more accurately, since he'd been asked to leave – he'd been working for his dad, collecting the rent from the tenants and theoretically fixing anything broken. Though if the truth be known, Dean had trouble fixing anything more complicated than a broken lightbulb. Joe was a lot better at DIY stuff, and since he was unemployed too, he tended to accompany Dean and do most of the work.

Ellen nodded, and raised her eyes. "The two of them are. I don't mind Dean staying but Joe gives me the creeps. He just sits there, saying nothing. You have to force answers out of him. Anyway, Dean's still holding a candle for you."

"It's just like him to get one of those everlasting candles . . ." I shook my head slowly. "I've tried to let him know that I'm just not in the mood for going out with anyone. I mean, we're only twenty – I think he's ready to settle down for the rest of his life."

"You know what day it is next Tuesday?" Ellen asked, suddenly looking very serious. "It's two years since you and Dean got together. That means it's a year and seven months since you broke up. It's about time you decided one way or another." She knocked back the last of her drink, and almost slammed the glass down.

"Well . . ." I started, but she interrupted me.

"Andi, you wouldn't like it if someone kept you hanging on all this time. Dean's made it clear that he's ready to get back with you, but you're just stringing him along. It's not fair."

"I know. But it's not that simple." I wanted to tell Ellen that there was no way on earth that I'd ever get back with Dean. There might have been before – well, there *might* – but in recent months he'd become extra creepy . . . Pretending that he was knowledgeable in the things that interest me, for example. He'd also managed to avoid talking about computers or football when I was around. He'd taken to wearing his good clothes whenever we met.

He was always neatly groomed and smelling of Lynx.

He was making an effort, but that only served to emphasise how much I didn't want to go out with him. A boyfriend who was boring, untidy, unshaven and smelling of socks was something that no sane woman would put up with. But if you take those negative attributes away and you're *still* left with someone you wouldn't touch with a baseball bat, that means he's "unsuited" right down to his DNA.

I couldn't ever say anything like that to Ellen – he was her brother, after all, and she was my best friend.

As I was thinking about it, and remembering how Dean and I broke up, an idea began to form . . . The problem with Dean would be solved if he found someone else to pine about.

Unfortunately, there wasn't anyone I could set him up with. Apart from Ellen, I hadn't kept in touch with any of my childhood friends – even those who still lived on our street. Most of my friends from secondary school had moved away or were already attached.

Okay, so there were one or two unattached females I sort of knew, but none of them were the sort Dean would be interested in.

If only Claire was a few years older, I said to myself. Claire was my niece, Roddy's daughter. I hadn't seen her in about a year, but from what I'd heard she was growing up into a really good-looking girl. And she was nice, too. Good fun to be with.

On the negative side, she lived in Cork and was only

fifteen. That was only five years younger than Dean, but it was more than enough to make a difference. Besides, Roddy would have had a fit if Claire started going out with someone five years older than her. Not to mention that I wouldn't wish Dean on someone like Claire.

"What are you thinking about?" Dean suddenly said, appearing beside me with drinks in his hand.

"Claire," I replied. "You know, Roddy's daughter."

He grinned, and nudged Joe. "Fifteen with the body of a twenty-year-old, Joe. You'd like her."

Joe blushed and looked away.

"That's disgusting," Ellen said.

"It won't be disgusting in a couple of years, though," Dean said, still grinning.

We were saved from more of this by the arrival of another comedian. This one was a Harry Hill-wannabe: his material was incredibly surreal, and he kept wandering all over the place, and coming back to odd ideas . . .

"I'm fed up. We have names for the days of the week, and the months of the year, but we don't have names for the hours of the day. So I've decided to name them based on the most important things about each hour. Eight o'clock, Brookside . . .

"You know, if it turns out there *is* life on Mars, I bet they come invading when they learn that we've named a chocolate bar after their planet . . . Two in the morning, Car Alarm . . .

"And what is it about Saint Patrick? I mean, *why*, exactly, did he banish all those snakes? What was the point of that? And did we get anything else in return?" Pause for laughter, which wasn't really forthcoming. "I was in the newsagents the other day, oh yes . . . My mother came in and caught me in the Horticulture section, flicking through a copy of PlayVeg. But mum, I only read it for the artichokes! Six am, Milkman!"

This went on for a solid twenty minutes . . . His tactic was simple, but it mostly worked – the shotgun method: pack as many jokes in as you can, on the basis that at least some of them will get a laugh.

"Four in the morning, Drunken Flatmate's Return!

"No, but think about it: where exactly did all those snakes *go*? And how did they get there? Did they go on boats? Were they, like, all queueing up at Dun Laoghaire trying to catch the ferry? Eight in the morning, Running for the Bus . . . And more to the point, why aren't there any snake skeletons? What about the snakes in the zoo? Do they have special exemption from the Pope? Maybe they're Catholic snakes and Saint Patrick only drove out the pagan snakes. All right, snake, you can stay in the country if you can recite the Lord's Prayer.

"So when the Martians come, and they're saying, 'How dare you degrade our glorious planet by naming a chocolate bar after it?', we can say, 'Hey, Mr Martian, that's not your planet it's named after. There's supposed to be an apostrophe before the S. This is Mar's Bar.' And they go, 'What, the guitarist who used to be with The Smiths? But there are two Rs in his name.' And we'll all go, 'There are? Oh no!' One o'clock, Queueing for Sandwiches! Oh, and by the way, Mr Martian, you haven't seen any snakes around, have you?'"

* * *

After we left the pub, the four of us walked towards the departure point at which I'd head for home and the others would go to Ellen's flat. I wasn't in the best of moods: Dean had insisted on sitting right next to me all night, and kept offering to buy me drinks and asking if I was all right, if I was too hot or too cold, if there was anything he could get me. Did I want peanuts or Bacon Fries? No? What about Scampi Fries? Was I sure I didn't want another drink?

It was a cold night, despite being in the middle of summer. There was no moon, and no cloud cover. The stars were fixed in the night sky like a photograph of falling snow.

"What time is it?" Ellen asked.

"It's just gone a Quarter Past Duvet," Joe said. It was the longest sentence he'd uttered all night.

Ellen stared at him. "What?"

"A quarter past twelve," he clarified.

"So you actually *were* awake tonight," she teased. "We thought you'd gone visiting the astral plane or something."

"Yeah," Dean joined in. "If you'd been any quieter

39

we'd have had you stuffed. You barely even laughed. Didn't you find *any* of them funny? What about the first guy?"

Joe shrugged.

"Well, *I* thought he wasn't bad," I said. "Definitely got potential. He needs to sharpen it up, though."

"That's true," Dean agreed enthusiastically.

Feeling suddenly mischievous, I stopped walking and turned to him. "Really? What did I mean? Give me an example?"

"Well, his timing. He didn't say anything for nearly a minute." From the look on his face, he knew he'd been caught out.

"Bollocks," Ellen said. "That wasn't timing. Yer man used to do the same thing . . . What was his name again, Andi? British guy, going bald, very sad-looking. Used to be in the thing with the lad who does *Robot Wars*?"

"Norman Lovett," I said. "Yeah, Andy Kaufman used to do the same thing as well."

"Okay," Dean said, "so what *did* you mean, then?"

"That bit he said about the dog screwing his leg? He said that the dog was interviewed for television, and that they had him in a darkened studio with an actor dog doing the voice, right? And the punchline to that whole bit is that the interviewer asks the dog a question, and the dog just barks . . ."

"So?"

"So he shouldn't have mentioned the bit about the

actor dog, because as soon as he did, the first thing you think of is that dogs can't speak. So then you anticipate that the dog is just going to bark."

Ellen started walking again, and the rest of us followed her. "Well, *I* didn't see it coming," she said.

"Me either," Dean admitted.

"I did," Joe said.

Dean turned on him, "Damn it, Joe! Will you just shut up for once!" He thought this was hilarious, but no one else was laughing.

"Dean, just leave him alone, for God's sake," I said. "I'm tired and I'm cold and I want to go home."

"Jesus, you're in a right miserable mood tonight, Andi," Dean said. "I'm just having a laugh. Joe doesn't mind, do you, Joe?"

Again, Joe shrugged.

"See?" Dean said, as if that was proof.

We reached the departure point. "Okay," I said. "I'm off. I'll see you in the morning, El." I looked at Dean. "Is someone going to walk me home?"

He grinned. "Sure."

Oh God, I said to myself. He thinks he's going to get more than a walk out of it. "Never mind," I said. "I'll go on my own."

"Be like that, then," Dean said, getting into a sulk.

Ellen thumped her brother on the arm. "Go with her, Dean."

"It's only five fuckin' minutes up the road," he said. "She'll be all right."

41

I started to walk away. "It doesn't matter. I don't need you."

"I'll go," Joe suddenly said, and caught up with me.

I couldn't think of anything to say to Joe as we walked, apart from, "Thanks." When we got to my parents' house, he said, "Good night" and turned to go.

"Are you going to be okay walking back to Ellen's on your own?"

Joe nodded, then said, "Look up."

I looked up at the night sky. The stars were a lot clearer in Kilkenny, where there wasn't quite so much light pollution, but it was still pretty amazing.

Joe said, "I have loved the stars too fondly to be fearful of the night."

"That's beautiful . . . Shakespeare, is it?" I asked.

But he didn't hear me. He was already halfway down the street.

* * *

I woke up on Friday at about nine. The shop was only a few minutes' walk away, and we didn't open until ten, so there was no rush.

My mother was ironing in the kitchen. "What time did you get in last night?" She didn't look up.

"About half-twelve," I said. I rooted through the cereals cupboard and was torn between Frosties and Cheerios.

"There's not much milk," my mother said. "You'd better have toast."

"I don't want toast," I said, putting the cereals back. "I'll get something on the way."

She tutted. "Chocolate."

"No, I'll get a breakfast somewhere." I poured myself a cup of tea, and sat down at the kitchen table.

My mother finally looked up. "You're not going to work dressed like that, are you?"

"What do you mean?" I glanced down at my clothes. "What's wrong with it?"

"You've got egg or something on your jeans. Are they the same ones you wore last night? Mother of God, Andi, you're never going to get on in that job if you don't smarten yourself up!"

"It's not exactly the sort of job you can really go *that* far in," I said, scratching at the dried egg – or whatever it was – with my thumbnail. "Anyway, I'm not going to be there forever, you know."

She raised her eyes, shook her head and returned her attention to ironing my Dad's huge Y-fronts. "So what are you going to do with your life? You're out of school two years now. It's about time you sorted yourself out and got a real job."

"How's Gran?"

"Don't change the subject . . ." she said. "She's fine. She was asking for you yesterday. Probably wondering why you haven't gone to see her in ages."

"I only saw her on Wednesday! Anyway, I don't know what the problem is. I go and see her more than anyone else does."

43

She finally finished the Y-fronts and fished another identical pair out of the laundry basket. If the iron had had a face, it would have been flinching. "Well, you can't expect Eimear to go – she's got enough on her plate as it is with the wedding. And John's far too busy in work."

"Well, Ciarán could go. It's not like *he* ever goes. Gran said that she can't even remember what he looks like."

"Your Gran says a lot of things she doesn't mean, Andi. Anyway, Ciarán's in Spain. Or somewhere. And your Gran's eighty. She won't be around forever, so you should go and see her."

"I'll go at lunchtime, then," I said.

"See that you do. And change out of those jeans before you go into work. I won't have one of my daughters going out looking like that."

Yeah, yeah, I said to myself. I turned away and focussed my attention on the previous day's newspaper. After some searching, I found the tiny ad for the comedy night:

Tonight!
Hilarious stand-up comedy from Dublin's best!
Bosco Byrne!
Dennis Clarke!
Mick "Mad Ranger" Murphy!
Tony O'Hehir!
No cover charge before 9:30. Adults only.

I tore out the ad, wrote the date on top. I kept them

all. It was important, I thought, to keep a record of who I'd seen. One day, one of them might become really famous – please God, don't let it be Bosco Byrne – and of course, one day *my* name might be there . . .

Chapter Five

My mother's name had been Sally Nolan until she married my father, John Quinn. She was twenty-three, and he was a year younger than her. Two years later, they had a beautiful son, and called him Roderick. The name never really stuck, and everyone ended up calling him Roddy. This lasted until he was a teenager and he started telling everyone that his name was Rick, which was altogether a lot cooler and didn't get him beaten up so much. Some of his friends *did* call him Rick, but everyone in the family always called him Roddy because it annoyed him.

A year after Roddy was born, along came another beautiful son. John was named after our father, leading to much confusion some years later when Brother John started receiving post, and Father John always opened it. Brother John got very sick of this and decided to get his own back: he started opening Dad's post. So then Dad started getting up earlier to make sure he was the first to catch the postman. Brother John saw the wisdom of this idea and he began to get up even earlier. It got so bad that for a while the two of them were getting up at six in the morning and sitting in the hall waiting for the postman to arrive.

Anyway . . . With two young sons, the family was happy, though not very well-off. Dad was a civil servant, Mam didn't work – it was traditional in those days for women to abandon their careers in favour of being a housewife. Things got tough when Brother John was about three years old: Ciarán was born. He was probably a beautiful son as well, but by that time Dad was holding down an evening job as well and my mother was running around like a blue-arsed fly after two toddlers and a baby and no one had time to take any photos.

Imagine their surprise a couple of years later . . . My mother discovered that – against all her prayers – she was pregnant again. I'm told that Dad strongly considered investing in a packet of condoms, but was talked out of it by my mother who told him that if he brought those evil things into the house he'd automatically lose any opportunity to use them.

Still, poor as they were, they were delighted when this new baby arrived and they found that the "boys only" spell had been broken. They called their little girl Eimear, after some almost forgotten friend of her mother's. For the first couple of years, she had to make do with hand-me-down stuff from her older brothers,

Jaye Carroll

but she was young and unlikely to get a complex about it.

Eimear was doted on and treated like a little princess, and was perfectly content with her place in the world. Until one day, when she was ten years old, her mother took her aside and said, "How would you like to have a little brother or sister?"

I'm told that Eimear screamed her head off and ranted and raved for weeks. Everyone said, "Poor little thing! All this time she's been the baby of the family, and now look what's happened." "Yeah, what's *that* all about?" "You'd think they'd know better." And so on.

By the time I came along, my Dad was forty and my mother was forty-one. I'm told that they went around with a shocked expression for the first couple of years.

I was named Andrea. I didn't like the name much and always told everyone to call me Andi.

* * *

Gran – Mam's mother – married Grandad when she was only eighteen. He was twenty. When I was really young, Gran told me how much her parents had disapproved of the marriage. Even though they were both of consenting age, there was a lot of trouble. Part of the problem was that Grandad didn't have what her parents considered to be a "proper" job.

Grandad was a stagehand with a travelling theatre company. I say "stagehand" but basically he did everything that the actors didn't – or wouldn't – do. He was the prompter, set dresser, make-up artist, tailor, director if needs be, lighting engineer – which is to say that he controlled the only spotlight the company had – occasional background extra, the man who took the money at the gate, and the official chucker-out of rowdy audience members.

Gran joined the company when she was seventeen, as an actress. By all accounts, she wasn't bad. She rarely managed to get a really good role – she was always one of Lady Macbeth's servants or something – but what she lacked in star quality, she made up in enthusiasm.

Gran and Grandad fell in love and a few months later they announced their engagement. Gran's parents went ballistic: they'd thought that her acting was only a hobby, something to do. They were fairly well-off so she wasn't expected to work. She never told me outright, but Gran hinted that her parents had thought that her mixing with the common folk would be good for her. Until they found out just exactly how much mixing she was planning to do. They considered theatre people – especially *travelling* theatre people – to be itinerants. Basically, my great-grandparents were classist scum.

On the other hand, Grandad was an orphan, so the theatre group was really the only family he had. Grandad had lost his left foot in an accident when he was a teenager, and that was even worse for Gran's parents: not only was she marrying a theatre person, he was a cripple as well. Gran's parents pretty much cut off all communications with her. They were proud

Jaye Carroll

people and wealthy enough to sustain a grudge for the rest of their lives – and even beyond, considering that they left her out of their will.

Shortly after Gran and Grandad married, the Second World War broke out. A lot of Irishmen of Grandad's age went off to fight in France, but Grandad's artificial foot prevented that. Times were tough during the war, and the theatre company was unable to keep going.

So now Grandad was an *unemployed* crippled theatre person. It was around that time that my mother was born.

I've seen a couple of photos of my mother and her siblings when they were kids . . . God, they were poor! I mean, *we* grew up in an ancient two-bedroomed house which for a long time didn't even have an indoor toilet, but compared to my mother's family, we were loaded.

Grandad and Gran worked whenever they could, but on the whole there wasn't much of an income. At one stage Grandad couldn't find any work for over two years. To make ends meet, Gran took in washing and became a cleaner for the local church – the pay was really, really bad, but it was still better than nothing – and when Mam was fourteen, she was pulled out of school and sent to work in the kitchen of a nearby hotel.

So my mother grew up with the very strong impression that a career in the performing arts was about as low as you could go.

It makes sense, from her point of view.

But on the other hand, *I* grew up with stories from

my grandparents about how much fun it had been in the theatre company. The thrill of the applause, the euphoria that comes with knowing that you've successfully entertained a whole bunch of strangers, the highs and the lows, the joy and despair . . .

From the age of about three, I knew that more than anything, I wanted to experience that.

Chapter Six

The boss was there when I got to the shop. He was asking Ellen questions and generally getting in the way. He normally didn't bother with the day-to-day running of the shop, so I knew that something was up.

As soon as he saw me, he called Ellen over and said, "Right, em, Andi . . . I want to talk to the two of you."

Gerry was in his mid-thirties, a very easy-going sort of person, and permanently stoned. He grinned a lot, never seemed to remember our names, and occasionally forgot to come in at the end of the day and collect the cash. He had such a casual approach to life that you couldn't help but like him. He was like a doddery old uncle, only much younger and funnier-smelling.

We'd never seen him annoyed at anything, even when the shop was making a loss, and he'd never called a meeting before.

"I'm selling the place," he said. "Sorry to have to

break it to you like that, but there's no easy way to say it."

"Shit," Ellen said. "I suppose that means you're going to have to let us go?"

"Not necessarily," Gerry said. "There's always a chance that the new owner will want to keep the shop as it is. But he'll only do that if he sees that it's profitable."

"Ah," I said. "So we have to work our arses off for the next few weeks or whatever, right?"

He shrugged. "If you want. I'm getting out of the retail game regardless, so it doesn't matter to me. The main thing is to shift as much stock as possible. Have a sale or something."

"What, you're leaving it up to us?" Ellen asked.

"Don't I always? Yeah, have a sale. Mark everything down. Get the punters in and make a big profit. He's bound to keep the place as it is then. From what I've heard, this guy doesn't know about the business; he's just doing it for an investment. He's loaded, apparently."

"So when's he coming in to look at the place?" I asked.

"Tomorrow."

"But tomorrow's my day off!" Ellen said. "I have plans!"

Gerry shrugged again. "Up to you. Whatever you want to do. If you do come in, it's not like you'd have to do a full day. Just wait until he's gone. Anyway, if you're going to have a sale, then you're probably going to be busy."

"Look," I said, getting a little exasperated as his apathy, "when is it you're selling?"

"A couple of weeks," he said. "Probably. Something like that."

Ellen asked, "Just out of curiosity, what are you going to do?"

"I don't know yet. I'll see how much I get for this place first. Then I'll probably go on a holiday. Did you ever go on a canoeing holiday? It looks brilliant! I've never been in a canoe, but it doesn't look that hard. I want to learn how to do that thing where they roll over in the water."

Before he could get any further into the intricacies of canoeing, I stopped him. "Look, if this guy is coming tomorrow, you're going to be here, right?"

"Me? No. I'm going to . . ." He looked blank for a second. "Oh yeah, Raheny. He'll probably just introduce himself and ask you a bunch of questions."

"Well, what's his name, then?"

Gerry had to think about this one. "I'd have to say, I can't remember. I've got it written down somewhere at home. I'll phone you later on and let you know."

"And he's never owned a shop before?"

"Nope. Well, I don't think so. I don't know. Maybe he has."

* * *

Gerry left a few minutes later. Well, he didn't leave so much as gradually wander away. That was his way – everything was taken at a snail's pace.

Business was slow for a Friday morning, so Ellen and I spent most of the time talking. And then she said something to me that really caught me out.

"Well, Gerry was even more stoned than usual this morning." She sighed. "I can't *believe* he's selling the place!"

I didn't know what she was so upset about – it wasn't like Ellen actually needed a job. As for me, I suddenly had a vision of myself standing outside the post office on a wet Tuesday morning waiting to collect my dole money.

"I meant to ask him if he's selling the Clontarf shop as well," Ellen said, then shrugged. "Ah, fuck it." She took a bag of Fun-Size Crunchies down from the wall, opened them, then sat on the counter swinging her legs. "So what are *you* going to do?"

"I don't know. What about you?"

"I don't think I'll stay, no matter what the new owner is like. A hundred pounds says he won't be as easy-going as Gerry." She suddenly laughed. "I can't imagine *anyone* being as easy-going. You know, I've *never* seen him straight. He's been stoned every day for God knows how long."

"How did he ever get the money to buy this place, then?"

"They're rich," Ellen said. "He told me the whole

story one day. His da has some big pub out in the country, worth a fortune. They had loads of land as well, and a few years ago they sold a few acres for over a million." She offered me a Crunchie. "Anyway, Gerry was just bumming around, and his da told him to get a job and straighten himself out or he'd be in trouble. So Gerry got the idea that there was real money to be made in pound shops, so he got his da to lend him the money."

"And did he pay it back?"

She nodded. "Mostly. I think that's probably why he's selling now, so that he can pay off the rest and doss around for a few more years. Maybe he's only selling this one and not Clontarf as well."

I checked the time on the oversized Swatch watch that was hanging up beside the door. Dave the sullen security guard was due to arrive at twelve. He rarely spoke, unless he was throwing someone out or telling Ellen he was going to report her for stealing sweets. "Do you think he's told Dave?"

"Probably forgot. I suppose we should tell him."

A tired-looking young woman came in towing three little kids behind her, two girls and a boy. The boy decided that he wanted a toy sports car, but his mother told him to put it back. She spent a few minutes browsing through the discount hair-care stuff, breaking off a couple of times to pull toys from her children's hands and put them back on the wrong shelves.

She came up to the counter with two bottles of some

foreign shampoo that smelled like burnt roses, a shower cap, a packet of cheap plastic hooks that had sticky pads on the back, and a Pokémon toy.

From the look of this woman – lank hair, dull clothes, overweight, with hollow, dark eyes – she wasn't a member of the jet set. She looked like she could barely afford to belong to the bus set.

Ellen climbed down from the counter and stood behind her till. We exchanged glances, and I could tell what she was about to do. "A pound, please," Ellen said.

The women looked surprised. "What, for everything?"

"Yeah," Ellen said. "The boss has just told us he's selling up, so we've got to have a sale."

"Well, thanks . . . I was going to ask you were there any jobs going, but I suppose there's no point."

"Sorry," I said. "But look, leave your name and phone number and if anything comes up, we'll let you know. The new owner might want to keep the shop going."

The woman looked eagerly around the shop. "So, *everything's* on sale?"

* * *

When Dave the security guard arrived, Ellen told him about Gerry's plans to sell the shop. He just nodded and said, "Right. Well, I'm going to check with the agency," and then left. Half an hour later the receptionist from the security agency phoned us and said that Dave wouldn't be coming back. We asked her if we were getting anyone else, and she said that we would, but only after Dave had been paid; apparently Gerry was well-known for his financial tardiness.

We tried to get in touch with Gerry to let him know, but his mobile wasn't on. Either that, or he'd lost it again.

"So," Ellen said, "what about this sale, then? What should we do?"

I took a deep breath and looked around. "Well, we could put up a big sign in the window. Mark everything down. I suppose we'd better tell Jimmy about it." Jimmy was our Saturday boy. He was about seventeen, lanky and clumsy, with a face made entirely out of spots and tufts of hair. Ellen and I had alternate Saturdays off, and Jimmy covered for us. He wasn't very good, but he didn't cost much and was fairly easy to boss around.

"Will three of us be enough? Suppose we get a mad rush? And what are we going to do without Dave?"

"Get Dean in," I suggested. "Tell him to wear a blue shirt and a tie. Does he have a tie?"

"Probably," she said. She gave me a sly grin. "Interesting that you thought of *him* first . . ."

"Well, he's the biggest person I know," I said, unwilling to get into a discussion about whether or not I was still interested in her brother. "Or you could phone Robbie and ask *him*."

She gave me a look. "I don't think so. Dean will do it."

"What should we offer him for coming in for the day?"

Ellen grinned again. "If *you* ask him, he'll probably do it for nothing."

"Yeah, right. Last night you were criticising me for stringing him along. Anyway, you should phone him and ask him to come in today as well, if Dave isn't going to come back. I don't want to be here in the afternoon with all the kids nicking stuff if we don't have anyone on the door."

Ellen was silent for a few moments, then she said, "We could just close up the shop and take the day off. Even if Gerry finds out, what's he going to do? Fire us? And we have a good reason now that we don't have anyone on security."

I had to admit it was tempting. "No," I said. "Look, I don't know about you, but I need this job. Where else am I going to get something like this? Gerry's the best boss that you could hope for. He never interferes."

"Yeah, but he won't be our boss for much longer. I wonder what the new guy's going to be like?"

"Well, I think we should do what Gerry said, and have a sale. If we do, you'll *have* to come in tomorrow."

"All right, but I want Monday off."

* * *

So we spent the morning restocking the shelves and marking down most of the prices. We had a look at all the stuff that never seemed to sell, and knocked the prices way down. Ellen phoned Dean, and he arrived in the afternoon in a reasonably clean shirt and a tie, and stood by the door with his arms folded and trying to look tough.

We hung a "SALE NOW ON!" sign in the window. We'd made it by cutting up a "Merry Christmas!" and a "Bon Voyage!" and taping the letters together – to make the W we just turned an M upside-down, and chopped up another M to make the second N. The L was easy enough: it was the B with the curly bits cut off.

We were flooded with less than ten people for the whole afternoon.

"This is a pile of shite," Ellen said, painting her nails with Tipp-Ex. "The sign hasn't made any bloody difference."

"The problem is," Dean said, "you've had a sale every week for the past year. Why should they believe this one?"

A customer came in and Dean quickly put down the *Noddy* book he'd been flicking through and went back to looking fierce.

He was right, of course. "We need a gimmick to get people in," I said. "Something like 'Every tenth customer gets their money back'."

"Yeah, but you still have to let everyone know about it," Dean said. "And you have to get the word out as early as possible. Hang on, I'll ask Joe if he has any ideas." He pulled out his mobile phone, and was about to phone Joe when he realised that he'd save money if he used the shop's phone. "Joe? It's me. Yeah, listen, we're having a sale and we have to get people in. What do you think?" Dean paused, listening, then said, "That sounds good . . . Go on." He paused again.

Every couple of seconds he muttered, "Yeah," and resumed listening.

Ellen and I looked at each other and laughed. "That can't be the same Joe," Ellen said.

After a few minutes, Dean hung up. "Right, Joe says that for about a fiver he can get a whole bunch of flyers printed up – he knows a guy who has access to a photocopier when his boss isn't around – and we can get someone to hang around outside the shop and hand them out. He also said that we should phone one of the radio stations and ask them to park their outside broadcast van in front tomorrow and get them to keep announcing the sale. He says we can phone NTL and get them to put up an ad on the community pages. Though it'll probably be too late for that one. Or the radio one. He has a friend who can do mime, and we can get him to walk up and down outside and hand out the flyers. He'll dress up as an alien or something and that'll get the kids interested. Joe says his mate will probably do it for twenty quid."

Ellen was impressed. "I'd no idea that Joe was able to speak in sentences of more than three words."

"I'd no idea that he had any other friends," I said.

"He said that if we want to shift some of the crap stuff we should bundle it with a few good things and sell them as sort of lucky bags. A pound each. What's the most expensive thing we sell?"

"Walkmans," I said. "Well, fake ones. They're a tenner."

"Right, what's the markup?"

"What, the profit margin? I've no idea. Gerry bought hundreds of them a few months ago."

"Are they any good?"

"Not really."

"Well, they still work, right? Joe also said that a good trick would be to wrap up a lot of things that are about the same size, and stand outside with a big box and tell everyone it's a lucky dip, a pound a go. We don't have to give away too much, as long as it *looks* like we're giving away good stuff. Most of the stuff won't be worth a pound, but a few things will be worth a lot more, like the Walkmans."

I nodded – this was beginning to sound like it would work. "So, if we get the flyers printed up, we can hand them out at the same time."

"Yeah. You mightn't make much of a profit, but it'll get a lot of stuff moving."

The Tipp-Ex on Ellen's fingernails had dried, and now she was colouring them in with a pink highlighting marker. "I don't know . . . It sounds like a lot of work."

Dean went on: "Say you stand outside with a box full of stuff, and everything's wrapped up so people don't know what it is, right? *You* know, of course, but you tell everyone that it's a lucky dip. Everything should be about the same size, so they can't easily tell. Charge a pound a go."

"We get the idea, Dean," I said. "You don't need to explain it any more."

The phone rang and Ellen grabbed it before I could. "Hello, Sound as a Pound, how can I help you? Oh, Hi Gillian. Yeah, she's right beside me. Hang on." She handed me the phone. "It's Gillian from the Clontarf shop."

Gillian was a few years older than us, and had been working in the Clontarf shop for years. I'd only met her about twice, but we spoke on the phone about three or four times a week.

"Hi, Gillian, how's it going?"

"Not so great, Andi . . . Listen, Gerry was just in here. He said he's thinking of selling the shop. Was he in with you?"

"Yeah, first thing this morning. He's selling this one as well. He never said that he was selling both of them. What are you going to do?"

"I don't know . . . Gerry says that he has to find a buyer first."

"Well, he told us that he's already got one for this place. He's coming in tomorrow to look the place over."

"I was talking to Jack about it. He says that maybe we should invest in it. There's a friend of ours who's an accountant, and we're going to go over all the figures with her."

"Wow. That's a big step."

"Yeah . . . Well, we haven't decided on anything yet. Anyway, let me know what happens after tomorrow, okay?"

I said goodbye and hung up.

Ellen was serving a customer who had bought a whole pile of stuff. "That's twenty-two fifty," she said. "And if you come back tomorrow with a load of people, I'll give you an even bigger discount."

The customer left with a satisfied "Yes! I've beaten the system!" expression.

"So, what are we doing tonight?" Dean asked.

"There's a karaoke night in a pub in Lucan," I said. "I wouldn't mind going to that."

"It's way too far," Ellen said. "We'd never get home."

"Well, yer man who was on last night is doing a gig in Camden Street," Dean said. "You know, the first lad."

"Tony O'Hehir," I said. "Yeah, I wouldn't mind going along to that."

* * *

Gerry came back to the shop to collect the money earlier than usual. As soon as he left we closed up – Friday evening was always a quiet time anyway – so I was home at half-past six. My mother collared me on the way in, and there was a furious look on her face.

"You said you were going to see your Gran today."

"Oh yeah. I forgot. Sorry. I'll go and see her tomorrow."

She gave me that look of utter disappointment and

hurt, as though she'd just caught me shoplifting or something. "Andi, I don't ask much from you, do I? But can you even do that? No, you're too busy swanning around with your friends."

"Mam, I wasn't just dossing around the whole day. I was at *work*," I said, getting annoyed. I didn't want to tell her about Gerry's plans. At least, not until we knew one way or another whether the new owner would want to keep the shop as it is.

"And I suppose you're off out now for the night."

"Yes, I am as a matter of fact."

"Well, Eimear's coming over. She wants to talk to you about the wedding."

I raised my eyes. "Then why didn't she tell me? Why didn't she just phone the shop?"

"Look, if you're going to be one of her bridesmaids you have to know what's going on. The wedding won't just organise itself."

"It's still ages away. All Eimear probably wants to do is talk about her dress or something. I'll call in to see her during the week," I added, heading upstairs to my room.

My mother called up after me: "She's depending on you, Andi. Don't go letting her down on her big day. And it's *not* ages away."

I closed the door to my room. Eimear's wedding was the biggest event to happen in the family since Claire was born, and that had been fifteen years before. Roddy got married when he was only twenty, and John was living in sin with a married woman. Ciarán was single at the moment, but John always said that Ciarán was the only person he knew who could live in sin on his own.

Actually, Eimear was also living in sin, and that's probably why my mother was getting so worked up about it. I got the feeling that Mam was worried that Eimear would be hit by a bus before the wedding and end up going to the special Hell that Mam believed was reserved for co-habitors.

* * *

By the time we got to the pub in Camden Street, Tony O'Hehir was just starting his show. He opened with the routine about falling asleep in the cinema. It got a better laugh this time, but I still thought it was pretty weak.

After that, he had a few shaggy-dog stories that didn't get much of a laugh at all.

I could tell from the look on his face that he was beginning to panic. He hadn't been heckled yet, though, so that wasn't a bad sign.

"The thing about families," he said, adjusting his glasses, "is that you *always* have a cousin who's doing better than everyone else. But that's just because his parents are good at public relations. It's like my cousin Seán, the gravedigger. I met his mother the other day. 'How's Seán?' I asked. She grabbed my arm, the way they do, and told me how wonderfully he was getting on. 'Of course,' she says, 'Seán's *always* been good at digging. You know he got a B-plus in gravedigging in the Leaving Cert? He would have got an A only he forgot that he was supposed to dig it in Irish. He's thinking of doing a night course in dirt management and shovel handling. He was also talking about going out on his own.'" Tony paused, and took a sip of water. "My cousin Seán, the freelance gravedigger. I can just see him doing those cheap ads on telly . . ."

Tony stepped to the left and leaned on an imaginary shovel. As he spoke, he kept pointing at the "camera", spoke in a thick Dublin accent and emphasised all the wrong words. "Hi, here at Seán's Discount Graves, we're havin' a special offer. Buy one, get one free. Die now and we'll also throw in this beautiful marble-style headstone! And that's not all! If your next-of-kin can find a grave cheaper in the same area within seven days of burial, we'll dig you back up and clean you off for the other funeral, at no extra charge! So, come on down to Seán's Discount Graves, where we *do* know our arses from a hole in the ground!"

This went down pretty well, and Tony introduced the next act: a middle-aged woman trying to be Shirley Bassey.

At our table, Dean announced that it was my turn to get the drinks in.

"Let's just wait for the girl to come around again," I said.

"No, I'm thirsty now. Go on."

"All right. Who wants what?"

"Tennents," Ellen said.

"Guinness," said Dean.

I looked at Joe, but he just shook his head. "I'm all right."

As the barman was handing me back my change, I noticed that I was standing right beside Tony O'Hehir himself. He noticed me looking at him, and nodded. "All right?"

"You're not bad," I said.

He smiled. "What, you mean the comedy, or how I look?"

"I meant the comedy," I said. I couldn't help smiling back. "We saw you last night as well. You were the best of the lot."

"Thanks. But I thought Dennis was the best. Five in the afternoon, Watching the Clock! I love that sort of stuff. I can't do it myself, though. He was sort of like Harry Hill."

"He was almost exactly like Harry Hill, only not as funny," I said. "Listen, how come you didn't do the bit about your leg being raped by the dog?"

"I'm going to," he said. "One of the other acts didn't show up, so I've got to go on again after this one. Yeah, the one about the dog . . . it went down well last night. I thought I'd close with it."

"Do you want my advice about it?"

He hesitated, looked me up and down, and said, "Maybe . . ."

"You should change it around . . ." I explained how

I thought he'd get a better laugh from the punchline if he dropped the bit about the actor dog.

"I see what you mean," he said, "but I don't want to drop that. I just love the idea that they get some other dog in to bark for him. Like that Section 31 stuff when they couldn't interview Gerry Adams."

I had no idea what he was talking about, and said as much.

"Ah, you're a bit young to remember it. There was a law that said members of Sinn Fein couldn't be interviewed on the television, so they used to get around it by interviewing him and getting an actor to dub the lines."

"Oh, *now* I get it!"

At that moment, Dean arrived looking for his pint. "What's keeping you?" He noticed Tony, and his expression changed. "Oh, hi, how's it going? Great set, by the way. Loved the bit about the heads in the bin bags from last night. How come you didn't do that one tonight? You should have. It was great. And you'd want to watch Andi here picking your brains. She thinks that *she's* going to be a stand-up comedian one day." He laughed after he said the last part.

I pushed his pint into his hand. "I'm busy, Dean. Here, take these back to the others. I'll be there in a minute."

I watched Dean sulk his way back to the table with drops of Guinness all over his shoes. "Sorry about that," I said to Tony.

"It's all right," Tony said. "Boyfriend?"

"Used to be," I said. "But he can't take 'get lost' for an answer."

Tony drank half of his pint in one go. "All right, I'd better get back up there. Nice to talk to you, Annie."

"Andi," I corrected. "But hang on a minute . . . The stuff about the ghost writer is good, but it's an anti-climax after the rest of it. So, put that whole bit before the bit where they're interviewing the dog on telly, and drop the 'actor dog' bit." I gave him my best serious look. "Trust me. It's better that way."

Tony paused, then smiled again. "All right, I'll give it a go."

* * *

After Tony's set, he came over to our table to thank me. The routine *had* worked better my way.

We invited Tony to join us, unless he had other plans.

He said that hadn't any major plans; he just had to get his money from the manager. He came back to us a couple of minutes later, a fresh pint in his hand, and sat down next to me.

Dean wasn't too happy about that, so he tried to monopolise the conversation. "So, Tony, how long have you been doing the comedy circuit?"

"Since last night," Tony explained.

"That's what yer man meant last night when he said it was Tony's debut performance," Ellen said sarcastically.

"Ha ha," Dean said, even more sarcastically. "How did you come up with the material?"

Tony stretched his arms out in an exaggerated "I've no idea" gesture. "It's just sort of freewheeling. You just start with a topic and look at it from different angles and see where it goes from there."

I was about to say something, but Dean butted in again. "What does it feel like, making everyone laugh? I bet it's great."

"Yeah," Tony said. "It's amazing." He laughed. "You know, I haven't slept for the past four days, I was so worried about last night's show. And I couldn't sleep last night because I was on such a high. So what about you, Andi? You want to do stand-up?"

"Sure she does," Dean said. "You should see her bedroom; it's packed with tapes and books and videos. Steve Martin, Steven Wright, Eddie Izzard, Bill Hicks, Seán Hughes . . . It's all she ever talks about."

"So who's your favourite?" Tony asked me.

Dean jumped in again. "Eddie Izzard! She's mad about him."

Tony turned to him. "Look, just shut the fuck up for a few minutes, all right? I wasn't asking you."

Dean sat back as though he'd been punched in the face. From the corner of my eye, I could see him turning red with embarrassment and rage.

I tried not to smile. "Yeah, he's right. Eddie Izzard, mainly, but also Woody Allen, Victoria Wood, Groucho, Rich Hall, Jo Brand, Deirdre O'Kane, Stephen Fry, Johnny Vegas, Bill Bailey . . ."

"All the greats," Tony said. "Especially Bill Bailey. I

wish I could play the guitar like he does. And Ben Elton, he's the best. I saw him about ten years ago in London, and that was when I knew I wanted to do stand-up."

Ellen, who had been unusually silent all this time, suddenly said, "So, Tony, what's your next gig?"

"I'm doing the show again next Thursday."

"That's a good sign," she said. "They don't usually have a newcomer back two weeks in a row." Then she added, "We've been going there for nearly a year. We've seen more than a few people die up there."

Tony sat back. "God, don't even *say* that word! I was shitting bricks all week about it. I really expected that as soon as I got up there, I'd forget everything."

"You said nothing for nearly a minute," Joe said.

Tony looked at Joe as if he'd just noticed that he was there. "Yeah . . . I don't know what happened."

"We thought that you might have been doing Norman Lovett's trick," Ellen said.

"No, that never occurred to me." He thought about it. "I might do that next time, though."

I shook my head. "Nah, you haven't got the face for it. He can pull it off because he can look really serious and depressed."

Tony finished his drink, and stood up. "Well, I'm off home. I haven't slept in days. I already told you that, didn't I? So I'll see you all next Thursday, right?"

"Sure," Ellen and I said at the same time.

Joe nodded, but Dean wouldn't even look at him.

Tony noticed this, and said, "Look, sorry about snapping at you like that. I'm still a bit on edge. And I'm knackered."

"It's okay," Dean said, forcing the words out. "Forget about it."

"That's cool, then. Thanks again, Andi," Tony said, patting me on the shoulder as he went past.

We watched him go, then Ellen grabbed my arm and said, "Is he gorgeous or what?"

"He's not bad," I said, as a grin slowly spread across my face.

Dean didn't like that at all.

Chapter Seven

When I got home, I discovered that Eimear had decided to spend the night. Eimear was thirty, ten years older than me, and I didn't really know her all that well, even though it hadn't been that long since she'd left home. We were so far apart in age that we'd never really managed to connect.

She was sleeping in her old bed in our room, but woke up when I came in and turned on the light. I was well on the way to being drunk, but did my best to hide it.

"How's it going?" she asked. "And why weren't you in tonight?"

"It's Friday night, Eimear," I said, sitting on the bed and pulling off my shoes. "Mam only told me when I got in from work and I'd already made arrangements."

She sat up. "Well, I wanted to talk to you about the plans for the wedding."

I undressed and got into bed. "Okay then. Fire away."

"You have to organise the hen party and pick somewhere for afterwards, for a start."

"Sure there's ages yet."

"There's only five weeks. And I want you to organise the cake and the bridesmaids' dresses. And you'd better talk to the hotel and make sure that everything is set up. Mam's doing the invitations but I want you to give her a hand. And you have to organise the band. I don't want a DJ."

I made a face. "Eimear, if you get a band then all the old folk will want to sing their party pieces. It'll be ten renditions of 'I'll Take You Home Again, Kathleen' and the like. By the end of the night we'll be only too aware of *how* low the fields of Athenry lie. You're much better off with a DJ. At least then you won't be getting people forgetting the words and trying to drink and sing at the same time."

She was having none of it. "I want a *band*."

"All right, all right. But what sort? Please don't say you want a trad band! I can't take any of that diddly-idle shite."

"I *do* want a trad band. You have to find a good one and get a demo tape off them or something so me and Chris can hear them. And a lot of Chris's relatives are real republican, so the band will have to know all the Wolfe Tones' stuff and that sort of thing. And make sure they do requests."

"They *all* do requests," I said, "because the only songs anyone ever bloody asks them to do are 'Oh

Danny Boy', and the national anthem and the 'Armoured Tanks and Cars and Guns' one. And anyway, how am I supposed to know whether they're any good or not? They all sound the same to me."

"Fuck's sake, Andi, you have to complain about everything, don't you?"

I sighed. "All right, I'll do it. What about the cake, though? I thought you were getting Chris's granny to make it."

"She decided she can't do it any more. She says she's too old." Eimear looked really pissed off. "You know how much a wedding cake costs these days?"

I had no idea. "A million pounds?"

She ignored me. "And you and Lorna and Audrey" – the other bridesmaids – "have to go and get fitted for your dresses next week. I can't get time off so you'll have to take care of everything. And don't fuck it up."

"Okay . . . What was it you wanted me to do about the hotel?"

"Just phone them and check that everything's okay. Chris's cousin's friend got married a few years ago and they just assumed that everything was fine and two days before the wedding they checked with the hotel and discovered that the place was double-booked."

"Okay."

Eimear was silent for a few seconds, then said, "I nearly forgot. You have to organise the Mass book as well."

"The what?"

"The Mass book. You know, for the ceremony."

"What, you mean all the priest's words and the readings and everything? Sure how would I even go about doing that?"

"I don't know. You'll have to get it sorted. We'll need about a hundred of them. And you need to get it done quick, because the priest has to approve it."

I switched off the light, pulled the duvet up over my head and turned my back to her. "Jesus," I muttered, "I have to do *everything*. You should have had all this done ages ago. But now, you leave it all till the last minute and get *me* to do it. You'd think that I was the one getting married."

She heard that. "Look, Andi, I've never asked you for anything before, have I?"

"You asked me to lend you twenty quid two weeks ago," I said.

"I meant anything important."

"Yeah. You're always getting me to do your dirty work."

"Look, this is *really* important to me," she said. "It's hard enough as it is. I don't want to have to fight with you about it as well."

I relented. "Okay, okay. I'll do whatever I can."

"Good. Thanks."

Neither of us said anything for a long time, but I could tell from her breathing that she was still awake.

"Eimear?"

"Yeah?"

"This lad goes to the doctor because he's been farting like mad. All day long it's just fart, fart, fart. But after less than a minute the doctor asks him to leave. 'Sorry,' the doctor says, 'you have to go – the smell is just too bad.' 'But you have to help me!' the man says. 'Sorry, I can't help you. You'll have to see a specialist.' He gives him a business card. 'Go and see this man – he knows all about flatulence. I'm certain that he can cure you.' So he goes to see the specialist . . . 'Well,' the specialist says, 'you've got the worst case of flatulence I've ever encountered. But I can help you, if you trust me.' 'Of course,' the man says. 'Whatever it takes.' 'Okay,' says the specialist. He gets up and retrieves a six-foot-long pole from behind the door. The pole has a large, wicked-looking brass hook on the end. The man almost faints. 'Oh my God! What are you going to do?' 'Well first,' the specialist says, 'I'm going to open some windows . . . '"

Eimear laughed, and said, "I think I've heard it before. I'll have to try and remember it for Chris. I can never remember jokes."

After a few more minutes' silence, I said, "Eimear?"

"Yeah?"

"Are you scared about getting married?"

She paused. "Yeah."

I sat up and looked in her direction. I couldn't see much, but we'd shared the same room for about seventeen years, so I knew where to look. "It'll be fine. Chris is all right."

"I'm not worried about the marriage. Just the wedding."

"It's only one day. As long as you both turn up and say 'I do' at the right time, it doesn't matter what else happens."

"I know that. But I've had thirty years to wonder what getting married will be like. I want it to be perfect."

"Well, you can count on me."

"I know that too."

* * *

The next day at work, Joe's mime-artist friend arrived carrying a huge lumpy sports bag. He was about five-ten, not bad-looking, though he seemed a little nervous. He asked if there was anywhere he could change, and Ellen pointed him towards the toilet. He came out fifteen minutes later dressed as the sorriest-looking alien I'd ever seen.

He was wearing a shiny tracksuit with hundreds of old CDs glued to it – he said that they were America On-Line disks that came free with computer magazines. He'd painted his face and hands silver, and his blond hair was now green. He handed me a black marker. "You have to draw large black circles on my eyelids," he said. "I can't do it myself."

His eyelids had already been painted yellow. I drew two large black circles for him. "How does it look?" he asked, keeping his eyes closed.

79

"Weird," I said.

"Yeah, but do I look like an alien?"

No, I said to myself, you look like a steel clown who's been on the booze all night. "Yeah, just like an alien."

"Deadly," he said, and opened his eyes. "So what do you want me to do?"

"Just walk up and down a bit outside, and hand out these flyers."

"That could be awkward," he said. "I can't move around much when my eyes are closed. I'll tell you what I'll do, I stand out the front and do my robotics." He demonstrated. It was shite. "How's that?"

"Brilliant," I lied.

At the far end of the shop, Ellen was silently killing herself laughing.

"So is Joe coming along today?"

"I don't know," I said. "Dean will be here, though."

He frowned, and cracks appeared in his silver face. "I don't know him. I only know Joe. He said you'd pay me for the day's work."

"Sure . . . Only it depends on how much business you bring in. If we do well, I'll give you twenty quid."

He looked panic-stricken, as though the responsibility was too much for him.

"But either way, you'll get at least a tenner," I added, out of compassion.

That suited him a little better. "Okay. Only, it'll have to be that much at least, because this silver paint is expensive. Will you phone Joe and ask him to come over?"

"I'll ask Dean to do it," I said.

A bit more satisfied, he took the flyers and went outside. Ellen came up and we watched him through the window. He was really, really bad . . . He tried moon-walking, and it just looked like he was trying to get shit off his shoes. Then he did a little more of his "robotics": his arms and legs went stiff and he moved around very slowly, occasionally turning his head left and right.

Little kids stared at him as their mothers dragged them past and avoided the offer of the flyers. A trio of builders working on a shop across the road broke their hearts laughing at him, and the other passers-by regarded him with some suspicion.

Ellen was still laughing as she started piling the wrapped "surprise" packages into a cardboard box. There were about a hundred packages, of which eight were worth more than a pound: the rest of them were bottles of men's aftershave or cheap toys. "When Jimmy gets here we can get him to stand outside and do the lucky dip," she said. "I don't want to be standing out there with that eejit."

"Or we could get the robot alien to do it," I said, "and call it a Lucky Dipshit."

"What's his name again?"

"I can't remember," I said. "I'll ask Dean when he comes in." That reminded me of something. "Listen, was Dean all right last night? He seemed a bit pissed off with what Tony said."

"Can you blame him?"

"Well, yeah. I mean, Tony was trying to talk to me and Dean kept answering for me. If Tony hadn't told him to shut up, *I* would have."

Ellen was staring out at the alien robot again, and was still giggling. "What is he *like*?"

He turned around using a move that made me think of t'ai chi performed by a someone who had all the grace of a ballet dancer with concrete shoes, and was now facing us. With his eyes closed, he couldn't see us making faces at him.

"I have to admit," Ellen said, "those eyes are really creepy. I can't look away."

"That's because it looks like he's not blinking," I said.

The alien swung back around again to face away from the shop, and marched forward a little. He almost collided with an old woman dragging a shopping trolley, but didn't even notice. The old woman glared at him and stomped off.

Next, he turned to the left and started the famous "shiny blind alien robot trapped in an invisible glass box" routine.

We must have spent about half an hour staring out at him. Occasionally he opened his eyes a little to check where he was or to track down potential flyer-takers.

No one was the slightest bit interested in the flyers.

A few groups of people stopped now and then to watch him, but edged away when he approached. During the whole time, not one customer entered the shop.

"He's scaring them away," Ellen said. "We're actually *losing* customers."

The best part happened a few minutes later, when he was awkwardly flying an imaginary kite and backed into someone. The flyers spilled to the ground and a gust of wind – a much more gentle wind than the pretend one he'd earlier been struggling to walk through – blew most of them away. The lads working across the street were practically doubled over with laughter as the alien ran around picking up the flyers and losing CDs every time he bent down.

Then we saw Jimmy heading towards the shop. Daydreaming as usual, he almost walked into the alien before he noticed him. Jimmy almost jumped out of his skin, nervously accepted a flyer, and darted into the shop.

"What the fuck is yer man up to?"

"He's helping us keep our jobs," I said. "Well, he's trying to." I explained all about Gerry's plan to sell the shop, and how he'd suggested we have a big sale to try and persuade the new owner to keep the shop as it is.

Jimmy wasn't bothered about losing the job. "My da said that I have to give it up before school starts again anyway." He looked around. "God, it's quiet today."

"It's him," Ellen said, nodding towards the entertainment department. "Any time anyone comes near

83

the door he goes after them and they run away." She was laughing again. "I'd tell him to stop, but it's too funny."

* * *

When Dean arrived shortly after noon, he had Joe tagging along with him. The alien spotted them and decided it was time for a break: It was a fairly hot day, and his silver paint had started to run.

Dean barely said hello to me, then took up his post beside the door. Ellen was on her lunch, and Jimmy was in the storeroom "tidying up" – his special code word for smoking a joint.

That left me to talk to Joe the Silent One and his very odd friend. "So," I said to Joe, "how are things?"

"Okay."

The alien dabbed at his silver sweat with a hanky. "I'm melting."

"*And* you haven't got a heart," Joe said.

His friend laughed, and it took me a few seconds to realise that it was a reference to *The Wizard of Oz*.

"What are your plans for the day, Joe?"

He shrugged. "Don't know."

"Are you going back tonight or tomorrow?"

"Tomorrow."

I abandoned my journey down this particular conversational cul-de-sac and turned to his friend. "Sorry, I can't remember your name."

"Niall," he said, extending a wet silver hand to be shook. "Oh, sorry. I'm still dripping."

"So what do *you* do?"

"At the moment, this," he said, indicating his get-up. "I'm a performance artist."

I had to stifle a snigger. "Been doing it long?"

"A couple of years. Everyone said I'd never get anywhere, but I'll show them."

"That's the spirit," I said. "Keep going against all the odds and negative comments. Don't let the bastards get you down."

"Joe says you're thinking about a bit of performance work yourself," Niall said. "If you need any advice, I'm your man. I've got a lot of experience. I've done dance, theatre, the lot. I don't dance much any more, though."

"Why not?"

"Accident. I was knocked off my bike and the truck ran over my foot. I'm more or less okay, but my tendons are pretty weak. It could be years before I dance again."

Joe started laughing, and I suddenly realised that I'd never heard him laugh before. He'd been coming along to the comedy nights for nearly a year, and I couldn't remember him laughing.

"What's so funny?" I asked him.

Niall looked disgusted. "Shut the fuck up, Joe." He let out an exasperated sigh, and said to me, "The truck that hit me was delivering office supplies."

"So?"

He slapped Joe – who was still laughing – across the back of the head. "Everyone else thinks it's so fucking funny, so you might as well hear it. I was run over by a stationery truck."

* * *

After Ellen came back from lunch, I went out. I'd promised my mother I'd go and see Gran, and I didn't want to let her down again.

Gran's house was about fifteen minutes' walk from the shop. She was in – she was *always* in – and happy to see me. As soon as I walked in she nodded to me and charged off to the kitchen, talking all the way.

"Andi. Will you have a cup of tea? Have you had your lunch? I'll just do you some sandwiches. Look at the state of you – do you never eat? When I was your age we made sure we had a proper breakfast every morning. Eggs and rashers, that's what you want. None of this Special K with strawberries cut up into it. That's not a proper breakfast. Your mam said that you'd be coming yesterday. I was a bit worried when you didn't show up. I thought that you might have had an accident or something. Your grandad, Lord have mercy on him, always said that a proper breakfast is a good foundation for the day. Even when we had nothing, we always made sure there was porridge at least."

She went on, and on, until the sandwiches were made and the tea was sufficiently drawn. She loaded a tray with the teapot, the little milk jug I'd bought her for her seventieth birthday, cups and saucers, plates of sandwiches and the sugar bowl.

I offered to carry the tray for her, but she brushed me away, saying, "The day I get too old to carry a tray is the day you can put me in a home."

Gran had turned eighty earlier in the year. We'd planned a surprise party for her, but she'd anticipated it and gone off on a pilgrimage to Knock to deliberately scupper our plans.

Her hair was completely white now – "I've never been the sort to colour my hair," she'd say, "not like some people whose names I won't mention. Like your mother. Airs and graces, that one. Don't say I said that." – and she looked old, but then she'd always looked old to me. That said, even at eighty, she was still fairly strong and healthy.

"Your mam says that you're going to help organise Eimear's wedding," Gran said, pouring the tea.

"So it appears. They never really *asked* me if I'd do it. They just assumed I would."

"Family duty. It's important that you all help each other out."

"That's a laugh. I can't even remember the last time I saw Ciarán or John."

"Well, you'll see them at the wedding, then." She said it as though she'd just solved a complex problem. Well, maybe she had.

"Gran, you know that they're never going to help *me* out . . ."

She said nothing, just picked up one of her famous and feared butter sandwiches – "I can't be having with wafer-thin slices of ham and whatnot. Ham is for the dinner table, not the lunchbox." – and munched on it thoughtfully.

"I still haven't told Mam what I want to do. I think Dad will be all right with it, but *she's* going to lose it altogether."

"Andi . . . the stage life isn't for everyone. Do you honestly think that you can get up there day after day and not have a single person laugh at your jokes? I'm not saying that *will* happen, but it could. You have to be prepared for that. And you can't just give it up when it starts going bad. Liberace never gave up, did he? No, he kept playing, and eventually he became the most famous piano player in the world." Gran never could bring herself to use the word "pianist". "Comedy is one of the hardest of all the stage arts, did I tell you that? Different people find different things funny. How can you ever be sure that you're going to make even one person laugh?"

"Gran, you tell me that every time I come here. I don't need to hear it. What I do need to hear is that you're behind me. I mean, none of my friends think I'm going to be able to do it, and the rest of the family will just think I'm mad. But you . . . well, you've been there. You were on the stage and you acted in plays and even sang, in front of hundreds of strangers. I mean, you're the one who used to tell me bedtime stories about plays that you and Grandad performed in. I thought that *you* at least would understand and support me."

She looked shocked that I'd even mentioned it. "Andi, I do understand, and I'll always support you. Look, it takes two things to make it on the stage: determination and talent. You have both. All you really need is to stop talking about it and start doing it. You can't learn to swim if you don't get into the water."

Gran was right, as always. I'd wanted to do stand-up comedy ever since I was in first year at school and discovered that I could make people laugh by doing impressions of the teachers.

But it wasn't as easy to get started as Gran seemed to think. I was going to be busy over the next couple of months, what with Eimear's wedding and all the stuff that was happening at work.

"Uh oh," I said, jumping to my feet. "I'd better get back to work. There's a lot going on at the moment. Thanks for lunch, Gran."

"Don't mention it, dear. Just remember what I said. If you want to do it, ignore all the begrudgers and just *do* it."

* * *

The new owner was in the shop when I got back. He was a tall, very good-looking middle-aged man, all shiny suit and immaculate grey hair. From the look on his face, he wasn't very impressed with what he saw.

Ellen was being bombarded with questions about turnover and stock, and her face lit up when she saw me. "Oh, here's Andi now! She's the manager."

That was the first *I'd* heard about me being the manager. The new owner turned to me, and behind him Ellen was nodding vigorously.

I offered my hand. "Andrea Quinn," I said. "Everyone calls me Andi."

He shook my hand and looked around again. "How long have you been working here, Andi?"

"Just over a year now."

"I see . . . I suppose Gerry's told you that I'm thinking of buying the shop from him?"

"He did . . . He said that he didn't know whether you'd keep it as it is, though."

He stepped aside and looked around, sizing the place up. "I don't think I will. I was thinking about an Internet café . . ." He turned to me again. "Do you know anything about the Internet?"

I glanced at Ellen, and she was nodding again. "Oh yeah," I said. "I'm not an expert, but I know a bit."

"It makes no difference anyway. I'd be hiring an experienced SA." He wandered around as he talked, trying to examine the walls behind the shelves. "What's the power like here?"

- I had no idea what he meant. "It's fine."

"Steady?"

"Like a rock."

This seemed to be the right answer, because he nodded and looked a little happier. "We'd be getting a good UPS anyway, for the Linux server. How big is the storeroom?"

"I'll show you." I brought him into the storeroom, and luckily all evidence of Jimmy's herbal indulgence was well-hidden.

"It's big enough," he said. "We can knock out part of this wall and set up the deli counter here. Do you have any experience in the catering industry, Andi?"

"Some," I lied. "But it's been a couple of years."

He didn't seem to be really listening. "That's fine . . . We'd be open from eight in the morning until midnight. Maybe two or three on Fridays and Saturdays. Probably wouldn't need anyone on security, but we'll have to see how that works out." He wandered back out into the shop. "That'll be an SA on full-time, say eight hours a day, plus call out . . . And at least two behind the counter at all times, another on the floor. Maybe four or five in total during busy periods. That's seven days a week, of course," he added, looking at me like I knew what he was talking about.

"Naturally."

"We can get ten iMacs in here, maybe twelve. All the shelves will have to go, and maybe the counter . . . Put a long high bench at the window with a few stools, attract the passing trade. We'll need a couple of printers too." He gestured towards the back of the shop, in the direction of the toilets. "How many cubicles are there?"

"Just the one."

"No, that won't do. We'll need at least one other."

He said nothing for a couple of seconds, then turned

to me again. "All right, I think it's doable. So, Andi, are you on board?"

"Try and stop me!" I said with fake enthusiasm. "I'm really looking forward to it!"

"Okay. We'll have to draw up proper plans, and the renovation will probably take at least a month. We'll do the walls and ceiling black, hidden lighting, dark grey carpet, good solid furniture. Not counting the IT material, it shouldn't come to more than five or six thousand, if I can get it at source. Catering licence on top of that, plus the catering equipment. I'll get the SA to organise the computers and the rest, of course. Can you handle the interviews for the staff?"

"Certainly," I said, though I'd absolutely no idea if I could.

"Excellent," he said, which made me think of Mr Burns from *The Simpsons*. "I should have everything sorted out vis-à-vis the transfer of ownership by the end of next week, if everything goes well. As for the stock . . ." he said with a wink, "good idea to sell it off cheaply. It'll make Gerry that much more eager to sell."

"That's what I thought," I said, nodding.

"And of course you'll need uniforms. Nothing fancy, just a skirt and blouse with the logo. Which reminds me, we need to come up with a name. Never mind, that can wait for a week or so. But put your thinking cap on anyway. Say a budget of twenty thousand for the renovation and catering . . . A decent couple of coffee machines. *And* a cappuccino machine . . . Refrigerated units. Maybe a Coke machine. Or Club, whichever is more likely to be popular."

He was looking at me expectantly.

I took a chance. "Coke, I think. I'd need to check it against the running costs."

"Perfect." He grinned and shook my hand again. "I'll be in touch during the week. If you have any questions, here's my card." He said goodbye to us all, had a last look around, and left.

We gave him thirty seconds, and then huddled together.

Me: "What's an SA?"

Dean: "Andi, I didn't know you knew anything about the Internet."

Ellen: "You bloody liar. You don't know anything about catering. You can't tell the difference between cappuccino and Al Pacino."

Me: "What's a UPS?"

Dean: "Does he mean that *you're* going to be in charge?"

Ellen: "You jammy sod. Are you going to give me a job?"

Me: "What's an iMac?"

Ellen: "You have no idea what you're doing, do you?"

Dean: "I bet yer man is absolutely loaded. Did you see his suit? Armani, that was."

Ellen: "How would *you* know?"

Me: "What's a Linux server? No, forget that for a minute . . . What the *hell* just happened here?"

And then Niall – who was still dressed as an alien – spoke up . . ."An SA is a Systems Administrator, someone who knows how to install the computers and all the cables. A UPS is an Uninterruptable Power Supply. Basically it's a big battery that'll keep your server up and running if there's a power cut. Think of the server as a sort of gateway to the Internet. All the computers connect to it, it connects to the Internet. Linux is the server's operating system – if the server was a person, the operating system is the mind." He paused. "Oh yeah, and iMac is the make of the computer that the customers will be using. And that was *never* an Armani suit."

I might have hugged him for that, if he wasn't so scary.

"What does 'vis-à-vis' mean?" Ellen asked, but Niall didn't know that one.

However, Joe did. "It means 'with regard to'."

I had to have a sit-down. "God, that was intense. And it's all your bloody fault, El. You told him I was the manager."

"Yeah, blame me for getting you another job."

"I've never even used the Internet," I said. "What the hell am I going to do?"

"Don't worry," Niall said. "I've got a computer at home with an Internet connection. You can come over and I'll show you what it's all about. And you should check out some of the other Internet cafés around Dublin."

"As if I don't have enough on my plate . . ." I looked around. "Where's Jimmy?"

"Lunch," Dean said. "Speaking of which, I'm going to get something to eat. Are you coming, lads?" He looked at Niall's outfit. "Or maybe you should both stay here until I get back."

"Go ahead," I said. "We'll be fine."

They didn't need to be told twice.

Now that Ellen and I were left alone, we stared at each other. "What am I going to do, El?"

She picked up the business card. "You could phone him and say you've changed your mind."

"Then I'll be out of a job. No, I don't know . . . It could be okay, though. I won't really need to know any technical stuff. What was your man's name anyway? You never introduced him."

"That's because I forgot it as soon as he said it . . ." She read the card. "Here it is: Bernard Parker."

"Well, he seems nice enough."

Chapter Eight

I phoned Gerry on his mobile and let him know that it looked like Mr Parker definitely *would* be buying the shop.

"That's great," Gerry said. I got the feeling that he was nodding slowly to himself. "That's cool. Listen, I was thinking, sorry if you guys all lose your jobs."

"Nice of you to think of that *now*," I said, dripping with sarcasm. "I'll probably be all right – he wants me to manage the place – but I don't know about Ellen and Jimmy."

"They'll be fine. Sure they're young."

"What does that have to do with anything?"

Gerry was stuck for an answer. After a long pause, he said, "Well, *you* could hire them."

"Maybe. Look, Gerry, do you know anything about running an Internet café?"

"You know, Andi . . . I don't."

"What about an ordinary café then?"

"Yeah . . . Okay, see there's this lad I know who used to work in a pub. I know it's not the same but they did lunches. He might be able to help you. No, wait, he's not there any more. I think. Or maybe he is."

I was really beginning to lose my temper with him. "Forget it, then. Look, what I want to know is, what are we supposed to do for the next week?" Before he could tell me that he didn't know, I added, "Do you want us to keep the shop open? What about the stock? And should I just let Jimmy and Ellen go? If I do, should I pay them redundancy money?"

He made a sort of panicky strangled noise, and I realised I was bombarding him with far too many questions.

"Okay," I said, "forget all that too. I'll sort it out. Will you stand by whatever I decide to do?"

"Ah yeah, why not?"

"Right. Are you coming in this evening to collect the cash?" Not that there was much to collect, since we'd had only a handful of customers all day.

"Not tonight. I was going to come in in the morning instead. About half-one."

"Half past one in the morning? Are you mad?"

"I mean, half-one tomorrow. After lunch. Is that cool?"

"Yeah, sure . . . But if the place gets broken into tonight and all the money gets robbed, it'll be your fault."

Gerry agreed that it would be his fault, but, hey, that was cool too. He said goodbye and I hung up.

"What's the story?" Ellen asked.

"He's a wanker," I said. "He doesn't have a clue what's going on."

"He never did. So what are you going to do?"

I shrugged. "There's not much we can do until we hear back from Mr Parker. On Monday I'd better cancel all the deliveries, though. We're going to have a hard job getting rid of all this crap as it is."

Ellen was staring out the window at Niall again. "He's playing imaginary basketball now."

I shook my head. "I don't even want to look at him."

"He's all right, though . . . I mean, he can't do mime for shit, but he's okay. At least he's a lot more cheerful than Joe. And he's not bad-looking under all that paint."

Jimmy wandered back in. "I've been out there for ages and only made eight quid."

I made a decision. "Right, here's what we'll do. What time is it?"

"Nearly three."

"When Dean and Joe get back, we'll close up and go to the pub." I opened my till and counted the cash. "Gerry won't be here until tomorrow afternoon. Let's borrow some of his money and all go out and get pissed. Consider it a bonus."

* * *

We were delayed in getting out of the shop because Niall insisted on changing back into his human form before we left. He had some trouble getting the silver paint off his face, so Ellen offered to help him. The two of them disappeared into the toilet, and Ellen came out a few minutes later to get a bottle of make-up remover.

Dean and Jimmy stuffed their pockets with sweets, on the grounds that it wasn't really stealing because the sweets weren't likely to be sold by their "best before" dates. In fact, Dean was surprisingly efficient at it: he also took a kid's rucksack and filled that with sweets too.

Joe stood by with his hands firmly in his pockets.

When Niall was finally ready – his face was red from scrubbing and his hair was still wet – we locked up the shop and piled into the nearest pub.

It was fairly quiet for a Saturday afternoon. There was a television on in one corner, so we sat in the opposite corner.

"Right, lads," I said. "The drinks are on Gerry! Who wants what?"

It was doubles all round, except for Joe. "I'm okay," he said.

"Ah, Joe, you have to have something," Dean said as he opened the rucksack and emptied the stolen sweets onto the table. "You should never turn down a free drink."

"I'm okay," he repeated.

"Suit yourself, then," I said.

Gerry's money ran out at about six in the evening, but we didn't let that stop us: we delved into our pockets and pooled our own money on the table.

Ellen counted it. "Thirty-three quid. That's . . . seventeen drinks. No, that's wrong . . . I don't know. Is this all we have between the six of us?"

Dean nudged Joe. "Here you, cough up."

Even though he hadn't had anything to drink, Joe pulled a ten-pound note out of his pocket and added it to the pile.

"Hang on a minute," Niall said to me. "You said that you'd pay me for the day's work!"

"Yeah, well I said you'd get a tenner at least, more if you got lots of customers for us."

"So where's my money?"

"Niall, we had less customers than usual because you were scaring them away."

He looked hurt. "Well, where's my tenner, then?"

"You've already drunk it," I said. "What, did you think that you're getting these drinks for nothing?"

"Jesus, Andi, that's not fuckin' fair!" Ellen said. "You should of told him!"

When Ellen's had a few drinks her diction goes all to hell. "You mean 'should have', El, not 'should of'," I corrected: when *I've* had a few drinks, I get really pedantic.

"Ah fuck off! You know it's not fair."

"All right, all right . . . Come to the shop tomorrow, Niall, and I'll pay you then."

* * *

By the end of the night, my suspicions about Ellen

being interested in Niall were reinforced when I came back from the toilet and noticed that both of them were missing.

Jimmy and Joe were also missing. This meant that I had to face Dean on his own.

"So, where's everyone?" I asked.

"Ellen and Niall have gone off for a snog. Jimmy's outside puking his ring up and Joe's minding him."

I groaned. "Jimmy's mother is going to come down on me like a ton of bricks. He's only seventeen. She gave me a bollocking once when he came home a bit wobbly after *one* drink."

"Then tell her that we've all got food poisoning," Dean suggested. "You could phone her now and say that we went out for something to eat and we're all sick. Jimmy can kip on the floor in Ellen's place tonight."

Joe and Jimmy came back. Jimmy looked really, really sick, and Joe was more or less holding him up. "I'm goin' home," Jimmy said. He looked like he was about to cry.

"I'll make sure he gets there," Joe said.

"Grand," Dean said. "We'll wait for you."

Joe nodded and steered Jimmy towards the door.

"So it's just the two of us," Dean said, looking at me.

"So it seems."

"You know what day it is on Tuesday? It's two years since we started going out. We should go out and celebrate."

"What? But you'll be in Kilkenny."

"I don't *have* to go back tomorrow. I mean, it's not like I have a real job to go to."

"Well, no one forced you to resign" – Dean didn't know that Ellen had told me the truth about Dean's job in the factory – "and no one's stopping you from going out and getting another job somewhere else."

"*You* could give me a job in your Internet café."

"I could, but I'm not about to. You don't know anything about the Internet. And you've never worked behind a counter."

"Well, neither do *you* know anything about the Internet. Anyway, what do you say about Tuesday? Where do you want to go?"

"Dean, we broke up over a year and a half ago. Why would we go out and celebrate?"

"Yeah, but it's not like we're *really* broken up. You just wanted some time to get yourself sorted." He drained the last of his pint. "If you ask me, you've had plenty of time. You have to make your bloody mind up one way or the other."

That was the last straw . . . I decided that it didn't matter how annoyed Ellen was going to get, I wanted to spell it out loud and clear for Dean: "I *have* made my mind up. I made it up about a month after we started going out, only I couldn't tell you because I didn't want to lose Ellen as a friend. But here's the story . . . I don't like you any more. I haven't liked you for a long time. I think you're a complete prick and you treat people like shit. You're selfish and vain and boring and you're a bully too – I've seen the way you treat Joe. God only knows why he hangs around with you."

Dean nodded slowly. "I see. This is about Tony, isn't it?"

"What the fuck are you talking about?"

"I saw the way you were looking at him the other night."

"Ah, just sod off, Dean. You don't know anything. But in case you're still not clear on the subject, we're *not* going out. We'll never be going out again. It was a mistake to begin with. So you have to just get a grip and forget any ideas you have about us. There *is* no 'us', understand?"

Dean said nothing, just stared over my shoulder, and then I looked around to see Ellen and Niall standing behind me.

"You fucking *bitch*," Ellen said. "You have no fucking right to treat him like that! Stringing him along! I warned you to sort it out!"

I stood up, and faced her. "I am bloody sorting it out! That's what I'm doing! Only your thick brother here can't get the fucking hint!"

"Don't fucking take it out on me!" Ellen said, screaming right into my face.

I suddenly realised how close we were to a fight, and I forced myself to calm down. "All right, I'm sorry. I'm not taking it out on you."

It didn't make that much of a difference to her. "You have no fucking right to treat him like that!"

"Yes, I do," I said, as calmly as I could. "I've been trying to break up with him for nearly two years. I've hardly even looked at another man in that time, because if Dean's around he gets mad jealous, and if he's not, *you* keep going on about how I should sort it out with Dean."

Beside her, Niall shook his head in disgust and walked away. Ellen stared after him in shock.

"Ah, would the two of you just shut up and sit down?" Dean said. "You're making a scene."

He was right about that: all the customers and staff in the pub were looking over at us. I sat down, but Ellen remained standing.

Very quietly, so that only I could hear her, she said, "You had to do it tonight, didn't you? You *knew* I fancied Niall, but you couldn't let me have him. You had to do your best to ruin everything. Well, I hope you're fuckin' happy now."

She stormed off, and Dean got up and followed her. I was half afraid that he'd say something, but for once in his life he knew when to keep his mouth shut.

I could feel the eyes of everyone in the place on me, and I wanted to run out too, but I didn't want to bump into the others. I sat there without moving, wishing for the ground to open and swallow me. I could feel the tears of anger and frustration building up.

After a couple of minutes, Joe came back. Without a word, he sat down opposite me and offered me his hanky.

I blew my nose and wiped my eyes. "Sorry," I said. "There was a fight. They've all gone home."

"I know. I met them down the road."

"What did they say?"

"That you broke up with Dean."

"I broke up with him a year and a half ago."

"I know."

I looked up at him. "What have I *done*?"

He said nothing.

"I mean, Ellen is my best friend. I didn't want to hurt her by hurting Dean. Jesus, I never should have gone out with him in the first place. It's been a nightmare, Joe . . . Well, you probably don't see that. But from my point of view, I've been trying to get rid of Dean and he just wouldn't go. He honestly thought that we'd get back together." I leaned my elbows on the table and put my head in my hands. "And now Ellen probably won't show up for work and she'll never speak to me again. And on top of everything I've got to organise my sister's wedding and now there's all this stuff going on with Bernard Parker and his bloody Internet café. My whole life is turning into shit." I looked up at him. "What am I going to do?"

"Survive," he said.

"What?"

"You'll survive, Andi. You're a strong person. You'll get through all this and come out stronger. Remember what you said to Niall . . . Keep going against all the odds and the negative comments. Don't let the bastards get you down." He stood up. "Come on. I'll walk you home."

As we left the pub, I smiled. "You're a dark horse, Joe. You don't say a word most of the time. What was that you said the other night about the stars?"

"I have loved the stars too fondly to be fearful of the night."

"That's beautiful . . . I suppose it means that you can face anything, if you live your life to the fullest and just get out there and start giving it loads. Is it Shakespeare?"

"I've no idea. I read it in a comic."

* * *

The next day at work, I got a phone call from Jimmy's mother asking me to thank Joe for bringing him home. I explained to her that the shop was about to be sold, and that we didn't know if Jimmy would even have a job next Saturday. She said that wasn't a problem because he'd have to give it up soon anyway – he had to study for his Leaving Cert.

Without Ellen, and with no one on security, I didn't bother to open the shop. I just sat there for the day, reading and waiting for Gerry to show up.

At about one o'clock, there was a knock on the door. I jumped up and opened it, expecting to see Gerry, but instead it was Niall.

"Can I come in?"

"Sure." I stepped aside and let him in, then locked

the door behind him. "I forgot that you said you'd be calling for your money."

"Sod the money," Niall said. "I just wanted to talk about last night."

"Right . . . What did Ellen say after you left?"

"Not much. She was crying her eyes out. You two've never had a fight before?"

"Not like that. I really fucked it up, didn't I?" I sat up on the counter. "I don't know whether I should phone her or not."

"I wouldn't, yet."

"You like her, don't you?"

He nodded. "Yeah. She's okay. But last night when you two were screaming at each other . . . Well, I didn't expect to see that." He seemed to be a little nervous talking to me, and I realised that Ellen had probably sent him.

"She's my best friend," I said. "I couldn't make a clean break with Dean because I didn't want her to be hurt. And the longer I left it the worse it got."

"Ellen said that she knew you didn't want to go out with him. That was why she kept telling you to sort it out. I mean, they're twins, right? They grew up together and they're still very good friends. But she says you're her closest friend, and that she'd rather lose Dean than lose you."

I was surprised. "She really said that?"

"She did." Niall paused, and seemed to take stock of the situation. "I'm still trying to figure out how the hell

I got mixed up in all this. I mean, I've only known all of you since yesterday, except Joe."

"What's his story?" I asked. "I've known him for years, but I still don't *know* him, if you see what I mean."

"If you want Joe's story, you'll have to ask him yourself."

I laughed. "Yeah, like he'd tell me."

"He might if you ever bothered to ask him."

Ouch! Well, I deserved that. "Why does he hang around with Dean?"

"You mean, why does Dean hang around with Joe . . . Talk to Joe, ask him what's going on. You might be surprised at the answer."

Before I could respond, there was another knock at the door. This time, it *was* Gerry.

"Hi, Andi . . ." He looked at Niall. "How's she cuttin'? Andi, there's something different about you today . . . What is it? No, don't tell me. Your hair is different."

I frowned, and said, "What?"

"No, that's not it." He went around behind the counter, opened the tills and took out the cash. "Slow day?"

"Very," I said. "Listen, Gerry, we need to talk about what's happening with the shop."

"Okay."

"Well, Mr Parker said that he'd be finalising the sale by the end of the week."

Gerry beamed. "Deadly!" It was clear to me that

he'd already forgotten the phone call I'd made the previous day.

"Yes, but what do you want us to do? Is there any point in even opening the shop?"

"Ah! I *knew* there was something different! The shop isn't open." He looked around. "And Ellen isn't here." He took a deep breath and let it out slowly, nodding to himself as he did so. "It's all changing . . . I remember when I bought this place. It was a pound shop then, too, but it didn't have such a cool name. Did I ever tell you how I thought of it?"

I shook my head.

"I was in a pub with my mates, and I said that I couldn't think of a good name for the shop, so one of them said, 'Call it Sound as a Pound'."

Niall laughed. "*That's* how you thought of it? By someone else suggesting it?"

"Yeah," Gerry said. "There's a lot of memories here. I still remember the very first thing I sold. Mars Bars, thirty pence each or three for a pound, they were . . . I'll be sorry to see the place go, but that's business. Okay, Andi, here's what to do. There's no point in opening the shop during the week. I've decided I'll definitely probably keep the shop in Clontarf, so we can shop the stick there. I mean, ship the stock. So you might as well spend the week inventoryising everything." He pulled a sheet of paper out of his back pocket. It was one of the flyers that Niall had dropped the day before. "I found this down the street. How did the sale go?"

"Not well. No one was interested."

"Ah well, never mind. Good effort all round."

"We owe a fiver for the flyers, and this man has to be paid twenty quid. He came in to help us out yesterday. Plus, me and Ellen and Jimmy still have to be paid."

"And Dean," Niall reminded me.

"Yeah . . . Ellen's brother came in to do security for us for two days. He has to be paid too."

Gerry took the cash back out of his jacket pocket and handed it to me. "There should be enough there. Will you sort it out?"

"Sure. Do you want receipts?"

He shrugged. "Nah. Okay then, see you round, right?"

I let him out and waved goodbye.

"You know," I said to Niall, "there's a good chance I'll never see him again." I felt a little sad. "I always liked him, even if he is a doper."

"I liked the joke about the Mars Bars," Niall said. "Thirty pence each or three for a pound! Good one that."

I didn't have the heart to tell Niall that Gerry hadn't been joking.

* * *

Niall left shortly afterwards. I'd given him his twenty pounds, plus Ellen and Dean's wages. I phoned Jimmy's mother and asked her to send him in on Monday to collect his money. Then I set about making a list of everything in the shop.

It was tiring, lonely work, and I wasn't nearly finished at eight, when I decided to call it a day.

I started again on Monday morning. The only distraction was when Jimmy arrived: he still looked hung over.

I took Tuesday afternoon off to get fitted for my bridesmaid dress. The other bridesmaids, Lorna and Audrey, were about Eimear's age, and took the whole thing very seriously, as though they'd been charged with a mission from God.

I spent all Wednesday finishing up the stock list, then I posted it to Gillian in the Clontarf branch. Then I phoned Bernard Parker's answering machine and told him that I wouldn't be in the shop for the rest of the week, but that he could reach me at my home number.

And then Thursday evening came, and it was time for the weekly gathering at the pub to watch the stand-up show.

* * *

I'd spent all day wondering whether I should call Ellen, and whether I should even go to the pub. I didn't want to miss the show, but at the same time I didn't want to sit there on my own like a complete gobshite.

In the end, I decided to go. If the others turned up, great. If not, I'd stand discreetly at the bar and try not to look lonely.

They weren't there when I arrived, so I found a quiet spot where I could watch the door in case they showed up.

As with the previous week, Tony O'Hehir was first up. He looked a lot more confident this time, though his material wasn't quite as good.

"I've had a strange week," Tony began. "On Monday I was on a special assignment in the jungle, and I got attacked by a tiger. He didn't kill me, though. He just dragged me through the jungle to this three-bedroomed semi-detached house. I didn't realise that tigers lived in houses, but there you go. So he dragged me in, and dropped me in the sitting-room. There were little porcelain people on the mantelpiece. Then another tiger came in, and the first one said, 'There y'are now, watch this!' and he grabbed my by the legs and swung me around in a huge circle. My head hit off the wall and then he dropped me and looked embarrassed, and said to the other tiger, 'Okay, so you were right'.

"I staggered out of the room and climbed out through the human-flap. I had a massive headache. But you can never find any aspirins in the jungle, because the parrots eat 'em all . . ."

This old joke was greeted with a chorus of groans, plus a few laughs from those who'd never heard it before.

"Anyway," Tony continued, "on Tuesday I went around to my mate's house because he said he was feeling depressed, but there was no answer when I rang the bell. I looked in through the window and I saw a note on the kitchen table. 'Oh no!' I said. 'He's after doing himself in!' So I picked up a rock and smashed the window, climbed in and read the note: 'Tony, gone to the shops. Back in a few minutes. Make yourself at home. P.S. the key is under the mat'."

The crowd liked that one a lot, and Tony seemed pleased with himself. Next, he did the routine about his cousin Seán, the freelance gravedigger, and it went down a storm.

After his set, he came up to the bar but was immediately surrounded by people telling him how great he was. I decided to hang back for a while, until I could talk to him more easily.

The next comedian was a rare one: a woman. "The trouble with men is that they think they run the world, don't they girls?" All the women in the audience – except me – cheered. "And they think they're so great in bed. Every man boasts that he's a great lover *and* a great driver. Now I know what those furry dice hanging from the mirror are supposed to represent."

For this one, she got a big laugh from the women, and even a "Woo!" I decided that I'd leave if someone shouted, "You go, girl!"

"I was going out with this guy for ages, and he says to me, 'Jenny, we've been together for years. We're good together, you know that. We like the same things, we understand each other, the sex is great . . . and, well, I think we should take our love to the ultimate stage.

113

Jenny, will you marry me?' And I said to him, 'No, I won't.' He was heartbroken. 'But why? Why won't you marry me when you know everything between us is perfect?' And I said to him, 'Because my name's not Jenny.'"

Even the men laughed at that one . . . I was a little relieved. After her first couple of lines I'd been afraid that she was just going to pick on men for the whole night – it's an easy way to get a laugh, but God it can get tedious.

"I went out the other night and got really, really drunk. I staggered home and did my best to be quiet coming in, so as not to wake up my parents. So I crept up the stairs as quietly as I could, and just before I got to the top, the landing light came on, and my mother was standing there with a fierce look on her face. 'You're drunk again, aren't you?' 'No, I'm not,' I said. 'What makes you think that?' 'Because you moved out three years ago.' But she's great, my mam. A good Catholic woman. And she did a fine job raising the eighteen of us."

By now, the crowds around Tony had thinned, so I felt it was time to approach him.

He spotted me coming, and smiled. "Andi, isn't it?"

I looked puzzled. "Isn't it what?"

"Your name . . . Oh, very good. So what did you think?"

"Not bad," I said. "I don't think everyone got the bit about the tigers, though."

"Yeah. Well, you can't win them all. I had a hard time trying to think of a way to get that one across." He looked at me expectantly. "Any ideas yourself?"

"A few . . . It might work better if you strip it right down and speed it up, so that they don't get a chance to anticipate it . . . Change it from the jungle to the zoo, that way the audience isn't side-tracked into trying to picture what a tiger's house would look like." I had a little think. "Okay . . . I went to the zoo and I fell into the tigers' pit, and one of them dragged me into the cage and swung me around by the feet, and my head kept hitting off the bars, and the tiger turned to the zookeeper and says, 'See?' and the keeper said, 'Okay, you're right. I'll get you a bigger cage.'"

Tony laughed, and then said, "I don't know why I'm laughing. I knew the punchline."

"The head hitting off the bars works better because it makes people think of when they were a kid walking along holding a stick and let it rattle off the railings."

"You know your stuff, all right. What are you drinking?"

"Bacardi, thanks."

When the drinks appeared, Tony said, "Listen, I want to pick your brains, but we can't talk in here with all this noise. Do you fancy getting something to eat?"

* * *

We went to the local Burger King. It was busy, but not as noisy as the pub had been. Tony asked me what I wanted, ordered something for himself as well, and paid for it: I couldn't remember the last time a man had voluntarily bought me a burger.

"So where are your friends tonight?" Tony asked as we sat down.

"Don't ask. We sort of had a fight. It's a long story."

"Okay. Something to do you with your man, then?"

"Dean? Yeah, it's everything to do with him. So, you wanted to pick my brains?"

Tony nodded and bit into his burger. "I wanted to ask you a few things about stand-up," he said as he chewed. "Sorry, I'm a messy eater." He swallowed his mouthful. "Okay, so tell me this for a start . . . How come you know so much about what works and what doesn't?"

I dipped a chip into my ketchup. "I'm not sure how I know. I just do. Like, sometimes we'll be watching something on telly, a comedy, and my dad will be killing himself laughing, even though I can see the jokes coming a mile away. My mam doesn't laugh much, but now and again she cracks up. I don't understand why they don't see them coming."

He nodded, and indicated that I should continue.

"For something to be funny, it should be unexpected. Not always, of course, but if you've already heard a joke, it's less likely to make you laugh, right?"

"Right."

"I mean, you can put an unexpected twist into a simple statement, and there's a pretty good chance that you'll get some sort of a laugh."

"Like what?"

"Why did the monkey fall out of the tree? Because he was dead."

Tony went "Hmm . . ."

"Okay, I know it's not a great joke. Or even a good one, but that's the sort of joke that really works on an eight-year-old. As people get older, it's harder to come up with something unexpected, because their subconscious is telling them, 'This is a joke . . . There might be something unexpected at the end. What should I expect?' So to get past that, you have to either get bizarre, or you stretch a joke out and put in lots of references to things that everyone will recognise. That way, they're on safe territory and when the punchline comes, they mightn't expect it."

Tony finished his burger. "Right. But there's more to it than that."

"Oh, I know . . . Look at that woman tonight. She started off by slagging men. When you're in front of an audience who've had a few drinks, you can get them on your side pretty easily by bonding like that. And once they're on your side, they're more likely to laugh at other stuff. Listen to what Billy Connolly does . . . Most of his jokes are pretty bad, but he spends so long telling them, throwing in loads of little one-liners, that by the end it doesn't matter."

"Well, you know the theories, but can you put them into practice?"

"How do you mean?"

"Write me a few routines for next week – they've booked me for another month, by the way – and if I like them, I'll pay you a fiver for each one I use."

I smiled. "So, you're offering me a job as your joke-writer?"

"Yeah. Well, for a probationary period. What do you think?"

"Okay," I said. "I'll give it a go."

Chapter Nine

My mother woke me up in a state of panic on Friday morning. "Jesus, Andi! Get up! You're going to be late!"

Her panic was contagious: I hopped out of bed and was half-dressed before I remembered that I was taking the day off again.

According to the clock, it was only half past nine. I sat on the end of the bed and debated whether I should get back under the duvet or go forth into the day.

Mam shouted up from the kitchen, "Andi! Get a move on!"

So I finished getting dressed and went down. Mam was ironing again – I sometimes got the feeling that she'd been cursed with a never-ending laundry basket. And that was only from herself, me and Dad – I couldn't imagine what it must have been like when all seven of us were in the house.

"I'm taking today off, Mam. I forgot to tell you."

She looked at me with suspicion: "Two days off during the week? Is something wrong?"

"Well, no . . ." I decided that I'd better tell her what was happening with the shop. I knew she wouldn't be happy about it, but the longer you leave these things, the worse they get. As I'd recently discovered.

"Gerry's decided to sell the shop, Mam. The new owner is going to turn it into an Internet café. And he wants me to run the place."

"But sure you don't know the first thing about running a café," she said.

I sat down at the table and yawned. "I know. But I'll learn. If I don't do it, he'll only hire someone else and I'll be out of a job."

"So who's running the shop now that you're skiving off?"

I raised my eyes in a "give me strength" kind of way. "I'm *not* skiving off, Mam. The shop is closed."

"You'd better sign on then," she said.

"No, I'm still employed until the new owner takes over. I just don't have anything to do at the moment. Well, actually the new owner wants me to organise the uniforms and get a Coke machine or something. I suppose I should make a few phone calls. It'll look better if I have stuff done for him when he phones. I gave him the number here, all right? So when he phones, don't start telling him stuff about me. He thinks I know what I'm doing."

She tutted. "You're going to get yourself into a right

bloody mess, Andi, you know that? Still, it's good that you have some time to yourself, because you've got a lot to do for Eimear's wedding." She paused, her hand reaching halfway into the laundry basket. "That reminds me, Eimear said to tell you that Lorna's *not* going to be one of the bridesmaids. They had a fight about something. So she wants you to ask Ellen to do it. I don't know . . . fighting with her friends at her age. She ought to know better."

I bit my lip. "Right . . . Well, I don't know if Ellen can do it . . ." I had a sudden inspiration. "What about Claire? She'd make a good bridesmaid."

"Good idea. You should phone Eimear and tell her that. She'd have to come up to Dublin to be fitted for her dress, though. Or maybe she can just send up the measurements."

"So, any word from Ciarán?" Ciarán was the second oldest, after Roddy. He was currently backpacking his way around Europe.

"We got a postcard yesterday . . ." She fished it out from behind the kettle and handed it to me.

Ciarán, ever the wit, had cut the pictures off last year's Christmas cards and was using them as postcards. This one featured the three wise men following a particularly pointy star. He'd crossed out "Merry Christmas" and written "Greetings from Somewhere!" on the front. This card was posted in Italy: *"I've just been to Rome. It was cool. I went to see the Pope, asked him did he have any openings for a cardinal, but he said the best he could do for me was a bishop. I* went to the Colosseum but I must have missed the gladiator show. Home in about three weeks. Love, Ciarán."

"So he'll be home in time for the wedding, anyway," I said.

"He'd better be," my mother said. "Which reminds me, I have to phone John today. Make sure that him and that girlfriend of his are coming."

My brother John was thirty-five. "That girlfriend of his" was a woman who was separated from her husband. Naturally, my mother didn't approve of the relationship. I'd only met her a couple of times myself, but she seemed okay. At least she didn't have any kids – my mother wouldn't have stood for that. Not that it would have made any difference to John.

* * *

I spent the morning going through the Golden Pages and phoning soft drinks companies. When I explained that we were going to be setting up an Internet café, they fell over themselves to be involved. I took notes on the prices, running costs and expected sales figures – even if they were exaggerating, a drinks machine looked like it was going to be quite a little earner.

Then I phoned a few places about uniforms. We'd need blouses and skirts for the girls, shirts and trousers for the lads. It was all way more expensive that I'd anticipated, so around lunchtime I went to the local Dunnes and priced everything. I guessed that it would probably be cheaper to just buy ordinary blouses and shirts and get sew-on patches made with the logo.

I returned home feeling very pleased with myself. A good morning's work. I went into the kitchen and saw my mother sitting at the table having a cup of tea and a chat with Ellen.

"*There* you are," my mother said. "I didn't know where you'd got to. You've left poor Ellen here waiting for ages."

"It's okay, Mrs Quinn," Ellen said. "This is a surprise visit."

"It is," I agreed.

Ellen and I looked at each other, neither of us knowing what to say.

"So," I finally said. "Any news?"

My mother seemed to sense that there was something up, so she told us to get out of the kitchen because she was far too busy to be sitting around gossiping.

"Let's go for a walk, then," I suggested.

We went out and just began to wander around, with no fixed destination in mind.

"So, how are things with Niall?" I asked. "Is that still going on, or what?"

"Yeah . . . We went out a couple of times. I like him a lot. I'm seeing him tonight."

"I like him too . . . I didn't know what to make of him at the beginning, with his silver paint and his CDs. And marching around with his eyes closed and pretending to be a robot alien."

We both laughed, and I could feel the tension easing up a little.

"He takes it so seriously," Eimear said. "It's weird to think that for the first four or five hours I knew him I was breaking my shite laughing at him . . . I don't think Dean likes him much, though. And I know that Niall doesn't like Dean – after Saturday night he decided to tell me right out, so that, well, the same thing wouldn't happen like it did with you and me."

There was an awkward silence while we both tried to think of something else to say.

"I met Tony last night," I finally said.

"At the stand-up show?"

"Yeah. He's doing really well. He said they've booked him for another month."

"That's good. What's happening in work?"

"Nothing. We didn't open during the week. Gerry told me to do an inventory of the stock and send it to Gillian. So that's it for the shop. Mr Parker's probably bought the place by now."

"And what's happening with *that*?"

"I'm not sure. It's all still up in the air a bit. The shop will have to be remodelled and everything. I think Parker will want me to oversee everything. What about you? Are you going to come and work there?"

She smiled. "Are you offering me a job, then?"

We stopped walking. "Look," I said, "I'm sorry about

what happened with Dean. I didn't mean for it to get so bad. I was just afraid that if I broke up with him you'd get hurt."

She said nothing, so I continued.

"Dean's all right, but he's just not my type."

"So, what *is* your type?" Ellen asked.

"I don't know . . . Well, someone who makes me laugh. Dean never made me laugh." To myself I added, he made me cry a couple of times. "Someone who makes me feel safe, too."

"He's really cut up about it, you know. He really expected that you'd get back together."

"Well, I tried to tell him often enough. So he hasn't seen anyone else since we broke up?"

"It's only been a week, Andi."

"No, I mean since we broke up nineteen months ago."

"As far as I know, he still thought you were going out. You were just, like, in a holding pattern."

I'd been out with other guys once or twice after Dean, but even Ellen didn't know about them. I wasn't going to tell her.

We walked on. "So anyway you were talking to Tony again?" Ellen said.

"Yeah. He asked me to write some stuff for him. He said he'll pay me a fiver for each joke he uses. I know it's not much, but he probably doesn't get more than thirty quid a night. I don't know if he has a day job or anything. At least, he never said. I'm going to do it anyway. I know it's not the same as getting up on stage and doing it myself, but it's a start."

"You're still thinking about that, then?"

"El, it's all I've wanted to do for the past ten years. Maybe longer. At least this way, I'll know if I'm able to produce the material. If that goes well, I'll think about doing a spot or two myself."

"It'll be a hard life," she said. "Probably ninety-nine per cent of stand-up comedians don't make it. I mean, for every Alan Davies there are hundreds of comedians who can't even get a gig at Butlin's for the summer. And they don't always last . . . Remember that time you were talking to Roddy about comedy? And he was naming all these comedians who were big in the seventies and early eighties when he was growing up? Where are *they* now?"

"Well, Tommy Cooper and Eric Morcambe are dead, Stan Boardman went too far . . . But you're right, of course, but you can't just not do something because you're afraid you won't be a success."

"Andi, do you *really* think you're going to make it?"

"I don't know . . . but . . ." I grinned, "but I have loved the stars too fondly to be fearful of the night."

* * *

Later, after Ellen had gone home, I called around to my grandmother's.

I was plied with cups of tea and plain biscuits while she filled me in on who in the area had recently died, bought new curtains, gone on a holiday they couldn't really afford, or mysteriously become pregnant. These wouldn't necessarily have all been the same people, of course, though there did seem to be a connection between death and new curtains, for some odd reason.

I told her about my new arrangement with Tony, and she was delighted.

"See what I was saying, Andi? You have to get out there and do it. Don't listen to your mother when she tells you it's not going to work. If it doesn't work, then it doesn't work. That's all there is to it."

"That's what I was thinking," I said. "I know it's not going to all fall into place overnight, but if I don't try, I'll never know."

"I'll tell you something now . . ." She said, leaning close to me and almost whispering. "Now, your mother would go into conniptions if she knew I told you about this . . ."

This was intriguing. "Yeah?"

"It was before long you were born. It was around the time Ciarán was born, I think. I was in my late forties, and your grandad hadn't been able to find work in ages. He applied for a job working with this company that had just set up to make ads for television. Well, he didn't get the job, but while he was there he heard about an ad which they needed a middle-aged woman for. He told them about me, and they called me in for an audition. I got the part, and did the ad, and your mother was mortified."

127

"Why? What was it for?"

"It was a slimming drink. I was the 'before' model. They had another woman who looked sort of like me, and she was a lot slimmer than me, so she was the 'after' model. They dressed us both the same, and set it up to look like it was the same woman who lost a lot of weight."

"Wow! So how come I've never heard about this before?"

"Well, you know what people are like . . . They gave me a terrible time about it. All in fun, of course, so I wasn't offended. But your mother was mortified. People kept saying to her, 'I saw your mam on telly again last night,' – that was all they said to her, but she was . . . I suppose she was ashamed of me." Gran shook her head sadly. "She'd only barely talk to me for nearly a year. There was only one Irish television station in those days, so if the ad was on, *everyone* saw it. Anyway, the slimming company went out of business, so the ad wasn't shown again. When she found out I was telling you about my theatre days, she made me promise not to tell you about the ad. She didn't want to have to go through the same thing with you."

"But that's not fair!"

"I know, but there you go. You can't blame her, though. She had a tough time growing up because me and your grandad hardly ever had regular work. She thinks it's a foolish way to spend your life. So in some ways she's like *my* mam and dad were."

She suddenly sat back, her great secret revealed. "So anyway . . . What we're all wondering is, who are you going to bring to the wedding?"

Her question completely caught me off-guard. I'd never even given it a thought. "I've no idea."

"You're not going to bring young Dean, then? Are you finally over him?"

"Gran, I'm so far over him I can't even see him any more. The problem was he couldn't get over me."

"Is there any other young fella you're keeping on the side, then?" she asked with a wicked grin.

"I wish. No, there's no one."

"Not even someone you fancy?"

"Well, yeah, but David Boreanaz lives in America. He's someone from the telly," I explained.

She looked at me like I was being stupid. "I know *that*."

"Gran, I didn't know you watched those sort of shows."

"I don't, really. But sure what else would I watch? I can't abide all those soaps, especially the Brit ones. They're all full of middle-aged plain people who can't pay their gas bills. If I want to see people like that, all I have to do is open the front door. No, I'd much rather watch good-looking young rich people."

"But I thought you'd be more interested in, I don't know, all the old black and white Cary Grant movies. That sort of thing."

"Andi, I've seen them all a million times."

"Next you're going to tell me you watch cartoons as well."

"Not at all. And don't go telling your mam or anyone else about what programmes I watch. They'd have me in a home quicker than you can say 'Bite my shiny metal ass!'"

I laughed. "I thought you said you didn't watch cartoons?"

Gran just winked at me and gave me a sly grin.

* * *

On Saturday morning, Mam woke me around ten and told me it was high time I got up. I explained that I respected her opinion, but I'd rather be hugged by Mr Duvet for another couple of hours. Using a great deal of scientific research as her basis, my mother told me that if I didn't get out of bed, she'd tan my hide for me. I countered this argument by pretending I'd fallen asleep, and she retaliated by poking me in the shoulder until I got up.

In the hope that whatever Mam wanted wouldn't take long, I didn't bother with proper clothes: I just dressed in my dressing-gown and slipped into my slippers.

I followed her down to the kitchen, where there were hundreds of pieces of expensive cream-coloured paper all over the table. "What's all this?"

"The wedding invitations. Eimear said you're to help me with them."

"Am I now?" I sat down and yawned. "What do we have to do? Do we have to decide who's getting them and who isn't?"

"No, your sister's already done all that." She waved a list at me. "What we have to do is write the cards and the envelopes."

"Aw Mam! It'll take ages! And she should be doing this herself! Or she should be getting Chris's sister to do something. I have to do everything."

"Just stop whingeing and start writing. Anyway, you have good handwriting, that's why Eimear wants you to do it. Chris's sister can barely write her name. I'll do the envelopes if you do the cards." She handed me the list and her "good" pen.

"This should have been done ages ago, Mam," I said as I started writing. "It's only four weeks to the wedding."

"I know."

"Well, what's Eimear been doing, then? They've been planning this wedding for a year now. What were they doing all that time?"

"Look, don't ask me, Andi. Your sister couldn't organise anything to save her life. I'll tell you something – and don't go telling anyone I told you this . . ."

"I won't," I said. I was getting used to people telling me stuff I couldn't tell other people.

"Remember two years ago when they went to Ibiza? Well, Eimear called me the night before they left because she couldn't organise her packing, and she had a fight with Chris about it. I nearly died when I saw what she wanted to bring. She had three bikinis and a full swimsuit, about eight pairs of shoes, five skirts and two pairs of jeans. And she was bringing her hairdryer, you know, the big noisy one, and her iron. And I don't mean a little travel iron, either. And on top of that was all her make-up, shampoo and conditioner – two big bottles – curling tongs, four different bottles of sunblock, three bath towels . . . *Piles* of stuff. Enough for a whole family."

"I'm not surprised Chris went nuts. Damn! Now I've just written an invitation to 'nuts'! Hah, I suppose we could send it out to Dad's family, they're all nuts anyway."

"I heard that!" came my Dad's voice from the hall.

He came into the kitchen and playfully hit me across the back of the head with his racing paper. "What's all this? The invitations?"

"Yeah. Dad, what sort of a dowry are you going to give Eimear? I was wondering because I might get married myself if it's worth it."

Dad poured himself a cup of tea. "I'm giving her a bloody good kick up the arse, that's what she needs. Imagine leaving off getting married until she's thirty!"

"So, what age *should* someone get married at, Dad?"

"Seventeen," he said. "It should be mandatory. And men should be able to take a pill so they can't have babies until they pass an intelligence test."

My mother rounded on him. "John, that's no way to talk at the dinner table!"

"I'm not at the dinner table. You are. I'm just near it. Anyway, dinner is hours away."

"So, Dad, are you going to hire a suit for the wedding?" It was great fun getting him started on stuff like that. Dad had an opinion on absolutely everything, and most of those opinions were likely to change from day to day, because he was never happier than when he had something to complain about. He never meant any of it, of course. He just loved saying things to see other people's reactions.

"Hire a bloody suit? Are you mad? I'll go as I am, and to hell with anyone who says anything about it." As he said it, he winked and me and looked towards my mother for her reaction.

She was having none of it. "John, you'll either wear a suit or you can sit at home and we'll just tell everyone you've been run over by a bus."

I laughed when she said that, remembering what had happened to Niall. "Hey, Dad, you'll like this . . . I met this lad last week and he said he'd been in an accident and was run over by a truck. But the thing is, it was a truck delivering office supplies."

"I don't get it," he said.

My mother tutted and raised her eyes. "Yes, very clever, Andi. A stationery truck." Mam rarely laughed, even though she did appreciate a good joke.

Dad thought it was hilarious, and wrote it down in the margin of his newspaper so that he could tell his mates in the betting shop later on.

"Have any other new jokes, Andi? I can never remember them."

"This lad goes to the zoo and he falls into the tigers' pit, and one of them drags him into the cage and starts swinging him around by the feet, and his head's hitting off the bars and everything, and then the tiger turns to the zookeeper and says, 'See?' and the keeper says, 'Okay, you're right. I'll get you a bigger cage.'"

Dad liked that one, too. "I've remembered one you'll like, Andi. This man goes into a pub and he sees a really gorgeous woman at the bar. He's going to go over and chat her up, but the barman says, 'I wouldn't bother. She's a lesbian.'"

My mother interrupted him. "All right, now that's enough, John. We won't have any talk of lesbians in this house. We never have and we never will."

"I'm pretty sure we did have before the lads moved out," I said under my breath. Aloud, I said, "Already heard it, Dad. That joke is older than you are. Damn! Now I've addressed this invitation to 'Lesbian'!"

Dad thought that was great. Still laughing, he took his cup of tea out to the back yard.

"I wish you wouldn't encourage him, Andi," Mam said. "He's hard enough to cope with as he is."

"Ah Mam, sure you wouldn't have him any other way, would you?"

"'Course not. But just don't tell *him* that."

* * *

Bernard Parker phoned after lunch. "Hello, Andi . . . How are things?"

"I'm fine, Mr Parker. How are you?"

"Well, never better, never better . . . I'm just calling to say that the sale has been agreed and we're all well on the way to getting the café up and running."

"Great. Well, I've not been able to do much on my end" – because I don't know what I'm doing – "but I did check around for drinks machines and uniforms." I gave him all the important details, and he seemed particularly pleased with my idea of just purchasing ordinary clothes and sewing on patches with the company logo.

"Have you given any thought to a name for the place? I've had a few ideas myself, but nothing seems right."

I actually *had* been thinking about that, but I wasn't too happy with any of the names I'd come up with. "Well, my ideas aren't great . . ."

"Let me hear them anyway," Parker said. "They might give us a jumping-off point."

"Okay. Beans and Bytes – that's bytes with a 'Y'. That one probably won't work because people will think of baked beans. Coffee-mail. Again, I'm not mad about that one, because people will pronounce it as 'cough e-mail'. Net Results." That was it for the names I'd come up with. Now I was starting to get desperate and I just threw out the ideas as they came to me. "Em . . . Sip and Surf. Brews and Browse. Robocoffee."

"Wait! Stop! That's perfect! Brews and Browse! I love it!"

"Thanks," I said. "I'm just worried that people will associate it with brewing alcohol, rather than coffee."

"So much the better if they do . . . Okay, here's what we'll do. Are you free for lunch on Monday?"

"Let me just check." I paused while I flicked through my imaginary diary. "Yes, Monday is fine."

Parker hummed and hawed for a few minutes, then finally picked a restaurant. "I'll make the reservations – I know the chef personally so there shouldn't be any problems. How does twelve-thirty suit you?"

"Perfect," I said. "Is there anything you need me to do in the meantime?"

"No . . . not that I can think of. Apart from getting some staff for the café, of course. I presume you already have that in hand?"

"I've started," I said. "I've already got one almost definite. I've worked with her before, so I know I can trust her." Thinking quickly, I added, "I'd rather not go to one of the agencies just yet."

"No, of course. They charge an arm and a leg. Best to work without them as long as we can. I've been talking to a few systems admin people, and I'm sure we'll have one signed up by the end of the week. All right, then. Good work, Andi. I'm glad you're on board. We can talk about the finer details on Monday."

He said goodbye, and hung up.

I almost collapsed. So far, I'd successfully managed to bluff my way, but sooner or later he was going to find out I had no idea what was going on.

Chapter Ten

An hour later – I was still in my dressing-gown – Eimear arrived. She looked me up and down, and said, "Would you look at the state of you? Andi, it's the middle of the day and you're still not dressed. Have you no shame?"

I put on a thoughtful look, and said, "Eimear, I'm going to take a wild guess, and say that you *didn't* come here to insult me. You came here because you wanted to get me to do something for you."

I didn't know why I bothered. She'd been vaccinated against sarcasm when she was a kid. "Right," she said. "We have to go and organise the cake. I was going to send you to do it by yourself but you'd only end up picking the wrong one or something."

"That's true," I said. "I'm so stupid I'd probably get one with Happy Birthday written on it by accident. In fact, I'm so stupid I think you'd be mad to even let me go with you."

"Oh, sure, you *say* you're stupid but you really think you're clever, isn't that it? Well, let me tell you if you were twice as clever as you are, you still wouldn't be half as clever as you *think* you are."

"You forgot to say 'So there!' at the end."

"Look, just don't start with me. I've got enough to worry about as it is."

"So people keep telling me. All right, I'll get dressed." I started up the stairs. "All your invitations are done. Don't mention it. They're in the envelopes all sealed and stamped and ready to go."

"Good."

"No, it's okay. No thanks are needed."

She looked up at me. "What?"

I shook my head and continued up the stairs, muttering loud enough for her to hear, "I just *hope* all the invitations are in the right envelopes."

* * *

If I'd been a couple of years younger, Eimear would have been dragging me along by my arm. "Come on! Hurry! This place closes at five on a Saturday! What time is it now?"

"Four minutes to five," I lied.

"Sweet fuckin' Jesus!" She tore off down the street like a madwoman.

I sauntered along after her at a leisurely pace.

She was waiting outside the cake shop with a face on that would have stopped a wedding. "You little bitch!"

138

"What? What was all the rush? Sure there's an hour to go yet."

"I know that *now*! You said it was four minutes to five!"

"No, I said it was *five* minutes to *four*. You're just getting yourself into a panic. You'd want to slow down, Eimear, and let someone else do some of the work for a change." Just because she was immune to sarcasm didn't mean I wasn't allowed to torture her.

I decided that my little trick was payment in full for all the work she'd made me do. After all, it's funny when you can make someone panic, but it's not so funny when they strangle you for it.

We went into the shop and went "oooh!" and "that one's gorgeous!" a lot, until she settled on a boring, traditional three-tier cake with a badly painted plastic bride and groom on top.

"You should get something a little more unusual, Eimear," I said. "Something without so many horseshoes. Why *do* wedding cakes have horseshoes?"

"Shut up, Andi. You're distracting me."

"I'm only asking. Okay, so you're sure that's the one you want?"

"Definitely."

"Shouldn't Chris be here for this?"

"Chris doesn't know the first thing about weddings. He wanted to have a barbecue."

I thought that was a great idea, but I wasn't about to say that out loud: Eimear was on the edge as it was.

The woman behind the counter agreed that the cake was absolutely beautiful, and then recommended another one that looked almost identical to me, but was a lot more expensive. Eimear wouldn't budge from her decision, until the woman started going on about how the wedding cake should match the bride's dress.

I saw that Eimear was starting to be swayed, and I was suddenly faced with a dilemma. If I insisted that Eimear's choice was the right one, she'd probably go mad when she realised that her dress *didn't* match the cake. On the other hand, if I agreed with the saleswoman, then Eimear would end up spending a lot more on the cake than she'd planned.

In the end, I decided to avoid that decision entirely. "I heard it was bad luck for the cake to match the dress."

The saleswoman fixed me with her stare. "That's nonsense."

"No, it's not. The dress represents the purity of the bride" – that was a laugh for a start – "so if the cake matches it too closely, what does that mean when the cake gets chopped up?"

She could see that she was up against a professional bullshitter. "The cake represents the love of the couple, which should be shared with everyone present."

"In which case, the cake should also match the groom's suit."

She had an answer for that one too: "The inside of the cake is dark, representing the suit."

Damn! "But the icing on the cake is purely

decorational. It's only there to look nice, but it doesn't mean anything. You're not telling me that my sister's wedding is a fraud?"

Eimear had been observing this exchange with fascination. "I think I'll stick with my original choice," she said. "After all, it's only a cake."

The saleswoman knew when she was beaten. She got Eimear to fill out an order form, and told her that the cake could be inspected three days before the wedding, and picked up any time after that. Or, for an extra fee, they'd deliver it to the hotel.

On the way home, Eimear kept staring at me.

"What?"

"Did you just make all that up?"

"Yeah."

"The purity of the bride . . ." she laughed. "Now you know why I wanted you there. You're much better at dealing with people than I am."

* * *

On Sunday afternoon, my brother John phoned. "Andi, are you up to anything at the moment?"

"Nope. Why, are you coming over?"

"No, but I was wondering if you wanted to meet in town. I've something to ask you."

"Sure. When and where?"

John picked a pub that was conveniently close to him, but inconveniently far for me. I agreed to the location anyway.

141

Jaye Carroll

John was thirty-five. For the past three years, he'd been living with a woman who was separated from her husband. None of us really knew the whole story. Eimear was convinced that the woman had been happily married until she met John, but according to Ciarán she was already separated when they met.

John's girlfriend, Betty, had only been married for a couple of years. She'd been about twenty-six when she met John. Mam had no problems with her for the first few months, because John and Betty knew better than to tell her. But these things are always found out, and Mam was even more disgusted then because she'd had to hear it from a neighbour.

I'd expected Betty to be with John in the pub, but he was on his own. He was sitting there quietly drawing a smiley face on the head of his pint of Guinness.

I bought a drink and sat down beside him. "Hi. What's up?"

"What? Nothing's up. I just wanted to talk to you."

"Yeah, I'm *sure* nothing's up, all right. Where's Betty?"

"Gone to her mother's."

"So you were lonely and decided I could cheer you up?"

He smiled. "Something like that . . . Listen, I have to talk to Mam about something but I want your advice before I do."

"Okay then."

"How would you like to be an auntie again?"

142

My mouth dropped open. "You're kidding! But you always said that you'd *never* have kids!"

"It turned out that my sperm weren't of the same opinion," John said. "So, what do you think? Should I tell Mam now, or after the wedding?"

"Well, I'm wondering if you should tell her at all . . . She'll probably be dead before she gets to a hundred, and the kid will only be about forty. You might get away with it." I bit my lip and had a good think. "I can tell her, if you prefer." It occurred to me that that could be what he wanted me for. John wasn't good at confrontations with Mam. In fact, none of the lads were.

"No, I'll do it myself. But I haven't seen her in ages and I don't know what sort of mood she's in these days."

"She's getting more and more worked up about the wedding. So's Eimear. Between the two of them they have me run off my feet. If I ever get married, I'll do it on the sly and not tell anyone."

"So I can't tell her yet . . ." He sucked in breath between his clenched teeth. "This will be awkward."

I looked at him. "You're not going to tell me that she's eight months pregnant already, are you?"

"No, only four months. But she's starting to show. Everyone will be able to tell at the wedding."

I drummed my fingers on the table while I thought about it. "Okay, then, here's what you have to do. You should go to see Mam, and tell her that you suspected but you've only just found out for sure. Ask for *her* advice on what to do. That should make her feel a little better about it. And explain that you know she won't be happy, but that you want her to know that you and Betty are happy, and stuff like that. I take it you *are* happy about it?"

"We are," he said, but his shell-shocked expression told me that it wasn't so simple.

"Really?"

"Well, we weren't expecting it. And in five months' time I'm going to be a Daddy."

"On the bright side, Claire will finally have a cousin. So, does Betty's family know, or is that why she's visiting them?"

"They've known for about six weeks. Betty's mam is delighted. She's been knitting like crazy."

"So what does Betty's husband think about it? Or has she seen him?"

He shrugged. "I know she bumps into him from time to time, but I don't think she's told him. I mean, how could she? He's still crying that she left him."

I decided it was time to finally get the true story. "Why *did* she leave him?"

"He had an affair with some young one he was working with."

"The bastard!"

"Yeah, well it wasn't that simple. Betty was having an affair at the same time. That wasn't with *me*, before you ask. That was with someone else. Anyway, then they both found out about each other. She said she could forgive him, but he couldn't forgive her. He seemed to think that it was okay for the husband to sleep with someone else, but not for the wife."

"I see. When in reality it's the other way around."

"Right," John said, nodding. "Wait, what did you say?"

"Never mind. So listen, here's a question. You don't have to answer it if you don't want to . . ."

"Fire away. But I know what you're going to ask, anyway."

"What am I going to ask, then?"

John picked up his pint, looked at it for a second, then downed half of it in one go. That was the way he drank: he rarely supped or sipped, he just poured it down his throat. Ciarán had a theory that John didn't actually *like* the taste of Guinness. "Okay, you're going to ask me who the other person was she had an affair with."

"No, I was going to ask you this . . . If she went off and had an affair behind her husband's back, how do you know she won't do it behind *your* back?"

He shrugged. "Well, I don't know for sure. I just have to trust her. But sure that's the way it is with everyone, right? Just because someone's done it before, that doesn't mean she's more likely to do it again."

I didn't really agree with him, but I decided not to mention that. "Good point," I said. "So, how is she anyway? Any morning sickness?"

"There was a bit, but not as much as she thought she'd have."

145

"And I presume she's happy about becoming a mother?"

"Yeah, we're both over the moon. But still, you know . . ."

"You're a bit worried about it?"

"A bit. More worried about what Mam's going to say, though."

This was John's way of letting me know he wanted to stop discussing girly things like "happiness" and "worry" and get back to the reason he wanted to see me.

In the end, we both agreed that it was best to let her know as soon as possible, so that she didn't have to find out about it from a third party like she had when John and Betty got together.

* * *

As we'd arranged, I met Bernard Parker for lunch at twelve-thirty in his chosen restaurant. It was a very exclusive tiny little French-Irish place called *Chez Healy*. If it had been a less up-market place, I suppose it would have been a themed restaurant, like one of those restaurants in the heart of Dublin that pretend to be Mexican. From the outside, it was very low-key – another good indicator that it was expensive – but through the windows I could see that the inside was decorated with lots of French and Irish things. Fake strings of onions hung from the ceiling, there was a real turf fire, ancient, ragged posters told me that Guinness was good for me, there were paintings of Charles de Gaulle and Eamon de Valera on the walls. Plus there were lots of French and Irish street signs, battered and faded for extra authenticity.

As I reached out to push open the door, the doorman beat me to it, and politely ushered me inside. After one look at the other customers, I silently thanked my mother for forcing me to wear my best clothes. Everyone looked loaded: even the waiters looked like they could afford to eat there.

The head waiter was very, very good at his job: I gave my name at the door and he sprang into action immediately. "Good afternoon, Ms Quinn. Welcome to *Chez Healy*. Mr Parker has informed us that he will be a *tad* late – no more than three or four minutes – for which he apologises, so perhaps you would like a drink from the bar?"

"Thank you," I said. "A Perrier, please." That was another of Mam's ideas – she'd said that I didn't want to give Mr Parker the impression that I drank during the day. "You'll only end up giggling at things and you'll ruin your chances of ever getting that job," she'd told me.

Without turning around, he raised his right arm in a gesture that – incredibly – managed to say to the other waiters, "Please bring the young lady a Perrier this *instant*, and make sure it's in a clean glass."

"My name is Clifton," he informed me, "and if there's anything I can get you, please do not hesitate to ask."

I was tempted to say, "I want a pony" but thought the better of it, and informed him that he was very kind.

He steered me to our table, and held out my chair as I sat down. I felt like I was going to meet Cary Grant in one of those old black and white movies that Gran didn't watch any more.

"Would you care to see the wine list, Ms Quinn?"

"No, thank you, I'm fine." Clifton bowed slightly and returned to his post by the door. I was fascinated with the whole place, but particularly him. He hadn't just turned away, he'd stepped backwards a few feet before turning around, presumably in case I became offended that he'd turned his back on me.

My Perrier arrived promptly, delivered by a gorgeous young waiter. He was shortish, with dark skin and very black hair, and, by the way his jacket moved I knew he had incredible muscles. As I waited, I looked around the restaurant and my eyes kept returning to him.

As I've said, the place was tiny. There were only about seven tables, and it looked like there was a waiter for each one. It was busy – every table was occupied – but still very quiet. Every table had a man/woman couple, and I got the impression that at least half of them were there on, as Ellen once put it, "illicit liaisons".

Bernard Parker arrived about five minutes after me, apologising profusely. I explained that it wasn't a problem – I'd often had to wait an hour or more for my ex-boyfriend.

He was dressed pretty much as he had been the last time I'd seen him: expensive suit, silk shirt and tie, good shoes, perfect hair – I didn't know much about the man, but I got the feeling that if his hair hadn't already been silver, he'd have had it dyed that colour.

Our gorgeous waiter waited exactly a minute after Bernard arrived before zipping over with the menus. He said, "The menu, miss?" and held the first one out to me. I blushed like mad, but he didn't seem to notice. He handed the other menu to Bernard and disappeared.

"I love this place," Bernard said. "Have you been here before?"

Yeah, sure, me and Ellen come here all the time . . . I put on my "thinking about it" face and had a look around. "No, I don't think I have."

"The food is excellent. I'm sure you'll enjoy it."

I opened the menu and wasn't at all surprised to see that it was handwritten. There didn't appear to be much in the way of choice, and everything was either in French or Irish, or both. Fortunately, I'd taken French in school and remembered every single class in perfect detail. I could clearly remember spending each class just staring out the window and wishing I wasn't there. Somehow the language itself slipped me by.

Okay, I did remember enough to interpret some of the stuff, but it looked odd: for a starter, we had a choice between *pain* and *poissons*. I didn't fancy being poissoned so I decided to go for the *pain*.

"I'm afraid my French is a little rusty," I explained.

"That's fine," he said. Everything was always fine with him. "Anton – the chef – will cook anything you like. The menu is really only a serving suggestion, as it were." He laughed politely at his own joke.

"I wonder how he'd react if I ordered a bowl of cornflakes," I said, and suddenly remembered that I was supposed to be *impressing* this man, not being a smart-arse.

He seemed to like that anyway. "Shall I order for both of us, then?"

"Yes, thank you."

He scanned quickly through the menu. "I take it you're not a vegetarian? No? Perfect . . . How does this sound? *Soufflé Tarbh* to start, followed by *Banbh avec Sücre agus Champignon Galimafrée*?"

"It sounds lovely," I said, wondering exactly who it was I was supposed to be. This wasn't like me at all – normally my lunch consisted of a Twix, and on special occasions, two Twixes.

Bernard called the waiter over somehow. I wasn't sure what he did, exactly – perhaps it was a subtle twitch of the neatly-trimmed eyebrow, or he'd put the menu down on some specific spot on the table that acted as a signal, but the waiter got the message that we were ready to order and he darted back over.

"For the young lady?" he asked, looking right at me.

I blushed like mad again, and Bernard made the order. When he was done, he said to the waiter, "How would Anton react if someone ordered a bowl of cornflakes?"

The waiter thought about this. "I think he'd be delighted, Mr Parker. It's not every day one has a chance to meet a connoisseur of the famous Mr Kellogg."

Parker laughed politely again, and the waiter headed off for the kitchen. I watched his arse as he walked . . . very nice indeed.

"So," Bernard Parker said, "to business . . . Andi, I have to say I'm very impressed with what you've done so far, especially considering that you had to wrap up in Gerard's place."

"Thanks," I said, and wondered who Gerard was for a few seconds, until it hit me that he was talking about Gerry.

"I'm meeting with a designer tomorrow morning, at the café, and we're going to start sketching out some ideas. I'd like you to be there."

"No problem," I said.

"We'll go through some ideas, kick them around for a while, and see what we can come up with. I've already got her working on a logo – she was very impressed with your suggested names, by the way – so with luck she'll have a few sketches with her tomorrow. We'll be meeting there at about ten, if that suits you."

"Sure. That reminds me in fact, I still have my keys to the shop. I never got a chance to hand them over to Gerry. I mean, Gerard. I have them with me if you want them."

He smiled. "No need. We'll be changing the locks . . . One thing I'm certain I would like to do is take out the entire front window. At the moment the door is on the left, and I'd prefer to have the door in the centre. Probably with your desk tucked in at the right . . . Anyway, we'll go over all that in detail tomorrow."

I was thrilled at the thought of getting my own desk. "Well, I do have a few questions, Mr Parker . . ." I hesitated, trying to remember exactly how my mother had put it. "We've never had a chance to discuss the terms of my employment."

"This is true, and it's one of the reasons I wanted to meet with you today. Now, I've been going over the first-year budget with my accountant, and we've broken everything down into categories. Obviously, the remodelling and the installation of the equipment is taking the lion's share, and then there's maintenance, the SA, beverages and so on. What we're left with, to cut a long story short, is about forty thousand pounds."

For a split second, I thought that he meant the forty thousand pounds was all for me, and then I realised that there would be other members of staff.

He continued: "Which isn't bad, considering that we've not taken income into account. Now, we'll be running sixteen hours a day – that's minimum, but let's leave it there for the moment. That's one hundred and twelve hours a week . . ." He did the calculations in his head. "Just under six thousand hours a year. Now, if we assume that we're going to have an average of three and a half people on at all times, what does that come to at say six pounds an hour?"

He was asking *me*? I had no idea. I had enough trouble trying to imagine what the half-person would look like.

I was just about to say that I didn't know, when he answered himself. "About a hundred and twenty-five thousand . . . Of course, I don't know *why* I'm still thinking in pounds. I'm having a hard time coming to terms with euros."

"Perhaps that's why the pound shop wasn't doing so well," I said.

Parker thought that was hilarious. He laughed like a drain and then stopped rather abruptly. It was as though his sensors had reported a "Joke Alert" and he'd carried out the appropriate action on autopilot.

"But back to the point . . . Obviously the manager of a café would be paid more than the staff. But, naturally, that's because the manager will have much greater responsibilities, if you see what I mean. To manage the place means having more or less a free hand running the café – reporting only to me – so that means almost certainly putting in more than forty hours a week."

The starter arrived, and it turned out to be a sort of meat pie – it was delicious. I stopped short of licking the plate clean, but only just.

Throughout the starter, Bernard went on about a manager's responsibilities, and I began to get the feeling that he was avoiding the issue of how much money I'd be getting, and then, out of the blue, he said, "So the basic manager's package comes to about seventeen thousand, to start with. That's pounds. Call it twenty-one and a half in euros. Obviously if the first year goes well it'll increase dramatically. How does that sound?"

Compared to how much I'd been earning in the pound shop, it sounded like an absolute fortune.

* * *

We were in the restaurant for over two hours. By the time we left I was getting hungry again. To boil it all down, Bernard said stuff about the café and I agreed with him.

It occurred to me several times that I might as well not have been there. He didn't seem to require any input from me at all. He didn't even chat about himself, or ask me about my background, nothing like that. He discussed the merits of carpet tiles for about ten minutes, and spent another ten on whether it would be sexist to hire only women for the café part.

He kept coming back to technical stuff that I got the feeling he didn't understand himself, but he was using the words so that I'd think he knew.

When he'd finally decided that we were done, he called for the bill and the gorgeous waiter delivered it. I've no idea how much it came to, but I was sure glad it was Bernard paying and not me.

"So," Bernard said as we left, "what do we have to do? Tomorrow morning we'll meet with the designer at the café. You've still got to start the interviews proper,

and you should also start working out the duty roster.
Uniforms and such I think can wait for now, until we've
decided on a colour scheme."

And that seemed to be that. He thanked me again
for all the wonderful work I was doing, offered me a lift
home – which I declined – and said he'd meet me in the
morning.

* * *

I wandered through town feeling a bit overwhelmed by
the whole thing. Bernard Parker seemed to have an
amazing faith in my abilities even though I'd never
done anything to deserve it. I mean, he only knew me
as the manager – and I wasn't even that – of a pound
shop that had never really done very good business.

Without realising that I'd even been heading in that
direction, I found myself outside Sound as a Pound for
the first time in nearly a week. I peered in through the
window and saw that most of the stock was gone.

I was just about to walk away when I realised I still
had my keys with me, so I went in and had a last look
around, just in case I'd left anything of my own behind.

The shop looked like a bomb had hit it. The shelves
were mostly empty, but whoever Gerry had hired to
move the stock hadn't done a very good job – there
were bits and pieces all over the place. Nothing worth
nicking, unfortunately.

Even the tills were gone. I went behind the counter
and started rummaging through the mess, and then I

found something I'd completely forgotten about . . . The name and phone number of the woman with three kids who'd asked for a job. She was the first customer to come in after Gerry had told us he was selling the shop. Ellen had taken pity on her and let her have a whole bunch of stuff for a pound.

I sighed. It seemed like months ago. The poor woman wouldn't be getting a job *now*. I crumpled up the note and threw it on the floor.

Seconds later I was cursing myself and down on my hands and knees searching for it among the debris.

I finally found the note, and straightened it out as well as I could. The phone in the shop had been cut off, so I went home and called from there.

* * *

A little girl answered the phone. "Hello?"

"Hi, can I speak to your mammy, please?"

"Hang on," she said, then yelled "Ma! Phone!" at the top of her voice.

A minute later, "Ma" came to the phone. "Hello?"

"Hi, is that Donna?"

"Yes, who's this?"

"Hi, Donna . . . This is Andrea Quinn, from Sound as a Pound. You gave us your name and number, in case we had any vacancies?"

She perked up. "What, you've got a job going? I thought you said that your boss was selling the shop."

"Well, yeah, he is. What's happening is that the new

owner is turning the place into an Internet café, and he's asked me to stay on to run the place. Anyway, I was wondering if you'd like to meet up for an interview."

"But sure I don't know the first thing about the Internet."

"Neither do I," I said, "but we're looking for people to work behind the deli counter. You know the sort of thing, making up sandwiches and rolls, pouring coffee and everything. Would you be interested in that?"

"Well . . . Andrea, is it?"

"Yeah. But everyone calls me Andi."

"Andi, I worked in a bloody café for seven long *years* and I swore I'd never do it again. I mean, I'm tempted, but it'd be like taking a step backwards. And on top of that, I've got the kids now."

Seven years! I *had* to have this woman! "Well, the thing is, Donna, it's not like an ordinary café. The customers are all very quiet, usually come in on their own. There's never any rowdiness or anything like that. Plus, the café will be open from eight in the morning to midnight, so you could work the hours that suited you."

"Okay . . ." she said, sounding like she was seriously considering it. "What about the money?"

"I'm not entirely sure about that yet, but I do know we're going to be over the minimum wage. For someone with your experience, though, we might be able to go a bit higher. I'll have to check that with the owner."

"All right, then . . . I'll meet you. When and where?"

"Well, at the moment the shop is in bits. How about we just meet somewhere for lunch tomorrow? Would that suit you? I'm meeting the owner tomorrow morning, so I'll see how high he's willing to go."

"Sure . . ."

* * *

So that was staff member number two! I'm doing well, I told myself. I went back over Bernard's calculations and tried to figure out how many people we'd need in total . . .

Sixteen hours a day, times three hundred and sixty-five days, times three and a half people – say three to make it easier – and then assume that everyone works forty hours a week, for say forty-eight weeks . . .

I figured we'd need nine full-time people. I wasn't sure whether that included me or not. I decided that it didn't.

So, that meant I had another seven people to hire before the café opened. Bernard had said that the remodelling wouldn't take more than three or four weeks, so I had a lot to do and not much time in which to do it.

* * *

At about eight in the evening, I remembered that I was supposed to have been coming up with some material for Tony.

We'd arranged to meet on Tuesday evening, so that he'd have a couple of days to learn it before the comedy show. He didn't say it, but I knew that he also wanted to have time to make any changes that might be necessary.

So I went up to my room and sat down on the bed with a pen and notebook, and tried to think of something funny to write.

I started with a list of topics: politics, families, religion, clothes, kids, animals, television, tourists, shopping . . .

It was tough going. Every time I thought of something that would work, I remembered that it had already been done.

I decided to just pick a topic at random and start writing whatever came into my head, on the grounds that I could go back over it later and take out the bits that weren't funny.

"Tourists," I wrote at the top of a blank page. I double-underlined the word and sat back for a few seconds, then started writing . . .

"Americans coming over here and expecting us all to be carrying around sods of turf for the fire. Saying 'top o' the morning' to us, as though *The Quiet Man* was a documentary or something. Leprechauns. Shamrocks. Shillelaghs – no person who actually lives in Ireland has them, only American tourists. Going on about 'The Craic' as if they knew what it meant. Claiming to be Irish because one of their great, great grandparents was born in Co. Clare. Identical anoraks. All the male American tourists are called 'Gene'. All the women are called 'Darla'. They have kids called 'Tiffney' or 'Tyler'. Waiting for the bus on the wrong side of the road. Saying 'You're from Ireland? My ancestors on my mother's side were Irish! Do you know the O'Hanlons?'"

I felt guilty about picking on the Americans so much – after all, they are the people who gave us Chris Klien – so I decided to focus on other types of tourists . . .

"Foreign students shouting to each other from opposite ends of the bus. Invading the city every summer. Everyone knows that they only come over here so that they can smoke. More identical anoraks. Cologne."

That one was a dead end, and I was beginning to worry that it all sounded a bit racist, so I wrote down absolutely everything else I could think of about tourism. In the end, I managed to get a couple of routines – there were a few old jokes thrown in, but I hoped that wouldn't be a problem.

I went to bed at midnight, having spent four hours coming up with less than five minutes' worth of material. I hoped that wasn't a sign of things to come.

Chapter Eleven

Tuesday morning: I turned off the alarm clock, climbed out of bed and yawned my way towards the bathroom.

It was nine, and I'd arranged to meet Bernard and the designer at ten, so that meant I had plenty of time to cook myself a good healthy breakfast. However, I was wise and used that time to watch Breakfast television instead.

I decided that since we weren't going to a posh restaurant today, jeans and a jumper would be more appropriate attire. Plus, my feet were still killing me from having to wear proper shoes the day before.

I arrived first at the shop – sorry, the *café* – and since I still had my keys I let myself in and started doing a bit of tidying. The plan was that Bernard would arrive and *see* me tidying up, and that would further convince him that I was a good worker.

I collected about thirty pounds worth of stock from underneath and behind the shelves. Most of the things were covered in a thick layer of dust, indicating that they had been there since even before Gerry bought the shop. I half expected to see price stickers with "2/6" on them. I did find a bar of chocolate that was six years past its sell-by date. I was half-tempted to open it to see whether it was still edible, but since it had been in a box next to the heater I decided against it.

I put all the non-perishable goods to one side, and threw out the rest. The floor was still covered in bits, but Gerry had taken the vacuum cleaner so there wasn't much I could do about that.

The storeroom was almost bare, even the kettle was gone. When I noticed that I had a sudden craving for a cup of tea, and that gave me another Bernard-impressing idea. I went down the street to the café and bought a box of doughnuts and three coffees, and made sure I kept the receipt. The girls in the shop told me that they hadn't seen me in ages. I didn't tell them that I was soon to be working for the competition.

Bernard and the designer arrived a few minutes after I got back. I was in mid-tidy when they knocked on the door, and I was pretty relieved to see them because I'd been stretching out the tidying to make it last.

"Morning, Andi. This is Nora. She'll be coming up with some designs for us."

Nora was about my height, and looked like she'd been kidnapped right out of art college. She was dressed in fashionable rags and her red hair was all over the place – shaved on one side, long and straggly on the other, in dreadlocks at the back. Her skin was the colour of milk that had been left in the sun. She had her ears pierced about a million times, a stud in her nose, rings through her lower lip, a bar through her left eyebrow, and – I later spotted – a stud in her tongue.

She was dressed in a denim skirt over a pair of jeans – unconventional *and* unattractive, I observed – and a thick Arran cardigan whose buttons had been replaced with pieces of Lego.

I shook her hand and said that it was nice to meet her, then I offered them coffee and doughnuts. This was well-received and I mentally put another notch in my bow.

Bernard gave Nora a rough description of what he wanted done to the place, and she immediately disagreed with everything and whipped out a drawing pad.

"Look," she said, "if we put the door in the centre, then we can have . . ." she drew some circles "six, seven, eight computers, and four tables in the middle. This is assuming that you want to have the food counter over there . . . Now, if we move the door over to the *other* side . . ."

This went on for some time, the two of them arguing back and forth, and I began to wonder what I was doing there.

Eventually, Bernard looked at me. "What do *you* think, Andi? You've been quiet so far."

I made a few suggestions, all based on the idea that

we should do as few structural changes as possible, to keep the cost down and make sure that we'd open on time.

Nora didn't like that at all. "No, no, you have to have a partition *here*, and another one *here*, for privacy. And the door has to move to the right, then there'll be a flow from the door to the food counter. Now, the window is facing east-south-east, which means that you get the early-morning light. To optimise our utilisation of that, we should put four computers here along the window, which means that we *have* to move the door to the right." She looked pleased with her decision.

"That's all very well," I said, "but on bright mornings there'll be so much light coming in that anyone sitting at one of those computers won't be able to see the screen. You know what it's like when you're watching telly and the sun is coming in through the window . . . well, it'll be ten times worse than that."

Nora was back to not being happy again, and argued in favour of flow, consistency and *feng shui*. From the look on Bernard's face, I could see that she wasn't convincing him.

"Look," I said, "leaving the door and window as they are will save a fortune. Even supposing you're right about the 'flow' and the 'good vibes' and all that, do you really think that your ideas will draw in enough customers to justify the investment?"

She had no answer for that one. Bernard, however,

did: "You're right, Andi . . . After all – worst case scenario – say we don't get *any* customers. Where are we then? I'd rather not go off the deep end. Not over something as trivial as this."

Nora looked like she was about to burst into tears, and suddenly I realised what she didn't just *look* like an art student, she *was* one. She was only about my age, and she probably thought that this was going to be a great commission for her.

"That's not to say that we can't utilise the window in some way," I said, backpedalling like crazy. "And of course Nora's right about the flow . . . There probably won't be many casual customers – I mean, if someone's out shopping and they decide they're in the mood for a coffee, they're not going to come to an Internet café – so we should do our best to make sure that the regular customers start to think of the place as a second home. How can we do that, Nora?"

"Well, there are several ways . . ."

We listened to the several ways, and they all sounded either way too much work, or just plain stupid. We didn't tell her that, however.

On the plus side, she'd come up with half a dozen logos for the shop, and they weren't bad at all. Bernard enthused over them, so I did likewise.

After we'd been there for an hour and a half, Nora seemed a little more satisfied. She went off promising to come up with detailed sketches and that she'd be in touch in a couple of days so we could go over them.

When she was gone, I told Bernard that I was meeting an interviewee for lunch, and explained about Donna's experience in the café trade.

"So, I think she'd be a great asset," I said. "I don't actually know her, but on paper she sounds ideal."

"Well, I'll leave it up to you to decide," Bernard said. "But you think that she should be paid more because of her experience?"

"Definitely," I said. I noticed the hesitant look in his eye, and I added, "If she passes the interview and has good references."

"All right, then . . . The highest we can go is seven pounds fifty an hour. Don't offer her that, of course, but that's the upper limit. If she insists on more than that, then we don't need her."

* * *

I'd arranged to meet Donna in the Bewley's on Westmoreland Street, and the minute I walked in I realised my mistake – the place was absolutely huge and I couldn't really remember what she looked like. I wandered around hoping that one of us would spot the other, and was on my second pass when I felt someone tugging at my sleeve.

I looked down and saw a tiny little girl looking up at me. "Missus, are you Andi?" She couldn't have been older than five.

"I am," I said.

"That's a boy's name."

"No, it's short for Andrea. What's *your* name?"

"My mammy said to get you. She's over there." She pointed towards where Donna and the other two children were sitting. Oh my God! I said to myself. She's brought her kids to a job interview!

Donna waved at me, and I let her daughter bring me over.

"Good girl, Kylie," Donna said. To me, she said, "Sorry, I couldn't get someone to mind them at the last minute. I know how it looks, though . . . But you didn't leave your number, so I wasn't able to cancel."

"Sorry, I never thought of it." I sat down and smiled at the kids, who were all staring up at me. The little boy had chocolate on his face, fingers and everything within arm's length. The girl who'd been sent to rescue me was like an older clone of the other girl, and both bore a remarkable resemblance to their mother.

My one fear about Donna disappeared when I saw her. The first time I met her she'd looked exhausted, but now I saw that I must have just caught her on a bad day. She was good-looking, a little on the large side, and seemed cheerful enough.

"So, Andi . . . this is Kenny, Trisha and Kylie. Say hello to Andi."

The kids mumbled a chorus of hellos.

Donna handed me her CV. "It's a bit out of date," she explained. "I haven't had a chance to add to it."

Donna was twenty-eight, married, provisional driver's licence – "but no car at the moment," she told me – with very few academic qualifications, but a hell of a lot of work experience. She'd left school at sixteen and had worked in a newsagent's for a year, then in a dry cleaner's for eight months, a café for two years and a different one for five years. "The last couple of years there I was really only part-time," she said. "Kylie was a toddler and I was pregnant with Kenny." She'd included a list of references at the end.

"Can I hang onto this?" I asked.

"Sure. Though like I said, it's a bit out of date. I've worked on and off part-time since then."

I started telling Donna about the plans for remodelling the shop into a café, but she stopped me.

"Sorry," she said, "I don't mean to be rude, but none of that matters . . . I just want to know what I'll be expected to do, what the hours will be, and how much I'll be getting."

Caught off-guard, it took me a couple of seconds to gather my thoughts.

"Okay . . . The café will be open from eight to midnight – maybe one or two at the weekends. So we're obviously going to have to do shifts. Now, I haven't decided yet whether we'll just have day people and night people, or if we'll move everyone around. What about you? Would you prefer to do mornings, afternoons, evenings, or a combination?"

Donna was clearly prepared for this question: "Well, a couple of hours in the morning while this lot are at school. Say from nine to one. Then maybe a couple in the evenings as well. I should be able to do most Saturdays and Sundays, but not all the time. I'd need a weekend off at least once a month."

I wrote all this down in my notebook. "Okay . . . I hadn't actually thought about breaking up someone's work day like that, but it might work out for the best. As for your duties . . . like I said on the phone, there will be a deli counter, and several coffee machines. We haven't decided what model or style yet." I added that because I had absolutely no idea about coffee machines and I didn't want her to ask me any questions I couldn't answer. "So, general duties will be making sandwiches and rolls, doing coffee, tea, hot chocolate and the like, tidying up, hoovering, washing up – though there will be a dishwasher – and working the till."

Donna nodded. "Okay, that –"

"Mammy, I'm hungry!" said Kylie. Or was it Trisha?

"Shush, Mammy's busy at the moment. What was I saying? Right, that all sounds fine. There's nothing there I haven't done before."

"The only other thing will be taking bookings. Most people will book the computers for an hour at a time, and we'll have to make sure that they're off them when they're supposed to be, and if anyone is waiting, they're called in turn. There'll be technical people there if anything goes wrong, so we needn't worry about that."

"So how much per hour are we talking about?" She certainly didn't hesitate when it came to the important points.

"We'll be starting everyone off at six pounds an hour. That's before PAYE and PRSI, of course. After three months we'll go up to six twenty-five, six-fifty in exceptional cases." And here comes the "hmm . . . I don't know" bit, I said to myself.

But I was wrong: she paused for a second, then said, "I'll do it for six-fifty."

It was my turn to pause, to make it look like I was wondering if she was worth it. "Okay."

"When did you say the café is opening?"

"Not for another three or four weeks. Is that convenient?"

"It's perfect. This lot will be going back to school around that time. So, will I be able to arrange my own hours?"

This was a tough one. "Well, we'll have to talk about that when the rest of the staff are on board, but at a guess I'd say yes, at least to some degree. We don't want –"

She interrupted me. "You don't want everyone taking the same night off," she said, nodding. "Fair enough. Okay, Andi, give me your number and keep me filled in. I presume I'll be getting a letter offering me the job?"

I hadn't even thought of that. "Before the end of next week," I said. "We're still designing the company logo, so we don't have any letterheads yet."

Kylie tugged at her mother's sleeve again. "Mammy . . ."

"What, pet?"

"I'm *hungry!*"

"We won't be much longer, pet." Donna looked at me. "We are almost done, aren't we?"

Uh oh, I said to myself, realising what had happened. "Donna, I don't know where my mind is! I completely forgot this was supposed to be lunch."

I also completely forgot to get any cash from Bernard, so I had to buy lunch for the five of us with my own money.

But it was worth it . . . Donna's initial abruptness had been due to nerves. She told me that she hadn't been able to get a suitable job since Kylie was born. Most places weren't flexible enough for a working mother.

After half an hour, Kylie and Trisha were fighting over who got to sit next to me, and Kenny – who was remarkably silent for a little boy, I thought – had offered me a look at his treasured Pokémon card collection. I wasn't allowed to actually *hold* them, but he was willing to show me.

Donna's husband worked in a petrol station, which meant that until recently he'd had to work very odd hours, but since he'd been promoted to manager he was working a regular nine-to-five. "I'd love a nine-to-five myself, if it wasn't for this lot," Donna said. "But I suppose I'll have to wait until they're a few years older."

Trisha and Kylie started fighting again, and Donna

pushed them apart like a boxing referee. "That's enough! Behave yourselves or we'll go straight home right now!"

Donna nodded towards Trisha, and said, "*She's* the real troublemaker. You know how it is, the youngest is always spoiled."

"Em . . . well, *I'm* the youngest in our family."

She laughed. "Sorry. By how long?"

"There's ten years between Eimear and me. And three boys older than her. I have a niece who's only five years younger than me."

"Ah, that's different . . . with such a long gap it's almost like a second family. I'm the middle child. Supposed to be the artistic one, but I can't even draw a straight line without a ruler."

"Well, that's what rulers are for," I said.

We exchanged addresses and phone numbers when we parted. Donna told the kids to kiss me goodbye, and the girls did, but Kenny was too shy. Which is just as well because he'd managed to get hold of some more chocolate from somewhere and was now covered in it.

I left Donna spitting onto a tissue and trying to wipe Kenny's face.

* * *

I met Tony O'Hehir at eight that evening in the local pub. It was busy but we managed to get a table to ourselves where it was fairly quiet.

"So, what have you got for me?" Tony asked, once all the 'how's it going's were completed.

I took out my notepad and flicked back through the pages. "I did this one this afternoon," I said, handing it over.

Tony read: "I hiked my way up to the north pole because I wanted to test my theory about time-travel. You see, every time you cross the international date line from west to east, you go back a day. So I found the exact north pole, and spent about an hour running around in little circles. I must have crossed the date line a couple of hundred times. Then I realised that there are twenty-four time zones, and every time you cross one of them, you go *forward* an hour. I was devastated. So I hiked my way back home, and went into the house, and my mother was there. She said, 'How did the time travelling go?' I said, 'I don't think it worked. I mean, I left in September . . . What month is this?' 'It's January,' she said. "My God! It *did* work!' 'I don't think so,' she said. 'You've been gone for four months.'"

Tony looked up at me. "You're kidding, right?"

"I know it's not very good, but . . ."

"I don't mean to be rude, Andi, but this is, well, it's crap. I mean, it's probably very clever, but it's not funny."

"It's hard to be clever *and* funny," I said, which was a lame excuse.

"Well, if you can only do one, go for funny. Anything else?"

I felt like it was being told off by a teacher. I was tempted to give up there and then, but I flicked through the notebook and showed him another. "Try that one."

He read: "I went into the local Internet café, and said, 'I'll have a large cappuccino and an Internet, please.' And the girl gets me the coffee, and looks in her Internet tray. 'Sorry, there's no more. Someone had the last one.' The thing about the Internet is, it's age-dependent. Old people have no idea what it's about. My mother says to me, 'Where *is* the Internet? It has to be somewhere.' So I said, 'Mam, it's everywhere. It's all around us.' And she says, 'Hah! They used to say the same thing about God!'"

Tony paused, lowered the notebook and started to speak, but I interrupted him. "It goes on. Next page. It's just a bunch of ideas, though."

He continued. "What exactly *is* the religious significance of hot cross buns? And are they actually holy? Do you get more and more holy the more you eat them? That'd be great. Imagine you were a murderer, and you're sentenced to bread and water for twenty years. You could insist on hot cross buns and holy water, and by the time they let you out you'd be fit to be Pope.

"I went to Mass the other Sunday for the first time in ten years . . . There was hymns and everything. 'Oh Lord My Soul I Give to Thee' . . . Why is it that all hymns sound like they were written by Yoda? In some churches they have the numbers of the hymns up on a little board. All the little old ladies getting confused between the church and the parish hall. They put on their Sunday glasses and read out the numbers: '314, 67, 203' and beside them there's another little old lady ticking off the numbers and getting ready to shout 'House!'

"The numbers on Sunday were 38, 24, 36. So I'm sitting there thinking, 'Yeah, I wish!'

"They really need to update it, you know? Mass should be like television . . . At the beginning they should give you a preview of this week's gospel. 'Ah, we heard this one before. What's on the other side?' 'Hell.'

"And it's been the same thing for the past two thousand years . . . Why don't they introduce new characters, like the religious equivalent of Scrappy Doo? Or they could do a version of Mass like the *Muppet Babies*. You know, have them all as kids. Jesus and all the apostles could be like five years old, and the headmaster would be Pontius Pilate.

"Or they could reinvent Mass like they did with *Star Trek* . . . *Mass: the Next Generation*. You could have a whole new set of characters and everything . . . Jesus could be a woman, for a change. And the Holy Ghost could be a robot. The Holy 'Ghost in the Machine'. Pilate would be a Klingon, Herod would be like Darth Vader.

"What if Mass was written by Spike Lee? And Moses came down from the mountain and he carried with him two tablets, and on the tablets were the ten commandments. 'I am the Lord thy God. Thou shalt not

```

put false Gods before me, or I'll go medieval on yo' ass!' 'Thou shalt not covet thy homeboy's honey.'"

Tony finished all this and stared at me.

"You're not laughing, I notice," I said.

He grinned. "You're going straight to Hell, you know that?"

"I'm not much of a believer. So, anything there you can use?"

Tony took a deep breath and let it out slowly. "I don't know . . . I mean, I liked where you were going with the hot cross buns, and I loved the bingo bit, but after that . . . The *Star Trek* stuff is pretty obscure. I don't know, a lot of people get offended at stuff like *that*. Some of them would be offended that I was even reading it."

"I know what you mean," I said. "If my mother caught me reading something like that she'd wash my eyes out with soap."

He laughed. "I like that . . . Why can't you put more stuff like that in?"

"Well, there's other stuff . . ." I took the notebook back, and found the finished version of the piece about American tourists in Ireland. "Try *this* one."

Tony skimmed through the routine, then went back to the top and started to read it out loud. "So I'm walking up Grafton Street and this middle-aged American couple stop me and say, 'Top o' the morning.' And I go, 'Excuse me?' And the man says, 'Top o' the morning. It's an old Irish greeting.' 'No, it isn't.' He
```

looks at me. 'Yes, it is. It means that you're wishing the best part of the morning on someone.' So I said, 'Look, Gene or whatever your name is, the only people who actually use that phrase are American actors *pretending* to be Irish. I've lived here all my life and I've never known an Irish person to actually say that.

"Then they asked me if I know where the Book of Kells was. I asked them if they meant the hardback or the paperback. Then they explained that they'd come all the way from America just to see it. So I said, 'You're from America? Wow! I have a friend in America! Do you know Brian?' Then the man wanted to know where he could buy a genuine Irish shillelagh. He said that he's only seen them in tourist shops, but he wants an authentic one. So I had to break the news to him that there was no such thing as an authentic one, and no self-respecting Irishman would have a shillelagh in the house. 'Why not?' he asked me. 'Because *shillelagh* is the Irish word for the Devil's Cane. They're all cursed. That's why we have to send them abroad.' So the man said that he didn't want one now, seeing as he was Irish too. Apparently one of his ancestors left Ireland hundreds of years ago. So I said, 'Really? Well, one of my ancient ancestors was from Egypt. That means *I'm* Egyptian.'"

Tony looked up. "I like it. I'll use that. Though I'd like you to change the bit about the shillelaghs. It's not as tight as the rest."

I felt a bit happier. "Okay . . . I'm relieved that you don't think I'm completely shite at it."

"It's a lot harder than it looks, isn't it? Once you hit on something that works, you can usually get some good stuff out of it. It's like shaking the tree to see if you can get any apples: it only works at certain times, and only when you shake in the right way . . ."

"And then only if you can *find* an apple tree," I said.

"So, are you happy enough with making some changes?"

"Sure. When can I get them to you?"

"Tomorrow night would be the latest. I'll need a day to rehearse." He sat back and sipped at his drink. "So tell us, what do you do when you're not writing blasphemy?"

I told him about the job in Sound as a Pound, and everything that had happened recently.

"You seem to be a little tense about the new job. I'm sure you'll be fine."

"Tense isn't the word. At the moment I could eat coal and shit diamonds. Every time I meet the new owner I feel like I have to put on a show for him, so that he won't find out I don't know what I'm doing. I mean, I've never even really *seen* the Internet, except when there's a thing on the news about it. I probably don't *need* to know much about it, but it would be nice to have at least some idea of what he's talking about. And on top of all that, my sister is getting married in a few weeks and I've got to do tons of stuff for her. She wants me to do the Mass book for her, and I don't even know where to begin."

"Well, I can help you there. I've got a computer in the flat, and it's hooked up to the net. And I did the Mass book for my mate's wedding a couple of years ago – I'll print you out a copy and you can show it to your sister." He thought about this. "Okay, that's what we'll do. You come over to the flat tomorrow evening and I teach you all about the Internet and show you how to do the Mass book. How does that sound?"

"Great, thanks! Give me your address . . ."

* * *

Bernard phoned early the next morning to say that Nora wanted to meet up with us. We arranged to meet in the shop again, and spent a couple of hours going over the designs. She'd done a pretty good job, too, though she kept trying to sneak in stuff that was arty and clever and completely impractical.

Afterwards, I told Bernard that I'd hired Donna, and I showed him her CV. He was even more impressed with me when I told him that I'd managed to hire her at only six pounds fifty an hour. He said he'd send her a letter officially offering her the job.

As we parted, Bernard thanked me again for my input. I was growing more and more confident. I can do this, I was saying to myself. It won't be so bad.

If only I'd known . . .

Chapter Twelve

There are moments in your life around which everything pivots. It can be like walking up a seesaw: when you get to a certain point, the whole thing moves.

This is all very well if we're talking about seesaws which move in an predictable path. You can see the point coming at which everything will change.

Life is not like that. In life, you can only see the point after you've passed it. You can plan ahead all you like, but there will always be times when life takes an unexpected shift and all of a sudden everything looks different.

I didn't realise it at the time, but my life had changed quite dramatically. I wasn't aware of it yet, but had I been looking around I could have noticed. And – if I'm going to be totally honest about it – it was mostly my own fault.

Over the previous few weeks, I'd met a good number of people. I've no problem with that, because

I'm not shy in the least. However, sometimes a little caution is a wise thing . . .

My world got completely fucked up by one of the people I'd just met, and by someone I'd known for a long time. And I got hurt pretty badly.

I'm sure that no one deliberately intended to hurt me, to make my life absolutely hell when all I wanted was to help them out. And I'm sure that if *they'd* taken some time to step aside and see just what they were doing, they wouldn't have done it and everything would have been fine.

But they didn't step aside and take a look, and everything was far from fine. And because I didn't have my eyes open, I had no idea until it was too late.

* * *

I spent the afternoon rewriting some of the material for Tony, then I called around to his flat.

It was in the basement of a huge old terraced Edwardian house. The walls had at one stage been covered with some sort of stone cladding, and this was now so patchy and crumbly it looked like the house had eczema. The garden – if you can call it that – was some sort of magnet for broken bricks, old mattresses and wrecked shopping trolleys.

This was bad enough, but the houses on either side of Tony's place were magnificent: beautifully pointed brickwork and immaculate gardens without a hint of a mattress.

It was a perfect example of "bringing the neighbourhood down".

Even the gate into the garden of Tony's house didn't fit right: there was a rusty arc in the ground where the bottom of the gate was losing a battle of friction to the paving stones.

I negotiated my way around the mess and found the door to the basement flat, set under the worn steps to the rest of the house.

The paint on the door was peeling, several of the windows were cracked, and the doorbell had come loose from the frame and was dangling limply on its exposed wires. I decided to knock instead.

A minute later, Tony opened the door. "Andi! Come in, come in . . ."

I gingerly stepped over the threshold, half afraid that the whole place would come crumbling down around my ears.

"Any trouble getting here?"

"No trouble until I got to the gate," I said. "What happened to your garden?"

He looked surprised. "We have a garden?"

Tony showed me into the kitchen: It was a good match for the garden. There was a very old table covered in scratches and pits and piled high with dirty dishes. The table was accompanied by two uncomfortable-looking chairs, one of which had at some stage lost a leg – it had been replaced by a length of two-by-four, badly nailed and glued into place. That struck me as funny, but creepy . . . A chair with a wooden leg.

The kitchen cabinets were all unique, in that no two of them were alike. Many of them did share similar attributes, though: three were missing doors, two had been painted bright yellow in the recent past, and three had padlocks. I made a mental note *not* to ask Tony what was in those ones.

"Tea?" Tony asked.

"Sure, thanks."

"Do you take milk and sugar?"

"A drop of milk, one sugar," I said, looking around. I peered back out into the hall, estimating the distance to the door, just in case. "So how long have you been here?"

"About two years . . . Anyway, go on inside into the sitting-room, and I'll be with you in a minute. First on your left."

The sitting-room was enormous. There wasn't much in the way of furniture, so that probably made the room seem that much bigger. There were large French windows opening out onto the back garden. I couldn't actually *see* the garden through them, because someone had erected a huge shed right in front of the windows.

The furniture in the room wasn't much better than that in the kitchen. There was a single three-seater sofa that bore the marks of many drink-aided late nights, an armchair with so much stuffing gone from it that it looked like it was anorexic, and one of those foldy director's chairs. That one looked the newest and safest, so I sat down there.

The room also contained an expensive stereo system. I didn't know much about stereos, but Dean did and when we were going out he was forever flicking through the magazines in the newsagents' and getting excited over various decks.

Right in the middle of the room was the largest set of speakers I'd ever seen outside of a concert. They were arranged back-to-back, a couple of feet apart, and an old door was resting on them. The door held a large number of crushed cans, empty pizza boxes, overflowing ashtrays and copies of *FHM*.

Tony came in carrying two mugs of tea and a packet of biscuits tucked under one arm. He had a large bag of crisps between his teeth, and he did a sort of slow-motion catering-ballet pirouette thing as he tried to close the door with one foot.

He cleared a space among the debris on the "table" and put the "refreshments" down. I sat there watching him and praying that my face wasn't showing him just how horrified I was.

Tony collapsed onto the sofa and a small cloud of dust came out of it. I tried to smile politely and not breathe at the same time.

"So, how's things?" he asked.

"Fine. You?"

"Grand. Busy today?"

"Yeah? What did you do?"

"No, I meant, were *you* busy today?"

"Oh, sorry . . . Well, not too busy. We had another meeting with the designer for the café. She actually did some pretty good stuff."

"So it's all going according to plan, then?"

"I think so. I've still got to hire seven more people for the café, though. Know anyone with that sort of experience who's interested in a job?"

Tony scratched his stubble. "Yeah, one or two. I'll ask around and see if they're interested."

I was suddenly relieved that he didn't offer himself for the job. Having now seen the state of his kitchen, I didn't like the thought of him being anywhere near food.

"So what do you do yourself? Apart from the stand-up?"

"At the moment, nothing. Me and the lads had a band going for a while, but we didn't get anywhere. We played a few gigs, wrote most of our own stuff, but we just never clicked, you know?"

"Yeah. Well, it's a hard life on the stage, as my Gran always says. She used to be in the theatre when she was my age."

"How long ago was that?"

"About sixty years," I said, and then copped on that this was Tony's way of figuring out how old I was. "She's eighty now."

"So you're twenty . . . When's the big day?"

"What, you mean, when am I twenty-one? Not till November. How old are you?"

"Twenty-two. I know what you're going to say, I don't *look* it."

He certainly didn't: the first time I saw him, I'd assumed that he was about thirty. Of course, that was when he was on stage at the comedy night. He'd looked handsome, and dashing, and suave. In the dinginess of his flat, Tony looked like a complete slob who had absolutely no idea of where he wanted to be in life.

Desperate to keep the conversation going, I said, "So what's the story with the speakers?"

"Oh yeah. The guy who was here before me broke the table, apparently, so he had to buy a new one. And then he took it with him when he left. But I'll tell you this: you put a Metallica CD on, turn it up full blast and stand on the table . . . it's fuckin' amazing! Your whole body shakes right down to your bones, and it's a complete high. Your hair stands up on end and afterwards you get the shakes!"

I stared at him. "And do you do that sort of thing often?"

He nodded. "Whenever *Coronation Street* is on. It drives the woman next door mad."

"I'm not surprised."

"But then the bitch complains about everything. It's always the smell, or the noise, or the mess, or something. She just can't leave us alone."

"Us?"

"Me and whoever else has decided to crash. We usually end up here at the weekends. It's one long party. You should come with us some time, bring your mates. We'll get smashed, do some blow, maybe some E. And then we can go out and nick a car. You ever nick a car, Andi? It's deadly. Once we nicked one while the guy was still in it. It was gas. We're driving up the M1 at like a hundred and he was banging on the window trying to get out! We nearly *shat* ourselves laughing. And then this cop tried to pull us over, and we crashed and we all died and went to hell."

I laughed. "You really had me going there for a while, you bastard!"

Tony was grinning like mad. "When did you twig it?"

"You used the word 'deadly', when it should have been 'fuckin' deadly'. So how much of that was true?"

"None of it. Look, the speakers aren't even connected. In fact, they aren't even speakers any more. They're just empty boxes." He tapped one with his foot. "See? Hollow. Anyway, the stereo has its own speakers."

He was right. I hadn't noticed them before, but there they were: two small speakers mounted on either side of the French windows.

"And there isn't a single Metallica CD in the whole place," he added. "At least, I don't have one. Maybe one of the other lads does."

"Ah, so you share this place, then?"

He nodded. "Yeah. Sure it's huge." He pointed towards the windows. "If that bloody shed wasn't there you'd see how far back it goes. Yeah, there's two others here. Real slobs. This is *their* mess, not mine." He was grinning again. "Sorry about that. I got here just before you did, so I didn't have time to clean up. I was just going to say, 'Sorry about the mess', but I thought this would be funnier."

"Scarier, more like," I said. "So are you really only twenty-two?"

"No, twenty-nine. And I was never in a band. What else did I tell you?"

"You said you were here about two years."

"Yeah, that was a lie too. I'm only here a couple of months, and I'm not going to be here much longer . . . I hate this place."

"I don't blame you. What are your flatmates like?"

"The very essence of hygiene, as you can see . . . I *hate* it when someone comes and they see the place like this. That's why I was trying to get home early, to clean up before you got here. But as usual I was held up at the last minute."

"Ah, so you do have a day job, then?"

"Yeah. I work in a furniture warehouse in Cookstown. Yeah, yeah . . . I know what you're thinking. You're thinking that this place doesn't look like anyone living here knows the slightest bit about furniture. But I wouldn't bring anything good into the flat – the other lads would just ruin it. The stereo is Nick's brother's, so it's about the only thing in here that's safe. Nick's too scared of him to do anything to it." He nodded towards me. "That chair you're sitting on is mine, I usually keep it in my room. And speaking of which . . ." He got to his feet. "Come on, I'll show you what the Internet is all about. I keep the computer in my room as well. I wouldn't want the other two morons anywhere near it."

I was a bit reluctant to go into his room – after all, I barely knew him, and he was nine years older than me – but I decided that if anything untoward was going to happen, being in the bedroom or the sitting-room wouldn't make any difference.

"And you can bring your tea and the bikkies and crisps, if you want," Tony added. "Don't worry. The mugs are clean – I keep them in my cupboard."

"So *that's* why you have padlocks."

"Yeah, the lads think that anything not locked away is public property. I even have to keep my bathroom stuff locked in the bedroom. I did have combination locks, but they managed to crack them."

True to his word, Tony's bedroom *was* locked. "See these scratches?" he said, pointing to the lock. "I came home one night to find that they'd tried to pick the lock. Bastards." He unlocked it and ushered me in.

Not counting Dean or my brothers, this was the first time I'd been in a man's bedroom. I didn't know what to expect. I thought that there might be posters of Britney Spears or Posh Spice or Manchester United on the walls, no bedclothes except a crumpled, stained sheet, dirty socks and underpants all over the place, a weird smell coming from somewhere, that sort of thing.

But his room was clean and fairly neat. There was a small, full bookcase against one wall, with a couple of snooker trophies on top of it. A couple of Salvador Dali prints were on the walls – Tony said they were there when he moved in – along with a small poster advertising his debut night at the stand-up show.

The computer was smaller than I'd expected, and was tucked into one corner. Beside it was a printer and a small pair of speakers.

"Hang on a sec," Tony said, turning the computer on. "I'll just get the other chair."

I watched as the computer threw up lots of incomprehensible text, then the screen flickered a couple of times, and showed the Microsoft Windows 98 logo.

"I'm lost already," I said to Tony as he came back. "How do I make it go?"

He sat down beside me. "*You* don't make it go. *I* do . . . Watch."

Tony showed me how to use the mouse, how to open the word processor and edit and save a document. He showed me how to run the Internet program – though he explained that the set-up in the café would be a lot simpler – and we spent the next hour surfing the net.

It was, in Tony's words, fierce fun.

* * *

Afterwards, we were in the sitting-room talking about

the material for Tony's gig when his flatmates came back. They barrelled noisily into the room and stopped dead when they saw me.

The first one couldn't have been any older than me. He had "student" written all over him. Well, not actually, but if it had been, it would have been badly spelled and in shaky handwriting. He was dressed in a frayed jumper about ten sizes too big for him, jeans that were too small, and sandals. His hair was down to his shoulders and looked like it hadn't been washed in months.

Tony later told me that in fact the guy's hair *hadn't* been washed in months, because he'd heard of the theory that if you don't wash your hair for ages it will eventually clean itself.

The second flatmate wasn't any more attractive. He was incredibly thin and stood with a stoop, so his shoulders were higher than his neck – which I could see in all its spotty, pale, angular glory. He was dressed much like his companion, but without the sandals. Instead he wore an old pair of boots with string for laces.

Tony turned around to look at them. "Lads, this is Andi. Andi, Nick and Dick."

The stoopy one nodded. "It's Nicholas, actually."

"How's it goin'?" enquired Dick.

Tony got to his feet, so I did likewise. "You just caught us on the way out, lads," he said. "So, been up to anything interesting?"

They couldn't take their eyes off me. "Yeah . . ." Dick mumbled. "We were with Benny."

"Yeah," confirmed Nick. "And Pete."

"And Shaner."

"And Joxer."

"And Joxer's mate."

"Mel."

"Yeah, Mel."

"Sounds like a laugh," Tony said. He winked at me. "Ready to go?"

I nodded. "Try and stop me," I said, quiet enough that the others wouldn't hear.

* * *

After making sure that his bedroom and the cupboards were securely locked, we headed out. "Sorry about that," Tony said. "But I know what those two are like when they catch sight of a good-looking woman. They'd just sit there and stare at you for the night, then snigger about it once you left. In fact, that's probably what they're doing now."

"I gather that neither of them are currently going out with anyone?"

He shuddered. "God, I'd hate to meet the sort of woman who *would* go out with them."

"So where are we going?"

Tony shrugged. "It's a nice night. We could go for a walk along the quays."

"Tony, I've lived in the heart of Dublin my whole life. Why would I want to walk along the quays?"

"Because it's a nice straight walk and we probably won't get lost. Besides, I'm broke so we can't go to a pub. Get paid on Thursdays, you see."

He was right, though: it was a nice night. It was about ten o'clock, and the sun was rapidly heading towards the horizon. The sky was a damn good shade of red and the air smelled clean and pure, despite the fact that we were only yards away from the Liffey.

"What's the story with your man Dean?" Tony asked.

"*That* one came out of the blue," I said. "What made you think of him?"

"Dunno."

"Well, I broke up with him. We started going out two years ago – I've known him and Ellen since we were kids – but I knew pretty much from the start that it was a bad idea. And I couldn't think of a way to break up without upsetting Ellen. She was my best friend."

"Was?"

"Well, maybe she still is, I'm not really sure. See, after five months I finally told Dean that I didn't want to go out with him, but he didn't really get the hint."

"Aw, you never told him that you just wanted to be friends, did you?"

"Well, yeah."

"Andi, that's the worst thing you can say. Look, there are one or two who'll get the hint and just piss off, but the rest of them are divided into two types: the ones

193

who think you really do want to be friends and they never leave you alone, and the ones who think that you're really in love with them but things are just moving too fast. That lot won't leave you alone either, because they're willing to wait." He shook his head and let out a long sigh. "I should know. I used to be like that."

"Really? You don't *seem* like the stalker type."

"I was lucky – things happened that made me see sense. That might happen to Dean, but then again it might not."

"I'm pretty sure he's got the message now," I said. "We had a huge fight and I told him right out that I didn't want to see him any more, and Ellen overheard me and then I had a fight with her."

"They're very close for brother and sister."

"They're twins," I explained. "They're not identical, though . . . What's that word?"

"Different?"

"No, it's about twins . . . fraternal. That's it. They're fraternal twins. But anyway, what's your story, then? Who broke *your* heart?"

"Ah . . . This girl I was seeing for ages. It was a strange situation. Liz, her name was. It turned out that she was actually in a relationship with someone else at the same time. I went nuts when I found out. But I'm cured now. I've sworn off women for life."

"Really?" I said, trying not to sound too disappointed.

"Yeah, I thinking of joining the Californian Foreign

Legion. They're like the French Foreign Legion, only a lot more mellow."

"Or you could break all religious conventions by becoming the world's first male nun. After all, there are women priests now."

"Sister Tony," he said. "Or even Mother Tony, if I get promoted."

"If you really want to swear off women, you only have to bring Nick and Dick with you everywhere. God, what are they *like*? And the state of their clothes!"

"All students dress alike," Tony said wisely. "They do it to emphasise their individuality."

"You should have seen the state of the designer Bernard got to do the café. She'd fit right in with them."

"So are you feeling any better about the whole thing? Think you can hack it?"

"Probably not, but I'm hoping to learn enough to get by before I'm found out. Is that how it's done, then, in the real world?"

"You're asking the wrong person. I've no concept of the real world. For years I thought that Erasure's song 'Oh L'Amour' was an Irish song all about a big drink. Someone asked me what my *raison d'être* was, and I thought he was talking about a laser for killing fruit. Until I was about ten I didn't know that America and the United States were the same place. I've spent my whole life wondering what's written on Dennis Nordern's clipboard. And I still can't figure out what all the millennium fuss was all about. Sure, didn't we already *have* a millennium in 1988? A millennium is supposed to last a thousand years, not twelve."

"Something tells me that all that's from your routines . . . But I don't get that last one."

"Dublin was a thousand years old in 1988," he said. "I suppose all you young folk don't remember that. Ah, it was a great time. Taxes were abolished and only *good* weather was allowed and Ireland won every match they played and there were parties all night long. The Celtic Tiger was only a kitten in those days, but we lived our lives to the full and we walked the streets with a song in our hearts."

"And everyone was your friend and you were able to leave your door unlocked at night, that sort of thing?"

"Exactly . . . Shite. If people of your age don't remember that, I'll have to drop it from the act."

"What's your all-time favourite joke, then?"

Tony had to think about this one. "Okay . . . An Englishman, an Irishman and a Scotsman walk into a bar. The barman looks up and says, 'What the hell is this? Some kind of joke?'"

I groaned. "Heard it a million times. Okay, here's one of mine: Two little kids, aged six and eight, decide it's time to learn how to swear. So, the eight-year-old says to the six-year-old, 'Okay, you say *damn* and I'll say *hell*,' All excited about their plan, they troop downstairs, where their mother asks them what they'd like for breakfast. 'Aw, hell,' says the eight-year-old, 'gimme some cornflakes.' His mother backhands him off the chair, sending him bawling out of the room, and turns to the younger brother. 'What'll *you* have?' 'I dunno,' says the six-year-old, 'but I sure as hell don't want any damn cornflakes.'"

Tony laughed. "Good one! I'll have to add that to my list of polite jokes . . . I keep a mental list of jokes that are safe to tell in front of my mother."

"This lad is sitting outside his local pub one day, enjoying a quiet pint and generally feeling good about himself, when a nun suddenly appears at his table and starts going on about the evils of drink. 'You should be ashamed of yourself, young man! Drinking is a sin! Alcohol is the blood of Satan!' He gets pretty annoyed about this, and goes on the offensive. 'How do *you* know, Sister? Have you ever had a drink yourself? How can you be sure that what you're saying is right?' 'Don't be ridiculous – of course I have never taken alcohol myself.' 'Then let me buy you a drink – if you still believe afterwards that it's evil I will give up drink for life.' 'How could I, a *nun*, sit outside this public house drinking?!' 'I'll get the barman to put it in a teacup for you, then no one will know.' The nun finally agrees, so he goes inside to the bar. 'Another pint for me, and a triple vodka on the rocks,' then he lowers his voice and says to the barman '. . . and could you put the vodka in a teacup?' So the barman says –"

Tony interrupted me. "Heard it a *billion* times."

"Well, I still like it. So what made you want to do stand-up?"

"Ben Elton . . . I saw him ten years ago in London. He was going on about really trivial stuff, and getting so worked up about it . . . it was a revelation. You know when you have one of those moments when everything suddenly becomes clear? That's what it was like. What about you?"

"I suppose being the youngest had a lot to do with it. I was usually the centre of attention. Plus, my brother Roddy was telling me about Tommy Cooper."

"Ah! One of the few true geniuses in the comedy world!"

"Yeah. He was dead long before I ever heard any of his stuff, but once I heard it, that was it."

"He was dead long before you were *born*, kid . . ." Tony said with a grin. "There was a tribute programme about him a couple of years back, and whoever it was who was being interviewed said the best gag he ever heard was one time at the start of a show, the announcer goes, 'Ladies and gentlemen, Mr Tommy Cooper!' and the curtain rises and there's no one there. Then Tommy's voice comes over the PA: 'Good evening, ladies and gentlemen . . . ' he pauses ' . . . I'm locked in the dressing-room.'"

I laughed. "My favourite is the one with the duck . . . He had this little wooden duck, and when you pulled a string the duck's head bobbed down and picked a card out of the deck. Tommy explained that the duck would pick a card selected by a member of the audience. 'And to make it extra hard . . . ' he says, and then he takes out a tiny little piece of cloth and blindfolds the duck!" I broke up laughing again.

"There was another duck trick he did. I thought you were going to say it. He holds up this large white handkerchief. 'Ladies and gentlemen, from this handkerchief I shall now produce a flock of ducks.' Then he crumples up the handkerchief, waves his magic wand over it, and with a flourish he opens the handkerchief and a big ragged hole has appeared in it. 'Damn! They got away again!'"

By the time we got to Heuston Station, Tony and I had each other in fits of laughter. At one point I wasn't even able to walk, and I'm sure that passers-by thought I was having a heart attack or something.

Tony looked at his watch. "It's getting late. Better get you home before your mother sends out a search party."

We turned around and headed back into town. "Did you ever notice," I asked, "that when you come in late, your parents are always *just about* to call the police and phone all the hospitals?"

"Yeah. If everyone came home two minutes later, the cops would be swamped with calls."

We walked in silence for a while.

Eventually, Tony said, "So you're coming to the gig tomorrow night, then? See your material in action?"

"I wouldn't miss it for the world."

"Grand."

I glanced at him just in time to see him taking a quick look at me. "So . . ." I said, wondering whether I should just bite the bullet and ask him out, "we could meet up before the show if you want, to go over everything."

"I don't know . . . I'm usually pushed for time. I don't get home from work until after seven."

"Okay," I said, when what I meant was, "Shit!"

"Or we could meet up afterwards, and go over the whole thing. See what worked and what didn't. And try and come up with some ideas for next time."

"This is assuming that you'll even want to see me again after tomorrow night when all my bits have everyone booing and throwing stuff at you."

"Now, I doubt that'll happen, Andi."

We walked in silence again. I was wondering if he was actually interested in me, or if I was just imagining it. He hadn't exactly asked me out for after the show, but maybe that was what he meant. But then, he'd turned down the offer of meeting up *before* the show, so that might mean he wasn't interested.

On the other hand – always assuming that I could get a third hand from somewhere – he might have been interested but worried about the age gap. Nine years is a pretty big gap.

I wondered if I should try the stumble-trick . . . It was something Eimear told me about years ago. In a situation such as this, you pretend to stumble and if he catches you and remains holding on, it's a pretty good bet that he's interested.

Then I wondered what *he* was wondering, and wondered if I should ask him. I was turning into Wonder Woman.

But before I could ask him what was on his mind, he asked me what was on *mine*.

"Stuff," I said.

"That's funny – I was just thinking about stuff as well."

"What kind of stuff were you thinking about?"

"Stuff like . . . Oh, all kinds of things. Like I'm hoping that tomorrow night is a success in the way I want it to be. Like I hope I don't forget to make my lunch for tomorrow. Like I'd better do a bit of rehearsal when I get home. Like I'm hoping that the gig tomorrow night is a success."

"You already said that one."

"No, I didn't."

"Yes you did. You said that . . ." Slowly it dawned on me. "I see."

"Do you?"

"I think so."

"And?"

"And I'm hoping that tomorrow night is a success in the way I want it to be."

He nodded. "Well then."

We walked on for a bit.

"Where, exactly, do you live? I know it's around here somewhere."

"We passed it a few minutes ago."

He stopped. "You should have said. I could be on my way home by now."

"Is that what you want?" I asked.

"That depends . . ."

We turned around and stopped outside my house. I quickly checked it for signs of twitching curtains.

"Well, thanks for walking me home."

"It's my pleasure . . . So. Tomorrow night? All prepared for the big event?"

I nodded. "*And* for the show."

He looked at me, took a deep breath, and seemed to come to a decision. "Andi . . . you're nine years younger than me."

"I know that."

"Well, it's awkward. I mean, when I was your age, you were only eleven."

"What does that have to do with anything?"

"I don't know . . . it just feels weird. I'm sorry. I thought I could do this, but it's not right. And it's not *you*, you're great. You're perfect. It's just, well, *nine years*."

I stepped back from him. "Okay. No problem. I understand. I mean, I'm only twenty. I'll get over it. It's not like I'm even old enough to know what I want."

"Look, I didn't mean anything like that."

I sighed. "Sorry . . . I know you didn't. I just wish I was a few years older."

"And I wish I was a few years younger."

"So if we were closer in age, it would make a difference, right?"

He nodded. "Definitely."

"Why, though? *What* difference would it make? Would I be more mature, is that it? Or is it because you're worried what people might say?"

He suddenly smiled. "You're right, you know . . . There's no real difference. I'm being stupid."

I smiled back. "Okay then. Shut up and kiss me."

He did.

Chapter Thirteen

Ellen phoned me the next morning. "It's me," she said. "Listen, how are things?"

"Okay . . . Great, in fact."

"Remember you were talking about the café, and wondering if I wanted to work there? Well, I think I do. At the moment I'm okay, but the folks have been getting on at me to get another job. Dad says it's bad enough that I'm not paying him any rent as it is."

"Do you want to meet up, then? I can fill you in on what's happening. Make it a sort of interview. I'm sure we could both do with the practice."

"Sure. Do you want to come over here, or should I go over to you?"

"I'd better go over to you . . . Mam's in a bit of a mood at the moment. I'll be there in about an hour, okay?"

We said goodbye and hung up. When I went back into the kitchen Mam was looking at me.

"What?"

"Who was that?" she asked.

"Ellen."

She made a "hmph!" sound and said, "I'm sure."

"No, really it was."

"So what's this I hear about you carrying on with some young lad right outside the hall door last night? You should be ashamed of yourself. Out there for hours you were."

I was tempted to point out that Tony wasn't a *young* lad, but I knew that would only make her worse. "That was Tony," I said.

"So does Dean know about all this? No, I'm sure he doesn't. He's a nice lad, Andi. You shouldn't be treating him like that."

I lost it. "Jesus! Will no one ever fucking *listen* to me!? Dean and I broke up over a year and a half ago! Mam, I've been telling you that for ages! Just because Dean still hangs around doesn't mean we're going out!"

She gave me her special look, the one that she used to reserve for the lads when she caught them watching porno movies. "Watch your tongue, Andi. You're not too old to get a clip around the ear from your father."

I calmed down a little. "I'm sorry . . . It's just that no one seems to be able to understand that I'm not in the slightest bit interested in Dean."

"Well, if you're not interested in him, why didn't you tell him?"

"I did! Look, Mam, I don't have time to go into this now. I'm going over to Ellen's."

"And I suppose you're going to tell her all about this Tony, too?"

"Probably."

She suddenly looked really sad. "There was a time when you felt you could tell me everything, Andi. And now you can't tell me *anything*. What happened?"

I decide that Ellen could wait. I sat down opposite my mother. "I'm sorry, Mam. Things are complicated right now . . . I met Tony in a pub. He's really nice, Mam, you'd like him a lot. He's a bit older than me, though."

"How much older?"

"A few years," I said, though I doubted *that* would work.

I was right. "How old is he, Andi?"

"Twenty-nine."

"Mother of God, Andi! He's half your age again!"

"I *know*."

"What sort of a man is he to be going out with someone as young as you?"

"That's not fair. Just because there's only a year between you and Dad doesn't mean that everyone has to be so close in age!"

"Fair has nothing to do with it, Andi. There's right and there's wrong. And going out with someone nine years younger than you is wrong. Plain and simple. I mean, *look* at you! You're barely over Dean and now you're after some older man!"

"I'm not 'barely over Dean'! That's what I've been trying to tell you! I've been over Dean for ages, but because I didn't want to upset Ellen, I had to go easy on him. So in all that time I've had *no one*. Well, now I do have someone and you can't stop me from seeing him!"

"As a matter of fact, I *can*." She paused. "But I won't. I just want you to be careful, Andi. A twenty-nine-year-old man knows a lot more about life than a twenty-year-old girl."

I moved towards the door. "I'd better get going. Don't worry, though. I'm not stupid. I'm not going to come home pregnant or anything."

"You'd better not."

* * *

Ellen was full of the joys of spring when I arrived at her flat. She looked happier than I'd seen her in ages.

She ushered me into the flat and I collapsed onto the sofa.

"Do you want a cup of tea, or something?" Ellen asked.

"Yeah, thanks. So what's happening with you and Niall?" I asked. "Is all that still going on?"

"Yeah . . . He's great. We see each other almost every night. And during the day sometimes, too."

"Great. How's everyone else?"

"Dean's okay. He's still kind of in shock that you broke up with him, though."

Jaye Carroll

"El, I'm not going through that argument *twice* in one day. I've just had my mother on at me about it."

"Well, he's getting better, anyway. So there's no chance that you'll change your mind, then? Only he asked me to ask you."

"Yeah, that *really* sounds like he's getting better, all right," I said, shaking my head. "You know, at one stage I was considering setting him up with someone, just to get him off my back. I couldn't think of anyone, though."

"That wouldn't have been a nice thing to do, anyway."

"Not nice to him, or not nice to her?"

"You see? You're doing it again! Stop picking on him!"

"Sorry . . . Anyway, to answer your question, there's no chance of me and Dean getting back together. Besides, I'm sort of spoken for now," I added, watching her face for her reaction.

"Really? Who?"

"Tony."

"Tony . . . What, Tony the *comedian*? Andi, he's way older than you are!"

"Here we go again. I had this conversation with my mother this morning as well."

"So how did it all happen?"

I told her everything that had happened between me and Tony, right up to the previous night's extended snogging session.

"What was it like, then?"

"Great," I said. "Amazing. Toe-tingles and everything. I mean, I haven't kissed many people, so I don't really know, but God it was good! And he was polite about it too. I mean, he didn't let his hands wander too much. The only thing was he hadn't shaved, so my face was all sore when I woke up."

Ellen made a face. "Hate that!"

"It was worth it," I said, grinning. I stretched out on the sofa. "He's incredible!"

"You sound like you're in love, or something."

"I bloody hope I'm not."

"You hope you're *not*? What do you mean?"

"Because if it feels this good and I'm *not* in love, imagine what it's going to feel like when I am!"

* * *

For a laugh – and because we really did need the practice – Ellen and I decided to do the interview properly. We sat at opposite sides of her coffee table.

"Okay," I said. "You don't know me and I don't know you . . . Let's just assume that you've come to the interview dressed normally, and not like that."

She looked herself up and down. "What's wrong with the way I'm dressed?"

"Well, you wouldn't go wearing jeans and your brother's old sweatshirt to an interview, would you? Anyway, let's get started. Okay . . . You're coming in for the interview . . . I'm the interviewer."

"Can I be me?"

"Why not? Okay, you knock on the door."

She just sat there. After a few seconds, she said, "You're supposed to tell me to come in."

"But you didn't knock yet!"

"All right! Fuck's sake! Knock, knock, knock."

"Come in. Have a seat."

"Thank you."

"It's Ellen, isn't it? Now, Ellen, I see here from your CV that you used to be the bearded woman in a circus."

"Ah piss off, Andi! You're the one who wanted to do this seriously."

I laughed. "Sorry, sorry! Okay, so I see from your CV that you worked in a pound shop. No, wait!" I cleared my throat. "I see here from your *resumé* that you have extensive experience in a retail outlet."

She nodded. "That's right."

"Now, tell me why you think you'd like this job."

Ellen looked at me. "Because . . . Because . . . Shite, this is hard! Because if I get the job I won't have to go on any more interviews."

I sat back. "Hmm . . . Well, thanks for your time. Can you send in the next candidate please? And don't let the door hit your arse on the way out."

We tried again: "Tell me why you think you'd like this job."

She was a lot more composed this time. "I've always wanted to work with technology."

"Let me save you the embarrassment of being fired by not hiring you."

The third time was a lot better: "It sounds like a challenge," Ellen said. "And a lot of fun. I like the flexible hours, and I like the idea of serving people, making them happy."

"I see. And tell me this: what special qualification do you bring to the job?"

"Well, as you can see from my resumé, I've had a lot of retail experience, so I know how to deal with customers. I think that customer relations are very important in a job like that."

"*Much* better," I said, slipping out of character.

"Yeah?"

"Definitely. Only one thing: the hours aren't exactly flexible, there's just lots of them. It's not going to be like flexitime."

"So how's it going to work?"

"I'm not a hundred per cent sure at the moment. If it's not busy in the mornings, then we'll only need one person to start at eight. They can work until four. Then we'll have two more from nine until five. And someone will come in at four and work until eleven. And another two from five until midnight. If it *is* busy in the mornings, we'll have two people starting at eight, and one at nine. Something like that, anyway."

"And what about the days?"

"Well, again we don't know which days are going to be the busy ones. At the moment I'm assuming that every day will be more or less the same. And I'm also assuming that we won't have any part-timers. So that means everyone will have to do Saturdays and Sundays. So one week you'll work Monday to Friday, the next it'll be Sunday to Thursday, then Saturday to Wednesday, and so on."

Ellen frowned. "Hang on . . . That means we're only getting one day off! That's a six-day week!"

"Oh yeah . . ." I thought about it. "All right, then, Monday to Friday, then Tuesday to Saturday. Then in on Monday, off Tuesday, in Wednesday to Saturday. So that way your day off would change from week to week."

Ellen got out a pen and worked this out. "That means I'll never be in on a Sunday."

"Shit! Hang on, let me have a think about this . . ." I gave it some serious consideration, and gave up. "No, it's too hard. I'll need to sit down and do a chart, or something. But whichever way I look at it, it looks like every now and again you'll have to do six days in a row. But on the other hand, every now and again you'd get three days off in a row."

"And you have to schedule in holidays and everything," she reminded me. "Plus you'll need to make sure that people are covered for sick days."

"Yeah . . . God, this is a lot harder than I thought it would be. And I've still got to find seven more people and interview them."

"So do I get the job, then?"

"Sure. But you're going to have to work under me, though. And I won't be able to go easier on you just because it's you. So, listen, do you know anyone else who might be interested?"

She shrugged. "I don't think so. But if I find anyone, I'll let you know."

* * *

Because Tony didn't know what time he'd get home from work, we'd agreed to just meet at the pub.

So I spent the afternoon alternating between getting ready and panicking. My mother wasn't talking to me, so I wasn't able to ask her opinion on what I should wear.

I must have gone to the toilet about a hundred times, but I still felt the need to go when I got to the pub.

I had a quick look around and there was no sign of Tony, so I dashed into the loo and did the business. On the way out, I bumped into someone who was vaguely familiar.

"Andi! I thought it was you! You walked right past me!" she said, clearly overjoyed to see me.

"Oh my God! What are *you* doing here?" I had absolutely no idea who she was. She was about twenty-six, good-looking, with red hair that was just about shoulder-length, John Lennon glasses and a Donegal accent. There was something about her that told me I should know her, but it wouldn't come to me.

"We're over there," she said, pointing towards the

front of the pub. "We heard about this lad who's on tonight. He's supposed to be pretty good."

"Who, Tony O'Hehir?"

She nodded. "Yeah . . . A friend of Jack's knows him or something. Have you seen him before?"

As soon as she said "Jack" I knew who she was: Gillian, from Gerry's other pound shop in Clontarf. "Yeah, I've seen him a couple of times . . . Actually, we're sort of going out."

She nudged me and grinned. "You sly little thing, you! Why did you never say? No, hold on, what about your man, Ellen's brother? Is he gone off the scene or what?"

"God, don't talk to me about that man! Anyway, what's up with Gerry these days? I haven't seen him in ages, now that the shop is gone."

"He's fine. Well, you know him, going around in a daze the whole time. He was only saying yesterday that we should all get together, a sort of farewell party. Anyway, wait right here and I'll be back in a minute." She dashed into the Ladies' and I stood there like an eejit looking around for Tony.

When Gillian returned, she grabbed my arm. "Look, come on over and meet Jack! He's always complaining that he never gets to meet the people I talk about."

She steered me towards her gang: I was a bit put out when I saw that they were sitting where *my* gang used to sit.

"Hey, everyone, this is Andi! She used to work in

Gerry's shop in town, until he sold it. Andi, this is Jack, Susan, June and Barbara."

Feeling very self-conscious – which was unusual for me, and I put it down to anxiety about meeting Tony again – I said hi to them all.

"Jack works with Susan and Barbara, and he used to work with June."

They seemed like a nice enough bunch, but I wasn't in the mood to join them. "Well, it's nice to meet you all, but I'm sort of waiting for someone."

Gillian nudged Susan. "She's going out with your man."

"*My* man?" Susan asked. "The bastard!"

"No, I mean the lad we came to see. Vince's mate."

"Tony O'Hehir," June said. She looked up at me. "He used to live in the same building as Vince. Have you seen his new place yet? It's supposed to be a right dump!"

"It is," I said. "I don't think he's too happy there. Listen, I'd better go and wait for him. I said I'd meet him at the bar."

Barbara looked towards the bar, which wasn't more than twenty feet away. "Yeah, you might miss him. Hang on, isn't he like *thirty* or something? How old are *you*, Andi?"

Susan thumped her. "Shut up, you. I'm going to get a drink. Anybody want anything?" She got to her feet.

They all had full drinks in front of them, including Susan. "Okay, then I'll get crisps."

Susan walked me over to the bar. "It's a good thing the rest of them aren't here yet. They'd tear you apart." She looked at me in a big-sisterly kind of way. "First date? Or something like that?"

I could feel myself turning red. "Well, we're just sort of starting off, you know."

"Don't let anyone say anything about the age difference, okay? What the hell do *they* know?" She looked concerned. "You're really worried about it, aren't you?"

"Sort of."

"But then you're probably not as worried as *he* is. You'll be fine. Look, are you sure you don't want to join us? I promise to keep the hyenas off your back."

I laughed. "What, are you in charge of them or something?"

"Well, I'm Jack and Barbara's boss, so I'll give them hell in the morning."

"So what do you do, then?"

"Office manager, in Complete Office Solutions out in Phibsboro."

I had an idea. "Listen, I'm supposed to be the manager in the shop now that it's going to be turned into an Internet café, but between you and me I've got absolutely no idea what I'm doing. Can I pick your brains sometime? I need to make up schedules and do interviews and everything, and so far I've been making it up as I go along. I don't even know where to *start* with the schedules."

"Sure . . ." She rummaged around in her pocket and produced a business card. "Phone me tomorrow or Monday, and we can talk about it. I'd better get back to that bunch. You don't want to sit with us?"

"Nah . . . I feel uncomfortable enough as it is."

She nodded. "Okay, maybe I'll see you later, then?"

* * *

At nine, one of the barmen set up a mike and announced the first act. There was still no sign of Tony.

The crowd cheered as Dennis Clarke stepped up to the mike. I remembered him from the first night we'd seen Tony.

"So anyway, the Martians attack and we're going, 'What are we going to do?' Well, *I* have a solution! When they say, 'Take us to your leader', we say, 'Steve? He's not here right now.' 'Well, when will he be back?'" Dennis sucked breath in between his teeth. "'Oooh, I don't know. Steve is like that.' And the Martians will say, 'Is it all right if we wait?' and then we can say, 'He could be a while. Go back to Mars and we'll let you know when Steve gets here.'"

Then Dennis went off on one of his tangents: "I went to the doctor, and I said, 'Doctor, it hurts when I raise my arm like this.'" Dennis demonstrated by pointing his left arm straight up. So the doctor says to me, 'Okay, hold your arm there for a second while I go and check my medical book.' And that's the funny thing about doctors: they spend all those years training and they still have to refer to the manual. And then I heard about these intern doctors who do thirty-six-hour days. Are they *magic*, or something? Where do they get extra twelve hours from? I reckon it's some medical secret and they won't let the rest of us in on it.

"So, what's the deal with crunchy peanut butter? What's the point of going to all the trouble of grinding up a load of peanuts if you're just going to put in some more lumps? If the lumps are too big, then when you're spreading the peanut butter on your bread they kind of tear it up a bit, so here's a tip: use toast.

"Now, some people think that the Martians won't fall for that one, so probably the best thing to do is this: we apologise. 'Mr Martian, on behalf of the people of Earth, we're very sorry and we promise that Mars Bars will be taken off the market.' And then what can they do? They can't come in with their guns blasting if we've already apologised, can they? So the doctor comes back to me, and says, 'Is your arm tired yet?'"

Dennis's left arm was still pointing straight up. "And I said, 'Yes, it is.' And he said, 'That'll be from keeping it up in the air like that. Let it down now.'" Dennis lowered his arm. "'How does it feel now?' 'Much better, thanks.' 'That'll be twenty pounds, please.' So I said to the doctor, 'Listen, I'm not paying you twenty pounds! You haven't done anything!' 'Ah, but I have,' he said. 'You see, the pain in your arm was caused by too much circulation.' 'Too much circulation? Are you mad?' And he said, 'Yes.'

"But sometimes the toast cracks, so that's no good. No, what you need to do is make sure that the toast is only done on one side. That way the other side is flexible and acts as a kind of shock-absorber. Now, if you're using a toaster, the best way to get the toast only done on one side is to slip a small piece of asbestos in beside the bread. Just tuck it in there safe and snug."

It was absolutely exhausting listening to Dennis – he went all over the place and it was just way too hard to keep track of everything. The audience loved it, though, and cheered like mad when he was done.

I looked around for Tony again, and jumped when I saw that he was standing right next to me.

"Sorry," he said. "I saw you examining the opposition and I didn't want to distract you. How was he?"

"Okay . . . His material isn't that good, though. It's his presentation that makes it."

"Still, at least *he* gets to go before Bosco Byrne."

"They're putting you on *after* Bosco? Wow! They must think you're okay, then."

We looked at each other.

"You look good," Tony said.

"You too. You shine up nice." He had shaved and showered and dressed in his best clothes.

He grinned. "Well, I had to make an effort, seeing as it's a special occasion."

"How long did it take you to get home last night?"

"About half an hour, I think. I don't really remember the walk. Cloud nine, and all that."

"So you haven't changed your mind again? Still okay with the idea of going out with someone who's only twenty?"

"*More* than okay," he said. "I'll tell you this. When I got in last night Nick and Dick were all over me, asking questions about you. They're mad jealous. Nick said you were the best-looking woman he'd ever seen. Now, I know that lads like him don't get to see many women who don't have staples in their tummies or phone numbers covering their nipples, but it's still a good compliment."

"It'd sound better coming from *you* . . ." I hinted.

"Well, I'd have to agree with Nick on that one . . ." He glanced at the stage area. "Aw, shit! Here comes Bosco!"

"You're not a fan, then?"

"He's an idiot. Actually, that's not true. In real life he's sound. Just on stage he's an idiot. If you met him on the street you'd go away thinking that he was one of the nicest people you've ever met."

Bosco started his act by telling a very old joke about a cat and a cockerel trying to cross a lake. Then he gave us several samples from his "old people having sex" repertoire. This was followed by some jokes about homosexuals that were in even worse taste.

As before, his fans loved it. He didn't need to tell any jokes: all he had to do was stand there and say "bollocks" and they broke up laughing.

As Bosco was winding up his set, I noticed that Tony was starting to sweat.

"I don't know if I can do this," he said. "The place is packed with Bosco's crowd now and they're not going to put up with me waffling on about tigers and tourists and that sort of thing."

"They will," I said. "Look, just open by telling them a few old jokes. Like the one about the nun and the drink. Once you get them on your side, you can fall back to your prepared stuff. It'll be fine."

He took a deep breath, and stared at me. "I'm going to die up there tonight. I can just feel it."

"You won't," I said. "Look, at the very least *I'll* be laughing. And there's an old friend of mine around here somewhere with a bunch of her mates. They all came to see you, so *they'll* enjoy it."

On stage, Bosco was explaining why his mother-in-law was a bitch.

"That's about it," Tony said. "He's almost done. I'm supposed to go on straight after him. If we leave a break Bosco's fans will lose interest."

I took a tissue from my bag and wiped the sweat off his forehead and neck. "Okay . . . Deep, slow breaths. You'll be fine. You'll be great."

He nodded. "Okay. Okay. Jesus, this is worse than the first time."

I put my hand around the back of his neck and pulled him down for a kiss. "That better?"

He laughed. "Yeah. Now I've got a hard-on as well! All right, here we go." He started to move away, then turned back for another quick kiss.

221

Then Bosco said, "Thanks very much, lazies and germs! You've been a fuckin' great audience!"

And then something remarkable happened: Bosco noticed Tony approaching the mike, and he must have noticed the fear in Tony's eyes, because he said, "Ladies and gentlemen, put your hands together for a very good friend of mine, a comedy genius, the one and only Mr Tony O'Hehir!"

The crowd cheered louder than they had all night. Tony went straight into a bunch of old, slightly off-colour jokes, and the audience loved them.

I stood by the bar, watching him. All trace of his nervousness was now gone, and he performed like a professional. I glanced over at Gillian and her gang, and they seemed to be enjoying it as much as anyone.

On stage, Tony was finishing up the joke about the nun and the drink: "So the barman says, 'Oh no! It's not that bloody nun again, is it?'"

Chapter Fourteen

After Tony's set was over, we hung around for a few minutes while everyone told him how good he was, then he grabbed my hand and almost pulled me out of the place.

Outside, the cold night air hit us like a breath of fresh air. Which, of course, it was.

Tony was in shock – he'd put all his energy into the performance. He stood there trying to remember how to breathe, and muttering over and over, "Shit shit shit . . ."

I was starting to seriously worry about him when he suddenly snapped out of it. He calmed down, took another few deep breaths, and looked around. "So how did it go?"

"You couldn't tell? Tony, it was brilliant! You were amazing! Even the barmen stopped serving drinks and just stood there laughing. Not that anyone was trying to *buy* a drink."

"I don't know if I can do that again," he said. "That was just too hard. God, I feel like I'm going to puke!"

"You'll be fine," I said. "It's just stage fright. They loved you!"

"What about your material?"

"I think they liked it . . . They seemed to be laughing at the right bits."

A trio of half-drunk lads fell out of the pub. One of them spotted Tony. "Hey! It's yer man!" He staggered over and shook Tony's hand. "That was fuckin' brilliant! American tourist *bastards*! You fuckin' showed them w – wankers!"

His friends – who luckily were a little more sober – grabbed hold of him and pulled him away from Tony.

"Good gig tonight, bud," one of them said. "Don't mind this lad. He's had a few too many. You'll be here next week?"

"Yeah," Tony said. "Thanks for coming."

"Ah, it was good crack. I didn't know what yer man was on about with the Martians and the toast and all that. It was, you know . . ." He passed his hand back over the top of his head.

"Me too," Tony lied, "but I still thought he was pretty cool."

The drunkest one spotted me. "Is this your bird . . .? Jaysus, you lucky b – bastard! Here, lads, get a load of yer one! Hey," he said, addressing me, "if you ever get tired of this lad let me know an' I'll fuckin' show you what a real f – fuckin' m – man can do."

The three of them staggered away, and Tony stared after them. "It's a glamorous life, show business."

"How are you feeling now?" I asked.

"A hell of a lot better after seeing *them*! Are you hungry? I haven't eaten a thing all day."

"Don't tell me you forgot to make today's lunch when you got home last night?"

"Oh, I remembered all right. I just left it at home. Do you fancy a pizza? I know this great little out-of-the-way place . . ."

* * *

The pizza place wasn't that great, in my opinion, but it *was* out of the way. It was designed to look like a genuine Mediterranean pizza parlour, complete with murals on the wall painted to show fake views from fake windows. We were seated at a table in the corner – they tried to seat us at a table right next to the door, but Tony insisted on the corner.

The table couldn't have been much more than two feet square, and most of that was taken up by an empty wine bottle that had what looked like a decade's worth of melty candle bits all over it. Tony moved the candle to one side so we could see each other better, and when the waiter brought our pizzas he moved it back. Tony put it on the nearest empty table.

"Quattro Fromaggio with extra cheese," Tony said. "That's the first time I've seen someone order that."

"Well, I *like* cheese. What's yours supposed to be?"

"Four Seasons," he said.

"I thought that a Four Seasons pizza had four different things, one for each season. Yours has olives and almost nothing else."

"This is the Irish version – all four seasons are the same."

"Feeling any better now?"

He nodded. "It's coming back . . . As soon as I stepped away from the mike it was like my mind just went blank. Input overload, or something. Yeah, it went well. They liked *your* stuff the best. I think I'll keep you."

"So you're not going to give me away to that drunk, then?"

"Not for nothing at any rate. Hey, you never introduced me to your friends. You know, the ones you brought specially to see me."

"I didn't bring them," I said. "They turned up themselves. Besides, I only knew one of them. The others were her boyfriend and her friends."

"Which one did you know, then?"

"Gillian. Red hair, little round glasses? Though I'm glad I met her – one of her friends is an office manager and she said she'd give me advice on running the café. I'm to phone her tomorrow or Monday."

"That's handy."

"How come none of *your* friends ever come to the gigs?"

"Because I don't tell them. It's hard enough without having them slagging me in front of everyone. I might tell them in a couple of weeks, though. They know I'm interested in doing stand-up, but they don't know I've actually done four shows now. Well, Nathan knows, but he lives in London so it's a bit of a commute for him." He looked thoughtful. "Wow! Four shows already! No, I'll wait until I'm a bit more polished before I tell anyone."

"Hah! Earlier you said that you didn't know if you could do it again!"

"I know. But I was shitting bricks all day. And not just about the gig . . . I got this sudden mad feeling in the middle of the night that you'd change your mind about me and not show up."

"Funny, I got the feeling that you were going to change your mind about *me*."

"So, listen, do you want to go out tomorrow night? On a proper date? Go to the pictures, or something?"

"Okay . . . Yeah, definitely. Only I don't know what time I'll be home from work tomorrow – the builders are coming in to the shop to start tearing out the old shelves and all that."

"Well, look . . ." He tore the edge off a paper napkin and started writing on it. "Here's the number of the warehouse. I usually leave about five on a Friday, so give me a ring before then if anything changes."

"Wow! Your work number! This *is* serious!"

He grinned. "Only, if you *do* phone, tell them you're from the gas company or something. Otherwise they'll be slagging me for weeks."

* * *

I had to open up the shop early the next morning to set aside anything we wanted to keep – which wasn't much. Bernard had had the idea that some of the shelves could be used for storing equipment and such, which would have saved us a bit of money if they hadn't been so tatty.

At about ten, two men pulled up outside in a van. "How's it goin'?" One of them asked. "We're looking for Andy."

"I'm Andi," I said.

He looked me up and down. "Oh. Right. Okay. We've to strip the place, yeah?"

I nodded. "Come in. Okay, pretty much everything has to go, except that pile over there. The carpet has to come up as well."

"Grand." He turned to his mate. "You get started on the carpet. I'll start shifting this stuff into the van." He looked back to me. "And it's all to be junked, right?"

"Yeah. Do whatever you want with it – throw it away, sell it, recycle it, whatever you like."

He nodded and started mooching around. His mate went out to the van and came back with a toolbox.

It was fascinating watching them at work. The one in charge looked at everything and poked at stuff, while his pal started going around the edges and pulling up the carpet.

After about ten minutes, the one in charge actually decided to do some work. He opened the toolbox and went to work on the free-standing shelves. A few deft turns of the spanner later, he declared that he'd "never get the fucker into the van in one piece", so he went at it with a hacksaw in one hand and a hammer in the other.

There was a lot of "Would you ever fuckin' move? You're in my way" and "Ah, would you look at the fuckin' state of this now? It's knackered."

"I told you not to go near that. I said I'd do it, didn't I? You never fuckin' listen, do you?"

"Look, just watch where you're swingin' that yoke."

For all their complaining, it took them less than two hours to strip the place, get it all into the van, and drive away.

So that's it, I said to myself, looking around. Apart from the counter and the few things I'd salvaged, the place was bare. When Nora had shown us her sketches, I was doubtful that we could get everything into the shop without it being too cramped, but now it looked huge.

Bernard arrived at noon, and looked around. "Okay . . . We're well on the way now. How long did it take?"

"A couple of hours." I pointed towards the storeroom. "When are they coming in to break down the wall?"

"This afternoon, I think. That reminds me . . ." He took a mobile phone out of his pocket and handed it to me. "I realised yesterday that you'll need this to check up on anyone working in the place."

"Great, thanks!" I turned it on and started pressing buttons to see what would happen.

"It's not a toy, Andi."

"Sorry."

"Nora's going to come in – she should be here in a few minutes – and she'll direct the builders. What they have to do is take out the entire wall. It's not a supporting wall so there shouldn't be any problem. Then they have to build a little alcove in the right corner. That's where the SA is going to be."

"So do we have anyone for that yet?"

"We do. I've asked him to come around this afternoon. The shopfitters are coming on Monday, so he'll need to have all the cables in by then. And he's dealing with the phone company for the data line, so there shouldn't be a problem with that."

"Okay," I said. "But I've just had a thought . . . If the builders are going to demolish the wall, are they going to take away the rubble as well? Only, if they're not, it would have made more sense to get the wall down before the lads got here this morning."

Bernard made a stern face. "Good point. I'll check with them. If they won't take the rubble away, we'll have to get a skip or something."

* * *

By the time I left for the day, the builders had knocked out the wall to the storeroom and built the little alcove Bernard wanted, Nora had come in and bossed me around a lot, and the system administrator – an obnoxious little fart called Bruce – had arrived with a whole pile of stuff: cables, little sockets for the walls, computery things, and so on.

As we were closing up, Bruce said, "Right. So the data line is going to be installed over the weekend."

"So you want me to come in, then?" I asked, silently praying that he'd say no.

"Not really. You'll only be in the way. Just give me your keys."

I handed them over. "Do you want my home number in case you need me for anything?"

He smirked. "Like what?"

"I don't know. Advice or something."

He nodded towards Nora. "Sure she'll be here looking after the painters and the lads doing the new carpet, won't you, Nora?"

"Yeah. What time?"

"About ten."

"Sure, no problem."

Without even saying goodbye, they walked away.

I wasn't bothered. I had enough on my mind as it was. Plus, I now had a completely work-free weekend. *And* a mobile phone to play with.

As I walked home, I phoned Tony's flat.

Either Nick or Dick answered: "Yeah?"

"Hi, is Tony there?"

"Tony?"

"Yeah. You know. Tall guy. Shares your flat."

231

"Oh, right, yeah, *Anto* . . . Yeah, he's here."

There was a pause, and I could still hear his breathing on the other end.

"Can you get him for me, please?"

"Hold on." I heard the phone drop, then a loud knocking sound. "Anto? Man, there's some woman on the phone for you!"

A minute later Tony said, "Hi!"

"Who was that?" I asked. "Dick or Nick?"

"Dick. The hairy one. He's stoned again. When I got in he was just sitting there laughing at the telly. I asked him if he wanted me to turn it on, but he said he was fine. So, what's the story?"

"Well, I'm just on my way home now. What time do you want to meet up? And where?"

"Hang on, have you got a mobile phone?"

"Yeah! Bernard gave it to me."

"Great! What's the number?"

"Ah." Bernard hadn't actually told me the number. "I've no idea."

"Phone someone you know who has one of those caller-ID boxes. Get them to tell you. Or someone else with a mobile."

"Clever thinking, Sherlock . . . Anyway, what are we doing?"

"Should we just meet up and worry about it then?"

"Sure. Do you want to come over? My folks will be there, but it should be okay, if you don't mind meeting them."

"Okay . . . I'll be there in about an hour and a half – I want to have a shower and get changed and all that."

* * *

When I got home, my mother was waiting for me in the kitchen. She had a face on that would have made Hannibal Lecter hide if he saw her coming.

"I want to talk to you," she said.

Oh shit! I said to myself. *Now* what have I done?

"John phoned this afternoon. He said that that girlfriend of his is pregnant."

"Really? Wow! That's great!"

"Don't play the innocent with me, Andi. He told me that you knew already. Why didn't you say something?"

"Mam, he told me in confidence. If *you* told me something in confidence, you wouldn't want me to go blabbing it all over town."

"I see." A classic line that mothers use when they know you're right, but they're still annoyed.

"So what do you think?" I asked.

"I think he should know better at his age. If that one left her husband, she'll leave him. And then he'll be stuck with a baby."

"Unless she takes the baby with her," I said, and suddenly wished I hadn't.

"I don't know what's happening with this family. First you start going out with an older man, and now John's got himself into trouble. Ciarán can't settle down and Roddy had to go and move to Cork. Where did I go wrong?"

"Mam, there's *nothing* wrong. John's happy. I'm happy. Neither of us are being hurt. And you know Ciarán . . . he'll sort himself out. And Roddy's been in Cork for years. You're just getting yourself worked up over nothing."

"Well, the wedding is only three weeks away, and nothing's done."

"That's not your problem. That's Eimear's. Okay, so she's dragging everyone else into it, but it's still her wedding, so it's her responsibility."

She sighed and got to her feet. "What do you want for your tea? Your Dad's not even home yet. I don't know where he's got to."

"He probably just stopped off at the pub," I said. "Do you want me to go and get him?"

"No, he'll be home in his own time." She pointed towards the counter. "We got another card from Ciarán. Now he's in France."

"At least he's getting closer to home." I picked up the home-made postcard. This one showed a fat Santa Claus face down on the sitting-room floor, an empty bottle marked "Poteen" in his hand. A family – all dressed in pyjamas and dressing-gowns – were standing over him. The mother was saying, "I *told* you that you should have left out a bottle of beer. Santa can't take the hard stuff."

"Hey!" I said. "This was the card I sent to him last Christmas!"

On the back, Ciarán had written, "Hi all. We're in France. Not entirely sure which part of France, but it has a lot of hills. Bumped into Bob Moore from school, which was weird. He's on his way to Greece. Home soon."

"Do you want waffles?" Mam asked. "Only they've got to be eaten by last Wednesday."

"Okay. What else?"

"Rashers, beans . . . do you want an egg?"

"Yeah, but I don't want any beans. I'm going out tonight."

"You're not seeing your man again, are you? That's two nights in a row."

"I am seeing him again. You'd like him."

She started banging around at the cooker. "I suppose you're going to bring him to the wedding?"

"I probably will."

"And what's everyone going to say when they see you with a man who's nearly old enough to be your father?"

"Mam, he would have been only eight when I was conceived. I don't think that eight-year-olds are capable of making babies. Anyway, you can meet him for yourself. He's calling over."

"Oh my God! Look at the state of the place! And we've nothing in!"

I looked around – everything was spotless. "Don't worry, Mam. We're not staying in or anything."

While she was getting the tea ready, I went upstairs

and had a shower. I was barely in there for a minute when she knocked on the door. "Andi! Did you say you did or didn't want beans? Only they're on now so you might as well."

* * *

My mother complained and moaned about everything – just like my Dad, in fact. But while he always had a smile on his face, she was the opposite. She took things way too seriously.

Maybe it was because of her upbringing – Mam thought that the worst possible thing in the world was someone doing what they wanted to do instead of what they should be doing. She agonised over trivial things, worried constantly about money, about what other people might think, about whether I was ever going to get a proper job. She worried about the weather if it was bad. She worried about the weather when it was good, in case it *turned* bad. Every year she'd wait for about a week after Midsummer's Day and then she'd start going on about how early it was getting dark.

Dad had a more happy-go-lucky attitude. He ambled through life with just a smile and the words "fair enough" never far from his lips. He was forever spouting his theories on life, religion, politics, sports . . . He had opinions on everything that he absolutely never budged on, unless he felt like it, or if he thought it would be a laugh to take a contrary opinion to someone else. He could argue for and against every argument, often in the same conversation, armed with absolutely no knowledge of anything other than how to wind people up.

The lads were all very different from each other: Roddy, being the oldest, always took charge of the rest of us – which meant that he bossed us around and got us to do all the things he was supposed to. He grew up to be a warehouse manager, got married very young, had a daughter, moved to Cork, and was rarely heard from. I was barely able to talk by the time he got married, so I didn't really know him at all.

John was the artistic type. In his early teens he dreamed of a career as a musician, comic book artist, sculptor, song-writer, and so forth. Basically anything that didn't look like a lot of heavy lifting or thinking was involved. He also grew up to be a warehouse manager, but he didn't like it and now alternated between being a decorator and a plumber. He wasn't much good at either occupation.

Ciarán, the youngest, was the clever one. He taught himself how to use and program computers and ended up getting a job writing computer games. This made John incredibly jealous and they wouldn't talk to each other for years. Of the three lads, Ciarán was the most like Dad. He took everything in his stride and if he didn't like something, he just didn't bother about it.

Then there was Eimear: good-looking, intelligent, very capable, with a chip on her shoulder the size of a Volvo. She was the only girl for ten years – when I came along – and I think that's one of the reasons she had such a hard time settling down. She had to be the centre of attention at all times. The upcoming wedding was a perfect example: she didn't need me or Mam or anyone else to do stuff for her. But by involving us and panicking about it, she was able to give the impression that her wedding was on the same scale as the Olympic Games.

* * *

Mam and I were halfway through dinner when Dad arrived home smelling strongly of Guinness.

"Your dinner's in the oven," Mam said. "What kept you?"

"Ah, you know how it is. Sorry I'm late." He shrugged off his jacket and hung it on the door knob. Mam would remove it later and hang it up properly, and ask him why he couldn't do it himself.

Dad retrieved his dinner from the oven and sat down next to me. He nudged me with his elbow. "Shift out of the way a bit."

I shifted.

"No, that's too far. Shift back."

"Sorry, Dad. It's a one-way chair."

"So I hear you're going out with some lad." He glanced at me and noticed that I was in my dressing-gown. "I suppose you're seeing him tonight?"

"Yeah."

"Good for you. As long as he's better than that

feckin' eejit Dean. I swear to God, Andi, if I never see him again it'll be too soon. I don't know what you ever saw in him."

Mam said, "Now don't start on him, John."

I don't know why she did that. Telling Dad not to start picking on someone had the same effect as pushing someone on skates down a hill.

"Now, his sister's all right," Dad said. "I like her well enough."

This was his diversionary tactic: pretend that he's changed the subject for a while, then bring it back on course. Unless someone could distract him . . .

"They're a lot different, Dad. Everyone thinks that they should be the same person or something just because they're twins."

"Not at all," he said, waving his cutlery around. "It's a well-known fact that when you have twins one of them is always evil."

"Is that right?"

"It is. You see, what happens is that everyone has a certain amount of goodness and badness in them. Some people have more of one that the other, but for most people it's roughly the same. Now, with twins – and there's been *years* of scientific research into this – one of the twins somehow sucks the goodness out of the other one, and gives it its badness instead."

"Is that right?" I asked again.

"Well-known scientific fact," he said, nodding.

"And is it done deliberately?"

"Yep. People think that babies don't know what they're doing, but they do."

"Well, if the good twin deliberately steals the goodness from the other twin, doesn't that mean that the good twin is evil as well?"

He laughed. "Shite! You've got me there!"

Even Mam laughed. "That'll teach you! You've met your match in this one, John."

"I know. I regret the day we ever found her."

"Found me?"

"Did no one ever tell you? You were abandoned on the doorstep. I was going out to work one morning and there you were, with the milk. And there was a note as well. Something about you being a princess and inheriting a million dollars when you turned twenty-one."

"Great! That's only a few months away!"

"But we lost the note," Dad said. "So now I don't know who to contact."

"Ah well," I said. "At least I'm still a princess."

He shook his head sadly. "Not any more. The royal family was dethroned and a republic was set up."

I raised my eyes. "Nothing *ever* goes right for me!"

"That's right. That's because of the gypsy curse . . ."

* * *

After tea, I went up to my room to get dressed.

I realised that this was going to be the first official

240

date I'd been on since Dean and I broke up. And when I realised that, I also realised that I was putting myself under a lot of pressure.

That didn't mean the pressure went away, though.

I opened my chest of drawers and had a look through. My first instinct was to wear something light and summery, something really girlish, but I couldn't find anything I liked enough.

I opened the wardrobe. Some of Eimear's old clothes were still there, but they were something like five years old and – apart from the fact that they hadn't been washed in that time – they were right out of fashion. Not that I was really fashion conscious – on my wages I couldn't afford to be.

As I mooched around, I heard my Mam and Dad arguing in the kitchen. They never really fought, but they did have disagreements from time to time. I heard my name mentioned a couple of times, and I guessed that my mother was expressing her disapproval of Tony.

* * *

I still wasn't ready when Tony arrived. I heard my mother answering the door and going, "Yes?"

"Hello, Mrs Quinn. I'm Tony. Is Andi home?"

There was a pause, during which I imagined her checking him for weapons. "She's just getting ready . . ." After another pause, she added, "Come in, and I'll get her for you."

241

Well, I said to myself, she's let him into the house. She's obviously decided he's not all bad.

I heard Tony go into the kitchen, and the start of a muffled conversation between him and my Dad, and then Mam came up the stairs and into my room.

"Right. He's here . . . You're not going out looking like *that*, are you?"

I looked in the mirror. I was wearing a white blouse, black skirt, tights and proper shoes: real 1980s chic, which was on the way back. "What's wrong with what I'm wearing?"

"That skirt's far too short, for a start. And look at your hair, for God's sake!" She picked up my hairbrush. "Sit down and I'll do it for you."

She hadn't brushed my hair for me in years. I sat facing the dressingtable mirror while she attacked my hair.

"So what do you think of him? Ow!"

"Stop fidgeting! He looks all right." She nearly took my left ear off. "We'll see what your father has to say about him."

"Dad'll be down there telling him jokes."

"Well, even so, the more you talk to someone the more you get to know what they're really like." She sniffed the air. "Is that my perfume?"

"No, it's mine."

"What did you say his name was again?"

"Tony O'Hehir."

"And where's he from?"

"Mam, I'd really love to give you his life story, but he's been waiting long enough."

"Hold on . . ." After a couple more brush strokes she stepped back. "All right, stand up."

I stood there getting more and more anxious as she brushed imaginary bits of fluff off my skirt. Oh my God, I said to myself, my mother's getting me ready for a date!

"You'll do," she said.

I told her to wait a few minutes, then I went down to the kitchen.

Tony and my Dad were laughing about something. Tony looked up when I entered, and did a double take. "Hi."

"Hi . . . I suppose Dad's been boring you with his stories?"

"Not at all."

Dad turned to me. "You never said he was a comedian, Andi."

"Didn't I?"

"No. So that's where you met, then?" he asked Tony. "At one of those comedy nights she's always going to?"

"Yeah. We got talking about one of my routines, and Andi was able to tell my why it wasn't working as well as it should. She knows more about it than I do."

"That's our Andi, all right."

"The stuff she wrote for me was great," Tony said. "Better than any of my own material. She'll make a damn good comedian herself." He was about to continue when he saw the look on my face.

Dad's smile faded, and he gave me a long stare. "Not if her mother has anything to say about it."

"I mean, if she ever wanted to. Which I don't think she does."

"You're only digging yourself in deeper, lad."

We heard Mam coming down the stairs, and Dad said quietly, "We'll talk about this again, Andi." Louder, he said, "So, Tony what do you do?"

Mam came into the kitchen.

"I work in a furniture warehouse, out in Cookstown."

"Isn't that in Northern Ireland?" Mam asked.

"There's one out on the west side as well, Mrs Quinn."

"So could you get us a discount, then?" Dad asked. His mischievous grin reappeared. "A really *good* discount?"

Tony didn't know my Dad well enough to be able to tell that he was just winding him up: Tony looked from Dad to me to Mam and back. "I'll do my best. What are you looking for?"

"Anything, so long as it's cheap."

"Well," I said, "we'd better be going. See you later, Dad."

On the way out, Mam said, "Are you going into town?"

"Yeah. I think so, anyway. Are we?"

Tony nodded.

Mam handed me a photo album. "You can drop this in to your Gran on the way, then."

I knew better than to give her a plaintive look and say "Aw, Mam!" She would have just given me a lecture filled with phrases like "you're not too young" and "you're far too young" and "pulling your weight" and "not a hotel".

* * *

"This'll only take a minute," I said to Tony as I knocked on Gran's door.

I was wrong.

Gran took one look at Tony and her eyes lit up. She dragged us in and forced tea on us.

"If she offers to make you a sandwich, say no," I muttered to Tony.

Gran had a quick flick through the photo album. "Ah, this is when Roddy got married. I asked your Mam for a lend of this because I couldn't remember most of it . . ." She held the album open and pointed out a photo to Tony. "There's Andi when she was four."

I groaned. "Please, don't!"

"Even then she was an entertainer," Gran continued. She flicked through another few pages. "Here she is again, dancing with Roddy. I don't think I've ever seen Roddy as happy as he was that day."

In the photo, Roddy had me in his arms as he spun around the dance floor. In the background, I could see Eimear looking on with extreme envy.

245

Gran then turned back to the first photo, and went through the entire album. There were three photos on every page, and thirty-two pages – I counted.

She pointed out who everyone was, explained what they did and whose children they were, who they were currently fighting with and every ailment they had suffered in the sixteen years since the wedding.

Tony made all the right sounds. "Really?" was the most common one, but now and again he said "You wouldn't think it to look at him" or "Isn't he the one who . . . ?"

Gran was in her element: explaining the entire history of the extended family to someone who was pretending to be interested and too polite to tell her he didn't care about a bunch of people he'd never met.

After an hour, I stood up. "We'd better get going, Gran. You must be getting tired by now."

"Not a bit of it. Now, Tony, this is Andi's mam's cousin Seán."

Tony nodded. "The one who went to Australia."

"And he's married to . . . Hold on, she's in here somewhere . . . Oh, look, Andi! It's your uncle Pat and he's giving you a piggy-back." She put her hand on Tony's arm for emphasis. "They were all mad about Andi. They thought she was a lovely child."

Tony grinned at me. "Oh, I'm sure she was."

After another hour, I got up again. "Right, we *really* have to go, Gran."

She finally got the hint, and closed the photo album.

"Right you are, so. You will be coming to Eimear's wedding, won't you, Tony?"

"I haven't been asked yet," he said. "But if Andi doesn't ask me, I'll go with you."

Gran playfully slapped his arm. "Get away out of that!"

* * *

"You didn't have to encourage her," I said as we left. "She's bad enough as it is."

"I was enjoying myself. My own granny died ten years ago. I never really knew her anyway."

"On your mam's side or your dad's?"

"Ma's. I never knew my dad or any of his family. I mean, I don't even really know who he was."

I didn't know what to say, so I said, "Oh."

"It's not a big deal," Tony said. "Ma raised me on her own for a few years, then she met this lad and married him, then he left just after my brother was born."

I said, "Oh" again. "I didn't realise. Actually, now that I think about it, you've never said anything about your family. Where's your brother now?"

"Scotland, last I heard. In Glasgow. Ma said he's talking about coming home."

"And what about your mam?"

"She moved into her sister's place. That's my aunt Marian. She never got married. I see Ma about once a month."

"Wow . . . Sorry, I don't know what to say."

He shrugged. "Well, there's a lot of stuff I don't really talk about much. I can tell you, though, can't I?"

"Sure."

"Well, okay . . . I ran away from home when I was fourteen, and went to London. I lived on the streets for a couple of years, until I got caught nicking stuff from a supermarket. I wasn't old enough to go to jail, so they sent me to a sort of halfway house. There were lads there who'd been on the street since they were ten or eleven, and they were hard as nails. Most of them weren't too bad, but there was one who really didn't like me. A black kid, about fifteen, but big. He decided that all Irish people were complete fuckwits, so he took every opportunity to beat the crap out of me. And of course I couldn't report him – that was just something you didn't do. He kept on and on about how the Irish were lazy and stupid and greedy, all that kind of thing."

"Bastard!"

"Yeah. Then one day I'd had enough. I knew that I was going to get another beating, but I couldn't help myself. I just said to him, 'You know what you are? You're a racist.' And like that" – Tony snapped his fingers – "he stopped. It was like it had never even occurred to him before. From then on, we were best friends. We looked out for each other . . . I convinced him to go back home, and then he convinced me to do the same."

"So are you still in contact with him?"

"Yeah. He's back in London now. He works in a gym. I write to him about once a month. Sometimes I phone him, but it's pretty expensive. I've known him longer than anyone else . . . He's like the best friend you could have."

By now, we had reached O'Connell Street. We sat down on the edge of the fountain. "So, what do you want to do?" I asked.

"I dunno. We've missed the start of all the movies. Are you hungry?"

"Sort of . . ." I had an idea. "Look, I'll go over to Mickey D's and get something. You wait here, and while you're waiting . . ." I handed him my mobile phone. "Ring your friend. Don't worry. Bernard Parker is paying for the call."

Tony looked at me in surprise. "You're serious?"

"Yeah. I mean, he's probably not in, but you never know."

He opened the phone and dialled his friend's number. As I walked away, I heard him saying, "Hi, Nathan! It's me! Yeah, no kidding! No, listen, it's a mobile. Well, right now I'm in O'Connell Street. . . . My girlfriend's . . . Yeah, she's pretty cool, all right. Listen, how're you doing?"

* * *

So our first proper date was spent at my Gran's and sitting on the edge of the fountain in O'Connell Street, eating Fillets o' Fish and telling each other about our backgrounds.

Tony's life seemed amazing to me: he'd travelled all over Ireland and England, he'd been to almost every country in Europe, and had friends in every one.

"What made you come back to stay in Ireland?" I asked him.

"Well, I'm not sure that I'm going to stay here forever, you know . . . And sure when I'm famous I'll have houses in London, New York, San Francisco, Hong Kong . . ."

"Yeah, sure . . . No, but really, why did you come back? I mean, what's here for you? Apart from me, of course, but you didn't know me when you came back."

"I just got tired of wandering. In the past ten years the longest I've stayed in one place was about eighteen months. But now . . ."

I nodded. "You're getting old."

He smiled. "Something like that. No, the real problem with travelling is that you're never in one place long enough to make real friends. And you never manage to save any money."

"So out of all the places you've lived in, where did you like the best?"

"Germany. Westphalia, near a town called Bochum. It was great. Okay, so the shops all shut at four on a Saturday and aren't open on a Sunday, but it was a lot of fun. Met some great people there, went to a few gigs. The food was fantastic and the scenery was great."

"What about the worst place?"

He had to think about that one. "I don't know . . . Far too many bad places. London was a nightmare before I got sent to the Home. Actually, it wasn't much better *in* the Home, until I teamed up with Nathan."

"Has he ever been to Dublin?"

"A couple of times . . ." Tony said, then laughed. "The first time, Ma insisted we stay with her, because she'd heard all about him. But I must have forgot to tell her Nathan is black. I got so used to him, I stopped noticing what colour he is years ago, if you know what I mean, so why would I mention it? So Ma and Marian decided they wanted to come to the airport with me to collect him. And we're there at the Arrivals area, watching everyone filing out, and Ma's pointing out people. 'Is *that* him?' 'No.' 'Well, is that him?' 'No. Mam. Don't you know what he looks like?' And she says, 'You never told me.' And as I'm talking to her, Nathan comes out and I don't see him. Ma nearly has a heart attack as this huge black guy comes running at me and grabs me from behind!"

I laughed. "I can imagine how *my* mother would react!" I stood up and stretched. "My arse is getting numb from sitting there. Do you want to go to a pub or something?"

Tony got to his feet, and his knees cracked. "Nah . . . let's just go for a walk."

We walked down towards the bridge, through College Green, and up Grafton Street. We chatted about this and that, told each other bad jokes, and somewhere along the way Tony's hand slipped into mine and it seemed like the most natural thing in the world.

* * *

When I got home, Mam and Dad were still up. From the hall I could hear them arguing. Or, well, agreeing to disagree very loudly. I went into the kitchen just in time to hear my mother say, "You *agreed* that we wouldn't ever have to tell her!"

"Tell who what?" I said.

Dad looked around. "Eimear. About John's Betty getting pregnant. You know what your sister's like. She'd take it really badly."

"Do I *know*? She'll assume John did it on purpose to steal her thunder. But you have to tell her, Dad. I mean, John said she was showing already, and that was last week. By the time the wedding comes, everyone will be able to see for themselves. And anyway, it's good news. It's stupid to ignore it just because it clashes with *other* good news."

"She has a point there, Sal," Dad said.

"Well, I don't want to be the one who has to tell her," Mam said. "I've got enough to worry about as it is."

"I'll do it, if you want," I said. "But there's no reason John can't tell her himself. I mean, he shouldn't need us to take care of his dirty work." I thought about that. "But I suppose if Eimear's making us take care of *her* dirty work, why shouldn't he?"

I poured myself a cup of tea and sat down.

"What did you get up to tonight, then?" Dad asked.

"Well, we dropped the photo album in to Gran. Then we left. But that's the condensed version. In fact, there was about two hours between getting there and leaving."

Mam's shoulders sagged. "Sorry, pet. I didn't mean to ruin your evening."

"No, it wasn't too bad. Gran seemed to like Tony," I added, as a sort of signal that about now they should be showering me with compliments about him.

"He seems nice enough all right," Dad said.

I looked at Mam. "Well?"

"I don't know, Andi . . . He's a lot older than you."

Dad looked up in surprise. "Really? How much older?"

"Nine years," Mam said.

Dad shook his head. "Mother of God! *Nine years* . . . Ah well. As long as you're happy."

Mam gave him a look that would have given a more sensitive person an aneurysm. "John . . ."

"What? What did I do now? I only said that he was a nice lad. You can't blame *me* for him being nice. If you have to blame someone, blame him!"

"Now don't start, the two of you," I said. "Look, I like him and he likes me. That should be all there is to it."

Dad looked away meekly. "Sorry, Mammy," he said.

I gave him a stern look. "You'd better be. One more peep out of you and I'll slap the legs off you."

Dad laughed. "So anyway, you're going to tell Eimear, then?"

"Sure. I've got to talk to her anyway. Tony's going to help me with the Mass book for the wedding. He's got a computer in his b – in his flat."

Thankfully, they didn't seem to notice what I'd almost said.

"What else is there to be done?" Mam asked.

"Just the cake – it has to be picked up a few days before the wedding. Oh, and I've to check with the hotel that everything's okay. And the bridesmaids' dresses. I don't think there's anything else. Oh, and the hen party. All the invitations are posted?"

"All except Roddy's and Ciarán's. I'll just give Ciarán his when he gets back. And I'll give Roddy his when they come up for the week."

"Oh, so that's the plan . . . I was wondering what they were going to do."

"Claire can stay in your room," Mam said. "Roddy and Gráinne can stay in the lads' room."

"Hang on . . . There won't be any room for Claire. I thought Eimear was going to stay here the night before the wedding, so she can keep us up all night worrying?"

Mam looked surprised. "That's the first I heard about that."

Dad raised his eyes. "Here we go. I'm going to bed."

He drained the last of his tea and got to his feet. "Did you lock the door behind you, Andi?"

"No, I left it wide open, Dad."

"Fair enough."

After he'd gone up, Mam apologised again for ruining my evening.

"Don't worry about it," I said. "Look, if we'd gone to the pictures we wouldn't have had a chance to talk. So it worked out better in the long run."

"You're smitten with him, aren't you?"

I grinned. "Yeah, I suppose so. I've never met anyone like him before."

"It's just he's so much older than you are, Andi. That's the only problem I have with him."

To myself, I said, Yeah, until you find out that he wants to do stand-up comedy for a living. Aloud, I said, "Well, I was thinking about that . . . I grew up with three brothers who are much older than me, so it only makes sense that I'd have no problem getting on with an older man."

She gave me a thoughtful look. "That's true, I suppose."

"So if anyone's to blame, it's you and Dad." I gave her a smug look.

"I see he hasn't cured you of giving cheek to your mother."

* * *

The next week in work was murder . . .

The shopfitters arrived on Monday morning: by the time I got there, they'd unloaded their van and everything was propped up against it, ready to be fitted.

As I was explaining to them that they were a day early, another van pulled up. This one had painters and decorators.

As I was explaining to *them* that they should have been there on Saturday, I got a call from the plumber, who told me that the installation of the new toilet would go ahead perfectly on schedule, except that he wouldn't be able to make it until Wednesday.

Neither the decorators nor the shopfitters were happy about this. They were less happy when I told them that Bruce the systems administrator had my keys, that he should have been here by now, and that we couldn't get in.

But all was not lost: I phoned Ellen.

"Hello . . ." she said, sounding sleepy.

"It's me. Listen, sorry if I woke you, but I'm locked outside the shop. Do you still have your keys?"

"Yeah."

"Can you bring them over?"

"Okay . . . What time is it?"

"Eleven. You should have been up hours ago, anyway."

Whispering, she said, "Niall stayed over last night!"

I almost dropped the phone in surprise. "*Really*? What happened! Tell me everything!" Then I remembered where I was and that they were all listening in. "Uh . . . never mind. Just get here as quick as you can, okay?"

Ellen agreed that she'd do her best, and hung up.

I stood there smiling politely like an idiot as the decorators and shopfitters sized each other up as though one group was The Jets and the other was The Sharks.

By time Ellen arrived, the rain was coming down in buckets. The decorators and shopfitters had piled back into their respective vans. I was left outside the shop-fitters' van holding a Chelsea umbrella and trying to keep the rain off the new countertops.

Ellen took her time getting there. I saw her at the bottom of the street, and waved, but she didn't come running up. She sauntered along like there was all the time in the world. When she finally reached me, she handed over the keys. "I was going to pretend I'd forgotten them, but one look at your face and I decided to play it safe."

The occupants of both vans had stared at Ellen all the way up the street, and now that she was here they were only too willing to display their manliness by climbing out of the vans and getting rained on.

I unlocked the shop, stepped in, and stopped . . . "Well, *bollocks*!"

Ellen peered past me. "What's the matter?"

"There's no carpet. They were supposed to come on Saturday."

One of the shopfitters looked like he was going to

cry. "So you mean we can't even put this stuff *together*?"

"You'll have to," I said. "The carpet-fitters will just have to work around everything. It's their own fault, so there's no reason you should be put out. Except that you're a day early – by rights I should send you back."

The painters objected to this, on the grounds that they needed a lot of space in which to work, but I countered their objections by pointing out that they should have been there on Saturday.

Then the plumber phoned again, and said that Wednesday was off, and would Thursday be okay?

Chapter Fifteen

Nora the designer and Bruce the systems administrator arrived a few minutes later. I was of course immediately suspicious: they'd left together on Friday evening, and now they were arriving together . . . It didn't take a great leap of the imagination to picture them shagging each other senseless all weekend. I knew it probably wasn't true, but the truth should never get in the way of a good bit of gossip.

Nora looked around the shop, at what had been done – very little, really – and what was left to be done. She turned to me. "We're way behind, Andi." She said that as though it was my fault. "The carpet should be down and the walls should have been painted. Now look at the mess we're in."

I was about to reply when she started up again.

"Right, Andi, get on the phone to Bernard and tell him what's happened. I'll do my best to straighten everything out. Bruce . . . I don't know, you'll just have to try and work around everyone." She turned to the shopfitter's boss. "Can you work on one side while the other side is being painted?"

He nodded. "Probably. What happens when we get to the middle?"

"Worry about that then. For now, just get on with it." Next, Nora turned to the senior decorator. "Is that all right with you? Any problems?"

"No, that's fair enough," he said, looking as meek as his opposite number.

Nora turned to Ellen. "Who are you and what are you doing here? Look, if you've no business being here you're just going to be in the way."

Before Ellen could reply, I said, "This is Ellen. She's with the Office of Revenue Commissioners. She's here to make sure that everyone working here is on the level."

Nora's pierced face drained of what little colour it had.

"No, I'm kidding," I said. "Had you going, though."

Nora stared at me silently, then announced that she was going outside for a cigarette.

"Ignorant bitch," I muttered.

"What's her story?" Ellen asked.

"Bernard recruited her right out of Art school, or something. She thinks her work is the dog's bollocks. Well, it is, but without the dog."

"*You* should be bossing *her* about, not the other way around."

"I know. Look, let's go and get a cup of coffee or something, and you can tell me all about last night. And I'll tell you about my weekend."

On the way out, we passed Nora. "I've just got something to attend to, Nora," I said. "Why don't you take over until I get back? If you have any questions or something comes up and you can't deal with it, just give me a ring, okay?"

* * *

"So what's the story?" Ellen and I said at the same time.

"You first," I said.

Ellen picked up a sachet of sugar by one end and shook it in the traditional pre-coffee ritual. "Well, I've seen him every day for the past God knows how long. He's practically living in my flat as it is."

I grinned. "Excellent! So, what happened last night?"

"Well, we had a couple of drinks, and came back to watch a video, then after it was over we got talking, and next thing I knew it was three in the morning . . . I don't really know how it happened. One minute he was saying that it was late and that he'd better get going, and the next minute we were in the bedroom ripping our clothes off."

"So . . . Come on! Details! What was it like? What did he do? Did he even know what to do?"

Ellen leaned closer. "I'm not going to tell you *everything* that we did, but, yeah, he knew what to do, all right."

"What was it like?"

She smiled. "Well . . . it was different. Very sweet, gentle . . ."

"No, I mean what was *it* like?"

Now she understood. "Oh . . ." She made a few hand-gestures to indicate length and girth. "Not bad. But the sex itself . . . I don't know. Not as good as it was with Robbie, but since Robbie was always more concerned with making himself happy rather than me, it was a lot more enjoyable. But it wasn't like fireworks and all that. I don't think I came. Actually, I know I didn't come. I know what *that* feels like."

"What did you do? Fake it and say, 'Mmm, that was lovely'?"

"Jesus, Andi! I'm not going to tell you *that*!"

"So you finally got a half-decent shag, then . . . Well, good for you! It took bloody long enough! So what's the chances of him being Mister Right?"

She sat back and sipped her coffee. "He could be."

I was impressed, and a little jealous. Technically I was still a virgin: Dean and I had had more than a kiss and a cuddle a couple of times – and I'd had a couple of encounters before that – but it had never amounted to sweaty naked penetration. In fact, he had never even seen me completely naked.

"Tell me about Tony, then," Ellen said. "You're still going out?"

"Yeah. We were supposed to go out on Friday night, so he called around. Then Mam gave me a photo album to drop into Gran's on the way, and we were there most of the night. You know what she's like."

She laughed. "You should have just put it in the letterbox."

"We met up on Saturday afternoon, and got the bus out to Dollymount, and spent the day just walking around. Yesterday he went to his mother's. He wanted me to come along, but I wasn't in the mood for it. I mean, he doesn't get to see her often, so I didn't want to be in the way. I told him to tell her all about me, and then I could go next time."

"So when are you seeing him again?"

"Thursday, at the comedy show . . . You should have been there last week. He was brilliant. And he used a lot of the stuff I wrote."

"Did it work? I mean, did anyone laugh?"

"Yeah, it went down well."

"Shit. I wish I'd been there."

"Well, he's doing more of my stuff this week. You and Niall should come."

"Nah, we're going out. One of Niall's friends is in a band. They're supposed to be really good. What about next week?"

"Sure. He'll be on again. The two of you should come along, and we'll all go out afterwards. You'll like him, he's good fun."

"What about Dean?"

That was an awkward one. "Ah . . . Well, he can't still be pining after me. He's not, is he?"

"He is. Now he thinks you're just playing hard to get."

"Hah! He wouldn't believe *how* hard where he's concerned. There's no way it'll ever happen, El. You're going to have to tell him. God knows *I've* tried to let him know. Or get Niall or Joe to tell him, or something. How is Joe anyway?"

"He hasn't been around much lately," Ellen said. "Not since Niall came on the scene."

"That's odd, because he was Niall's friend. I mean, if it hadn't been for Joe, you wouldn't have met him." Something was right at the back of my mind, but it wouldn't come. "Wait a minute . . . You're not suggesting that Joe fancies you, are you?"

She shrugged. "I don't know for sure, but that's what it looks like."

"Ouch! Imagine what he must be going through! He fancies you for years and now you're going out with one of his friends!"

The something was *still* at the back of my mind, like a faint voice in the background calling for attention. "Something's not right . . ."

"What?"

I frowned. "Remember the day after the fight?"

"How could I forget?"

"Niall came to see me in the shop, and we got talking about Joe. I asked him, 'Why does he hang around with Dean?' and Niall said, 'You mean, why does *Dean* hang around with *Joe*?' What's all that about?"

She looked blank. "I've no idea. But Niall knows Joe much better than I do. I'll ask him later."

The niggle at the back of my mind still wasn't satisfied, so I mentally informed it to shut up for a few minutes.

Then I remembered something I'd planned on telling Ellen. "You'll never guess who I met at the comedy night on Thursday."

"Who?"

"Someone from Sound as a Pound."

"Jimmy?"

"Nope."

"Dave the security guard?"

"No."

"It wasn't Gerry, was it?"

"God, you're crap at guessing. It was Gillian from the Clontarf shop."

"Oh, right . . . How's she? Is she still with yer man?"

"Jack? Yeah. She was with him and a bunch of their mates, and one of them is Jack's boss, and she said she'd give me some pointers on how to manage people for the café. I'm supposed to phone her today."

"That was good of her. Listen, how are the wedding plans coming along? I suppose Eimear's all worked up these days?"

"When is she *not* worked up? She's the only person I know who agonises over whether to say 'laid-back' or 'easy-going'. I think everything is done. Well, everything that can be done now is done. We've to check with the hotel and make sure the cake is okay, but that's all. Oh, and Tony's going to give me a hand with the Mass book. He's got a computer. Actually, I was telling Mam and Dad about it the other night, and I almost let it slip that the computer is in his bedroom. He has to keep it locked away – you should see the state of his two flatmates. They're right bloody weirdoes. Anyway, where was I?"

"The Mass book."

"Right . . . Yeah, I think that's the last thing. Except that me and Audrey and Claire have to get our dresses. But there's plenty of time still."

"I thought that Lorna was going to be a bridesmaid?"

"Nah, she had a fight with Eimear about something." I looked at my watch. "Jesus, I'd better get back! Nora will be having kittens!"

* * *

I spent the rest of the week at the café, sorting out problems and making sure Nora was aware that she was working for me, not the other way around. By the time I locked up on Thursday evening, the café was really beginning to take shape, and I was feeling a lot more confident about the job. I'd spoken to Gillian's friend Susan a few times, and she was very helpful. It turned out that her company did a lot of recruiting for office jobs, and though we didn't need anyone for that, they had a lot of people on their books who they hadn't found work for, and who might be suitable for the café.

Bernard came by the shop a couple of times, mainly to speak with Bruce about the computers. He was pleased that I'd somehow come up with a long list of possible staff members – I wasn't about to tell him that I'd got the list from someone else.

On Thursday evening, I met Tony at the pub for the stand-up night.

It was a great thrill to see – for the first time – Tony's name larger than all the others on the poster in the pub window.

"Ladies and gentlemen," said the barman into the mike, "he's been called the best new Irish comic since Ardal O'Hanlon . . . and it all started right here!" A ragged cheer rose from the crowd. "Would you please put your hands together for the one and only Tony O'Hehir!"

The cheers grew louder when Tony approached the mike. "Thank you! Thank you!" He waited until the noise had subsided. "I've had a tough week . . . Someone ask me how tough my week was."

Someone near the front shouted out, "How tough was your week?"

Tony looked at him, and said, "What?"

For some reason, this went down a storm. From that point on, there was nothing he could do wrong.

"I love playing tricks on people," Tony said. "I went out and bought a bagel and put it into a box of Cheerios . . . You should have seen the look on my flatmate's face the next morning. He woke me up to tell me he's found a fuckin' *huge* Cheerio! So I'm going, 'No way! The one from the competition?' 'What competition?' So I tell him it's the 'find the giant Cheerio and win a million pounds' competition. And he's going 'Oh my God! I'm a millionaire!' for the next few minutes. And then I say, 'Of course, it only counts if the box has the competition printed on the back.'

"He got his own back on me, though . . . He slept with my girlfriend. So I slept with *his* girlfriend to get back at him, then he slept with mine again. Eventually the girls had enough of this, so they slept with each other to get back at the both of us. *And* they made us watch! Well, that sure taught *us* a lesson . . .

"I've seen a lot of stand-up comedians over the years," Tony went on, and I recognised this as another of my routines. "Did you ever notice how black comedians can take the piss out of white people, but if they do it the other way around, it's called racism? What's that about? And women comedians can pick on men, but we can't pick on women. Gay comedians are allowed to pick on straight people, but not the other way around . . ." He paused to take a sip of his water. "These two black gay women went into a bar . . .

"The best thing about doing comedy is that no one ever heckles you . . ." He paused again. "See?"

Again, this was remarkably well received. The thought occurred to me that Tony's real strength lay in working the audience. It seemed to me that they were all starting to think of him as a friend.

Towards the end of his set, someone *did* start heckling. The heckler was pretty drunk, and obviously thought it was an audience-participation show.

"I got on the bus the other day, at the terminus," Tony began.

"What number was it?" shouted the heckler.

Tony ignored him. "And as I was waiting, this guy comes up and –"

"What was his name?"

"His name was Irritating Git," Tony said. "And –"

"We all know this one! It's shite! Tell us another one!"

Tony stopped and stared at him. "Look, as much as I value your input, I'm working here, okay? So don't interrupt. I mean, I don't interrupt you when *you're* working. I don't come along and slap the sailors' cocks out of your mouth, do I?"

That got one of the best laughs of the evening, and later Tony confided in me that it wasn't original. "I heard someone else using it a couple of years ago."

"I suppose you have lots of other anti-heckle lines prepared?"

"Not really . . . It's pretty tough to think of something. You can say things like, 'Yeah, I remember *my* first drink,' and stuff like that. Another good trick is to get them to come up to the mike, but that can backfire if they're really drunk."

I thought about it. "I suppose you could say, 'Your Mammy phoned, and she wants to know if you want the pyjamas with the bunnies or the little trains.'"

"I'll remember that one," Tony said. "Any more?"

"Em . . . 'Ladies and gentlemen, meet the man who wrote the lyrics for *The Angelus*.' Or . . . Let's see . . . Oh yeah! You could look towards the back as if you were speaking to your manager, and say, 'Hey! I said I wanted a *plant* in the audience, not a vegetable!'"

Tony pulled out his little notebook and started scribbling. "Go on . . ."

"It's hard to think of them when you're on the spot."

"Well, that's when you need them the most."

"Okay . . . 'You'll be all right after a few more drinks and a nice drive home.'"

"I don't know about that one . . ."

"You could pretend to recognise him, and say, 'Don't you remember me? We were in school together for a couple of years, until they put you in the slow class.'"

Tony laughed. "Andi, you've got a strange imagination! There's a lot of weird shit going on up there."

"Hang on a second . . . Why am I telling you all my best lines? I'm going to need them myself one day." I shrugged. "I'm always thinking of things like that, but I never remember them."

"You should write them down like I do. So listen, what are you doing at the weekend?"

"Well, they're still working on the café, so I'll

probably be busy during the day on Saturday. What about Saturday night?"

"Can't make it. I'm supposed to be meeting some of the lads from work. I'd bring you, but girlfriends and wives aren't invited."

This was intriguing. "So what's happening? A strip club? Lap dancing?"

"Nothing like that. One of the lads is hiring a big-screen TV – we're all chipping in – and we're going to watch the match."

Having grown up in a house with three brothers and a father, I knew better than to ask "What match?". Ask a question like that and they're bound to tell you. At length and in detail. Give them a hint that you're in any way interested and you'll spend every night thereafter hearing all about football matches, the best and worst players, what the ref should have done, what the manager should have done, which team has the best strip and why, which player was sold for the largest amount of money . . .

My own interests in football were along the lines of which player had the best legs, and who was going out with who. Things I was sure that Tony wouldn't have cared about.

* * *

On Saturday evening, Ellen and Dean called around. When I answered the door, Ellen gave me a look that meant, "I accidentally let it slip that I was coming over

271

and Dean said he'd come along and there was nothing I could do about it. Sorry."

I ushered them into the kitchen, where my mother had a bit of a shock at seeing Dean. She kept looking from me to him and back, and then decided that she was going over the road to her friend Breda.

"So," Dean said, "how are things?"

"Fine. You?"

"Okay."

"How's Joe? I haven't seen him in ages."

"Me either. It's been a couple of weeks or something."

"Have you even heard from him?"

Dean shook his head. "Nah."

I glanced at Ellen, and she shrugged. "Maybe you should give him a ring," I said. "Make sure he's all right."

"Are we going to stay here?" Ellen asked. "Only I could murder a drink. Let's go over to the pub."

So over to the pub we went. I felt a little better about being around Dean there, because my Dad and his mates were there too, propping up the bar.

I told Ellen and Dean to find us a table, and went over to Dad. "How's it going?"

"Grand, pet." He looked around. "I see yer man's here."

"Don't start, Dad. Look, do you want a drink?"

Dad looked at his glass, which was almost full. "Ah, go on then. I might as well. Where's your mam?"

"She went over to Breda's."

On the other side of Dad, his friend Paddy – Breda's husband – grinned. "That's me here for the night then. So tell us, Andi, are you looking forward to the big day?"

"Yeah, it should be okay. It'll be great when Roddy comes up. We'll have the whole family in one place for the first time in ages."

"Not since your Gran's birthday, then?"

"Not even then . . . Roddy didn't manage to turn up for that. And Ciarán didn't stay around for long."

Dad sipped at his pint. "Sure, that's your brother all over, Andi. He's got itchy feet. We're going to have to tie him down to get him into a suit."

Paddy laughed. "I can't wait to see your oul' lad in a suit, Andi," he said. "That's the only reason I'm going."

"Ah would you ever *feck off*," Dad suggested. "They're pickin' on me, Andi. You sort them out."

On the far side of Paddy, another of his friends – also called Paddy – leaned forward and peered down at me. "Sure it's a big day. You have to dress up for it. When your only daughter's getting married, you have to put on a show."

I had to laugh. "Jaysus, you haven't a clue, Paddy! It's not *me* getting married. It's Eimear. The *other* daughter."

He looked puzzled. "What?" Slowly it dawned on him. "Oh, right . . . the older one. God, I'd forgotten all about her. What's she up to these days?"

Dad stared at him. "Paddy, you're a complete

fuckin' eejit. 'What's she up to?' my *arse*. She's gettin' married! That's what we're talking about!"

Embarrassed, Paddy nodded and returned his attention to his pint.

"So you're getting them in," Dad reminded me.

"Yeah. Well, only for you. This lot can buy their own drink."

I bought a pint for Dad, and the usual for me, Ellen and Dean. "Right, Dad, I'll see you later."

He nodded. "Hang on. Where's the other lad?"

"Tony? He's off with his mates tonight."

"No, yer man who's always with Dean. The quiet lad. The tall one."

"Joe? I don't know. He hasn't been around much these past few weeks."

Paddy – the less dumb one – nodded. "He's prob'ly shacked up with some bird somewhere."

"Probably," I said, though I very much doubted it.

When I got back to the others, Ellen asked, "How's your Dad?"

I handed out the drinks and sat down. "He's fine. Well, you know what he's like. He never changes."

We sat there in silence, surveying the pub. The silence stretched on, and on. Eventually, I said, "So what's everyone been up to lately?"

There was no reply, other than a grunt from Dean.

"I see."

Then Dean said, "Everything's changed and it's all your fuckin' fault, Andi."

"What are you talking about?"

"Ellen's got that fuckin' gobshite Niall around all the time."

Ellen thumped him. "Hey! Watch what you're saying!"

"Why is that *my* fault?"

"Because he wouldn't have come along to the shop if you hadn't wanted the sale."

"Yeah? Well, *you're* the one who phoned Joe and asked him for ideas."

Dean knew that I was right, and was man enough not to apologise.

"You're just pissed off because I'm going out with Tony now," I said.

"Is that right? Is that what you think?"

"Yes," I said. "Go on, prove me wrong. You can't, can you?"

Dean drained his pint. "Ah fuck this. I'm going home."

"Good."

"Don't go, Dean," Ellen said. "Look, we have to sort this out. The two of you are my best friends and I don't want you at each other's throat every time you meet."

"She's right," I said to Dean. "Look, I'm sorry if I hurt you, but I spent a year and a half waiting for you to get the hint."

"You could have just fuckin' told me, Andi! You didn't have to string me along like that!"

"Look, what's the big deal? Are you going to tell me

that in all the time since we broke up you really thought that it was just temporary? Didn't you get the hint after the first year?"

"It's not like that," he said.

"All we ever did was sit in a pub and you'd tell me what happened in work. You hardly ever even asked me how *I* was getting on. You didn't care about me. You just treated me like a diary."

"Of course I cared about you!"

"I wasn't happy, Dean. Couldn't you see that?"

"You *were* happy. You're just saying that now."

I was beginning to despair. "If I was happy, why did I break up with you?"

He didn't have an answer for that one.

We left the pub shortly before closing time. Ellen had said hardly anything for the night – she'd been stuck between me and Dean going back and forth over our relationship. I ended it all by getting up. "Okay, I've had enough of this. I'm going home. Dean, listen very carefully: I don't want to go out with you. Get the fucking hint. It's over. Over, over, over! And next time Ellen's coming to see me, don't bother tagging along unless you've got something else to talk about."

Ellen gave me the "phone me" signal. I nodded, and walked away.

* * *

There were times when I just wished the universe had a

Reset button, so that I could set everything back a few days and start over.

But the trouble with that was I'd start avoiding problems instead of dealing with them.

Take the situation with Dean; if, when he and Ellen arrived at the door, I'd told them that I was busy, they'd have gone away and I wouldn't have had to spend the entire evening arguing with Dean.

But that argument was there, waiting to be had at some stage. Now, at least, it was done. Okay, so it was possible that the argument would resurface, but I had a very strong feeling that it had been defeated. Dean wasn't stupid – the message would get through eventually. And sooner or later, he'd find himself interested in someone else, and I'd be nothing but a bitter memory.

I never imagined I'd find myself wishing I was a bitter memory.

When I got in, Dad was sitting in the kitchen. "Your mam's gone to bed," he said.

"I didn't see you leaving the pub, Dad."

"I'm not back that long. Andi, I want to talk to you about something important. God, Sal would kill me if she knew I was talking to you about this."

"Okay . . ." I sat down. I knew what it was going to be about. "Dad, what Tony said about me wanting to do comedy . . . well, he's right."

"He is?"

"Yeah. I know Mam will go mad, but I really, really

want to do it. And I think I can, too. Only, it'll take years."

"Well, you don't have to give up your day job," Dad said. "You could do it at night. I don't suppose she'd mind all that much then."

"Maybe not. But I'm still not ready to tell her."

"You've always been good at coming up with jokes and things. You might be able for it, all right. Now, me, on the other hand . . . I'm not up to that at all." He paused. "I've got to do a speech at Eimear's wedding."

"I know. What are you going to say?"

"I haven't a clue. I could say that she was a grand little young one until you appeared on the scene, and since then she's been like a demon. But I don't suppose that'll go down so well. Or I could say that Chris is a nice lad and it'll be nice to have a son-in-law, and that I only hope he can straighten her out."

"Was she really that bad when I was born?" I asked.

"Ah . . . sort of. She didn't really understand it. Asked a lot of questions, sulked a lot, fought with everyone."

"She was ten, Dad. She must have had some idea where babies come from."

"No, she understood that, all right. She just didn't want us to bring another baby into the house."

"Well, don't worry about the speech," I said. "I'll give you a hand with it. The main thing is to keep it short."

"God, I know *that*! When me and Sal got married,

her oul lad spoke for nearly an hour. But that's what he was like – he loved the spotlight. A bit like her mam."

I laughed. "Yeah, I can see Gran sitting there fuming because she doesn't get to say anything."

"Of course, Sal was raging. She thought that her dad was hogging the whole show."

"What about *your* parents?" Dad's parents had died long before I was born.

"My da just said that he wanted to welcome Sally to the family, and he hoped everyone was having a good time. Ah, sure they were just glad to see the back of me."

"Oh, I'm sure. Anyway, I'm off to bed. Let me know what you want to do about the speech and we'll work on it, okay?"

"Thanks, pet."

As I lay in bed that night, I went over the events of the day. The situation with Dean was – I hoped – well on the way to a resolution. And it was nice that Dad didn't seem to mind that I was interested in a career as a stand-up comedian.

Then I realised that Dad had been in the pub for most of the evening, and had probably overheard me arguing with Dean. So he stayed up to talk to me, and make me feel better about everything.

And it had worked: I *did* feel better.

So instead of going to bed miserable and annoyed at Dean, I was able to relax and worry about a completely different set of things: the wedding, the café, Tony . . .

* * *

The shit hit the fan on Sunday afternoon.

Or, to be more accurate, that's when the shit *started* hitting the fan. But it turned out that there was a lot more shit waiting in the wings.

Mam had sent me around to the shops, and when I got back Tony was in the kitchen, making small talk with her.

She seemed to be in a good enough mood, and was asking him about his family.

"Hi," I said as I came in. "Sorry, I just had to get some stuff."

"Tony was telling me about his mother," Mam said. "She's had a terrible time, poor woman."

Tony nodded. "You're right. And I have to admit that I probably wasn't much help, running away all the time. I never really got into too much trouble, but I was close a couple of times." He shook his head. "Ma always said that it would have been different if my dad had stayed around."

"And you don't even know his name?" Mam asked, fascinated.

"Oh, I know his name, all right. But that's about all I know. Ma barely knew him. She was only eighteen when she got pregnant with me, and I don't think he was much older. The thing is, she was actually going out with someone else at the time. My dad was a one-night stand."

I said, "You never told *me* that."

"Sorry. So when her boyfriend found out, he broke it off. Then her parents threw her out for, well, for being a slut."

"So you grew up with no Dad and no grandparents?" Mam said. "And look at you now. You've turned out fine."

I couldn't help a grin from appearing. She'd just complimented him to his face – there wasn't any higher praise from my mother.

"Thanks, Mrs Quinn," Tony said.

"So is our Andi going to bring you to the wedding, then?"

Tony looked at me. "I don't know. She hasn't asked me yet."

"Well, you have to come. It'll be good fun. Can you sing?"

Tony frowned. "Sing? Not really."

"Only we're going to have a band and everyone will have to do a piece."

I froze. "Oh *shite*."

Mam looked shocked. "Andi!"

"What's the matter?" Tony asked.

"The *band* . . . I'm supposed to be organising that. I forgot all about it."

"For God's sake, Andi! There's less than two weeks to the wedding!"

"I know, Mam! What am I going to do? Tony, you must know someone in a band?"

"Not really. Though I'll tell you what I'll do – I'll ask down at the pub. They used to have bands on Thursdays before they started doing the stand-up. What sort of band is she looking for?"

"Trad. You know, all that diddly-idle stuff." I slumped forward and rested my head on the table. "She's going to murder me."

Tony put his hand on my back and gently patted me. "It'll be fine. Sure, if the worst comes to the worst, I'll get up there and entertain the troops. Your sister will be the only one of her friends to have a comedian at her wedding."

Mam stared at him. "What's this?"

The cat was out of the bag now. I sat up, and looked nervously towards her. "Tony does a comedy act now and then."

Mam was silent for a few seconds, then said, "I *knew* I'd heard that name somewhere." She rummaged around in the pile of newspapers Dad kept under his chair, and pulled one out. She flicked through it, and then spread it out for us to see.

It was a review of Thursday night's performance:

New comedian Tony O'Hehir impressed the three-hundred strong audience with his special brand of jokes and clever observational humour. The show is definitely not for children, though . . . Almost all of the jokes were about sex and contained strong language. That said, O'Hehir's material – co-written, he says, with his girlfriend – was fresh and original, and stood out far above the other acts of the night. Could he be a star in the making? Well, everyone present seemed to think so. Definitely one to watch out for.

* * *

Tony didn't stay long – Mam made it very clear that she and I had a lot to talk about.

When he left, she turned on me. "Who the hell do you think you are, lying to me?"

"I wasn't lying! I just never told you."

"That's the *same* as lying, Andi! For God's sake, you know how I feel about that sort of thing! Look at what happened to your grandad! He wasted his life trying to break into showbusiness. And your gran's just as bad. If not worse. Because of them, we had *nothing*, Andi. Nothing."

"I know, Mam, but . . ."

"Shut up and listen to me for once in your life. I had to go to work when I was twelve, washing dishes in a hotel for five hours a day – and that was on top of going to school – just so we'd be able to put food on the table. And if my father ever managed to get some work, it was usually only for a couple of days, and he'd go out and waste all his money on stupid things to celebrate. He spent his whole life waiting for his chance to come, and he died a failure."

"That's not fair! He was just trying to do what he knew best."

"Oh, you're right there! What he knew best was to

sit around and tell us all how great it was going to be when he got his big break. But it never came, Andi. He was sixty-five when he died, and it was probably just as well that he did because he had no proper pension and no savings, and hard as it was to find work, at that age it would have been even harder." Tears began to build in Mam's eyes. "And look at your gran. She has nothing now."

"She has her pension," I said.

"That's only the state pension, Andi. It's barely enough to live on." She took a long, deep breath. "I've been paying her gas bills for the past twenty-six years, and she still comes to me every few weeks for a loan. And it's not like *we're* loaded. It's not like there's a huge amount of money coming in here every week."

"Well, what about Gran's house?"

"What about it? When she dies, it'll go back to the corporation."

"Oh. I thought she owned it."

"She owns the clothes she stands up in, and not much else. And you know why? I'll tell you why: because the two of them, her and Dad, they did what they wanted to do, and not what they should have done."

"But Mam, that won't happen to me. I'm not going to start going on the comedy circuit without a day job to fall back on."

She stared at me. "What did you just say?"

I swallowed. "Nothing."

"I don't believe it. I don't believe it . . . I was trying to warn you against getting involved with a man who's chosen to risk everything for a few moments of glory, like my parents did. I thought that what the paper said meant that you'd just given Tony a few ideas. And now you're telling me you want to do it for yourself?"

I decided that since it was all out in the open, I might as well be honest. "Yes. That's what I want to do."

"Well, you can think again."

"No."

"What?!"

"No. I'm not going to 'think again'. This is something I want to do, something I know I *can* do. I've wanted to do comedy for as long as I can remember. And I *will* do it. But not yet. I'm not ready for it."

"I see. And when do you think you'll be ready for it? Because let me tell you it won't be while you're living in this house. Maybe you'll be ready for it when you have your own place, with a rent or a mortgage and bills to pay. Maybe then you'll tell yourself that you don't need a proper job, you'll make enough money from telling jokes that you'll be able to pay all the bills."

"It's not like that, Mam. I said I'm not going to give up my day job. So I will have a regular income. What's wrong with it then? What's so bad about appearing on stage?"

"Because it's all *lies*," she said. "That's it, plain and simple. These people get up on stage and they tell lies about themselves, and their wives, just so that other people will laugh at them."

"You mean, just so they'll make people happy."

"Don't tell me what I mean, Andi. I'm quite well aware of what I mean or don't mean."

"So if it's the lies that bother you, what about *Coronation Street* or *Fair City*? You watch them. They're not true. What's the difference?"

"The difference is that they're pretending to be other people. Comedians tell all the stories about themselves as if they were true."

"So what if I go into acting instead? Would that be okay?"

She said nothing.

"You're just ashamed of Gran, aren't you? You're ashamed of her, so you're taking it out on me."

"Now you're being ridiculous."

"No, I'm not. She told me about that ad she did. She told me that you were embarrassed that your mother was on television for a slimming product."

"Yes, I was embarrassed. I didn't want people to know how low we had to stoop for money."

"Gran doesn't think she was stooping. She thinks it was one of the high points of her career."

Mam was silent for a long time. I got up and made us both a cup of tea.

Eventually, she said, "I don't want to fight with you, Andi. It's just . . . I don't like being lied to."

"Everyone lies, Mam. Sometimes you *have* to lie."

"I know. Sometimes you have to. But that doesn't mean you have to like it."

She's thinking about something else, I said to myself. I briefly wondered what it might be, and then decided that the best thing to do was to just ask her.

"So what are we talking about here?" I asked. "It's not just about me going on stage and making a fool out of myself, is it?"

"Andi, you're still very young. Oh, I know you *think* you're all grown up, but you're not. Sometimes it *does* matter what other people think. Sometimes you have to bury things in the back of your mind and try and forget about them."

"Well, whatever it is that's on your mind, you can tell me. I mean, I know we fight a lot, but we're still friends, aren't we?"

"I hope so . . ." She smiled. "One day I will tell you everything, Andi. I promise you that."

* * *

Afterwards, I thought a lot about what she said: sometimes you have to bury things in the back of your mind and try and forget about them.

I was in my bedroom, lying back on the bed and staring at the ceiling, when all of a sudden I thought of Joe.

I'd asked Niall why he always hung around with Dean, and Niall said, "You mean, why does Dean hang around with Joe . . . Talk to Joe, ask him what's going on. You might be surprised at the answer."

I found my address book and flicked through it. I wasn't even sure I had Joe's number – I couldn't ever remember calling him – but there it was.

I went down to the phone, and called the number.

"Hello?" It was definitely Joe's voice.

"Hi, Joe! It's me!"

"Me?"

"Andi. God, don't tell me you've forgotten me already!"

"No, of course not. How are you?"

"Great. But the thing is, how are you? No one's seen or heard of you in ages. I was getting worried."

"Yeah?"

"I thought that something might have happened."

"No, I've just been keeping to myself."

"Any particular reason?"

"There is."

"And . . . ? Come on, out with it!"

He paused. "Andi, this is the first time you've ever phoned me. I didn't even know whether you knew I existed except as Dean's friend."

I didn't really know how to respond to that. "Sorry," was the best I could come up with.

"And now you want to know what's going on. I realise that this might sound rude, but why? What do *you* care?"

"I care."

"So you say. What is it you really want to know?"

"Okay . . . Do you actually *like* Dean?"

"Between you and me, no. He's a fool."

"I should have realised that. I should have seen that a long time ago. Why do you hang around with him, then? Why do you put up with all the slagging and everything?"

"I don't. Not any more."

"God, I give up. Are you going to tell me anything or not?"

"It depends on what you already know, Andi."

"Which is?"

He laughed. "I'm not falling for that one."

A thought suddenly occurred to me. "Joe, you're not working at the moment, are you?"

"No."

"Well, you know about the shop being turned into an Internet café, right? I can give you a job there. The work isn't the best, but the pay's not too bad. What do you think?"

"Okay . . . Listen I have to know why you're offering before I say anything."

"Because I trust you. You walked me home twice when Dean abandoned me. You looked after Jimmy that time when he was drunk. Because you're smarter than any of the others. And because I've been thinking about the old gang a lot, and only today I realised you're the one I missed the most."

"And . . . ?"

I couldn't think of anything else. "And what . . . ?"

"When you think of it, Andi, phone me back. Okay, I've got to go. See you." He hung up.

Jaye Carroll

Mam called out from the kitchen. "Who were you talking to?"

"Joe," I said. I went in to her.

"You look upset, or something," she said.

"I'm not upset. I'm just confused. I offered Joe a job in the café, and he wanted to know . . . something."

Mam raised her eyes. "Another bloody oddball."

"No, there's something about him that I just can't figure out. I always thought that he hung around with Dean because he hero-worshipped him or something, but there's more to him than that. He just told me that he doesn't even *like* Dean. Ellen thinks that Joe might fancy her or something, and now that she has Niall he knows he's got no chance with her"

"Or maybe he fancies *you*," Mam said. "And since you started going out with Tony . . ."

I stared at her. "God. I've known him for years, and it's only in the past month I've started talking to him. In fact, the first time I ever spoke to him without slagging him was one night when he walked me home because Dean was in a sulk and he wouldn't do it."

"Well, there you are, then."

Something went *click*! in my mind, and I ran out to the phone.

Joe answered on the second ring. "Hello?"

"It's me."

"So you know what I'm talking about."

"Yeah. And you're right. What you said made a difference to me. That's why I want you in the shop.

290

I've known Dean for years and he never said anything important, but you said something that really made me look at myself."

"Let's hear it, then."

"I have loved the stars too fondly to be fearful of the night."

Chapter Sixteen

The next day – Monday – I went into the café and saw how much it had changed. The carpet was down, the walls and ceiling were painted, all the counters were in, and the Internet server was installed in Bruce's little cubbyhole next to where the deli counter was going to be. For the first time, it didn't seem like the Pound Shop with a new coat of paint.

There was still a lot of work to be done, but at least now it was starting to look like we'd be able to open fairly soon.

My main task for the week was to hire the rest of the staff. With Joe now on board – well, probably – that made four of us: me, Joe, Donna and Ellen. I knew I had to hire another five at least.

My secondary task was to work out a schedule, and that was proving to be incredibly hard.

I had it all written out on a large sheet of paper that I was now unable to roll up because it was covered in so much Tipp-Ex.

The best schedule I'd come up with was to treat weekends the same as work days, and have everyone in for five days on earlies, two days off, five days on lates, two days off, five days on earlies, and so on. Everyone's cycle started on a different day, so we'd always have at least three people in early and three on lates.

That wouldn't suit everyone, I knew, but we'd just have to deal with that as it happened.

I made a promise to myself that the schedule would be fairly flexible. If two people wanted to swap, that was no problem, as long as they checked with me first. If someone wanted to work overtime, that would also be allowed, as long as there actually was something for them to do.

Bernard promised that we'd have someone come in once a week to work out the wages, so that was something of a relief. I hadn't been looking forward to that.

So we were almost there . . .

The catering equipment was due to be installed later in the week, and someone from the company was going to show us how to use it all.

The only remaining things were to hire the staff and get their uniforms.

In the afternoon, there was a knock at the door: two guys had arrived with a huge sign for the front of the shop.

"So where do you want this, missus?" One of them asked.

"I was thinking of the front, unless you have any other ideas?"

"And I suppose you want it the right way up an' all?"

"That'd be handy."

While one of them attached the sign, the other fixed the letters to the window: *E-mail, Coffee, Sandwiches, Cappuccino, Access to the World!* And so on.

They were barely gone five minutes when there was another knock at the door. An eager young nerd stood outside. "Hi. When are you opening?"

"Soon," I said. "We're still waiting on the equipment. We'll probably open some time next week."

"Okay. What times?"

"Eight until midnight."

"Oh." He looked a little disappointed. "I hoped you'd be open twenty-four hours."

"We will, but not all in a row."

A few minutes after that, someone else called. Then another, and another.

This was a good sign, but it was irritating as hell. I wrote "Opening Soon!" in large letters on a sheet of paper and stuck it to the glass in the door.

Half an hour later, there was another knock at the door . . .

"*How* soon?"

* * *

All Tuesday morning I was plagued with people wanting to know exactly when the café would be open, how much it was going to cost, whether or not we'd have unrestricted Internet access, a few incomprehensible questions about "domain names" and "ISPs", and a teenage girl wondering if we had any jobs going.

This last was music to my ears. I interviewed her there and then, and offered her a job. She wanted to know when she could start. I told her, "Next week, sometime. But I'll be in touch before then."

I decided to phone Bernard and find out exactly *when* we would be opening.

He was happy to hear that so many people were interested in the shop. "We haven't even done any publicity yet," he said. "This is looking really positive. How are the interviews going?"

"Not bad," I said. "I only need another four people, and I've got a list of over twenty to check out."

"Great. The catering equipment will be delivered on Thursday, and on Friday afternoon there'll be someone coming out to show you how everything works. So if you can get all the staff together, it'll save time. The computers will be delivered and installed over the weekend. What else do we need?"

"Chairs and tables," I said. "I think that's all."

"Fine . . . Look, Andi. How can I put this? Nora tells me you've been bossing her around."

Uh oh. "Really?"

"She said that you were rude to her in front of the decorators."

"That's not *entirely* true, Bernard. In fact, it was the

other way around. She seemed to think that she was in charge of me."

"I see. Well, I don't want it to happen again."

"It won't. Besides, she's almost done here."

"No, she's not. She said she's dropping out of college, so I'm hiring her as the café's manager."

I felt like I'd been shot. "But . . . but Bernard, that's *my* job!"

"What? What makes you say that?"

"But you *said* that I would be!"

"Andi, I never said anything of the sort. You don't have any experience of managing a café."

"Neither does Nora," I said. "She's never done any sort of work apart from this. Look, when we had lunch in the restaurant, you said that I'd be paid a lot more than the staff, because I'd have much greater responsibilities. You said I'd have a free hand running the café and that I'd report only to you."

His normally even voice suddenly went hard. "I don't recall that. I think I would remember something as important as that."

I swallowed. "Well, what have I been doing for the past few weeks? I've practically organised this whole place for you."

"I'd hardly call making a couple of phone calls, interviewing a few people, and being there to let the builders in 'organising the whole place', Andi."

I felt like I was going to cry. "This is crazy. You *said* I'd be the manager!"

"Don't be ridiculous. I never said anything of the sort. Now, stop all this nonsense and just get on with your job."

"Well, in that case, what *is* my job?"

"It's doing what I *tell* you to do. And once the café opens, it's doing what *Nora* tells you to do." Without saying goodbye, he hung up.

* * *

On Wednesday morning, I interviewed two girls for the café, and offered both of them a job.

Neither of them had impressed me much, but I didn't care any more.

All Tuesday night I'd been in a total rage. I called Bernard Parker every horrible name I could think of, and quite a few I made up specially.

I guessed that Parker had never really wanted me to be the manager, but he had wanted someone to hang around and get everything started. So he'd just told me what I wanted to hear.

I wondered what he saw in Nora. From what I'd seen of her, she was a cold, self-centred bitch. Maybe that was it. Maybe he wanted someone tough to manage the staff. I would have been their friend, and perhaps he thought that meant I'd be weak.

When I got home on Tuesday evening, I was still in a daze. A dozen revenge scenarios went through my mind . . .

The first one I thought of – and the one that kept

coming back to me – was to just quit. Just leave and say nothing. Leave everything hanging, and see how he gets on without me there. That was the easiest thing to do, and – I was sure – the best thing to do.

But it wouldn't have been the most satisfying. My favourite idea for revenge was to contact everyone on my list and hire all of them, and tell them all to start at the same time on the same day. But of course that wouldn't have been fair to *them*. It wasn't even possible anyway, because Bernard was the one who sent out the letters of confirmation.

Another idea was to just pretend to have everyone hired, and then on the first day he'd be completely screwed when no one turned up. But that would never work because Nora would know about it.

In the end I decided that there was no way I could get my own back on him directly. The best thing to do was to hire people who were only barely competent. That way, it meant I still had a job, even if it wasn't as manager.

On Wednesday afternoon, after I'd hired those two girls, there was no one else in the café so I put a "Help Wanted" notice in the window.

By the end of the day I had more than my full quota of employees: another girl and two more lads.

On Thursday, as Bernard had promised, the catering equipment was delivered and installed: a fridge, a Coke machine, cool counters, work surfaces, the lot. After checking with the catering supplies people, I contacted all of my employees and arranged a training session for Friday afternoon.

Then, as I was about to leave for the day, Bernard phoned and had another surprise for me: "We're going to open tomorrow week. Everything should be in place by then."

I was about to tell him that it was a bit awkward for me, because my sister was getting married the following day, but I decided against it. After all, Nora was the one I should be asking for days off.

"How is the recruitment going?" he asked.

"All done," I said.

"Good . . . Now all you need is their uniforms."

"I'm going to arrange to get everyone together early next week, and we'll go shopping for them. Blouses and skirts for the girls, shirts and trousers for the lads, two of each. But I'll need money for that."

"Nora will sort that out."

"Fine."

"Is there anything else I should know about?"

"I don't think so."

He paused. "Don't tell me you're still annoyed about that misunderstanding?"

"I won't."

"These things happen in business, Andi. You'll have to get used to it." He sounded a little kinder this time.

"I know, but it just isn't fair. I did all this work for you."

"You can't go through life expecting everything to

be fair. Consider this a life-lesson, Andi. You'll thank me for it eventually."

"There's just one thing I want to know, Mr Parker . . . Why her? Why Nora?"

"What do you mean?"

"I mean, why did you choose her over me? She's no more qualified than I am. And I've had years of experience of dealing with the public. All she knows is how to order people around."

"Maybe that's what this job needs. Did you ever think of that?"

"As a matter of fact, I did. But she's not an easy person to get on with. She's going to make a lot of the staff very unhappy. And then they'll be less efficient." I was pleased with that – now I'd covered myself for hiring staff who might not turn out to be incredibly competent.

"I've been hearing things like that my whole working life, Andi. It's not true. Successful businessmen don't get where they are by treating their staff like pets."

"Well, I don't agree with that."

"Another thing successful businessmen do is follow their own instincts, and not those of a twenty-year-old girl who gets upset at the first little thing that goes wrong. That's why I hired Nora. She's able to get the job done without whining about it."

I could feel myself getting angry. "Do you *want* me to leave, is that it?"

"Of course not. What good would that do either of us? You'd be out of a job, and I'd . . . Well, I can't think of what harm it would do me. Look, I'm not saying that you'll *never* be the manager. I'm just saying that you're not going to be the manager now."

After that, there was little more I could say to him without losing it completely. So I told him I understood, and then hung up.

* * *

Thursday night at the comedy show had something a little different: a double-act. They were brothers, they called themselves Feck and Eejit, and, well, they were shite . . .

Feck: "I heard yer ma was on the telly the other night."

Eejit: "Yeah, she fell off and hurt herself, though."

Feck: "My ma was *really* on the telly."

Eejit: "Yeah?"

Feck: "She fell off and *really* hurt herself."

There was more like this. A lot more. They were desperately trying to be D'Unbelievables, and failing miserably.

Tony and I watched from the back. "What do you think?" I asked quietly.

"They're fecktacular," Tony said.

On stage, Feck – or maybe it was Eejit – was trying to entice a woman onto the stage. "C'mon up, now, missus . . . we're not going to hurt you."

"Not so it shows anyway," the other one said.

"Listen," Tony said. "I was asked to do another show tomorrow night."

"Here?"

"No, out in Sutton. Any chance you can knock something together for the show?"

"I'll give it a go . . . How long are you going to be on for?"

"Probably an hour and a half, fifteen-minute interval."

"Wow! A proper gig!"

Tony grinned. "Yep! Since it's so far out, there shouldn't be a problem using some of the old stuff. Tie it all together with some new bits . . . What do you think?"

"Well, it's all a bit Sutton," I said.

He elbowed me playfully. "Very funny."

"Okay, I'll give it a go. What time do you have to be there?"

"Nine."

"I'll try and get something done tomorrow in work. But just in case I can't, you'd better have something else prepared."

Feck and Eejit were just about to wrap up: they were embarking on their closing number, a nasty song about Charlie Haughey to the tune of "Davy Crockett".

"Okay," Tony said. "What am I doing tonight?"

"Moses, talking in the cinema, Tarantino doing Disney movies, real names for things, people in the bus queue, big books, drinking." Tonight, for the first time, it was all my own material. No doubt Tony would embellish it on the fly, but the essence of it was mine. So if it failed, it was all my fault.

"Which drinking one?" Tony asked. "The one with the cats?"

"No, the one with the beermats and kids in the pub."

"Grand . . . How do I get from Moses to talking in the cinema again?"

"Charlton Heston."

He nodded. "Got it. Okay, wish me luck."

"Break a leg."

* * *

"So Moses comes down from the mountain with the Ten Commandos. They were like the Dirty Dozen, only more biblical. The toughest of the commandos was number six, Thou-shalt-not Steel."

I hadn't told Tony what had happened in work. In fact, I hadn't told anyone yet. I wasn't even sure *how* I was going to tell my mother. I had a sort of vague plan along the lines of "I've decided not to take the manager's job until I get more experience" but I was sure that she'd see right through it.

One thing that was really beginning to bother me was that Bernard hadn't paid me yet. I was used to getting paid once a week, and I was starting to feel the pinch.

Bernard had told me that I'd be paid once the café opened. But then, he'd told me quite a few other things too . . .

I didn't have a single thing on paper saying that I worked for him. He could easily turn around on the first day and tell me that I didn't have a job at all.

On stage, Tony had progressed to the cinema routine: "What you have to do is turn around and just stare at them, like this" – he demonstrated, all googly-eyed – "until they notice you. They'll stop talking, but you don't turn back. Just keep staring at them. And eventually, they'll ask you what you want. So you tell them to come closer, and you say really quietly, 'I've got something to tell you.'" Tony said that quietly, and everyone leaned forward to hear.

"So they lean closer," Tony said softly. "And you say again, really quiet this time, 'I've got something to tell you.'" The audience leaned even further forward, and Tony beckoned them closer still.

"'What? What have you got to tell me?'"

Suddenly Tony roared at the top of his voice, "'*Shut the fuck up!*'"

Everyone jumped, and then broke into applause.

He is *really* good at this, I said to myself. They're lapping it up!

Tony segued into a routine about Quentin Tarantino's interpretations of Disney movies. It wasn't my favourite of my routines, but Tony liked it, because he was able to do damn good impressions of Mickey Mouse and Donald Duck.

It was a long routine, dealing with Mickey and Donald attempting to frame Goofy for the fake kidnapping of Donald. But it all goes wrong when Minnie walks in on their plan, and Donald decides that they have to get rid of her. Mickey disagrees, and Donald says he'll do it himself.

"Fuck you!" Tony said in his Mickey Mouse voice. "No motherfuckin' duck touches my bitch! What the fuck *you* know about offing someone, anyway?"

The audience responded well, but not well enough. The problem was that a lot of them couldn't understand what Donald Duck was supposed to be saying. Neither could I, and I was the one who wrote the material.

Still, I said to myself, at least tomorrow I should get enough time to work on Tony's routine.

Watching Tony on stage, I found the urge to get up there myself growing stronger by the minute. He was good, there was no doubt about that, but now and then he fluffed the delivery of a punchline, and occasionally he wandered too far off track with his ad-libs.

I didn't know if I could have done better, but I wanted to try.

I felt like I was almost ready . . . It was like the whole thing was building up inside me, ready to break out onto the world.

It would have been nice to pretend that the need to perform was like an orgasm waiting to happen, but that was a bit much: in reality, it was more like waiting for ketchup to come out of the bottle.

* * *

On Friday afternoon, the staff assembled in the café to learn how everything was supposed to work. I'd asked Nora to turn up, but she'd just told me that she didn't need to know anything about the catering side of the business – that was what the staff were for.

Donna already knew everything, but I asked her to stick around anyway, in case she had any questions. She did have a few questions, and so did everyone else, apart from Joe, who stood in silence at the back.

After the lesson was over, I made everyone agree to meet back on Monday morning so that we could all go shopping for our uniforms.

Ellen and Joe stayed behind, and I told them what had happened with my managerial position.

"The bastard!" Ellen said, predictably. "Why didn't you let us know?"

"Because I still don't know what to think myself. I suppose at least this way I have a job but I don't have to worry about the responsibility."

"He definitely told you that you'd be the manager?" Joe asked.

I nodded. "He did."

"Are you sure he actually *said* that?"

Ellen raised her eyes. "For God's sake, Joe! She just *told* you!"

I tried to think back over every conversation I'd had with Bernard . . ."He's right, El. Parker never actually said it. But he did tell me about all the responsibility I'd have, and that I'd be making more money than everyone else."

Joe said, "Did Parker tell you that *you'd* be making the money, or the manager would?"

I bit my lip. "The manager."

"He was stringing you along," Joe said. "He never intended you to be the manager. He just wanted you to think that you would be. I bet that if you tried to bring him to court and you had recordings of all your conversations with him, that you'd still have no actual proof that he promised you the job."

I felt so disappointed with myself. "I walked right into it, didn't I? I did everything he wanted, and got nothing in return." I shook my head. "God! I'm so stupid!"

"No, you're not," Ellen said. "There was no way you could have known. Look, come out with us tonight. Joe's staying over and we're going to go and get drunk. Well, Joe isn't, but me and Niall are." She paused, then added, "Dean's not around."

"Thanks, but Tony has a gig tonight. So, Joe, is that the story? You're going to stay with Ellen until you can get your own place?"

"That's the plan."

"Dad says that that it shouldn't be long before one of the tenants moves out," Ellen said. "At this time of year there's always someone moving out."

"Well, if you're ever stuck, you can stay with us. Only, not until after the wedding. Roddy and Gráinne and Claire are coming up during the week."

"So how are all the wedding plans going?" Ellen asked.

"Okay. The only major thing is the band. Tony's going to check around for one. Actually, I'd better get on his case about that. We're kind of running out of time."

"One of Niall's mates has a band," she said. "I could ask him. They're desperate for gigs."

"Well, they'd have to know all the Irish folk songs."

"I'll ask anyway."

"Thanks. Okay, now get out of here, the two of you. I'm still working on stuff for tonight's show."

* * *

I met Tony at his flat just after he got home from work. I was exhausted, pissed off, ready to kill, hungry, and in need of a good hug, and it must have shown on my face.

"Please don't tell me you were up all night working on stuff," Tony said.

"Not *all* night," I said. "I got to bed at about four. And I managed to get some done at work. If you can call it work."

"Look, come in, and sit down. I'm just going to have a shower."

So I sat in the disgusting sitting-room and waited, hoping that Nick or Dick wouldn't show up. The place wasn't as bad as it had been the last time – the "door on giant speakers" table was relatively free of mould-gathering food, and it looked like someone had done the rounds with a hoover in the recent past.

I had pages of notes ready for Tony to memorise. It was mostly older stuff, so that wasn't too bad, but I'd added a lot of linking material to tie everything together. The hardest part was making sure that there was enough material. If Tony rushed through a routine, or skipped one, it could throw the whole thing off, and we didn't have much in the way of spare material to fill any gaps.

Tony came into the sitting-room wearing nothing but a pair of shorts and a towel around his neck.

It was the first time I'd seen him so close to being naked, and I could barely take my eyes off him.

His chest was well-defined, and broad, though his stomach protruded a little and was so hairy it didn't so much resemble a six-pack as it did a wolf-pack.

He stopped. "What are *you* looking at?"

"Have you no modesty, Mr O'Hehir? Cover yourself up: there's a lady present."

"Really?"

"All right . . . How much time do we have for you to learn all this?"

"About an hour. Maybe less. I suppose we can go over it on the bus." He was about to sit down – again, I was on the only good chair – and then changed his mind. "Come on. We'll go to my room. Unless you'd feel more comfortable here?"

"Comfortable in this room? Are you kidding?"

So we went to his bedroom. I sat on the end of the bed, and while he dried his hair I started going over the material.

I was slightly disappointed when he started to get dressed, but he took my mind off it by making me choose his clothes for him.

From the way he was starting to panic, I guessed that sex was probably the furthest thing from his mind.

"This is the big one," he said. "This is make-or-break time."

"Oh, come on! It's not that big a deal."

"It is, you know. It's only me. They don't even have someone doing the warm-up. I'm going in cold to a new audience. And on top of that, they're paying me a hell of a lot more."

"How much? If you don't mind me asking."

"Two hundred quid," Tony said. He paused with his shirt half-buttoned and looked over at me. A smile crept across his face. "What do you think about that?"

I was impressed. "That's almost a week's wages for me!"

"Yeah, it's a lot. And there's going to be some press people there, they said. Probably someone from *Hot Press*, and maybe one or two of the big student websites. So you know what that means . . . ?"

"Yeah . . . You might get The Lounge next year."

"I hope so."

"Wow . . . So, listen, where does that leave me?"

"How do you mean?"

310

"Well, I don't want to get all mercenary, but at this stage nearly all of your material was written by me."

Tony nodded. "I know. Don't worry, I haven't forgotten about that. I was going to suggest we split the money fifty-fifty."

I couldn't help grinning. "A hundred quid! Yes!"

"You can go shopping tomorrow . . ."

"Sod shopping! A few more gigs like that and I can tell Bernard Parker to go and fuck himself!"

"What's this all about? I thought you liked him?"

"It's a long story. Forget it. I'll tell you later. For now, you have to concentrate on tonight."

* * *

"Ladies and gentlemen, Mr Tony O'Hehir!"

There was a smattering of polite applause, and Tony bounded up to the stage and grabbed the mike. "Thank you! It's great to be here!

"So, on the way here I got on the bus at the terminus, and sat down and waited. After a few minutes, this lad comes up to me. 'You're sittin' in my seat,' he says. I looked around and the bus was empty, apart from me. 'What? Sure there's loads of seats.' But he insisted. 'It's my seat. I always sit in that seat.' So I'm going, 'Would you ever fuck off out of it? You can't reserve seats on the bus.' But he kept on and on, and more and more people are getting on the bus. So one of them comes up and says, 'He's right, mister. He always sits there. That's his seat, that is.' I'm thinking, 'Great, now they're ganging

311

up on me!' So I said, 'Okay! Okay! You can have your bloody seat if it's that important!' And I got up. 'Sure I didn't want to drive the bus anyway.'"

No one laughed.

Tony's face sagged, and he looked over at me. I gave him the "keep going!" signal, and he went on.

"So I went to the zoo and I fell into the tigers' pit . . ."

After forty minutes of pure hell, Tony told them that they were a great audience – which was a lie – and that he'd be back after the interval. Then he rushed backstage.

I went after him, and found him in the tiny, squalid storeroom they were using as a dressing-room.

I couldn't think of anything to say.

Tony was slumped forward on the chair, his head between his hands. "They hate me."

I put my hand on his shoulder. "Look, everyone has a bad night. It's not your fault. The second half will be better."

He shook his head. "No it won't. Ninety minutes was too long. I wasn't ready. The material is okay for short sets, but it's not good enough for something this long." He let out a long sigh. "I should just quit now. Save them the trouble of booing me off the stage."

There was a knock at the door. I opened it to see the pub's manager wearing a very dour expression. "So how's it going?"

"It's shit," Tony said. "Fuck it. I don't know what went wrong."

"Well, you could try being funny. That might work. Your mate Bosco Byrne said that you were this great new comedian. What was it, a joke or something? Was he just having me on? Or did you lose a bet, is that it? Or maybe you're only great when your own mates are around. Jesus, I've seen funnier sermons in Mass."

"Just fuck off," Tony said. "You're not making it any easier."

"Is that right? Well, let me make it a *lot* easier. You're out. Don't bother going back on."

Tony raised his head and stared at him. "What about the money?"

"It's lucky for you everyone is drowning their sorrows at the bar. You'll get your money." He turned around and stomped away.

"Look, it wasn't all that bad," I said to Tony, who had slumped forward again. "They laughed a lot. They just didn't go nuts, that's all."

"Andi, I really don't need to hear that sort of thing right now."

"It was the first joke," I said. "It wasn't strong enough. Or maybe they'd heard it before, or something."

Tony raised his head and stared at me. "What do you mean, 'heard it before'? I thought it was one of yours."

"No, it's an old joke. But obviously not as good as I thought it was."

"You never told me it was an old joke. Jesus, Andi! For all we know there was someone in here last night who told the same joke!" He looked away from me. "Fuck!"

"Look, don't take it out on me. It's not *my* fault."

Tony stood up. "Well, whose fault is it, then? It's either yours or mine. And you've already said it's not mine."

"I had less than a day to prepare the material! You only told me last night about this gig! How was I supposed to work miracles in that amount of time?"

"What, you're saying it takes miracles now? What are you, my guardian angel or something? Well, you've lost your fuckin' halo tonight!"

I couldn't help myself: I lashed out and slapped him across the face.

Then I opened the door and walked away.

Chapter Seventeen

Mam woke me early next morning by repeatedly shouting at me to get up. This didn't have the effect she'd planned: I curled up under the duvet and tried to squeeze a few more minutes' sleep.

At least when I was asleep I didn't have to think about Tony. That was the plan, anyway, but I kept dreaming about him, about the fight, about Bernard Parker and his damn tricks. About the wedding and how if I didn't get a band Eimear would murder me.

Someone grabbed my feet and tried to drag me out of bed. "Come on, wake up, you lazy cow."

"Ah, piss off, Ciarán, I'm trying to sleep!"

A second later I was sitting straight up. "Ciarán! You're back!"

Grinning like mad, he sat on the end of the end of the bed. "So how's it going? Mam's been trying to wake you for ages."

"When did you get home?"

"I got back to the flat last night. I was going to come over, but the minute I got in I just crashed. So, what's the story?"

"Never mind my story – look at you! You have a tan and everything! And a beard! Shave it off, it doesn't suit you."

"I can't shave it off until my tan fades," he said. "Or the bottom half of my face will be white."

I grabbed him and gave him a big hug. "I missed you."

"That's shite," he said. "Sure I hardly ever even see you and I only live half an hour away."

"No, I mean it. The others are all going mental over the wedding and everything."

"Mam told me about your new boyfriend. I'm glad to see that you're not still hanging around with that fuckin' gobsite Dean."

"Don't *you* start."

"So what's happening there anyway? Mam said he's a comedian."

"Yeah. He does stand-up comedy."

"Any good?"

I nodded. "Yeah . . . Well . . ."

"Uh oh. Had a fight, did you?"

"We did. Last night. The show didn't go well. In fact, it was bloody awful. They hardly laughed at anything."

"So what did you fight about?"

"Well, I wrote most of his material for him. So he sort of blamed me. Though I can understand that.

316

Anyway, he lost his temper and said stuff he shouldn't have. So I hit him."

Ciarán suddenly looked serious. "He didn't hit you back, did he?"

"What? No, of course not. He wouldn't have had a chance anyway, because I walked away."

"Are you going to break up with him?"

I shrugged. "I don't know. I mean, he was under a lot of pressure."

"You're not in love with him, are you?"

"God, you ask a lot of questions! No, I'm not. I mean, I could be eventually, but I haven't known him all that long. He's way older than me, too. Did Mam tell you that?"

"She told me everything. Anyway, get yourself up and dressed, okay? We're all downstairs."

"All who?"

"Mam and Dad and Eimear and Chris." He got to his feet. "Don't go back asleep, or you won't get your present."

"What did you bring me?"

"Are you deaf? I said it's a present."

* * *

When I walked into the kitchen they all stopped talking at once. "Caught you," I said. "Talking about me again."

"Yeah, sure," Ciarán said. "That's because the whole universe revolves around you." He handed me a tiny – but expensive-looking – paper bag. It was one of those

317

made out of thick shiny paper with purple rope handles. I peered inside and saw a small bottle of perfume that he'd clearly bought in the airport on the way home.

"All the girls in Italy are wearing that at the moment," Ciarán said.

"Cheers, thanks!" I unscrewed the top and had a sniff. It smelled like hot butter. I put a drop on my wrists, and of course Mam and Eimear had to give it a try.

Eimear handed the bottle back to me, and said, "Where's my band?"

"Don't worry. They're coming. Trust me. In fact, I've got two bands at the moment, so I'm trying to get them both to give me demo tapes."

"And did you phone the hotel to check?"

"Of course I did!" I lied. "They said everything was fine, but I should check again early next week, just to be sure. I'll do it first thing on Monday morning."

"So how's the new job going?" Chris asked. I hadn't seen Chris – Eimear's fiancé – in ages. He was thirty, the same age as Eimear, but to look at him you'd think he was much older. He was getting very bald, and had permanent lines across his forehead. His goatee beard was mostly grey, and he even dressed old: thick jumpers and sensible trousers.

"Not bad. We're opening next Friday, if all goes well. But I'm beginning to think that I don't want to be the manager. It's a lot more work."

"You're better off," Dad said. "A manager is no sort of a job for a young lass like yourself."

"Well, if *you're* agreeing with me, then maybe I should take it," I said.

"Show your father at least *some* respect, Andi," Mam said.

Chris got up, and said, "Right, I'm off to the shops for some smokes. Andi, do you want to go for a walk?"

"Why?"

"So you can give me the last-minute warning about Eimear, just in case I'm making a mistake."

Eimear nearly fell off her chair. "*What*!?"

"Relax," he said. "I'm kidding."

* * *

"So what did you want to talk to me about?" I asked Chris as we walked to the shop.

"Your mam was telling me about your other job . . . writing jokes and stuff."

"A-ha! You want me to help you write your speech for the wedding!"

He looked at me in surprise. "How did you guess?"

"I'm psychic. What do you have so far?"

Chris pulled a crumpled and stained sheet of paper out of his pocket and handed it to me. It was covered in crossed-out sentences, and the only ones that remained intact were "thanks very much for coming" and "I hope I can make Eimear as happy as she makes me".

"So what do you want? Jokes, or stories, or what?"

"Whatever you can manage. Getting married is a doddle compared to speaking in front of all *your* relatives. I still haven't met most of them, and Eimear says your dad's brothers are even worse than he is."

"You'll be fine. Look, the most important thing is to keep it short. You have to thank Eimear, the priest, all the parents, and then you can just have a sort of blanket 'thank you' to everyone. Then you have to explain how you met – that's when you put in the first joke. And all of your jokes have to make you look bad and her look good."

"All right."

"It's up to you whether you want to thank the hotel people – you probably should, because the speeches come fairly early. It's not a good idea to thank anyone else apart from immediate family, because if you do someone will be left out, and that's how family feuds start. Oh, and you have to thank our gran, because she's old and it might be her last wedding."

Chris nodded. "Fine."

"Who's your best man again?"

"You know Mark?"

"Okay, he's all right. They'll like him. Just make sure he tones down the language and keeps it clean. No jokes about nuns in the bath or anything like that."

By now we had reached the shop and were standing outside it. "So," Chris said, "do you think I'm doing the right thing?"

"Sure. I mean, you love her, don't you?"

"Yeah."

"When the day comes, try and sound a *little* more enthusiastic."

He laughed. "You are something else, you know that? I can remember you when you were only fourteen. How did you get to be grown up so fast?"

"Hardship," I said. "Listen, I know that Eimear and I don't always get on, but she is still my sister. If I thought you shouldn't marry her, I'd tell you."

Chris nodded, and went into the shop. On the way back, I said, "Can I tell you something? In confidence?"

"Sure."

"I forgot to organise the band."

"Ah. I had a feeling about that."

"But I'm doing it now. So will you tell Eimear that I was telling you about the two different bands? Just make it seem like I've got everything under control. I mean, it's her fault anyway, she gave me way too many things to do."

"You'd better not have forgotten anything else," he said. "Or she'll tear strips off you."

"I know . . . If I ever get married, I'll make *her* organise it."

"Actually, the only thing she's really worried about is the bridesmaids' dresses. And that's only because Claire had to send her measurements up from Cork. So I reckon you'll live to see the week after."

"I only hope I can get the day off on Saturday."

He raised his eyes. "Jesus, is nothing *ever* easy with you?"

"Not lately."

* * *

Tony was in the kitchen with the others when we got back. Ciarán was giving him dangerous looks, but I guessed that Ciarán hadn't said anything, because everyone else seemed friendly enough to Tony.

We decided to go for a walk. As soon as we were outside, Tony said, "I'm sorry about what I said last night."

"Me too."

"I forgot how much pressure you were under. I only had the gig to worry about. You have that and the wedding *and* work."

"I'm sorry I hit you," I said. To myself I added, 'but you deserved it.'

"I deserved it," he said. Either he was reading my mind, or we both knew it was true.

"So where do we stand?" Tony asked.

"I don't know . . . To be honest, maybe we should just cool it off for a while. At least until after the wedding."

"Do you mean the working relationship, or the other one?"

"The other one. Look, I *have* been under a lot of pressure lately, and to be honest I don't need the hassle. And after last night, well, I don't know whether I want to go out with someone who can just snap like that."

Tony started to speak, then hesitated. After a couple of seconds, he said, "Okay. Whatever you want."

I smiled. "I promise that I won't leave you hanging on for a year and a half."

"That's a relief. I'd be middle-aged by then . . . But listen, I have to tell you what happened after you left."

"What?"

"I went up to the manager and apologised. I asked him if I could go back on."

"Wow! And what did he say?"

"He told me I had ten minutes, and if they weren't rolling on the floor laughing by then, I could forget about it."

"So were they?"

"Not exactly, but they enjoyed it more than the first half. I was on for another half an hour. And he asked me to come back in a couple of weeks. I said I'd let him know . . . I have to think about the whole thing. I'm not sure I could go through all that again."

"You have to. That's the whole point. Besides, when they're making the movie version of your life, you don't want it to be all plain sailing."

Tony reached into his pocket and pulled out a wad of notes. "Here's your half from last night."

"Yes! I'm rich!"

"Tell us, how come you smell like popcorn?"

"Oh yeah. It's this perfume that Ciarán bought me from Italy. *I* think it smells like butter. He says that it's the big thing over there right now."

323

"What, they have popcorn-flavoured women in Italy now? Deadly! As soon as they have beer-flavoured women, I'm emigrating. Anyway, tell me what's been going on in work."

So I told him that whole story.

Talking to him like that – especially after the fight we'd had – I realised that I wasn't seeing him as potential boyfriend material any more. We walked around town for a couple of hours, discussing ideas for his act, and by the time I got home I knew that it was over. It was like the fight had shown me that my relationship with Tony wasn't supposed to go in a romantic direction. But I still liked him, and I wanted us to remain friends.

It was like we'd automatically started going out because that's just what people do when they like each other. Clearly, being a couple wasn't going to work, but that didn't mean we *didn't* like each other.

He didn't say it, but from the way Tony seemed to relax I got the feeling that he thought the same way.

It was nice to know someone who had the same interests as me, and who wasn't going to follow me around the way Dean had. It looked like – for the first time in the entire history of the world – a girl had told a man, "I think we should just be friends" and he actually understood what she meant.

* * *

I was starting to feel a little better about what had

happened in work. I mean, I'd been dreading the responsibility of managing the staff, and now that wasn't a problem any more. Even if things did get bad, now I'd have Joe and Ellen with me.

Things with Tony had reached a low point and managed to survive – that could only be good. And the fact that he came to the house to see me was a damn good sign that he cared. Plus, he had the guts to go back on stage the night before to face a hostile audience – and they liked him enough to ask him to come back. That meant my material *was* working.

Okay, so I'd almost screwed up with organising Eimear's band, but Ellen was going to let me know if Niall's friends could do it, so I'd probably survive that one, especially since I had Chris on my side.

And the wedding was only a week away. Whatever happened, in a week's time it would all be over one way or another . . .

But somewhere not too far away, a nice big piece of poo was heading fan-ward at an alarming rate.

Chapter Eighteen

Ellen phoned on Sunday afternoon. "Niall's friends will do the wedding," she said. "You're off the hook."

"Thank God! How much do they want?"

"A hundred and fifty."

"Okay, that's all right. But what sort of stuff do they do?"

"Well, they're trying to be the next Hothouse Flowers, but Niall says they know all the old ballads and everything. One of them used to be in a ceilidh band."

"Do they have a demo tape? I want to be able to give it to Eimear."

"Yeah, I've got one here. Listen . . ."

She played a few minutes of the tape into the phone. "What do you think?"

They sounded okay . . . It was a bit heavy on the drums, and the singer didn't seem to be sure whether he was supposed to be Sting or Bono, but it was a damn sight better than no band at all.

"They'll do. Thanks, El. You're a life-saver."

"I'll drop the tape in to Eimear's, if you like. Save you a trip."

* * *

On Monday morning, I phoned the hotel where Eimear's wedding reception was to be held. I told the receptionist that I was just checking that everything was still on, and she seemed a little annoyed at that, like I was insinuating that they had the capacity for making mistakes.

Bruce and Nora showed up at the café quite early, and Bruce was in a foul mood: there was something wrong with the server and he wasn't able to fix it. "Look at this!" he said to me.

I looked, but I didn't know what I was looking at. "What's the problem?"

"The fuckin' thing will connect, and the domain is up and everything, but I can't get the bastard firewall up. Every time I think it's up, everything else stops working."

"What's a firewall?"

"It stops other people coming in and messing around with the server."

"Well, there'll always be someone at the deli counter, so that's no problem."

He looked at me like he thought I was stupid. "I meant coming in over the Internet. You know, a hacker."

327

"Oh, right . . . What's this knobbly little thing here?" I asked, pointing to the screen.

"That's a camera. You can use it to do video conferencing."

"Wow! Like a video phone!?"

"Yeah. Look . . ." He moved the mouse around, and all of a sudden the two of us were on the screen. It was weird – you expect it to be a mirror, so that when you raise your right hand, the image's left hand moves, but it's the other way around.

"If I click *this*," Bruce said, "it records the video. So you can play it back later or send it to someone, or edit it. Or you can add captions, or add in extra bits. It's pretty cool."

"You could make a movie with it," I said.

"You could, but a video camera is way cheaper and much better quality. Anyway, I'd better get back to this."

"Okay, just one thing . . . My sister is getting married at the weekend. Would I be able to put the video onto the computer and make changes and add captions?"

"Well, yeah, but it takes a *lot* of time. You couldn't do it on this one, because it'll be in use most of the time."

He went back to sorting out his "bastard firewall" . . . He sat there for the best part of an hour, typing like mad, swearing to himself and turning the computer on and off every now and then.

Nora, for her part, was also busy: she was drinking coffee. Okay, so she was pretending that she was checking out the different types of coffee from the machines, but basically all she was doing was sitting back and relaxing.

She saw me looking at her, and said, "Haven't you got anything better to do than stare at me?"

"Nora, anything is better than staring at *you*."

From his little cubbyhole, Bruce gave a short, sharp laugh.

She ignored him. "What time are the help going to come for their uniforms?"

"I told them to get here around ten-thirty," I said. To myself, I said, the *help*? Who does she think she is?

"There's been a change of plan. Bernard wants to make it more casual. So all he wants is T-shirts with the logo on them. He says everyone can wear their jeans."

"I see. When exactly were you planning to tell me this? Before or after we went out and spent a fortune?"

"Before, obviously. I'm telling you now, aren't I?"

"Nora, we don't need everyone to come in just for T-shirts! I can get them done on my own. When did he decide this?"

"Last week sometime."

"Well, you could have bloody told me before I arranged for everyone to meet here! Donna said she'd have to get someone to mind the kids!" I gave her a filthy look. "I'll have to phone everyone and cancel. Joe was going to go home to Kilkenny yesterday, but he stayed up for this."

"That's hardly *my* responsibility! You're the one who hired them."

I reached for the phone, and paused. "What else have you not told me?"

She shrugged. "Nothing *you* should be concerned about."

"There'd better *not* be," I said.

So one by one I phoned around. I was lucky, and most of them were in, but Donna's babysitter said she'd already left. "She should be there any minute," I was told. I thanked her and hung up.

"Nice going," I said to Nora. "Now I can see why Parker picked you – it's because you're so efficient."

"I don't want to have to talk to him about you again," Nora said. "You'd better not be so insubordinate when the café opens."

Bruce looked up. "Nora, you're a bitch. You know that? A complete bitch."

I laughed. Bruce was the only one who could get away with something like that, because Parker needed him more than he needed her.

Nora said nothing. She just got to her feet and stormed out of the café.

Bruce turned to me. "God, I hate that cow. You know what she's done so far? Nothing. Apart from complaining to Parker about everything that *we* do."

"Is there something going on between the two of them?" I asked.

"I don't know. Probably. Personally, I wouldn't

touch her without gloves on." He turned back to the computer and resumed pounding away at the keyboard.

"That's funny," I said. "Because I was sure the two of you got together the first weekend you were here."

The keyboard-pounding stopped.

"That was a mistake," he said coldly. He swivelled around to face me again. "I'd appreciate it if you didn't tell anyone."

"Of course I won't," I said, making a mental note to tell Ellen.

He swivelled back. "Good."

"What's the story with the other computers?"

"They're coming this afternoon. I hope. They won't take long to set up."

"So we're almost ready, then?"

"Almost. Once I get this fucking firewall sorted, I'll be a lot happier."

I left him to it, and returned to the front of the café. We had the door open now, and occasionally people stuck their heads in right past the "Grand Opening Friday" sign and asked when we were opening – so much for the idea that computer people are vastly intelligent.

A few minutes later, Donna arrived. She seemed to be in a great mood – probably relieved to be rid of the kids for a couple of hours – and I felt rotten about bursting her bubble.

"It's okay," she said. "I'd rather have a T-shirt than a uniform anyway."

"So do you have to head back, or do you want to come with me and get the shirts done?"

"Ah, sure I'll come with you," she said. "It's like having a morning off. I'll give you a hand carrying them back."

As we walked, I told her that I wasn't going to be the manager.

"You're not going to tell me that the job's off or anything?"

"No, nothing like that. It's just that Parker decided to give the manager's job to Nora. She came in to design the shop."

"And what experience does she have?"

"None."

"Is she good-looking?"

"Well, I wouldn't have thought so. But maybe she is from someone else's point of view."

"She's going to be trouble," Donna said. "But I'm not worried. I can handle her."

"I'm not sure *I* can. I gave out to her this morning for not telling me that everything had changed about the uniforms, and I bet you anything you like she's moaning to Parker about it right now."

It took less than an hour to have the T-shirt place make up twenty shirts. I wasn't sure about the sizes, so I got half of them done in medium, a couple of smalls, and the rest large. It came to a fraction of the cost of proper uniforms.

When we got back to the café, Bernard Parker was

there waiting for me. He didn't look happy. "Andi . . . I want a word with you."

This is it, I said to myself. I'm going to be fired.

But I was wrong. Not by much, though . . . He told me that the next time Nora had any sort of complaint about me, I'd be let go.

I was getting so tired of saying "it's not fair" that I didn't even bother. I was just going to have to accept things as they were.

"So are we clear?" Parker asked.

I nodded. "Yes."

"Good. Now, we're going to open on Friday morning, so I want you to have all the staff in here on Thursday afternoon. We're going to run through everything. We'll also have some people in pretending to be customers, as a sort of dry run."

From the look on his face, the pressure was getting to him.

"Okay," I said. "Do you want me to get some of my friends to come in?"

He nodded. "The more the merrier. Hopefully we'll be able to catch any major problems then."

"There's something I wanted to ask you about."

Parker didn't look happy at all. "What is it?"

"I still don't have a contract, or anything like that. Not even a letter offering me a job. I've been working for you for four weeks now, and I haven't received a penny."

"I said that you'd be paid when the café opens, didn't I?"

"You did. But I want at least some form of assurance that you're not just going to let me go as if I never worked here."

His eyes went wide and he bared his teeth – for a second I thought that he was going to throttle me. "Damn it, Andi. I don't need this now!"

"So I should take it up with Nora, then?"

"Yes! Tell her I said to give you a letter saying you had a job. Sort it out between the two of you! God damn it, that's what you're here for!"

Cheerfully, I said, "You mean, that's what you led me to believe I was here for, until you changed your mind. Okay, I'll talk to Nora about it."

I left him fuming.

Nora was reluctant to even talk to me, but after she took a look at Bernard's face, she did everything I asked. Using Bruce's laptop computer, she typed out a letter not only telling me I had the job, but also thanking me for my work – which was listed in detail – over the past four weeks.

"How can I print this?" she snapped at Bruce.

"You can't, until the printers come this afternoon. Leave it with me, and I'll do it then."

Nora turned to me. "Are you happy enough with that?"

"Fine. Thanks."

She went outside for yet another cigarette break.

"How's the firewall?" I asked Bruce.

"Jesus, don't *you* start," he said.

"Look, you told me about it earlier when I didn't even ask. You can't blame me for asking now."

We glared at each other. The first few times I met him, I thought he was a prick. Now, though, I knew him a little better. He was still a prick, but he was becoming just as frustrated with the whole place as I was.

"It's almost done," he said. "I've been on to the company and they're sending me a patch."

"What's a patch?"

"A program that'll fix the problem. Satisfied?"

I shrugged. "I won't be satisfied until Nora's gone."

"I asked her earlier if something was going on between her and Parker. She said there wasn't, and I'm inclined to believe her. I mean, look at the state of him . . ."

I looked. Parker was sitting near the door, talking quietly into his mobile phone. He didn't look good. He was still immaculately dressed, but he looked incredibly pissed off and was rapidly losing his self-composure.

"This is his last chance," Bruce said.

"What do you mean?"

"He used to own a software company, but it all went wrong."

I pulled over a chair and sat down next to him. "How do you know about that?"

"I was supposed to go for an interview there last year, but the agency cancelled at the last minute, and said that it looked like the company was going under, so I shouldn't bother. The next thing I heard they'd been bought out and Parker was . . . how did they put it? 'Dismissed.' And apparently he was told that if he didn't leave, legal action would be taken. There was all sorts of talk going around about how he used to treat his staff."

"I'm not surprised, if he treated them anything like the way he treated me."

"Why? What happened to you?"

So I told him about how Parker had led me to believe that I'd be the shop's manager, and how I'd done all that work for him, until he decided to let me know that Nora had the job instead.

Bruce shook his head. "That's a bad sign, Andi . . . I wouldn't stay here if I was you."

"I don't intend to," I said. "I'm going to give it a couple of weeks and then leave. Once I have my letter signed, I'll be a lot happier."

"You know, we could fix everything with that letter," Bruce said. "All we have to do is make some changes to it before he signs it."

This was an intriguing idea. "Like what?"

"Well, we could change it so that it says you're being offered the manager's position."

"No, he'll read it before he signs it."

"Not if we have two versions. The first one just as it is now, only with a typo in there. He'll read over it, and point out the typo. Then we pretend to fix it, and give him the altered version. He'll probably just check for the typo and sign it without reading the rest."

I had to admit, it was a very tempting idea. But that wasn't my sort of thing. Then again, Parker had tricked me. Maybe it was only fair that I tricked him back.

In the end, I was too scared to try it. When the printers arrived, Bruce printed out a copy of the letter, Parker signed it, and that was that.

* * *

When I got home on Tuesday evening, my oldest brother Roddy, his wife Gráinne, and their daughter Claire were in the kitchen with my parents and my grandmother.

Roddy jumped out of his chair when he saw me, and gave me a big hug. Then he stepped back and looked me up and down. "Look at you! God, you've changed!"

"*I've* changed? Listen to your voice! You've turned into a right bog-man! I didn't know you were here, because I didn't see your tractor outside."

I hadn't seen him in about a year, though I did talk to him every few months on the phone. Roddy was what Mam called 'the lucky one'. Apparently when he was a teenager he was always getting into trouble, but he'd managed to sort himself out. He and Gráinne had got married when they were twenty, and Claire was born less than a year later. I was always suspicious of that, but either they'd lied to me about Claire's date of birth, or she genuinely *was* a honeymoon baby.

Claire was fifteen now, and she reminded me a lot of myself when I was that age, though I had to admit she was better-looking than I ever was. I put that down to her mother's side of the family, even though Claire and Gráinne didn't look that much alike. What she saw in Roddy, who – to me anyway – looked very ordinary, I could never tell.

Gran creaked herself out of her chair. "You sit here, Andi, pet . . . You've had a hard day at work."

Dad grinned and winked at me. "Here we go. No one's paying her any attention so she has to fight for it."

Gran made a face at Dad, and got even more attention.

"So how's work, Andi?" Gráinne said. "Your mam's been telling us all about it."

"It's okay," I lied. "Though to be honest, the owner is turning out to be a bit of a . . . Gran, you'd better cover your ears. You too Claire. And Mam."

"We get the picture," Mam said.

"So I don't know how long I'll be able to stick working with him. How are *you*, anyway?"

After much talk along the lines of how everyone was doing, Mam told me to take Claire up to the bedroom and get her settled in.

"It'll be great having someone here again," I said as I hauled Claire's bags up the stairs. "Eimear's stayed over a couple of times, but it's not the same."

I used my elbow to open the door to the room. "That's your bed there on the right. If you're going to be sneaking out in the middle of the night to see some youngfella, the window rattles, so be careful."

I dumped her bags on her bed, and opened the wardrobe. "I've cleared out a space for you. It was mostly a load of Eimear's old things, but they'll have fallen to dust before they come back into fashion."

I sat down on my bed and pulled off my shoes. "God, that's better! Those bloody things are murder. I barely got a chance to sit down all day. And it's probably going to be worse when the café actually opens."

Claire opened one of her bags and started taking things out.

"Eimear was saying something about staying here on Friday night, so she can leave from here before the wedding. I suppose that means one of us will have to sleep on the camp bed . . ."

Claire nodded.

"Of course, the last person to sleep in that bed was murdered. You don't mind, do you?"

She looked up. "What?"

"Ah, you *can* talk!"

"Don't fucking start with me, Andi," she said, looking away.

"Now what have I done? Jesus, Claire, I haven't seen you in over a year! What have I done to deserve this?"

She sighed. "It's not you . . . not really." She cleared some space on the bed and stretched out. "Mam and Dad were on at me the whole way up in the car. 'Andi's done this, Andi's done that, why can't you be more like her? When she was your age . . . ' All that crap."

"I didn't know. Sorry."

"It's because you're his baby sister, that's why he does it. He probably still thinks you're only seven, or something."

"So how come they're giving you a hard time about it *now*?"

She let out an exasperated sigh. "They caught me smoking a while back, and decided I'd fallen in with a bad crowd."

"Is that all?"

"As far as *they* know. The thing is, one of the girls in school got pregnant a few months ago, and when they heard about that they went mad. The way they were going on you'd think that the school was a brothel or something."

"In *my* school, if a girl wasn't pregnant by the time she was fifteen everyone thought she was a snob."

Claire laughed, and for a second I saw the little girl she used to be. She rolled onto her side and propped her head up on her hand. "Dad was a bit upset about this lad you're seeing. He kept saying that he was too old for you."

"He's twenty-nine," I said. "Mam kept telling me the same thing. It's funny, but maybe when someone becomes a parent they automatically start disapproving of things. Though at the moment me and Tony are on a sort of break."

"Will you get back together?"

I paused. "Probably not."

"And is he really a comedian?"

"Yeah . . . He's only starting out, though. I've been coming up with some of his routines for him, actually."

Claire demanded to hear some, so I spent the next hour using her as a test audience. It was the first time I'd performed in front of someone.

* * *

By the time Mam finally called us down for tea, Claire was in a much better mood.

We all crowded around the table: me, Mam, Dad, Gran, Roddy, Gráinne and Claire. Seven people, and about eighteen different conversations all happening at the same time . . .

"So he says to me, 'John, if I ever get like that, I want you to shoot me' . . ."

"You should of seen the *state* of her . . ."

"When I was your age . . ."

"So it passed all the tests, except the clutch was sticking a bit. So I'll have to bring it back in . . ."

"If you hold the icing bag like *this*, and then squeeze it from the top . . ."

"I didn't check. I mean, you don't, do you? I just put it in and pressed the play button . . ."

"I never understood that. Why *can't* they just print more money?"

"So he comes in from the right, lashes the ball in, and, bam! Just *clips* the post!"

"Seventeen pounds fifty, and then on the way home I saw it for half that . . ."

"Hang on, wasn't she the one who tried to kill him last week?"

"And I said to her, 'Look, if it wasn't rewound when I got it home, and I had to do it myself, why are you charging *me* because I didn't rewind it?' She said that they had to charge everyone if the tapes aren't rewound, but they don't rewind them themselves."

It was the best of times . . .

* * *

. . . but the worst of times were on the way.

* * *

The next morning, Eimear called into the café so that we could go and inspect her wedding cake. She marched in, found me, and dragged me out after her, all without noticing that it wasn't a pound shop any more.

"We have to go to Mrs Murphy's and get the dresses after this," she said as she strode through the streets like she was the only person on earth who had anything important to do. "Audrey and Claire will meet us at the house and we'll walk over."

"Did Ellen give you the tape?"

"Yeah, we've booked them. No thanks to *you*," she added.

"What do you mean by that?"

"This is a bit late in the day for organising a band. You're bloody lucky I don't murder you!"

"So that's all the thanks I get! I had to listen to fifteen crappy bands just to find one good enough!"

She slowed down. "Fifteen?"

"Yes," I lied. "And to be honest, by the end of it I was ready to just give up and forget the whole thing. You *had* to have a band, didn't you? You couldn't have just got a DJ like normal people."

"That's bollocks. Everyone has a band at their wedding."

"Well, if they do, I bet most of them find the band for themselves, and don't have everyone else worrying themselves sick about it."

"All right. I'm sorry."

I tried hard not to smile. This was working a lot better than I'd expected.

"What about everything else?" she asked.

"Well, the hen party's tonight, like you wanted. I was going to book a nightclub, but since it's the middle of the week, there's no point. All the good clubs will be empty, so we can take our pick. I don't know what we're going to do with Claire, though. She might be all right in the pub, but bringing her to a nightclub is taking a big chance."

"Why does she have to come at all?"

"How would you like to be the only one left out? No, she has to come. Actually, the real worry is that Mam and Gran might invite themselves along."

"I've already taken care of that," Eimear said with a smug smile. "Mam and Dad are going out to dinner tonight with Chris's parents. I've told Mam that she can bring Gran as well."

"Nice one! You're paying for it?"

"Yeah."

We reached the cake shop. The woman behind the counter was serving someone else.

"What about the Mass book?" Eimear asked.

"It's more or less done. All it needs is for you to give it the once-over. Tony gave me a hand with it. I left one back at the café. Mark anything you want changed and get it back to me before Friday morning, then I'll get the rest of them done. It's a hundred copies you want, yeah?"

She nodded. "That should be enough . . . Hold on, what do you mean you left it in a café?"

"Not *a* café . . . *the* café."

She still didn't understand.

"Look, remember ten minutes ago when you collected me? Didn't you notice anything different about the shop?"

Eimear frowned. "Oh yeah. Right."

"It's not a shop any more. It's an Internet café. That's what I've spent the past month doing: I organised the whole place and set everything up." That last bit was an exaggeration, but she didn't need to know that. "Of course, that was on top of all the things *you* made me do."

This was lost on her, because the woman behind the counter chose that moment to pay attention to us.

"Hold on a second, Ms Quinn. It's in the back. I'll just get it for you."

We waited . . . The seconds dragged on, and I was half afraid that Eimear was going to have a nervous breakdown.

Then the woman returned, carrying the cake. She placed it on the counter in front of Eimear. "What do you think?"

Eimear swallowed hard, then sniffed and dabbed her eyes. "It's beautiful!" she whispered. "Oh my God, I'm getting married!"

The woman looked at me. "We get a lot of that in here."

* * *

After we paid and arranged for the cake to delivered to the hotel, Eimear and I left the shop and stopped outside.

"So are you happy now?" I asked.

She nodded. "Yeah . . . Look, sorry I was being so hard on you."

"Forget it," I said, by which I meant, don't *ever* forget it; you owe me for all this. "Come on, let's go and meet Claire and Audrey."

Audrey was Eimear's current best friend. Eimear went through best friends like a bus went through passengers. Her original plan – made over a year earlier – was that Denise and Lorna would be her bridesmaids, while I was to be an innocent bystander. However,

Mam had done her "not letting go of the argument" trick, and Eimear finally agreed to let me be a third bridesmaid. I hadn't wanted to be one, but Mam insisted that I did.

Denise was dropped from the playlist with only seven months to go – there was some fight about something someone might have said, or maybe it was about something that someone *thought* someone might have said – and she was replaced with Audrey. Lorna was then dropped at a mere four weeks, and replaced with Claire.

I didn't know Audrey all that well – she worked in the same factory as Eimear, but I'd only met her a few times. She seemed nice enough, though when she had a few drinks she got a bit giggly and after a couple of hours you just wanted to punch her face in.

Mrs Murphy, the woman who was making the bridesmaids' dresses, lived only a few streets away from my house. She was well-known in the area for her skill with the sewing machine, and it had become a tradition that every bride-to-be in the area would go to her. She was so busy that even though Eimear had booked nearly a year in advance, it was a close thing. Mrs Murphy didn't charge too much, but somehow it had also become a tradition that she was invited to the wedding itself, and bought a present.

We picked Claire and Audrey up at our house, and walked over. Claire didn't look happy.

"What's the matter?"

"I went out earlier, and when I came back Dad and Granny were fighting about me."

It took me a second to remember that when Claire said "Granny" she was referring to *her* grandmother – my mother, in other words – and not my grandmother.

"What were they saying?"

"Oh, I don't know. Something about me not being looked after properly, that sort of thing. They stopped when I came in, and they refused to talk any more about it."

"Well, I wouldn't worry," I said. "Mam's very fond of you. Maybe she was telling Roddy to stop comparing you with me."

"I hope it *was* something like that, because I've never even heard Granny shouting before."

I laughed. "Really? What, in all the years before you moved to Cork, you never heard her shouting? God, you were lucky! Sometimes I think that all she does is shout, iron and make chips."

We both laughed, and Eimear turned around and roared at us: "Hurry up you two! God, look at the state of you dawdling along and making a holy show of yourselves."

"Yeah, yeah, yeah," I said. "You should have seen her earlier, Audrey! Crying her eyes out over the cake, she was!"

Somehow, Eimear managed to glare at me even though I was behind her.

* * *

The bridesmaids' dresses were fairly simple, off-the-shoulder, fake satin, lavender with tiny red bows on the sleeves and the waist. Mrs Murphy had done a superb job, especially considering that Claire had sent her measurements up from Cork. When we tried them on, Eimear fussed and moaned and made us stand in certain ways – "Put your right arm up. No, your other right arm. Look, do this. Okay, now stand there and do *this*. No! Look! Watch me! It's on crooked, Audrey. Yes, it is. Yes, it *is* . . . Here, hold this . . . That's it. Now, walk this way. Yeah, very funny, Andi . . ."

Eventually I'd had enough. "I've got to get back to the café. What time is the rehearsal tomorrow?"

"Seven," Eimear said.

"Fine. I won't be able to stay around afterwards, though. Tony's on at nine."

"We should all go with you to see him," Claire said.

"Sure, if you like. And if you're let."

We paid Mrs Murphy, pleaded with her to come to the wedding even though we didn't want her to, then Audrey and Claire were put in charge of ferrying the dresses back home, while Eimear and I went back to the café.

I dashed in and found the prototype of the Mass book. "Everything should be here as you wanted, but if there are any changes let me know as soon as possible."

"Okay . . ." She flicked through it. "Chris said that when one of his friends got married, the priest just ignored their Mass book and did his own thing.

Everyone spent the entire time going back and forth through the pages trying to find where they were, and when they said 'I do' most of the relatives missed it."

"Well, that won't happen to us. After all the work I put into this, it had *better* be used."

* * *

In the café, all of the computers had been taken out of their boxes and set up, but they weren't all working yet: Bruce's estimate of an hour had turned out to be a lot more than that.

He was going from machine to machine, typing in stuff and swearing.

"Can I do anything to help?"

"You can get out of my way," he said.

"No, but . . ."

"Look, Andi, stop talking to me. I'm far too busy here."

"Okay then."

He whirled around: "Jesus *Christ*! I said *shut up*! Can't you get the hint? What does it take? Do you want me to tattoo it on your forehead, or something?" He turned back to his computers, muttering under his breath.

"I was only trying to help," I said.

Bruce paused. "Don't make me turn around, Andi. Don't. One more fucking *word* . . ."

From behind me, a man's voice said, "Bruce . . ."

We both turned around. Joe was standing behind me, staring at him.

Bruce looked relieved that it was only him. "Aw, just fuck off, Joe. Jesus, what does it take to get some work done around here?"

"Bruce, if you ever speak to Andi like that again, I'll break every bone in your body."

I looked from one to the other. Bruce looked manic, ready to snap completely. Joe stood solid, not even blinking, but his face showed an emotion I'd never seen on him before: pure, cold rage.

After what seemed like a year, Bruce's composure sagged, and he turned away again.

Joe put his arm around my shoulders, and brought me to the front of the café. "Are you okay?"

I shook my head.

"He's just under a lot of pressure right now," Joe said. "Don't take it personally. He'll apologise later."

I looked at my hands: they were shaking. "How . . . ?" I could barely get the words out. "How can you defend him like that? After what you just said?"

"When someone gets like that, the only way to get through to them is to be as mad as they are."

"He won't apologise, you know."

"He *will*."

"Will you really break every bone in his body?" I asked.

Joe smiled. "God no. He'd flatten me if it came to a fight. But his sort never fight. They just shout and whine and bitch about things. They can't cope if someone stands up to them like that."

I smiled back at him. "Thanks."

He just nodded. Back to being good old Silent Joe.

"So, how come you're here today? I thought you were going to go back home on Monday."

"There was no point. I'd only have to come back tomorrow."

"Are you staying in Ellen's?"

"Yeah."

"What about Niall?"

"He's there too, most of the time."

"Are you going to get your own place, then?"

"When Niall moves out, I'll get his flat."

That perked me up. "What? He's going to move in with Ellen?"

Joe nodded.

"When?"

"I'm not sure. Soon. They don't know themselves that it's going to happen, but it will."

"Well, how do *you* know?" I asked.

But Joe didn't answer me. He just smiled.

* * *

Bruce didn't really speak to anyone for the rest of the day. That suited me fine, because I had nothing to say to him anyway. He did look over in my direction from time to time, so I guessed that meant he was feeling guilty.

351

By half-past-four, everything was working perfectly. We could access the Internet from every computer in the place. Joe showed me how to go searching for stuff, and I was amazed at what I found.

"Most of the Internet is crap," Joe said, "but there is some good stuff out there, if you know how to find it."

By five o'clock, nothing at all was working.

And by half-past-five, it was fine again. By the time I left at six, it had stopped and started more than a dozen times.

Bruce was almost in tears. He was running back and forth, swearing and praying at the same time, going from a pure high when it was working to the depths of despair whenever it locked up again.

Joe left at the same time as me.

"He'll be happy now," I said. "It'll work fine for the rest of the night."

Joe raised an eyebrow. "How are you so sure?"

"Because maybe *he* wasn't watching you, but I was. I saw you plugging and unplugging that cable."

Again, his only answer was a smile.

I leaned forward and kissed him on the cheek. "Thank you."

Chapter Nineteen

The hen party is a tradition that goes back, oh, I don't know. Ages, probably.

In Dublin, it is part of the tradition that the bride-to-be is bedecked in strange attire, for comical effect: the most important item she should have is the "L"-plate, signifying that she's only a beginner. Other items include schoolgirl dresses, giant condoms, inflatable sheep, inflatable – and fellatible – men, anything that can be tied to a string and hung around the neck, and so on.

Eimear was having none of it. This was going to be a fairly quiet night, just a few friends out for a drink, maybe a nightclub afterwards, but nothing too wild. Eimear had made all this very clear to me. I was to be the responsible one, and make sure that everything ran smoothly.

So when Ellen arrived at our house to get ready, she and I had a disagreement over whether the stripper should be a caveman or a cowboy.

Claire – who by parental consent following a big row was allowed to come to the pub with us – maintained that the stripper should be a member of the Gardaí.

Claire's mother, Gráinne, thought that we were being needlessly childish, and that the stripper should be a priest.

My mother overheard all this and warned me that if anything happened to Eimear, I'd be the one who paid the price. And besides, the stripper should be a construction worker.

* * *

By the time we got to the pub, Eimear was already pissed. There was about fifteen other girls there, all cackling like idiots and making lewd suggestions to the lounge boy.

We forced everyone to bunch up and squeezed in beside them.

"I'll get them in for us," I said, calling the lounge boy over. "What'll you have, El?"

"A pint of Carlsberg."

"I'll have the same," I told the lounge boy. "Gráinne?"

"Smithwicks."

"Claire?"

Claire looked at her mother, who simply shrugged.

"A screwdriver," Claire said.

Gráinne gave her a look.

"What? I've always wanted to try one."

"You'll regret it in the morning," her mother said.

"I'm willing to take that chance, Mam."

I ordered a few more drinks for those still sober enough to let me know what they wanted, and it wasn't long before Eimear was drunk enough that she began telling me that I was the best sister anyone could ever ask for, and she didn't care what anyone said, I was her sister and that was that.

"Thanks," I said. "You're not the worst yourself."

There was an awkward moment when John's girlfriend Betty arrived. I hadn't actually been sure whether or not I should invite her, so I did anyway. Eimear was delighted to see her, she drunkenly announced, and that it was great that Betty was pregnant and going to give her *another* niece.

"Well, it might be a boy," Betty said.

"That's even better!" Eimear said. The way she went on, anyone would think that John and Betty were having their baby as their wedding present for her.

At about nine, Gráinne told Claire that it was high time she went home.

She told her the same thing at half-past nine, and at ten. By half-past ten, Gráinne was telling Claire that there was no way she was to leave without her.

Around that time, someone – it might have been Ellen, but I wasn't sure – called out, "Hey, Andi! Tell us a joke!"

I was just about sober enough to remember some of

the routines I'd written for Tony. I started off with the "Ten Commandos" routine, and went on from there.

To say it was successful would be an understatement: okay, so they were all drunk and most of them were people I knew, but even so, they laughed like a whole network of drains.

There was even an unscheduled interval, when Audrey had to be brought off to the Ladies because she'd been laughing so hard she wet herself.

Even the stripper – who had come dressed as a barman and surprised the hell out of us – waited until I was finished before he did his thing.

At closing time, everyone wanted to go off to a nightclub, but I declined. "I've got to get up in the morning!" I said.

"Aw, come on!" Ellen said.

"Yeah," Eimear said. "Don't be such a wet fuckin' blanket, Andi."

I looked at Claire, who seemed a little paler and a lot more barfy than usual. "No, you lot go on. I'll bring Claire home."

Gráinne decided she was going to bale out too. We got in at about half-past midnight. Mam and Roddy were still up.

"What time do we call this?" I asked.

"Did you have a good time, then?" Roddy asked, looking a little the worse for wear himself: he and Ciarán had planned to go out "for a game of pool".

Gráinne and I were holding up Claire between us.

"We did," I said. "The rest of them are gone off to a club."

Roddy got to his feet and examined Claire. "You didn't let her drink, did you?"

Gráinne shrugged. "I might have. Yes. A bit. She'll be all right."

He filled a pint glass with water, and handed it to Claire. "Drink this. All of it."

"This is the blood of the everlasting Christ," I said, giggling.

That made Claire laugh, just as she had the glass to her mouth. Water went everywhere.

Mam declared that we were all a bunch of messers, and ordered us to go to bed.

* * *

I woke up with what I thought was the world's worst hangover, until I saw Claire. She looked like a special effect: green skin, red eyes and lank hair.

I hauled myself out of bed, stood up too fast, and sat down again.

I spent the best part of an hour getting myself ready to go to work. A large chunk of that time was used up waiting for Roddy to get out of the shower.

Bruce was in the café when I finally arrived, but he didn't say hello. Nora was there too, poking around inside one of the coffee machines.

"What's the plan for today?" I asked.

"We've got the test run this afternoon. Everyone will

be here. Bernard's invited some media people over to see how it all works."

"And is the system up and running?"

She nodded. "Bruce says it's working fine."

There was something different about Nora, but I couldn't quite put my finger on it. "So how's the work schedule going?"

"It's okay . . . We'll probably have to make changes as we go along, but it's fine for the moment."

"So, who's in tomorrow?"

"You, me, Joe and Donna in the morning. Ellen, Seán and Carol are on lates."

"Okay . . . What about the food and everything?"

"It's coming in this afternoon. Though it'll usually come in at about half eight in the mornings."

It finally clicked with me what was different about her. "You've taken out most of your piercings!"

"Bernard told me to. He said that they looked unhygienic."

Without its piercings, Nora's face looked pale and bland, but I decided not to mention that to her because she looked upset enough as it was.

Nora went back to examining the coffee machine, so I sat down at one of the computers and logged on to the Internet. It was actually quite addictive, searching for things, though it was harder than I'd expected to find anything specific. It seemed that no matter what I searched for, at least half of the websites listed were pornographic.

Bruce came over and stood just behind me. "Look, sorry about yesterday."

I shrugged. "I know you were under pressure, but you didn't have to snap like that."

"I know. It won't happen again."

"Good . . . Now, tell me something about this . . ."

"What?"

"If I tell it that I want to search for something, will the computer remember what I looked for?"

"Well, no. It won't remember what sites you searched for, but if you actually *go* to those sites, they're logged. Why?"

"Just wondering. And if I wanted to do my own website, how would I do it?"

Bruce explained the process at length. I didn't understand most of it, but I was getting there. I figured that if I wasn't going to last long in the place, the least I could do was come away with a better understanding of computers.

* * *

At two in the afternoon, all the staff were gathered to learn how everything was going to work. Bernard Parker was there too, standing in the background.

Bruce explained the technical aspects of the Internet, which was completely pointless since most of us wouldn't get much further than wiping down tables.

Nora went through the staff rotas, and answered about a million questions about days off, sick days, swapping shifts, working weekends, extra hours, holidays, and so on.

It got a bit awkward when Donna said that she'd prefer to work a few hours in the morning, and a few in the evening. Plus, she'd be happy to work most weekends if it meant she'd be guaranteed afternoons off so she could collect the kids from school. That sparked a whole new round of questions.

In the end, a few changes were made to the schedule, and everyone agreed that for the first few weeks at least we'd give it a go and see what happened.

Nora finished off by telling us her fairly simple rules for the staff: "Never leave anyone waiting. As soon as a customer gets up, their table should be cleared and wiped. Any spills should be cleaned immediately. Always wear the disposable gloves when you're handling the food, and wash your hands every time you come back to the counter. If you find yourself with nothing to do, look busy. Everyone has to do their share of making the food and serving the customers . . ."

After that was done, the official testing of the system began. Basically, this involved everyone present playing on the Internet for an hour. Bruce went back and forth, sorting out little problems and answering questions like, "It says I need a plug-in. What's a plug-in?" and "It's warning me about security or something".

Ellen had a great time looking for photos of Tobey Maguire, and somehow managed to get her computer to freeze. Bruce came over and restarted it. A couple of minutes later it was locked up again.

"Were you on the same website?" he asked.

"Yeah."

"That could be it, then. There are some sites out there that just cause problems. It happens."

Donna called him over. "Bruce . . . how do I send an e-mail? I want to send one to my cousin."

"Well, you need an e-mail account."

"Oh. How do I get one?"

A few of us broke off early to help carry in the food for the deli counter. We hauled in containers of sliced tomatoes, potato salad, onions, ham, turkey, salami, corned beef, roast beef, chicken, peppers, various types of cheese, and sandwich fillers like tuna and sweetcorn, coleslaw and egg mayonnaise. There was also a couple of dozen bread rolls, about ten sliced pans, a huge jar of mayonnaise, an even larger tub of margarine, bottles of ketchup, brown sauce and mustard . . .

The cans for the Coke machine arrived at the same time, as did the bottled water, ice cream for the fridge, and the sachets of sugar, salt and pepper. There were croissants, Danish pastries, doughnuts, éclairs and caramel slices.

There was carrot cake and banana bread, crisps and Pringles, and oranges for the juice machine. There were three types of tea, eight types of coffee, and hot chocolate. There was crockery and cutlery, napkins, toothpicks, and a little jar for tips. The only thing we didn't have was milk.

Nora sent Ellen out to buy four litres of milk, then went through everything on her checklist, carefully noting down exactly what we'd received and how much of it. Then she went nuts because Joe was behind the counter making a sandwich.

"What the *fuck* do you think you're doing, Joe? The food isn't here for us! If you want a sandwich, you can pay for it like everyone else!"

"I'm timing myself," Joe said. "It'll be handy to know how long it takes."

Donna nudged me and whispered, "Nice save."

"Yeah, he's good at that."

Bernard Parker checked his watch, and said, "All right, everyone. The press people will be here shortly. I want to make sure that there's coffee and sandwiches for them."

So we began making sandwiches. Donna was incredible: she was working twice as fast as everyone else, and she was able to advise the rest of us at the same time. We had no idea about how much of anything to put on a sandwich or in a roll, so she started to come up with little rules, like three slices of tomato for a small roll, five for a large roll, and so on.

By the time the journalists were due to arrive, the tables were filled with refreshments and each of the computers was showing the café's logo. We were all in our T-shirts and standing ready to serve.

A bunch of people came in, and they were welcomed warmly and given the grand tour by Bernard, until he realised that they weren't journalists, just friends of the staff.

Then my mother turned up. I showed her around, but she didn't seem to realise that there was a difference between an Internet café and an ordinary café. I tried to get her interested in the computers, but they might as well have been light fittings for all she cared.

The first of the journalists arrived at about five-thirty, followed by a handful of others a few minutes later. They ignored everyone except Bernard, and asked him a lot of questions about his plans for the café: Was this only the start of a new empire for him? How, exactly, did he finance the whole operation? Did he have any problems getting backing after the failure of his last company? How long before he expected to make a profit? How long before he'd be able to pay off his debts?

Parker answered every question with an air of confidence I was sure he didn't feel.

After the questions, they hung around and ate our sandwiches and ignored the computers.

At about six, Mam told me that she was going, and I was to be home in half an hour, if I was going to make it to the wedding rehearsal in time.

* * *

Thankfully, we didn't have to dress up for the wedding rehearsal: it was bad enough with Eimear bossing everyone around and making sure we all knew exactly what we had to do and when. Chris stood where he was told with a bemused look on his face.

Since she had the only finished copy of the Mass book, Eimear stood behind everyone doing the readings and poked them in the arm if they made a mistake. She charged all over the place, and even the priest was jumping out of her way.

"I wouldn't want to be God if the weather turns out bad on Saturday," I whispered to Claire.

She laughed a little too loudly, and Eimear glared at her. "Get it out of your system now, Claire, because if you mess it up on Saturday you'll be very sorry."

I whispered, "Amen," and that set Claire off again.

Mam jabbed me in the back with her Bible, and said "Shhh!" so loud that everyone turned to look.

Finally, we were ready to run through everything. The priest skipped over the ordinary Mass bits, and did the marriage part. When it came to saying their vows, Eimear said "I do!" a little too soon, so they had to start over.

When it was all done, we gathered outside the church. "Right, lads," Chris said, slapping his hands together and rubbing them briskly. "Are you ready?"

Gran looked around. "Where's John? Did he not come?"

"No, Gran," Roddy said. "Betty wasn't feeling too good. She'll probably be okay for Saturday."

"She'd *better* be," Eimear said.

Chris looked at his watch, and turned to Roddy and

Ciarán. "Come on, lads . . . we're wasting serious drinking time."

It was Chris's stag party, and we decided that they didn't need to hang around for much longer. Eimear warned Chris not to come home too drunk, and he just looked at her, and said, "I promise I won't be any more drunk that you were last night – I mean, this morning – when you got home."

The lads went off, except for Dad who looked a little disappointed to be left behind.

There was some debate as to which pub was the best one to go to after a wedding rehearsal. Eimear wanted to go to her local, Audrey wanted to go to hers, Mam wanted to go home, Dad wanted to go to *his* local, as did Gráinne, Gran wanted to go with Eimear, and I announced that I wouldn't be joining them because I was going to see Tony at the comedy night.

As soon as Gráinne heard that, she changed her mind and wanted to come with me. So did Audrey and Claire.

Claire was told in no uncertain terms that she wasn't going to another pub, not after the previous night. She could go straight back to the house with her grandmother.

* * *

In the end, Eimear, Gráinne and Audrey came with me to see the comedy night.

Tony was waiting at the bar, so I told the others to find somewhere to sit and I'd join them shortly.

"Hi," Tony said. "I wasn't sure if you were going to make it."

"We're just finished the wedding rehearsal," I said, and pointed to the others. "That's Eimear – she's the one getting married, her friend Audrey, and Gráinne, my sister-in-law. Come on and I'll introduce you."

I dragged him over to the others. "This is the famous Tony," I said.

"How's it going?" he asked Gráinne. "Looking forward to getting married?"

She looked up at him. "You have the wrong woman here, Tony."

Eimear said, "I'm the one getting married. Gráinne's been married for fifteen years."

"Sixteen," Gráinne corrected.

Tony cringed. "Oh, sorry. I don't know what I'm saying. I always get like this before a gig, don't I, Andi?"

"He does."

"So what's everyone drinking?" Tony asked.

He had just enough time to come back from the bar with the drinks. "Okay . . . I'm on first. I've got about ten minutes."

I excused myself from the others and we went over to a fairly quiet spot.

"How've you been?" he asked.

"Okay. Busy, though. You?"

He shrugged. "Not bad. But . . . well, remember

what you said about us keeping our relationship on a professional level for a while?"

"I think I remember something about that."

"Well, you were right."

"Are you sure?"

"Yeah. I mean, I like you a lot, but the age difference is always going to be a problem. We'd be better off just being friends."

"I know. That's what I was thinking. Not about the age difference, I mean about being friends." I was silent for a few seconds, then said, "Tony, there will come a time when you and me are on the same show. You know that?"

"Yeah. I've thought about that."

"I'm going to go for it. I'm going to start making it happen. And if I'm doing that . . ."

He finished my sentence for me. "Then you can't be writing material for me at the same time. I've thought about *that* too. But still, give me a ring from time to time. Or maybe I'll see you at one of the festivals one day. Winning awards."

I smiled. "Maybe you will. Or maybe I'll see *you* winning the awards . . . Hey, guess what? I had my first public performance last night."

"Yeah? Where?"

"At Eimear's hen party. I was pretty drunk, but I think I remembered most of the routines without screwing them up. But don't worry, I didn't use any of your stuff, just my own."

"How did it go?"

"Great. It was a brilliant night. I didn't go on to the club afterwards, but Eimear did and she said they had a fantastic time."

"I meant, how did your performance go?"

"It wasn't bad . . . Claire was really impressed. But she's my niece, and she's only fifteen so she's easy to impress."

Tony glanced over at the barman, who gave him the nod.

"All right, I'm on in a minute."

"So what are you opening with?"

"Well, I was going to do some of your stuff, but . . . I don't know. Maybe it'll be for the best if I stick to my own."

I gave him a last hug. "Okay, then . . . I'll see you sometime, waiting in the wings."

He nodded. "And I'll see you up on stage, bringing down the house and giving it loads."

Chapter Twenty

I was in work at seven-thirty on Friday morning for the official opening of the café. I was the first one in, so I turned on all the computers and printers like Bruce had shown us, and I fired up the coffee machines. Donna and Joe arrived shortly before eight.

"So, who wants to serve the first customer?" I asked.

"You should," Donna said. "After all, if it wasn't for you, this place wouldn't be here."

We had to *wait* for our first customer; contrary to expectations, we weren't flooded with people.

A middle-aged man came in at about nine, and asked for a sandwich. "Do you have Sandwich Spread?" he asked.

"No, sorry," Donna said. "But we can make up anything you like."

"Thanks anyway." He left.

The first real customer was a girl who wanted to send an e-mail to a friend in America. Joe showed her what to do, and she happily sent the e-mail, and dawdled around on the web for a while.

Donna and I watched her in action. "Jaysus, she's a whizz on the keyboard," Donna said.

"Yeah . . . She looks like she knows more about it than we do."

"Are we supposed to charge them before or after?"

I shrugged. "I don't know. After I suppose. Nora would know, if she was here."

"You should phone her," Donna said.

"I will if there's an emergency, or something. Apart from a few minor questions like that, I don't know if we need her today. What do you think, Joe? Charge them before or after?"

"Before would be better," Joe said. "A lot of our business will be from regular customers, and we charge by the hour. If we get them to pay before, they'll stay the whole hour. Otherwise, they'll rush in once a day to check their e-mail, then argue that if they didn't stay for a whole hour, they shouldn't be charged for it."

By noon, we'd had about fifteen customers.

Donna looked at the deli counter. "God, it's painful to see all that food going to waste."

"I know what you mean," I said, munching on a slice of cucumber. "You know what we should do to get more people in here?"

"Have Niall walk up and down outside dressed as a robot?" Joe suggested.

I laughed so hard that bits of half-chewed cucumber

went everywhere. Donna didn't get it, so Joe had to explain.

When he was done, I said, "Hold on a minute, Joe . . . You *knew* that Niall was crap at mime and you still suggested him. Why did you do that?"

"Because he needed the exposure. How else was he going to find out he couldn't do it? Besides, he was single, and Ellen had just broken up with Robbie, and I had a feeling they might hit it off."

Again, he'd amazed me. "Well, you were right. Anyway, my idea was to bake bread. We could get one of those ovens, you know, where you buy the bread rolls already half-cooked. People love the smell of fresh bread."

"True," Donna said. "We did that in the last place I worked."

Eimear phoned shortly after that. "I've got the copies of the Mass book done," she said, "so you needn't worry about that. Listen, everyone keeps asking me about Tony. What'll I tell them?"

"The truth. That we're not going out any more."

"Okay . . . So who are you going to bring to the wedding, then?"

"No one. I've got enough to worry about as it is."

"Right. Well, I'll see you tonight, then? I suppose we're going to have to fight over who doesn't get the camp bed."

"I'll take it," I said. "You're going to need your sleep."

* * *

After lunch, it got a lot more busy. Bernard Parker came in, and saw the place buzzing. Donna, Joe and I were run off our feet, and Parker looked happy for the first time in weeks.

He came over to me. "Where's Nora?"

"She's hasn't shown up yet. I wasn't sure whether she said she'd be here or not."

"She *should* be here for the first day. I'll have to have a word with her." Parker looked around. "And Bruce's not here either?"

"He's been in and out. There haven't been any problems."

He nodded. "Okay. Well, it's looking good."

The phone rang, and I was nearest so I answered it. "Good afternoon, Brews and Browse . . . How can I help you?"

"Hi, I'm looking for Andi Quinn," a girl's voice said.

"Speaking."

"Andi . . . sorry, I didn't recognise you. This is Susan Perry."

"Oh, right. Gillian's friend. Hi, how's it going?"

"Okay. But listen, I've got the paper here, and there's an article about your café . . . You never said that the owner was Bernard Parker."

I instinctively glanced over at Bernard, who was poking around in the deli area. "Didn't I? Does it make a difference?"

"God, yeah . . . Andi, you wouldn't believe the shit that man put me through. And it was *nothing* compared to what he did to June Hogan. If I was you, I'd have nothing to do with him. Leave right now. Just walk away and forget you ever heard of him."

I laughed. "Why, is he the devil or something?"

She laughed too. "He's close enough. He's a complete user, Andi. You really don't want to be associated with him. He's dangerous."

"Oh, come on, Susan! It can't be all *that* bad!"

"It is . . . Look, you've worked with him for, what, a month?"

"Yeah, just over."

"What's the worst thing he's done in that time?"

I paused. I'd only met Susan once, and talked to her on the phone maybe three times. And now she wanted me to tell her stuff about my boss that should be private. "Nothing," I said. "He's all right."

Susan sighed. "Okay, if you say so. But don't forget that when the shit hits the fan, the shit is never distributed evenly."

"I'll remember that," I said. "I've no idea what you mean, but I'll remember it."

"Call me if you need me. You still have my number?"

"Yeah. Thanks for the warning anyway."

She said goodbye, and hung up.

Joe was passing me, and noticed the puzzled look on my face. "What's up?"

"Remember Gillian's friend Susan?"

"No, but then I don't remember Gillian either."

"Oh, right, you weren't there. Gillian worked in Gerry's shop in Clontarf. Her boyfriend works with this girl Susan, who I asked for advice on being the manager here. The odd thing is, she just phoned me out of the blue and said" – I lowered my voice so that Parker wouldn't overhear – "that I shouldn't have anything to do with a certain owner."

"Any particular reason?"

"She seems to think he's dangerous. She said he was a complete user."

"Well, he did deliberately mislead you about the manager's job."

"Yeah, but if Nora decides not to show up, I'm a dead cert for the job now."

"She's right, you know. He's dangerous."

I shrugged. "I think I can handle him."

Joe did his "silence" thing again.

"I *know* I can."

* * *

I was behind the deli counter when Parker came over to me at around three. Joe was using the Internet server to access the printer, and Donna was clearing off tables.

"How is everyone holding up?" Parker asked.

"Fine, so far. It's getting pretty busy, though. Did you manage to get in touch with Nora?"

"Yes. She's not coming back."

Hooray! I said to myself, and did my best to look disappointed. "Oh. Why not?"

"She's decided she won't drop out of college after all."

"So who gets the manager's job, then?"

"Donna. She's got the most experience."

"Okay . . . And where does that leave me?"

He smirked. "You can be the under-manager, for all I care. It's only a title, Andi. The work is more or less the same."

"But the pay isn't," I said.

"I'd appreciate *some* display of loyalty. I didn't think it was all about money for you."

I threw my cloth into the sink. "Look, the money shows how loyal *you* are to *us*. Besides, I've worked for you for over a month and still haven't received a penny. I think that shows loyalty on my part."

He sighed. "We're not going to have this argument forever, are we?"

"No, it'll stop when I get what I'm owed."

Parker turned his back on me and headed for the door. "I'll see you tomorrow, Andi."

"I won't *be* here tomorrow," I said. "My sister's getting married."

He stopped, and turned around slowly, and started back. "What?"

"I cleared it with Nora," I said.

"Well, with Nora gone we're a person down. You'll just have to miss the wedding."

I shook my head. "No, I won't."

"Of course you will," he said casually. "You won't have a job otherwise."

"You'd do that? You'd fire me just because it suits you?"

"Andi, what's the point of being the owner if you can't order people to do things they won't like?" Maybe he thought that was witty, or something. Maybe he though that I'd see his playful side. He was wrong: his smug grin was too much for me.

"Susan Perry was right about you."

Something in his manner changed. It was as though until then he'd seen me as an amusing diversion, someone he could push around just to see how much she would take. But now, he was about to find out that I was liable to start pushing back.

"*What* did you say?"

I'm going to the wedding so I'll be fired anyway, I said to myself. I might as well go for it. "I said that Susan Perry was right about you. She told me everything that happened between the two of you. And what happened with June Hogan. You're not a popular man, Mr Parker. Your enemies are talking to other people."

"You stupid little *bitch*!" Parker roared. "What the *fuck* do you know about that?"

Everyone in the place stopped what they were doing and stared at him.

When he noticed this, he regained his composure a little, and leaned over the counter, almost pushing his face into mine. "You listen to me, you filthy little *slag* . . . you are fired. I don't care how much work you've done for me, you can fuck off right now. And that goes for that whore of a friend of yours, Ellen, or whatever the bitch's name is."

If Parker had been around that night when Tony and I had the fight, he'd have known what was coming: I lashed out and punched him in the face.

Parker instinctively made a grab for me, and all of a sudden I was knocked to the floor. I looked up to see that Joe had grabbed Parker's wrists and pulled him forward so he was half-hanging over the glass of the counter.

"It won't take your weight," Joe said calmly. "Relax and I'll let you go. Otherwise, the glass will crack and rip your stomach apart."

Parker's look of anger suddenly turned to one of terror. Joe released his grip, and Parker dropped back to the floor.

Joe offered me his hand, and helped me to my feet.

"*You* can fuck off too," Parker said to him. "You're a friend of hers."

"I *am* her friend," Joe said.

"Then get the fuck out of my café right now, before I drag you out by your scrawney necks."

Joe stared at him. "I *am* Andi's friend."

"You already said that. What are you, thick as well?"

"And I *protect* my friends," Joe said.

Parker laughed. "Are you *threatening* me, boy? Come around to *this* side of the counter and show me what sort of a man you think you are."

Joe ignored him, moved to the Internet server and started typing rapidly.

"What are you doing?" Parker dashed forward and grabbed Joe's arm. Joe shrugged him off, and as Parker reached for him again, Joe stepped to one side.

"You're too late. It's out there now. Look." He moved the mouse and clicked on an icon.

Bernard Parker stared in horror as the computer played back the video of his entire tirade.

Joe turned up the volume on the speakers, and everyone in the place could clearly hear him saying, "You listen to me, you filthy little *slag*."

"I've just sent a copy of that to four of my friends, and asked them to pass it on to everyone they know. By this time tomorrow, it'll be all over the world."

Joe played the video again. "It's not bad quality at all, is it, Parker? There's no doubt that it's *you*. And look, you can even see the logo on Andi's T-shirt." Joe turned to me. "Andi, do you have Susan's e-mail address?"

Parker said nothing further. He turned and walked out of the café.

"Are you all right?" Joe asked. "I hope I didn't push you too hard."

I brushed myself down. "I'm okay. Thanks." I looked up at him. "The way you recorded that . . . was that even legal?"

"I don't know. I don't care. It's not like he can do anything about it now."

"So Susan *was* right," I said. "I should have listened to her . . . What do you think will happen to him now?"

Joe shrugged. "I don't know. You've got a good case against him if you want to bring charges of harassment."

Donna came up to the counter. "God, Andi . . . Are you okay?"

"I will be. Shit. I hope I haven't screwed things up for *you*."

"I'll be okay. It's just a job. Besides, things will go on here. Parker will probably sell the place to someone else. Do we know anyone with money?"

"*I* don't," I said.

"Yes, you do," Joe said. "Well, you know someone who knows someone. What was the name of the guy who used to own this place when it was a pound shop?"

"Gerry."

"Right. Ellen told me that his father bought him the pound shop. His dad is supposed to be really rich. This would be a damn good investment."

"Good idea . . . as usual. So, what do we do now?"

"We're fired," Joe said. "We might as well go home."

I looked at Donna. "I don't want to leave you on your own."

"I'll get rid of this lot and lock the place up until the late shift comes in."

"Except Ellen," Joe said. "We'd better let her know."

Donna went away to ask the customers to leave.

The shock was wearing off, and I was starting to shake.

Joe reached into the cooler and handed me a bottle of water.

"That'll be ninety-five pence, please," I said.

We both laughed.

Chapter Twenty-one

"I'll walk you home," Joe said.

"It's okay. You don't have to if you don't want to."

"I want to."

We walked in silence for a while.

Eventually, Joe asked, "What did Ellen say when you phoned her?"

"She went nuts. She says she's going to sue him for defamation of character."

"I don't think it's worth the trouble," Joe said.

"It's time," I said suddenly.

"Time for what?"

"The truth. You avoided it that time we spoke on the phone. What's the story with you and Dean?"

"Well, what do you know so far?"

"I asked Niall about you. I asked him why you hung around with Dean, when all he did was slag you. And Niall said that I should be asking why *Dean* hangs around with *you*. He said I should ask you what was going on, and that I'd probably be surprised at the answer."

"And what have you figured out for yourself?"

"You're not who you appear to be. I've known you for years, and it's only recently that I've seen what's beneath the surface."

"Which is?"

I laughed. "God, it's like getting blood out of a stone!"

"Go on."

"You stood up for me. Twice. Once with Bruce, and now with Parker. And you walked me home when Dean wouldn't. And you looked after Jimmy when he was pissed. And you told me that you don't even *like* Dean."

"Well, I'd never say that I can't stand him, but he's not one of my favourite people."

"So why do you bother with him?"

Joe shrugged. "I don't. Not now."

"And why's that?"

"Because I don't need him any more."

"I see . . . No, I don't. Why *did* you need him?"

"He kept me sane."

"What, all that slagging – and it wasn't just Dean: me and Ellen were as bad – that was supposed to keep you sane?"

"Yeah."

I shook my head. He really was incredibly hard to talk to sometimes. "I give up," I said. "I can't figure you out."

"Keep going," he said. "You're getting there."

"Yeah, but is it worth the effort?"

"It might be."

"At one stage I was starting to wonder if you fancied Ellen. That made sense then. Especially when you sort of disappeared after Niall came on the scene."

"That's a good theory," Joe said. "But it's wrong."

"And someone suggested that maybe you fancied *me*, and when Tony came along you gave up."

"Another good theory."

"So, if it's not that, then I don't know . . . And after seeing the look on your face when Bruce turned on me, I don't even know what to think. He was really scared of you. So was Parker."

"So was Dean."

I stopped. "What?"

"Dean was afraid of me. He's always been afraid of me."

"Then *why* was he hanging around with you? Why would he slag you if he was afraid of you? And what did he have to be afraid of?"

Joe sighed. "Look, I'm starving . . . Shite, we should have got something to eat at the café. Let's go somewhere and sit down, and I'll tell you everything."

* * *

All the good fast-food places were packed, so we had to make do with one of the lesser ones. Joe tucked into a cheeseburger and chips, and I opted for a chicken-burger.

As he ate, I watched him carefully. Not a move was wasted – this, I said to myself, is a man who thinks very carefully before he does *anything*.

When Joe finished his food, he sat back. "Ready?"

I nodded.

"I was twelve when I met Dean. He's a few months older than me. He had a gang he used to hang around with in Kilkenny – Ellen didn't know about them, so you can't tell her any of this. There were five of them, and they thought they were fairly tough, but they never really did anything other than make comments about girls going past, and occasionally they might nick something, like a magazine or sweets from the newsagents. They basically had nothing to do.

"I was small for my age. And a bit of a loner. Well, no, I was a *real* loner. They were forever teasing me, pushing me about, robbing my pocket money, throwing my schoolbooks into the mud, trying to jam sticks into the spokes of my bike, saying I was a girl, a sissy, a wimp, a pouf. That sort of thing. It didn't bother me too much at first: I just tried to avoid them, but they always seemed to find me, and things just got worse and worse. Once they even jumped on me and tore off all my clothes. I had to walk home in my underpants.

"And one day, after about two years, I just snapped. My dad had sent me to the shops, and Dean's gang stole my money." Joe looked away from me, and stared out the window. "I knew that if I went home and told my folks what had happened, the whole story would have come out. They would have gone around to Dean's house and demanded the money back, plus everything else he took from me. I also knew that if *that* happened, Dean would *never* leave me alone. He'd never grow out of it. So, well, I went crazy. I'd never been in a real fight before . . .

"I grabbed the nearest one by the neck and started punching him in the face. I just kept hitting him and hitting him. The others all scattered and ran."

I stared at him. "I'd no idea . . ."

He continued. "When he finally stopped screaming and starting sobbing, I dropped him. Then I went after the others. One by one I tracked them down. I beat the shit out of every one of them. Dean was the last. I couldn't find him anywhere, so I went to his house and waited across the road in the field. One of the other lads must have said something to his parents, because they phoned Dean's parents, and *they* called the police, who started searching the area. The police found me, and I said the first thing I thought of: I told them that I was with the others and that someone had attacked us, and we'd all run.

"They brought me over to Dean's house, and asked his parents to phone mine. It was only when I saw how distressed Dean's parents were that I realised what I'd done, and what I'd been planning to do." Joe turned away from the window and looked me right in the eye. "I was going to kill him. I don't mean that I was going to beat him up . . . When I'd finished with him, he would have been dead."

I swallowed. "Jesus . . ."

Joe reached out and put his hand on mine. "It wasn't that late in the evening, so my parents were still out. Ellen was staying with you that week, I think – she never knew anything about it. Dean's parents kept telling me that it was going to be all right, and that I could wait with them until my own parents came home. And that was when it hit me."

"What?"

"That they didn't *know* any of Dean's friends. And that he didn't actually *have* any real friends, just the gang. In a lot of ways, he was just like me. Except that he had Ellen, and you. Though of course at that time he wasn't in love with you. Anyway, Dean came home on his own, and almost shat himself when he saw me. But he's not entirely stupid – he immediately assumed that I'd come complaining to his folks, so he made a big show about him and me being friends, to give them the impression that anything I'd told them was just a story."

"I see," I said. "So that just made them believe *your* story?"

He nodded. "Right. His folks phoned the police and said he'd come home, and that he was fine. So they called off the search. I talked to Dean, and told him – in great detail – what I'd do to him and the others if they ever touched me again, or if they told the police who had beaten them. And after that, well, it was strange. The other members of the gang lost touch: I think they were ashamed. Not ashamed that they'd tormented someone younger and smaller for years, but ashamed that someone younger and smaller had managed to beat them."

"So you and Dean hung around with each other because despite your differences, you knew you had a lot in common?"

Joe suddenly laughed. "Not really. We hung around with each other because I wanted it that way. I was scared of losing control again, and I knew that if I ever felt like I was going to lose it, all I had to do was look at Dean, and remember how scared he was. And how close I had come to committing murder and throwing away the rest of my life."

* * *

Joe walked me the rest of the way home, and explained a bit more.

"I let Dean slag me because I had to convince myself that it didn't matter. Words are just words. Eventually, I think that we did become friends, of a sort. He was still a bit of a bully – well, you know that. He thinks that because his dad is rich he's better than everyone else. But he knew just how far he could push me. And because I was always there, he had a constant reminder of what he used to be like."

"I don't know what to think, Joe. It's like you're this whole other person I never knew."

"Everyone's like that, Andi. To some degree."

"I know, but with you . . ." I shook my head. "You've always been the quiet one. You rarely opened your mouth. You hardly ever touch a drink. A couple of weeks ago I realised I'd never even heard you laugh. You've never had a girlfriend that I know of . . . In fact, the only other person you've ever mentioned is Niall."

"His parents know my parents. I wouldn't say he's a friend, but I like him well enough."

We stopped outside my house. "Do you want to come in for a cup of tea or something?" I asked as I opened the door.

"Nah, I'm fine. I'm going over to Ellen's to pick up my stuff. I'm going to try and catch the early bus home."

"Okay . . . Look, phone me after the weekend, all right? You can come up and stay here for a few days, if you want. Once Roddy and the others go home."

He nodded. "Sure. Enjoy yourself tomorrow."

"I'll do my best . . . What are *you* going to do for the weekend?"

"Just crash at home. It'll be good to get back there and not have to worry about getting in Ellen's way."

"You're not going out with your mates, then?"

"No . . . but you probably guessed that."

"Joe, do you actually *have* any good friends?"

He nodded. "Yes. One."

I smiled. "It had better be me."

"It is . . . Okay, I'll see you soon, then . . ."

I could sense that there was something else he wanted to say. "What is it? Don't go all shy on me now."

"I've never told anyone the whole story before. Niall knows a bit of it, but not the whole thing. I just want to say thanks. For listening."

"You're welcome."

* * *

I decided not to tell anyone at home what had happened in work until after the wedding: they had enough to worry about as it was. Besides, I couldn't even think of *how* I was going to tell them. They'd all know in time, and then there would be serious repercussions.

Dad would go nuts, I knew that for certain. My brothers would want to go after Parker and tear him apart. My mother would insist on contacting a solicitor. Gran would almost certainly leave him out of her nightly prayers.

All that would come, but I wasn't ready to face it just yet.

Mam and Gráinne were in the kitchen when I walked in. Mam looked up in surprise. "You're home early."

"Yeah, I decided to take the weekend off."

She tutted. "It's well for some. You can give us a hand with this, then."

They were doing their best to sort out the seating arrangements for the meal. For the next hour, we argued over who was to be at the top table, who couldn't sit next to who because they'd fallen out, which people we didn't like and could lump together in the farthest corner, how we were going to squeeze in the extra people Eimear had invited since the last time she'd decided that we were at maximum.

When Claire came back, she was roped in too.

Dad and Roddy had been in the pub doing some emergency last-minute talking about football, and when they got in, they were also recruited.

At about seven, Mam ordered me and Claire to go to the chippy and return with food for the masses. By that stage, Eimear had arrived in a state of complete panic because her shoes weren't exactly the same colour as her dress, so Claire and I were only too pleased to get away.

Mam asked everyone what they wanted and carefully wrote it all down on a slip of paper, which I lost on the way to the chippy.

"Just get everyone chips," Claire said as we queued up. "How many of us are there?"

"Seven."

"Okay, so get four burgers and four fillets of cod as well. If anyone complains, we'll tell them that they were out of whatever they wanted."

"You're fairly devious, aren't you?" I asked.

"Look who's talking."

"So what did you do today?"

"I just went into town and wandered around. I went to your café but it was closed."

"Ah."

"What happened?"

I shook my head. "It's a long story. I'll tell you after the wedding. Just don't say anything to anyone else about it being closed."

On the way back, Claire asked me if I was nervous about the wedding.

"Not really. Are you?"

"Yeah. I don't want to do the reading. I'll probably get stuck on a word and have to spell it out. I used to do that in primary school. Everyone will be staring at me."

"That's because you're the good-looking one. You'll be fine, don't worry about it."

"It's easy for you to say – you're the one who wants to do stand-up comedy for a living. Whatever you do, don't start telling your joke about Moses and the Ten Commandos." She started laughing. "That was a good one, though. How do you come up with all that stuff?"

"It's not that hard . . . The hard part is making it look like you're just coming up with it a few seconds before you say it. You see some comedians and you'd almost swear they go on stage without the slightest idea of what they're going to do . . . Well, okay, some of them *don't* know, but most of them put as much time into creating that sort of casual approach as they put into their material."

"So what sort of comedy do you like the least, then?"

"I'm not mad about audience participation stuff. It's just too hard. You really *do* have to be able to make it up on the spot. Guys like Jon Kenny and Pat Shortt are just brilliant at it, but I couldn't do it."

"Dad thinks you're just going through a phase."

"Well, what does he know? He hasn't been around in years. It's not just a phase. I mean, you were there at the hen party. What did *you* think?"

"I loved it. I only wish someone had taped it. So, would you do movies and things like that?"

"I doubt it . . . I just like making people laugh. You can't hear them laughing when you're making a movie." We'd reached the front door, and I fished my keys out of my pocket. "Sometimes I don't know what I'm letting myself in for."

Claire burst out laughing. That was one of the things I really liked about her: she didn't know all the old jokes.

Eimear was in the hall, on the phone, and she shushed us as we came in. I couldn't tell who she was talking to, but she seemed upset. We went into the kitchen and closed the door behind us.

"What's going on?" I asked quietly.

Everyone looked uncomfortable. "It's Chris. It sounds like they're having a fight," Mam said.

"You're kidding! Today? They've been together for six years and *now* they're having a fight? What's it about?"

Mam shrugged. "With her, it's probably about the size of the tyres on the wedding car."

Roddy laughed and Gráinne nudged him and told him he wasn't helping matters.

Claire and I took a pile of plates from the press and unloaded the food onto them. We were all just about to start eating when Eimear came back in. She had a face on like you wouldn't believe.

"Chris wants to talk to you, Andi."

"What about?"

"I don't know."

"Well, is everything okay?"

"Ask him *yourself*."

So I went out to the phone. "Chris?"

"Andi . . . what am I going to do?"

"What do you mean?"

"I've been asking myself if I really want to go through with the wedding."

"Oh, for fuck's sake. Why not?"

"It's just such a big step."

"You still love her, don't you?"

"Yeah."

"And you've been living together for years, right? So what's the problem? You love her and she loves you. So get married."

"What if something happens? What if I'm there on

the altar and the priest asks me, and I can't say 'I do'? What happens then?"

"Then you run like mad. Chris, you've just got the jitters. You're not worried about the marriage, just the wedding. You'll be fine. Trust me. Did you get my speech?"

"Yeah, thanks. It's just what I wanted. I liked the gag about Eimear's Mam sizing me up the first time she met me. I can't wait to see how she reacts."

"Well, if you don't go through with the wedding, you'll never know, will you? So are you going to do it?"

"Jesus, Andi . . . I'm . . ."

"You're scared."

"Yeah."

"So's Eimear. And what are you scared of? Are you scared that you might fart when you kneel down? Are you scared that you might drop the ring? Chris, the fucking roof could collapse. The priest might have a heart attack. A million things *might* happen. The only thing that's certain is that if you don't go through with it, you'll be making a big mistake."

He was silent for a while, then he said, "You're right . . . Look, tell her I'll be there in the morning. Everything will be fine."

"Okay. Just phone me if you need anything."

We said goodbye, and I went back into the kitchen. Eimear was in tears, and Dad and Roddy looked fit to kill.

"What did he say?" Eimear asked.

"That he loves you, and he'll see you tomorrow at the church."

She sniffed. "Are you sure?"

"Yeah." I smiled. "It wasn't about you, you know. He was just nervous about the wedding. Afraid he'd screw it up and ruin your day."

* * *

Eimear cheered up fairly quickly, though she still had a few moments of panic now and then, which by this stage was par for the course.

Dad made a few suggestions along the lines of "Let's go to the pub," but Mam exercised her veto and announced that we were going to be busy enough in the morning without having to worry about hangovers.

Eimear kept watching the clock, and I could see her counting down the hours. She had another panic attack at ten, when she realised that in only twelve hours she'd be walking down the aisle.

It was around then that the phone calls started: Gran wanted to know what time she should come over in the morning. John couldn't remember whether they were supposed to meet us at the house or just go straight to the church. Chris's sister phoned to wish us luck. Audrey phoned to check that everything was okay, and to say she'd be there at eight in the morning. Then Audrey's mother phoned and said she'd come over and do our hair, if we wanted. Ellen phoned to say that she'd be getting up early, so if we needed her for anything, all we had to do was ring her. Ciarán phoned and said he was going out with the lads, so would we tape *Star Trek* for him.

And every time the phone rang, Eimear jumped. She thought that it was Chris phoning to cancel the wedding.

At midnight, Mam decided that enough was enough: we were all going to bed. We knew better than to argue with her, especially at a time like that.

Dad was ordered to get the camp bed from the shed. "Give us a hand with it, Andi," he said.

I followed him out, and once we were out of earshot, he whispered, "Did you do my speech?"

"Yeah. I printed it out for you and everything. I put it in the pocket of your suit. You should go through it a couple of times before the reception."

"Thanks . . . So, what do you think? Is Chris going to show up?"

"I think he will. He doesn't really have a problem with *being* married, only with *getting* married. He's shitting bricks that he'll screw it up somehow."

"So what about you? I heard that you and Tony weren't seeing each other any more."

"Yeah . . . Well, that's probably for the best. We had a bit of a fight and things weren't the same afterwards."

"Still, never mind. You're sure to find someone else."

"I know."

We hauled the camp bed out of the shed. After the

last time it was used, Dad had wrapped it up in a huge plastic sheet to keep out the damp.

"I hate this thing," I said. "It creaks and squeaks all night long."

"Then just use the mattress off of it," Dad said.

So I did. Dad helped me carry it up to the room, where Eimear and Claire were arguing over who got which bed.

"Thanks Dad," I said. "Goodnight." I closed the door behind me. "Right. Clear some space on the floor. And don't either of you fall out of bed tonight."

* * *

At about half one in the morning, Eimear said very quietly, "Andi, are you awake?"

"She's asleep," I said, hoping to throw her off the scent.

"Liar."

"What's the matter?"

"I can't sleep."

"That's because you're talking too much."

"I keep thinking that something will go wrong."

"It'll be fine."

She sighed. "God, I'm beginning to wish we weren't doing it. I'd be happy enough just living with him."

"What's it like, living with someone?" Claire suddenly asked.

I looked in her direction. "What? You're awake as well?"

"From the sound of the snoring, I think that only Dad and Grandad are asleep," she said.

"Well, that settles it, then," Eimear said. "I'm bursting for a piss only I didn't want to wake everyone up." She swung her legs out of bed and stepped on me.

"Watch where you're going!"

When she'd gone out, Claire asked, "Are you going to tell me what happened in the café?"

"No. Not yet. Besides, I'm still going over it in my head. You know, editing it so that it makes me look good."

From the bathroom, we heard a long, loud fart. Claire giggled, and that started me off.

When Eimear came back, she looked disgusted. "Grow up, the two of you!"

"Just think," Claire said, "that was probably your last fart as a single woman."

"I'm going to thump the living daylights out of you if you don't shut up," Eimear said, stepping all over me again as she got back into bed.

"So what's it like?" Claire asked again. "Living with someone?"

"Do you mean sleeping with someone, or living with them?" I asked.

"Sleeping with them, I suppose," she said.

Neither Eimear nor I responded.

"Well?"

"Don't ask me," I said. "I've never done it. Not the whole way."

Eimear sat up. "Really? What about Dean?"

"What about him?"

"You never slept with him?"

"No. I never wanted to. I didn't even really want to go out with him that much."

"I didn't know . . ."

"God," Claire said, "what does it take to get an answer?"

"Look," Eimear said, "it's not that great the first few times. The more you get to know him, the better it gets."

"Did it hurt? The first time?"

"A bit."

"And was that with Chris, or someone else?"

Eimear lay back down again. "I'm not going to tell you *that*. You must have friends who've had sex, Claire. Ask them."

"Yeah," I said. "It was too long ago for Eimear to remember."

"Very funny . . . I'll tell you this, Claire. Don't rush into it. That's the mistake Audrey made."

This was intriguing. "Really?" I said. "Tell us about it."

"She was seventeen or something, he was a couple of years older. He wanted to do it in the back of his car, and she let him. She said it was the most uncomfortable thing she'd ever experienced, and she's always regretted that she didn't wait. She said that any time anyone talks about their first experience, all she can think about is when he rolled up the window and trapped her hair in it. She didn't notice straight away, though. He was just about to come and she wanted to shift position, so she slid down and nearly tore all her hair out. She screamed, he jumped and knocked his head on the roof, and right at that second he came all over her."

I laughed. "No wonder she keeps her hair shorter these days."

"Like I said, he was fairly young, so he was able to get quite a distance. It hit her in the face and some went up her nose."

I was, quite literally, rolling around on the floor laughing.

Eimear reached down and thumped me. "Shut up! You'll wake up the whole house!"

Claire was puzzled. "I don't get it. What do you mean 'he was able to get quite a distance'?"

Eimear sighed. "You tell her, Andi . . . I've got to get some sleep."

So I found myself explaining the intricacies of sex – as well as I understood them – to Claire, until my mother knocked on the door and told us to stop whispering and giggling and to go to sleep.

* * *

Eimear woke me up at six in the morning: she was having another panic attack. "I had a dream that we were late."

"We *are* late – it's Sunday. We slept through the whole day."

For a split second she believed me, then she relaxed. "Bitch."

I crawled out from under the blankets. "I'll never get back to sleep now. I might as well put the water on."

When I came back into the room, Claire was sleeping like a baby, all curled up in my bed. "Look at her," I said to Eimear. "You wouldn't think that last night she was asking us all about penises."

Eimear got out of bed. "So this is it. The big day."

I nodded. "Yeah. Don't worry. It'll be fine."

"Did we forget anything?"

"No. And sure if we did, it can't have been anything important. The main thing is to make sure you and Chris are at the church at the right time."

"Will you ring him for me? I'm not supposed to talk to him before the wedding."

"I'm not bloody ringing him *now*! I'll do it at about eight."

"Right. Okay. So what's next? Should I get dressed now?"

"No, you have to have a shower and wash your hair. The car's coming at half-nine, so you should start getting dressed about half-eight. You need to get something to eat as well."

I made breakfast while Eimear had her shower, and by the time she was out, everyone else was up, apart from Dad.

Chaos was too small a word for it . . .

Roddy turned on the telly and watched the early-morning cartoons until Mam turned it off and told him to go and wash himself.

Someone was sent up to wake Dad three times, and each time he pretended he was getting up, and went back to sleep.

Gráinne and Claire had a fight over whose turn it was to have a shower.

My mother complained that no one had done the washing up from the night before, so she elected me to do it. Unfortunately, that led to much shouting of "Stop using the bloody hot water!" from Claire in the shower.

Gran arrived heavily laden with gossip about one of her neighbours, and was desperately trying to find someone to help share the burden.

Audrey arrived with her mother, who was a hairdresser. Unfortunately, Audrey managed to forget to bring her dress with her, so she had to go back for it. Eimear argued that she should have left her dress here in the first place; there was no need to bring it home with her.

Mam went up to get dressed and to order Dad out of bed and into his suit. She came back down looking relieved. "He's *finally* getting up," she said.

Roddy waited until I'd done all the washing-up and put everything away before he remembered that there was a whole pile of cups in the downstairs bedroom.

Gran cornered Gráinne and filled her in on the

gossip while Gráinne attempted to iron Claire's dress, which had somehow become creased overnight all by itself.

Claire, meanwhile, was getting her hair done by Audrey's mother, who spent the time complaining about Audrey and wishing that she was the one who was getting married.

Mam went back upstairs and roared at Dad to get up. Then she stomped back down.

Eimear told Roddy to get into his suit, and he told her to leave him alone, there was plenty of time. She then told him that if he made them late, she'd murder him. He told her to calm down. That just made her worse.

I went upstairs to change into my dress and discovered that Gráinne had ironed mine by mistake, and the creases were still in the other one. I went back down to let her know, and I was collared by Audrey's mother who started doing my hair.

Gran took Eimear aside for some advice on married life. Eimear by this stage was climbing up the walls with nervousness.

Audrey came back with her dress, and changed up in the bedroom, then Claire and I changed. Gráinne did our make-up – she always was good at that sort of thing – and told us she was very proud of us. Then she went off to get changed and to bully Roddy into his suit.

Claire and I went back down and Audrey's mother started making last-minute adjustments to our hair.

Dad wandered into the kitchen wearing his suit. "Jaysus, am I the only one who's ready?"

* * *

Eimear went up to change into her dress, and Audrey and I went up to help her. She got into her underwear and was just about to put on the dress when she had another panic attack: "What if I need to go to the toilet?"

"You'll be grand," Audrey said.

"Go now and you won't need to go later," I said.

"That's easy for you to say," Eimear said. "It'll take me an hour to get this thing off. Anyway, I don't need to go now. Did you phone Chris?"

"For the third time, yes, I phoned him. He's ready and waiting. Mark is there too. They're getting a lift to the church. They'll be there in plenty of time."

"What time is it now?"

"Just gone nine."

"Okay . . . I shouldn't have said we'll have the wedding so early. We wouldn't be in such a rush then."

"Then you'd only have more time to worry," Audrey said.

* * *

The car arrived a few minutes early, and Eimear almost fainted. We were still up in the bedroom, and Eimear peeked out through the curtains.

"Shite! All the neighbours are having a look!"

I looked out. Breda and Paddy from across the road were at their hall door. I couldn't see anyone else.

Eimear looked ready to burst with panic.

"Here, take this." I took her hand and put a small white pill into it, and handed her a glass of water. "It's a sedative," I said. "A really mild one. It'll stop you from freaking out."

She looked at it uncertainly.

"I went the chemist yesterday, and she said to give it to you. She said her daughter was in a right state before she got married, and she took one of these and it calmed her right down. It works almost immediately, and there's no side effects or anything. But apparently they're dead expensive. Film stars take them before they do a première, that kind of thing."

"All right," Eimear said. "I'll trust you not to poison me or drug me." She tossed the pill into the back of her throat, and drank half the glass of water.

"Feeling any better?"

She took a deep breath. "Yeah . . . yeah, I am. Thanks."

"Okay. Now, go downstairs and show everyone how gorgeous you are."

Eimear nodded, and opened the door. Then she looked back and gave us a huge grin. "Thanks, both of you. I'd never get through this without you."

She went downstairs and there was a round of applause from the kitchen.

Audrey looked at me. "Jesus! What did you *give* her?"

"A Tic-Tac," I said. "Want one?"

* * *

We went outside for the obligatory photographs before we got into the cars. Eimear, Mam, Audrey, Claire and me were to go in the wedding car, and Roddy and Gráinne were going to take Dad and Gran in theirs.

A tiny little kid came up to Roddy just as he was getting into the car. "Are yiz not goin' ta do the gushy, Mister?"

"Would you ever feck off," Roddy said, laughing.

"Ah, give him something, Dad," Claire said.

"Sure the whole point of the gushy is so that the kids won't go near the car." He looked around. "And he's the only one for miles."

"It's bad luck not ta gimme sumptin," the kid said.

"I'll give you a good kick in the arse," Roddy said.

Claire took pity on the boy, and handed him a pound coin.

He looked at it. "Is tha' *all*? Jaysus." He walked off in a huff.

"Right," Dad said. "Come on, let's get moving. If this wedding doesn't work out I'll still have time to get to the bookies."

"Dad!"

He laughed. "Sorry, pet. Come on, now. You look

lovely. Get in the car and make me the happiest dad in the world."

As luck would have it, we got to the church a little early, and had to drive around the block a few times.

"This is gas," Audrey said. "Everyone's looking at us."

On the fourth pass, I spotted Chris and his best man Mark getting out of a car. "Slow down!" I said to the driver. "There they are!"

"God, yer man Mark's not bad-looking," Audrey said. "So Eimear, who's the chief bridesmaid? Can I be? Then I'll get a dance with him."

"You might as well," Eimear said distractedly. "All right, they're going in . . . Is everyone ready?"

We all said that we were.

The steps outside the church were packed with friends and neighbours and relatives we hadn't seen in years. They cheered when they saw Eimear getting out of the car.

Dad was waiting at the door, and I couldn't remember the last time I'd seen him looking so proud.

"Okay," I said. "Audrey, you go first. Me and Claire will walk down together."

"I know, I know. We rehearsed this enough times."

"Eimear, put down your veil," Claire said.

Eimear linked arms with Dad.

"Are you ready, pet?"

She nodded.

"Okay then . . ." Dad looked at me, and winked. "Let's get rid of her, Andi . . ."

Everyone else piled into the church to take their seats, and the organist started playing.

I gave Audrey the nod, and she stepped in through the door. Claire and I followed her down the aisle, but no one was looking at us. They were all craning their necks to see Eimear. I winked at Ellen as I passed, and she stuck her tongue out at me and nearly made me laugh. My brothers were all sitting together near the front, and they grinned as I passed.

At the altar, Chris was waiting. I could see that he was resisting having a look until the last second. Then he turned to her, and smiled.

Chapter Twenty-two

After the ceremony, we stood around outside the church while the photographer ordered us about:

"Now, first can I have just the bride and groom together? That's fine . . . Move a little to the left. No, your *other* left . . ."

It took forever, and I swore that if I ever got married I wouldn't have an official photographer. The photographer insisted on every possible combination of people.

"Now the immediate families. Now just the bride's family. Now just the groom's family. Now the bridesmaids and the best man. Now both families together. Now all the people who are wearing their suits buttoned on the wrong side. Now all the unmarried mothers. Now all the people your parents said that you had to bring because they were very good to you when you were four. Now all the alcoholic relatives. Now all the people who are holding cigarettes behind their backs. Now all the people who always sing rebel songs at a wedding. Now all the people who are going to bitch about the wedding when they go home. Okay, now all the children who were sliding on their knees up and down the church aisles. Now all the people who wouldn't have come if there wasn't a free meal going. Now everyone who intends to steal silverware from the hotel at the reception."

Okay, maybe he wasn't quite that bad, but that's what it felt like.

When the official photos were done, it was time for the unofficial ones – it seemed like everyone present had three rolls of film that were about to go out of date. During all this, Eimear and Chris came over to me.

"We just want to say thanks," Chris said. "For everything you've done."

"And not just for talking sense into him last night," Eimear said.

"Well, I wouldn't do it for anyone else," I said, and smiled. "I'm really happy for you."

"No, we owe you," Chris said. "We'll make it up to you."

"Buy me a car," I suggested.

He laughed. "Yeah, sure."

Then Gran came up to us. "Come on, your Mam wants to take a photo of the whole family. It's the first time everyone's been together in ages."

Audrey was handed the camera, and she took over

"bossing us about" duties. Dad, Mam and Gran stood at the back, a few steps up. Roddy, Gráinne, Ciarán, John and Betty were next, with me, Claire, Eimear and Chris at the front.

"All right . . ." Audrey said. "Smile like you mean it."

Then Gran took hold of someone's Polaroid camera and started getting shots for her own collection. "Andi, come over here. I want a photo of you and Roddy and Gráinne and Claire together. Okay, now, Roddy, you stand behind Andi and put your hand on her shoulder, that's right. Now Gráinne, you put your hand on Claire's shoulder. Lovely!" She pressed the button, the camera went *click* and *whirr*, the photo came out, and – behold the miracle of modern technology – a couple of minutes later Gran was the proud owner of a photo of the four of us without any heads. So she had to take another one.

Then Ellen found me. "Your reading was great," she said. "You were the only one – not counting the priest – who wasn't shitting bricks."

"Thanks," I said. "So, what about the café? I suppose Joe told you everything?"

"Yeah . . . I'm still not sure what to do. Should we go to a solicitor, or something?"

"We probably should. Even if it's only to get the money we're due. Anyway, I promised myself I wouldn't even think about it now. I want to wait until tomorrow or Monday. Right now, I just want to enjoy the wedding. Oh, and don't say anything about the job to anyone else. I don't want to spoil the event."

"Okay." She peered past me. "It looks like you're wanted for *another* photo. I'll see you later, okay?"

After that, we finally got going towards the hotel. Chris had hired a bus for the occasion, and we all piled in, except for Chris and Eimear who of course went in the wedding car, and Gran who went with Roddy and Gráinne.

We were halfway there when Dad, who'd fought his way onto the bus first so he could sit nearest the driver, stood up and announced that there'd been a change of plans and we were all going to McDonald's instead.

Mam told him to sit down and stop making a show of himself.

The first item on the agenda was a champagne reception. Well, they *called* it champagne, but it seemed to me that the closest it had been to anything French was when the waiter was carrying the bottles through the kitchen and past the chips.

We all milled around, chatting to relatives and making the usual comments about how we never meet up except at weddings and funerals.

Eimear grabbed me and Claire and brought us over to meet Chris's parents. "This is Andi, and Claire."

Chris's mother told us how lovely we were, and said, "You probably get people asking you this all the time, but are you twins?"

"We're not even sisters," Claire said, sounding a little hurt. "I'm Eimear's niece. Roddy's daughter."

"Ah, I see. It's probably because you're wearing the same dress. And Roddy's the eldest, is that right? What's your other brother's name? I know John."

"Ciarán," I said. "He's the one who spent most of the summer travelling around Europe."

Chris's Dad said to me, "So you're the one who was doing all the jokes at the hen party?"

I nodded. "I was the free entertainment."

"Yeah, I heard about that. Some friends of ours happened to be in the pub. They said you were hilarious."

I felt a little embarrassed to be taking the spotlight away from Eimear. "Thanks. So, how does it feel to have a daughter-in-law?"

They went on about how delighted they were, and somehow they managed to get the conversation turned around so that we were talking about their local residents' association, and how one of the neighbours had managed to get planning permission for a two-storey extension even though no one else in the area had ever been able to get permission to even widen their gate.

It was about then that I noticed both Eimear and Claire had craftily slipped away. "I must introduce you to the rest of the family," I said. I pawned them off on Gran, and made my own dash for freedom.

Ciarán grabbed me as I ran past him. "Slow down a minute!"

"What?"

He looked around, then ushered me into a quiet spot. "I've got something to ask you."

"Let me guess . . . There's someone you fancy and you want me to check out whether she likes you."

"Am I that transparent?" he laughed. "Yeah. It's Audrey. What's she like?"

"She's okay," I said. "She seems fairly bright, but a bit giddy sometimes. She's able to put up with Eimear's bullshit, too, which can't be a bad thing. Only the thing is, she was asking about Mark earlier."

"Mark?"

"The best man."

"Oh. Him. Well, ask her anyway, will you?"

I started to say I would, then I paused. "Hold on. How come everyone gets *me* to do their dirty work?"

Ciarán grinned. "Because you're good at getting things done."

"No, I'm serious. Why is it always *me*?"

"Because you're one of those people everyone can rely on."

I took a deep breath. "Ciarán, I'm not kidding. I'm forever doing things for people. When was the last time I asked anyone else for a favour?"

He shrugged. "I don't know. So, are you going to ask her?"

"No. I'm not. I'm not doing any more favours until someone does something for me."

"All right. What do you want?"

"No, not like that . . ." There was something niggling away at the back of my mind, but I couldn't pin it down. "Look, I'll see you later. I've got a few things to sort out."

He held my arm to stop me from leaving. "Okay, okay . . . So what should I say to her?"

"Tell her she's absolutely gorgeous."

"Will that work?"

"It's more likely to work than just standing around and saying nothing to her."

I pulled my arm free and walked away.

To get from where I was to the door, I had to pass my mother, who was fiddling around with her bag. "Andi, come here a minute and give me a hand with this."

"Not now, Mam."

Just as I got to the door, Claire caught up with me. "Where are you off to?"

"Just outside. I want to get some air."

"Mind if I join you?"

"Well . . . okay."

We found a bench hidden away in the grounds of the hotel, and sat down.

"Mam and Dad had another fight about me," Claire said suddenly.

Part of me wanted to tell her to sort it out herself, but that was only a small part. "What were they saying?"

"I'm not sure . . . It was all about the way I behaved at the hen party, I think. Dad kept saying that he didn't want me acting like that, and Mam said that I was fine. I wasn't that bad, was I?"

"You barely opened your mouth, except to laugh or put drink into it," I said. "Look, you're only fifteen. By rights you shouldn't even have been in the place, let alone drinking. He's just . . . I don't know . . . getting worried about you. I mean, you're at the age where you could come home some night and announce that you're pregnant. That's got to be scary for any parent."

"I suppose."

We sat in silence for a while.

"So what's on *your* mind?" Claire asked.

"If I told you, you'd think I was either paranoid, or being a bitch."

"Tell me anyway."

"All right . . . Ciarán asked me about Audrey. He fancies her, and he wanted me to check her out, and see if she was interested in him."

"And is she?"

"I don't know. I told him I wouldn't do it."

"Oh . . . Why not?"

I looked at her. "Claire, you've been here since Tuesday, right? In all that time, how many people have asked me to do stuff?"

She shrugged.

"I'll tell you: everyone. Andi, do this. Andi, do that, Andi, write my speech for me. Get this. Fix that. Go here, go there, go everywhere. In the past six weeks I've organised most of this wedding. I got the whole café up and running – more or less – and didn't get paid for it, and I nearly exhausted myself writing stuff for Tony.

And what do I have to show for it? Nothing. Okay, so I don't expect to get anything out of the wedding, but the other stuff: I got fired yesterday – don't breathe a word of that to anyone – and me and Tony broke up."

"Wow . . ."

"You see, the thing is, Claire, it's all my own fault. Everyone expects me to help them because I never say no. And then they start to think of me as someone who can get things done, so no one ever offers *me* any help. If I'm ever in trouble, I'm on my own.

"I mean, look at all the shit I put myself through over Dean! I should have just told him to fuck off and leave me alone, but I didn't because I was too worried about how Ellen would react. He *is* her twin brother, after all."

"Andi, you're overreacting. People trust you, that's all."

"Sure, they trust me. But a lot of them *use* me. There's not one single person in the past year who actually did something for me without wanting a favour in return. And most people just want me to help them out without even checking to see whether *I* need anything. It's like I'm a free favour fountain. Even you – and please don't take this the wrong way – you've been coming to me for advice."

She looked hurt.

"God, I said don't take it the wrong way! What I mean is, you – and everyone else – automatically assume that I'm going to be willing and able to solve your problems."

She still looked upset.

"Claire, I'm sorry. I shouldn't have used you as an example. And I don't mind giving *you* advice. You're a good friend and I'll always be there for you."

Claire nodded. "So what you're saying is that you want someone to be there for *you*."

I laughed. "Yes! Exactly! Damn it, it took me ages to get to the point and you summed it up in a few words!"

"Don't patronise me, Andi. I'm fifteen. I'm not *thick*."

"Sorry. I know you're not thick."

"And you're wrong. You think there's no one who's willing to be there for you? How many times over the past few days have I asked you about what's going on in your life? You won't open up, though. Maybe you're starting to believe what everyone else does – that you're independent." She stood up. "Look, I'm going back in. The dinner will be starting in a few minutes."

As I watched her go, I realised that she was right. She *had* been trying to talk to me. And I had just put her off, because . . . well, because she was younger than me, and therefore she couldn't possibly know how to help. I'd been a snob.

And I'd been wrong. Even aside from Claire, there *was* someone who had been there when I needed them. Someone I'd overlooked all too often in the past.

When Joe was walking me home the previous afternoon, I'd said to him, "At one stage I was starting to wonder if you fancied Ellen. That made sense then.

Especially when you sort of disappeared after Niall came on the scene."

"That's a good theory," Joe had replied. "But it's wrong."

Then I'd said, "And someone suggested that maybe you fancied *me*, and when Tony came along you gave up."

"Another good theory," Joe had said.

But he'd never said *that* theory was wrong.

I smiled. All right, Joe, I said to myself. Now I know what's so different about you. And now I know why it's *you* that I want.

* * *

During the meal, I had the good fortune to be sitting between Gran and Claire. Well, that wasn't really just good fortune – I'd insisted on it when we were doing the seating plan.

Also seated at our table were, clockwise from Gran: John, Betty, Ciarán, Gráinne, Roddy and Claire. As I sat down next to Claire, I whispered, "Thanks."

"For what?"

"What you said. You were right. And you made me realise something else, too. But I'll tell you about that later."

Gran poked me in the shoulder. "Andi. It's rude to whisper at a wedding," she whispered.

"Sorry, Gran."

"So you and Tony broke up, then? That's a pity. I

liked him. I certainly liked him a lot more than that Dean lad."

"Me too," I said. "But it wasn't serious with Tony. At least, it ended before it could *get* serious. So I suppose that's almost the same."

John said, "Andi, what's all this I've been hearing about you being a comedian?"

"She was great," Betty said to everyone. "Wasn't she, Gráinne?"

"She was. We could have a star in the making here."

"I wish I'd been there," John said. "But for some reason they don't let men go to hen parties."

"They do," Claire said, "but only for the strip-o-gram."

Roddy looked at her. "What?"

She blushed, and stared at the tablecloth.

"What's all this?" Roddy asked Gráinne.

"There was a strip-o-gram. He stripped as far as his boxers, and that was that. It was just a bit of fun."

"She's only fifteen, for crying out loud!"

Ciarán – who loved a good fight – decided to join in. "Ah, sure I wouldn't worry about it, Roddy. She was probably too drunk to have seen anything."

Roddy and Ciarán started squabbling. John turned to Betty, and said, "Now you know why I love family gatherings so much."

* * *

During the main course – Roddy and Ciarán were

speaking to each other, but only on the safe topics of
football and PlayStation games – Gran turned her
attention back to me again.

"So you're really thinking of taking up the stage life,
Andi?"

"I'm thinking about it. I'll have to see what happens.
But I do know one thing: I wouldn't want to get to your
age and look back and start regretting all the things I
never tried." I smiled. "That's why I've always loved
you, you know . . . ? You were never afraid to go after
what you wanted."

She smiled back. "Oh, I was afraid all right. I just
never let it stop me. You know what my motto
was?"

"No?"

"It was a line from a poem by Sarah Williams . . ."

I interrupted her. *"I have loved the stars too fondly to be
fearful of the night."*

Gran was impressed. "How did you know that?"

"A friend said it. That's *his* motto. He didn't know
where it was from, though, so I looked it up on the
Internet."

"That was the first thing your grandad ever said to
me. The day I met him would have been Sarah
Williams's hundredth birthday, if she hadn't died at the
age of thirty-one."

Claire, who had been earwigging through all this,
asked, "What does it mean, though?"

Gráinne answered her. "It means that sometimes

you have to put up with a lot of bad things to get what you want."

* * *

After the meal, it was time for the speeches . . .

Dad stood up, looking a little nervous, sipped from his pint and consulted his notes.

"Right . . . Well, first of all, I want to thank everyone for coming. And I'd particularly like to thank the good Father here for such a great ceremony. When I was a lad, Mass was a lot different. We were all terrified of the parish priest. And Mass was a lot longer in those days. Sometimes it went on for weeks. And it used to be in Latin, too. Not the Latin you get nowadays, with all them fancy words. We had *Irish* Latin, which was a lot harder, and the priest used to come around to our houses at night and give us spotchecks to see if we knew the names of the ten apostles or all of the twelve commandments, and if we *didn't* know, we were whipped, and we had to wear sackcloth and a bag on our heads so people would know we were sinners."

I'd been a bit worried about that one, but the priest laughed his head off, so I knew I was safe.

"And I want to thank Chris's parents. They did a great job of bringing him up. The only thing is, now that he's around, he's making my own lads look bad . . . Look at the feckin' state of them!" Everyone laughed and looked at our table. Ciarán stood up and bowed, and John and Roddy joined him.

"Ah, they're all right," Dad said. "But at least now that I have a son-in-law as well as the three lads, we're starting a five-aside football team." He turned to Chris's dad. "We're looking for a sub if you're interested, Tommy.

"But mostly, I want to thank two special women . . ."

I perked up when I heard that. Dad was deviating from the speech . . . Good for him, I said to myself.

"First of all, Eimear. She's a damn good catch, so hard luck to all the single lads out there. She's been a great daughter, and I know she'll make an even better wife."

Everyone clapped and cheered. Dad waited until they'd finished before he continued.

"And I want to thank someone very special who put her heart and soul into helping Eimear with the wedding. Sal, stand up and take a bow!"

Mam blushed and shook her head.

"Well, anyway," Dad said. "My little girl is all grown up and married now. But I don't see it as losing a daughter as much as gaining a bit of peace and quiet."

When the laughter faded again, he raised his drink. "To Eimear and Chris. God bless them and protect them, and may they receive all the love that they deserve."

* * *

Shortly after Chris's speech – which went down very well, I was pleased to note – more photographs were taken, the cake was cut, and we were ushered out of the room so that it could be prepared for the evening part of the reception.

Claire and I went for another walk, and found ourselves back on the same bench.

"You were right," we both said at the same time.

Claire laughed. "Jinx!"

"What?"

"You have to do whatever I tell you for the next minute."

I raised one eyebrow and stared at her. "Do yourself a favour – don't tell me to do anything for the next minute."

"What was I right about?" she asked.

"You were right that there are people who will be there for me when I need them."

"Anyone in particular?"

"Yeah, I think so. I'll have to see what happens, though. So what was I right about?"

"Grandad thanked everyone and didn't even mention all the work you did for the wedding. Neither did Chris."

"Yeah, well that's because I wrote their speeches."

"Really? Then why didn't they even thank you for that?"

"Now, how would that look? 'I'd like to thank my daughter for writing this speech for me.'"

"But still, it sounded like they added their own bits. They could have said something."

I shrugged. "It doesn't matter. I'm just glad it's all over now."

"Well, there's the evening bit still to come," Claire said. "That should be a laugh. Do you think there'll be any cute guys there?"

"I'm just hoping that there'll be a band." I got to my feet. "Come on, let's go and find everyone else. I could murder a pint."

"Me too."

"Not a chance. Your dad would go nuts. You saw how he reacted to what Ciarán said. Anyway, you're far too young. Your body is only barely past puberty – it's not strong enough to absorb large quantities of alcohol."

"Ah, that's bollocks."

I laughed. "Okay, do whatever you want. I just don't want to be known as the auntie who turned you into an alcoholic."

* * *

The afters to the wedding was a lot more relaxed. Eimear and Chris had booked a room for the evening in the hotel, so Audrey, Claire and I took advantage of it to change into more normal clothes.

The band was in full swing when we got back downstairs, backing Chris's dad as he did his medley of Brendan Shine songs. Guests were pouring into the place, and Eimear and Chris seemed to be spending most of their time saying hello and accepting presents.

Audrey and Claire disappeared among the masses, and I hung around the door for Ellen.

But it was Niall I spotted first. He was carrying a huge present, and it looked heavy. He grinned at me, and came rushing over. "Andi . . . How's it going?"

"Great. Where's Ellen?"

"She said to meet her here. I'm glad I saw you, though. I don't know anyone else here." He lowered the present to the floor and rubbed his hands.

"So what's in the box?" I asked.

"Microwave oven," Niall said. "A real good one, too. It's from Ellen's folks. I'll tell you, I was tempted to keep this for myself and just get your sister a CD or something."

"So did Ellen tell you all about the café?"

"Yeah. Well, I knew already. Joe sent me an e-mail with the video attached." He shook his head. "If Joe hadn't been there . . ."

"I know. Parker might have killed me. Listen, don't mention it to anyone else. My folks don't know yet, and I don't want to spoil the wedding."

"No problem. What's your sister's name again?"

"Eimear. And her husband is Chris. But you needn't worry – here's Ellen now."

Ellen got me to describe at length everything that had happened since the ceremony, who was wearing what, who had sat where, what the food was like, who was turned up. After a few minutes I was strongly regretting that we hadn't invited her to the whole thing.

Not because she'd missed it, but because then I wouldn't have had to describe everything.

"Anyhow," Ellen said, "we'll go in and meet the happy couple. Are you coming?"

"Nah, I'll hang around here for a while. It's starting to get dark, and I want to look at the stars."

* * *

I had a lot to think about.

The hotel's car park was still buzzing with people, so I wandered around until I found a quieter area.

Everything's changed now, I said to myself. The wedding is over; the job is finished; Dean's finally out of the way. Maybe it's time I stopped organising everyone else's lives and started on my own.

I knew where I wanted to start, too . . .

I'd phone Joe in the morning. Maybe I'd even get the train to Kilkenny.

It was strange to think that I'd spent all that time with Joe and never looked at him as a potential boyfriend. Now, it seemed impossible *not* to look at him that way. As they say, it's always the quiet ones.

* * *

It was almost eleven before I finally went back inside. Mam caught sight of me and came charging over. "Where were you?"

"Just outside. Is everything okay?"

"Well, you missed Eimear and Chris going away.

And Claire's sick. She drank way too much and she's been vomiting all over the place."

"God . . . Where is she?"

"She's up in the room. Roddy's up there with her, and he's really upset with *you*. You were supposed to be looking after her."

"That's the first I've heard of it."

"Just go on up and see that she's all right."

So I went up to the room and knocked on the door. "It's me. Andi."

Roddy opened the door wide, grabbed my arm and hauled me in. "Look at her!"

Claire was sitting on the side of the bed, and she looked terrible. She had a plastic bowl on her lap, and her head was carefully positioned over it. Strings of saliva hung from her lips.

"Are you all right, Claire?"

She groaned.

"She's so drunk she doesn't even know where she is. That's your fault," Roddy said. "You're supposed to be in charge of her. You're supposed to be the responsible one!"

"That's just what Mam said. What the hell are you talking about? Why am *I* supposed to be the responsible one?"

"Because you're older!"

"Yeah, but only by five years. You're twenty-one years older than her, so why aren't you the responsible one? *And* you're her father." I sat down on the bed beside Claire, and gently rubbed the back of her neck.

"After what Gráinne said about you making a show of yourself at the hen party, I should have known I couldn't trust you."

I sighed. "Ah, for fuck's sake, Roddy. Did you never get drunk when you were a teenager? She's going to feel like shit for a couple of days, and then she'll be fine. And if she's lucky, she'll be put off drink for the rest of her life. It's not the end of the world, so just get a fucking grip for Christ's sake."

He looked like he was going to explode. "All right, that's it. I've had it up to *here* with you and your smart mouth. Just get out of my sight. Get your coat and go home."

I was disgusted with him. "Look, you can't order me about like that, Roddy! I mean, you're only my brother. It's not like you're my father."

"As a matter of fact, that's exactly what it's like."

Chapter Twenty-three

I ran out of the room, down the corridor, through the lobby and past the woman I'd always been told was my mother, and out into the hotel's car park.

Over and over, I kept thinking to myself, I should have realised, I should have guessed, I should have *known* . . .

It explained a lot of the odd things in my life – like why Mam and Roddy never really got on. It explained why some of the wedding guests thought that Claire and I were sisters – because we *were*. It explained the arguments between Roddy and Gráinne that Claire had half-heard and assumed were about her.

That was why Tony assumed that Gráinne was my sister, and not Eimear – because Eimear was only my aunt, Gráinne was my mother.

I kept telling myself that I wasn't going to cry, but I was crying anyway.

Again, I started thinking that I should have been able to figure it out, I should have guessed, I should have known . . .

Then something clicked inside me, and I realised that once again I was taking on someone else's responsibility: whether or not I should have guessed was beside the point – *they* should have *told* me.

I started to put the pieces together in my head, and for the first time, things began to fit . . .

Gráinne had been fifteen and Roddy a year older when she discovered that she was pregnant. Roddy's parents – my grandparents, I had to remind myself – probably went crazy, but in the end agreed to raise the baby as their own. I presumed that Gráinne's family had known about this, but I couldn't be certain.

At that time, Roddy had two brothers and a ten-year-old sister, the darling of the family and doted upon by everyone. And then she was told that there would be a new baby coming into the house.

And against all the odds, and something I guessed I should be grateful for, Roddy and Gráinne had stayed together. They got married quite young – maybe they'd planned to take me back, or something – and then shortly afterwards discovered that Gráinne was pregnant again.

* * *

Mam – I couldn't help but still think of her as that – came out looking for me, and found me in the car park, looking up at the stars.

431

"Are you all right?"

"No, I'm *not* all right."

She stood beside me, and looked up.

"What are you looking for?"

"Courage," I said.

"I don't understand."

"You said that sometimes we *have* to lie . . ."

She nodded. "Sometimes."

"But for how long?" I looked at her. "How long should a lie go on?"

"Andi, I don't know what you mean."

"Sure you do. You know, Dad knows, Gran knows, Roddy and Gráinne and Eimear and Ciarán and John know. I'm the *only* one who didn't know. No, that's wrong. I'm *not* the only one. My sister didn't know. She still doesn't."

Mam frowned. "Doesn't know what, love?"

"That she's my sister, and not my niece."

Mam's face fell. "Oh dear God."

"Should I start calling you Granny now, the way Claire does? I suppose I should start calling Roddy and Gráinne 'Mam and Dad', too?"

"Please, Andi . . . don't."

"Don't what? When were you going to tell me? Were you *ever* going to tell me? What was the idea? That I could go through life and never know who my real parents were? Jesus Christ, Mam! There are some things you just don't fucking lie about!"

Mam burst into tears. "Oh God forgive me, Andi.

I'm so sorry. We were going to tell you when you turned twenty-one. That was the . . . the plan."

"That really would have made a great birthday present, all right: a new set of parents and a younger sister." I turned away. "Look, just . . . just go inside. I can't talk to you right now."

Still sobbing, she went back inside.

I felt like shit for treating her like that, but I couldn't bring myself to go after her.

A few minutes later, Dad came out. Without a word, he put his arms around me, and just hugged me as I cried, my face pressed against his chest.

Eventually, he said, "I'm sorry, pet. I really am. I wanted to tell you years ago, but, well, they wouldn't let me. Look, you'll freeze out here. Come inside and we'll get you a cup of tea or something."

I shook my head.

"All right. We'll stay here. Hold on a second." He stepped back, and took off his jacket, then draped it around my shoulders. "We'll stay out here as long as you want."

I sniffed. "I'm sorry about what I said to Mam."

"She knows that."

"What am I going to do, Dad?"

"Andi, you can do whatever you like. You can stay with us as long as you want, but if you don't want that, we'll understand."

"I'm sorry if I've ruined everything for everyone."

"Don't worry about that. They probably think you're just upset about Claire."

433

I stepped back from him. "No. No, I don't want that. That's just lies on top of lies." I handed him his jacket back. "I want to talk to my mother. My *real* mother."

"Okay. I'll send her out."

He went back in. I turned away from the hotel again, and stood staring at the stars.

And then I heard footsteps behind me, and *she* was there . . .

"Andi. Your dad's just . . . I mean, your grandad has just told me."

I stared at her. "How could you *do* that? How could you just give me *away*?"

"God, Andi, I wasn't much older than Claire is now. What else could I do? My parents threw me out. They wouldn't have anything to do with me. They still won't. I haven't seen them since before you were born." She looked at me sadly. "It wasn't that I didn't love you . . . I did. And I still do, more than you could ever know. But it was the only thing to do."

"Gráinne, you ruined my life. What do you expect from me? Sympathy?"

"I *gave* you life, Andi. I carried you inside me for nine months, and then I had to give you away and pretend that you were never mine. Can you even imagine how hard that was for me? And when you were growing up, if you hurt yourself you'd come in crying and go straight to *her*, and not to me? It broke my heart every time I saw you."

I didn't know what to say.

"But God knows I love you, and I'm proud of you, and every night I pray that Claire turns out to be even half the woman you are. You're the best thing that ever happened to me, and the best thing I've ever done."

I started crying again.

"I'd hug you," she said, "but I don't know if you'll let me."

I shook my head. "No. Not yet. There's still too much . . ." I blew my nose. "I don't want to see him," I said. "Not after the things he said to me tonight. Tell him I'll see him . . . sometime. And Claire. My sister. I want you to tell her everything. She deserves that."

She nodded. "Okay, but I don't think that you'll be able to avoid Roddy around the house."

"I'm not going back there tonight," I said, looking up at the stars again.

"Where will you go?"

"I don't know." I suddenly whirled around and faced her. "Tell him that if he *ever* speaks to Claire the way he spoke to me, he'll regret it. I mean it, Gráinne."

"He loves you too, Andi. It was just as hard for him to give you up."

"Really? Well, tough fucking shit to him. He tried to blame *me* because Claire got drunk. He wouldn't even accept the responsibility for himself."

"Andi . . ."

"No, whatever it is, I don't want to hear it. Just leave me alone."

* * *

435

I was out there for a long time. Ciarán was the first one to come out after Gráinne.

"So now you know," he said.

"So how are you, Uncle Ciarán?"

"Don't give me that shite, Andi. Don't go gettin' up on your high horse about this. You'll end up blaming everyone in the world. Look, what else could they have done?"

"They could have told me before now."

"That's true. I've been on at Roddy for years to tell you. I even came close to it myself a couple of times."

"Then why didn't you?"

"Because I didn't want to lose my baby sister."

John was the next one to draw the short straw and have to try and talk me in from the edge of the gravel.

His approach was interesting. "Ah, it's all a load of shit, Andi. Who gives a fuck who said what and who didn't? You grew up with us, and you'll always be our little sister. Come on in and we'll get a drink."

"John?"

"Yeah?"

"Can I be the godmother?"

He grinned. "I wouldn't want anyone else . . . Are you coming in?"

"Not yet," I said. "Go on back in to Betty, and tell her I'm sorry if I've spoiled the wedding for her."

As he was going back in, Ellen passed him on the way out. She came bounding up to me. "I was wondering where you'd got to. I thought you might have snuck out here with someone."

"Roddy's my father," I said.

Her mouth dropped open. "Holy *fuck*!"

So I told her the whole story, and when I was done, I said, "Look, I need a favour. I can't go home tonight, Can I stay in your place?"

"It's a bit crowded at the moment," she said. "But I'll tell Niall that he and Joe will have to go to Niall's place."

"Wait. Joe didn't go home to Kilkenny last night?"

"No, he said he wanted to stick around for a few more days, in case you needed him."

"I see . . . Okay, change of plan. You and Niall go to his place. I'll stay in your place with Joe. That way you won't miss out on your sordid sex session with Niall."

"Are you sure? You don't mind being stuck there with Mr Silent?"

I smiled. It felt like years since I'd smiled. "I think I'll be okay."

* * *

Ellen had given me the keys to her flat and gone home with Niall when I finally went back inside. All of the guests had gone, and only my family – such as it was – remained, sitting in the lobby.

They all tried to talk me at once, but I ignored them and went straight to Claire, who was looking a lot better.

"Are you okay?"

She nodded.

"Come on," I said, and took her hand. I led her to the far side of the lobby. "They told you?"

"Yeah."

"Okay. Look, I don't know what I'm going to do in the future, but I do know this: you're my sister, and I love you. If you need me for anything, just let me know."

Claire smiled. "And the same goes for you. Sis."

* * *

Joe was asleep on the floor of Ellen's sitting-room when I opened the door to the flat. He sat up when he realised it was me.

"Hey . . . you were crying." In a second, he was at my side. "Come on, sit down."

I sat down on the sofa. "I'm a bit stressed at the moment," I said.

Joe said nothing.

"I've had the worst few days of my life. God, I thought what happened with Parker was bad, but tonight . . ."

"What happened?"

"I uncovered a secret that was hidden for almost twenty-one years."

Joe frowned. "Something about your parents?"

"How did you know?"

"I guessed. I mean, you're nearly twenty-one."

"Right . . ."

"So what happened?"

"To be honest, Joe, I don't want to talk about that now. I just want . . ."

"What?"

"I just want someone to hold me."

He sat down beside me, and put his arms around me, and held me until I fell asleep.

Chapter Twenty-four

A couple of months later, a Thursday afternoon . . .

Claire was up in Dublin, staying in the flat with me and Joe. She'd been badgering me for days to bring her along to the stand-up night in the pub, and I finally gave in.

I phoned Tony to see whether he was doing the show that night.

"No, not tonight. Where *are* you, anyway?" he asked. "And what the hell happened to the café?"

"What do you mean?"

"I went by there this afternoon, and all the computers are gone, and the name is changed. I would have gone in, only it was mad busy."

"So what's it called now?"

"Donna's, or something. Listen, I was going to phone you . . . Nathan called me from London. He says that one of his mates showed him a video on the computer of you and Bernard Parker in a fight. Nathan

440

says it's all over the place. Apparently they showed it on Channel Four."

I laughed.

"And he said that some guy saved you."

"That was Joe," I said. "I'm going out with him now."

"Hmm . . . fast work. What's he like?"

"He's the best."

"Well, tell him I said he's to duck if he ever gets into a fight with you."

"I will . . . So you're not going to the gig?"

"Nah. I'm taking it easy for a while. I'm not really that sure it's my thing any more. I had a couple of bad experiences and I'm kind of gone off it. But *you* should go. It's open mike night. Anyone can perform. It'll be like karaoke with jokes."

"Maybe I will."

"Okay, here's the deal. Promise you will, and I'll come along and heckle you. You can try out some of your lines on me. And bring Joe along. It'd be nice to meet him."

"You've met him already. The quiet one. Dean's friend."

"Oh, right." He paused. "Jesus, Dean must be pissed off!"

"He was, for a bit. But Ellen straightened him out. It's weird, though. Nowadays when we're all out together Dean just sits there barely saying a word. I think he's more embarrassed than annoyed. He'll get over it, though."

"So are you going to go? Get into the spotlight, and

441

just let loose with everything you've got. Give it loads."

"Okay," I said. "Okay. I'll do it."

* * *

From the point of view of the audience, it doesn't seem that tough: stand up on stage and tell a few jokes. How hard can that be?

I was about to find out.

The pub was absolutely packed, and more and more people were arriving as I nervously walked towards the makeshift stage. As soon as I stepped into the spotlight, the audience clapped politely.

The spotlight was shining right into my eyes, so even though I knew that Joe and Tony were standing at the back, I couldn't see them. Somewhere in the audience – I hoped – Ellen and Niall and Claire were silently praying that I didn't screw it up.

I stepped up to the microphone. "Good evening, ladies and gentlemen."

Not the most original start, I knew, but it was something.

"This is my first gig. They told me if I wasn't funny they'd flicker the lights to let me know to come off." I pulled a pair of dark glasses out of my pocket and put them on. This got a modest laugh, so I decided to keep going.

"They also said that if I didn't take the hint, they'd switch off the mike." I lowered the microphone. "Can you still hear me?" I shouted.

Someone called back, "Yeah!"

I raised the mike again. "Okay, so the thing that bothers me about television programmes is this: not that you never see them going to the toilet, not even that they never seem to finish any of their meals or drinks. What bothers me is that *they* never watch television! You never get someone on *Brookside* going, 'Shut up! I'm trying to watch this!' or 'Did you see *Coronation Street* last night?' If television programmes were anything like real life, the kids on them wouldn't ever get to see their favourite shows because their dads would insist on watching the news."

This little routine didn't have quite the reaction I'd been hoping for. The audience seemed to enjoy it, but they didn't really burst out laughing.

I made a fist with my left hand.

Niall spotted the pre-arranged signal and shouted, "Get off!"

I turned in his direction. "Get off? With *you*? Do I *look* that desperate?" A good few people laughed, so I felt a little better. "Isn't that just like a man? He sees a woman with dark glasses and thinks he's in with a chance. In the land of the blind, the one-eyed trouser-snake is king."

I was on stage for twenty minutes before the lights flickered. The overall reaction hadn't been brilliant, but at least no one had booed or thrown anything.

"Well, that's it!" I said, more than a little relieved. "Thank you very much!"

443

Dennis Clarke, the host for the evening, bounded onto the stage and took the microphone from me. "Well done! A big hand, ladies and genitals, for Miss Annie Quinn!"

"It's Andi," I corrected loudly.

Dennis made a big show of apologising. "I am *soooo* sorry, Andi!" He grinned at the audience as I stepped down from the stage. "Whew! That was lucky! I thought she was going to thump me! It was hit and run for a second there." He paused. "No, not hit and run . . . What's that other phrase? Oh yeah, touch and go." That got another laugh, and I was pleased with that, because Dennis and I had arranged it earlier – I'd even told him exactly what to say.

I was grinning like an idiot as I made my way to the back. Joe hugged and kissed me. "You were great!"

I turned to Tony, who grinned.

"Not bad at all," he said. "Just over twenty minutes. Most first-timers don't last more than five."

Ellen, Niall and Claire came up to us. "Loved it," Niall said. "Brilliant stuff about the Christmas songs!"

"I missed the last one," Claire said. "I was laughing too hard."

Niall repeated it for her: "Twas was the night before Christmas, and all through the house, not a creature was stirring, not even a spoon."

Claire laughed. "I have to remember that one!"

"You didn't do the one about Urethra Franklin," Ellen said. "I was looking forward to that."

"I couldn't remember how it ended," I said. "I was just about to start it and all of a sudden my mind went blank."

"Well, you covered up okay," Joe said. "I didn't even notice."

"God, I'm sweating! I didn't think I'd be able to go through with it."

"We had faith in you," Joe said.

I slipped my arm around his waist.

"It wasn't the best performance ever," I said. "I buggered up a couple of lines."

"That was just nerves," Tony said. "It'll get easier. If you're going to try again."

"I am," I said. "Dennis told me that if I lasted more than ten minutes I could come back next week."

"Are we going to stay for the rest of the show?" Claire asked.

"We should," I said. "See what the competition is like."

A woman's voice behind me said, "I don't think you have anything to worry about, Andi."

I turned and stared. "Mam. I mean, Granny. I didn't know you were here."

She smiled. "Claire asked me to come along."

I didn't know what to say.

Niall, Ellen and Tony stepped away, looking a little awkward.

"So . . ." I finally said. "How are things?"

"It's been quiet. Very quiet. Your dad – your grandad – misses you something terrible."

445

"I miss him too. Both of you."

"Are you going to come home?"

I shook my head. "No. But it's not because of what happened. I'm with Joe now."

She looked like she was on the verge of tears. "I'm so sorry, pet. We should have told you years ago."

"That's okay. You did what you thought was right. I don't blame you any more. I shouldn't have blamed you in the first place. But, well, things had been getting to me." I let go of Joe and hugged her. "I still don't know whether to call you Mam or Granny."

"Mam would be fine," She said, and stepped back, a smile beginning to form. "After all, you'd only end up confusing *my* mam even further."

"I called over to see her last week, but she wasn't in. How is she?"

"Well, she nearly wet herself when you told that joke about the three men in the helicopter, but apart from that she's in great form."

My mouth dropped open. "She's *here*?"

Mam nodded. "We're *all* here, Andi. All of us. You don't seriously think that we'd miss your first night? Look, here's Ciarán heading this way now. Eimear and Chris only just arrived before you went on."

I glanced at Claire. "You set all this up?"

She nodded. "Yep. I learned a few things about organising stuff from you."

Joe took my hand. "Come on, then. Reservations are in half an hour."

"Reservations for what?"

"The restaurant. I know your birthday's not for another couple of months, but when you decided you were going to perform tonight, we thought it'd be a good idea to celebrate your birthday and your debut performance at the same time."

Joe led me out and we held onto each other as the rest of my family and friends piled out of the pub; Ellen and Niall, Tony, Mam, Dad, Gran, Gráinne and Roddy – who both gave me a large hug, John and Betty, and lastly Ciarán and Audrey, who were keeping well apart and giving each other filthy looks. Clearly, something had happened between them. I could hardly wait to find out what.

We were about to set off when I suddenly realised that Claire was missing.

"She must be still inside," Gráinne said. "I'll go and get her."

"No, I'll do it," I said.

Claire was standing at the back of the room, watching the latest act. I poked her in the back. "Time to go, little sis."

She nodded, but didn't look around. "Yer man's nowhere *near* as good as you were."

"Thanks."

"I mean, look at him! He doesn't know one end of a routine from the other!"

I grinned. "And yet somehow you're still standing here watching him . . ."

Claire turned to me. "You know, I still can't believe you did that. You actually went up there on stage and started telling gags and made everyone laugh."

"I can only barely believe it myself," I said. "But they didn't *all* laugh."

"Believe me, Andi, it could have been a lot worse."

I nodded. "Come on. Everyone's waiting."

I had to practically drag her out of the pub. Just as we reached the door, Claire stopped and turned towards the stage once more. "One day," she said, a wistful look in her eyes, "one day that'll be me up there."

THE END